FAMILY
REUNITED

FAMILY REUNITED

J.R. BONHAM

The Book Guild Ltd

First published in Great Britain in 2021 by
The Book Guild Ltd
9 Priory Business Park
Wistow Road, Kibworth
Leicestershire, LE8 0RX
Freephone: 0800 999 2982
www.bookguild.co.uk
Email: info@bookguild.co.uk
Twitter: @bookguild

Typeset in 12pt Adobe Jenson Pro

Printed and bound in the UK by TJ Books LTD, Padstow, Cornwall

ISBN 978 1913551 940

British Library Cataloguing in Publication Data.
A catalogue record for this book is available from the British Library.

1

Surrey
A Thursday in late September

"Gan, Gan!" yelled Summer at the top of her voice. She had been playing and was now standing up in her playpen in the back garden, taking in the end of the summer sunshine before the autumn and then winter descended. Her great-grandmother was in earshot in the kitchen, busy preparing lunch. Jan had a new friend coming to lunch and she had in mind to give Summer her lunch separately before her afternoon nap. This would enable Jan and her friend some peace and quiet to enjoy each other's company.

"Hello, sweetheart. What is it? Are you hungry?" said Jan, popping her head out of the back door. It was a little too early for Summer's lunch but Jan was always talking to her with the hope that her language skills would develop. For a fourteen-month-old, Summer was advanced for her age, finding her feet at eleven months and she could manage the odd word. She certainly knew who "Gan" was and adored her. She was not so keen on the playpen, though, wanting to get out and run about

1

on her own. Jan insisted on the playpen as a way of keeping Summer safe when Jan was busy indoors or gardening.

"Gan!" Summer pointed towards the grass, where Sandal was busy chewing a long stick he had found.

Sandal, the labradoodle puppy, stopped chewing and bounded towards the kitchen and was soon by Jan's side, panting. He was just nine months old and a bundle of fun.

"Hello," said Jan kindly to Sandal as she bent down to stroke him. "Are you hungry too?" Jan thought that maybe the chewing of the stick was a sign. Or maybe he was bored. She put his bowl in front of him and he tucked into his midday snack. It was gone in seconds and he was soon looking around for more.

"You're just too greedy, Sandal. You'll have to wait until tonight for your supper," said Jan, while filling his water bowl and putting it down on the floor. He lapped thirstily at the water. "You're very thirsty too!"

Jan picked Summer out of the playpen and took her over to play on the swing. The rope swing had been put up for her by a friend of Jan's. The long ropes were secured to a branch of an oak tree set close to the ground. It had an ingenious seat made from plastic with a soft top and an extra attachment for safety. She liked to be pushed on her special swing but she had also perfected her own technique by laying her tummy on the seat and walking as far as she could then letting herself go. This was much more fun, although Jan worried when she first tried this. With supervision, Jan watched over her and could see just how much more fun it was than being pushed.

Sandal brought his ball over for Jan to throw for him and he never tired of retrieving it and Summer loved to watch, giggling every time Sandal dropped it at their feet. Summer ran over towards the owl sculpture and Sandal followed. He would follow her everywhere if he was given the chance.

Sandal knew he could easily far outrun Summer but he was so gentle with her and always let her take the lead. Summer was laughing at Sandal. She was always happy when Sandal was around.

The old tree stump was several feet high with the owl, in all his glory, perched on top. It had been an oak tree in its former life. Other tall oak trees were on the perimeter so the owl sculpture, in the centre, was the main feature of the large garden.

Summer felt along the smooth wood where the bark had been shaved off. There were oak leaves and acorns etched into the wood all around the sides as well as a "nest" of three baby owls. She traced her little hands over the baby owls and loved the feel of the wood under her fingers.

On further investigation, Summer noticed a little door around the back of the tree. It was about two feet high and eighteen inches wide. An ideal size for a small person. She tentatively stepped nearer for a closer inspection of the door. Sandal had come to investigate too and sat obediently by Summer's side but also ready for more fun. They did love each other so much; they had a great bond.

Jan lost all track of time as she watched over Summer and Sandal but suddenly realised she still had to feed Summer before her friend arrived. She picked up Summer and took her to the kitchen, where her lunch was ready. Sandal followed them hoping for another tidbit.

The modern kitchen had been revamped the same year that Jan had lost Mike, two years earlier. Jan loved her new kitchen. She had always said the old kitchen must have been designed by a man with no idea of how a woman works. There were now plenty of floor and wall cupboards, with doors of clean white, while the granite peninsula and work surfaces, with stainless steel hob and sink, complemented the whole look.

3

"I've got a friend coming to lunch so I'd like you to be on your best behaviour," Jan said to Summer as spoonfuls of food were being demolished. Summer loved her food.

She waited for her friend to arrive, with Summer in her arms, so she could introduce them before she put Summer in her cot after a nappy change. Sandal disappeared into the garden to find the stick he had found so tasty earlier. He searched and searched for it but did not know that Jan had surreptitiously thrown it over the fence into the woodland.

Rachel arrived a few minutes later. She was several years senior to Jan, greying at the temples with a kindly face. She wore rather old-fashioned clothes compared to what Jan would normally wear. Jan wore smart navy shorts and a pretty lilac top, her favourite colour. Her long legs showed off her tan that she had had all summer to perfect.

"Come in," said Jan affably as her friend stepped in through the front door. "This is Summer. Her mum is at school today. She missed out a lot of her education while having the baby but now she is going to catch up and take her exams."

"Hello, Summer," said Rachel and smiled. Summer rubbed her eyes in tiredness and started to suck her thumb. This was a classic sign that she was ready for her nap. "Lovely to meet you and... Oh, who is this?"

"This is Sandal," Jan divulged the dog's name as he came rushing into the hall, bumping into both Jan and Rachel, panting and wagging his tail. "He's only a puppy, just nine months old and rather boisterous, I'm afraid. They are both going for their afternoon nap now."

"He's gorgeous. I love labradoodles. And such a fabulous colour," said Rachel.

"Pretty, isn't it? They call it gold apricot," Jan explained.

"Oh, yes, he's beautiful. And knows it!" Rachel nodded knowingly. She loved all dogs.

"Now, come on through, I thought we would have lunch in the garden. It's still quite warm for the time of year."

"That'll be lovely. Thank you so much for inviting me. Yes, it's going to be lovely and sunny today, apparently." Rachel followed Jan into the kitchen and then through the back door into the garden.

"Apparently we are in for an Indian summer. Something to look forward to before the winter starts to snap at our heels," Jan told Rachel as they went into the back garden.

"Oh, wow!" Rachel exclaimed as she beheld the beautiful sight before her. "What a fantastic garden! That phormium is absolutely gorgeous. The whole garden is like a piece of parkland!" She was enraptured as her eyes drank in the whole scene. "It's ideal for Sandal and Summer to play. You are so lucky."

"Thank you, yes I am, although I find it is a bit too big at times. You're not the first person to say it's like parkland. I enjoy cutting the grass with my new ride-on mower; it's great fun. If you would like to have a look around, I'll be with you soon with our lunch once I've put madam to bed. We've got salad for lunch; hope that's okay with you?"

"My favourite," Rachel confirmed.

Rachel took herself off for a self-guided tour around the garden while Jan went to change Summer's nappy and settle her in her cot.

Rachel enjoyed wandering slowly around the garden, which is mostly laid to lawn with a large rockery in the centre, just a few feet away from the owl sculpture. The rockery contains a red acer tree at the back, flanked either side by two miniature ornamental fir trees. In front of the trees are several roses, pieris japonica, azaleas, montbretia and heathers, graded by height with the tallest at the back. In the front, growing over the rocks, are aubretia and rock rose in differing hues. This would give a blaze of colour throughout the year.

5

Behind the rockery, the garden extends some way back until it reaches a patch of rough ground which has been left to grow naturally under five tall oak trees. In the same area in springtime, the bluebells make a carpet of beautiful blue. These used to be Jan's husband Mike's favourite flowers. In his remembrance, Jan would wait until after the flowers had finished before giving the rough ground its annual strim to keep down the weeds and tall grasses. Two large variegated phormiums dominate the front of the area to mask the rough ground, together with some mixed-colour rhododendrons.

There are many different species of hebe all along the border to a woodland on one side of the garden with a small fir tree between each hebe.

Nearer to the house, next to a large patio, is a small water feature and a spreading acer. Also a specimen viburnum tree, which produces large white scented flowers in spring, is just outside the back door, with its wonderful perfume flooding the house.

The tall oak tree, with Summer's swing, is on the other side of the patio, next door to a vegetable patch, close by the house to enable Jan to keep an eye on her. Rachel ended her tour at the back door at the same time as Jan.

"I love your owl sculpture: what a fantastic feature. It's a really fabulous garden, isn't it? You are so lucky, although I expect it's a lot of hard work," said Rachel, several minutes after her lap around the garden after inspecting the plants.

"Thank you! I've been here nearly twenty years now and we liked that it is so secluded being right next to the woodland. And, of course, it is completely enclosed so no little'uns can escape! Yes, it is a lot of hard work but I do have some help, of course, but only since my husband passed away," said Jan. "A man comes in once a week to do the heavy work. I can do some pruning and weeding but I get backache very quickly.

6

Best to leave it to the experts, although I do have the last word in what needs doing. Then my granddaughter helps me too."

To this remark Rachel raised her eyebrows but Jan missed that and carried on without thinking. "I'll just show you around the side while we're here." Jan became engrossed in showing her friend all that there was to see. "It's the vegetable patch which Mike used to tend but this year I asked the gardener to dig it over. Then I just threw down some cottage garden flower seeds so I'd have some flowers to pick and arrange in vases to brighten up the house. Mike used to grow beans, carrots and lettuce in the open, plus tomatoes and cucumbers in the greenhouse, but that was far too much for me. The fruit bushes of blackcurrants, blueberries and gooseberries and a crown of rhubarb were here when we moved here so we would pick and freeze most of these or I would make jam if there was a glut of fruit."

Rachel was most puzzled to hear that Summer helped out in the garden but did not say anything for fear of being rude. She put Jan at a much younger age than was true, not thinking at all that Summer was actually her great-granddaughter rather than her granddaughter.

"Would you like tea or coffee or something a little stronger? We can have a glass of wine if you like. I have a bottle of New Zealand Sauvignon Blanc in the fridge or I have red wine if you'd prefer," said Jan as she brought out their plates of salad.

"Oh, yes, thank you, the white wine would be lovely." Rachel licked her lips.

"Good choice," said Jan. "My favourite!"

Rachel and Jan had met at their yoga class and did not know each other very well. There was certainly more to discover.

"Your granddaughter is really lovely," said Rachel and Jan smiled. "So sweet."

"Actually, she's my great-granddaughter! It's her mother who is my granddaughter! I never knew her when she was growing up so I'm making up for lost time now. Summer has been here all her young life and, because her mum calls me Gran, Summer does too! Well, it actually comes out as 'Gan' but I don't mind. I never ever met any of my grandchildren when they were growing up. I've only recently got to know them."

"Oh, really?" said Rachel, entirely curious and glad that her misunderstanding of who was who, was cleared up. Jan was obviously older than Rachel first thought. "How come?"

Jan was aged sixty-nine, nearing her seventieth birthday in a month's time. She hated the thought of going grey and colour washed her hair a light caramel colour, a much lighter and kinder hue than her natural dark brown when she had been young. She kept it in a short style and visited the hairdresser every six weeks to keep it trim. She could easily have passed for fifty-five, just six years older than her own daughter, Louise, would be now, if she had lived. She liked to keep as fit and healthy as she could by walking Sandal at least twice a day.

"Well, it's a long story," Jan explained. "Not always happy."

"I've got plenty of time. Only tell me if it's not too painful."

"I'd better start at the beginning but I'll try not to bore you. I became pregnant when I was nineteen and married the father. My parents weren't too pleased but accepting in time. I had Louise first and three years later I had Steven. Two of the loveliest kids, very well behaved."

"I can believe it. Like Summer?" Rachel wondered. "She seems a little sweetie; maybe you had influence there too?"

"Yes, a little, I'd like to think. She's a lovely little girl, so grown up for her age. I suppose that is because she's only been with adults. She started walking very early but her talking is not so advanced but all will come in time. I think she understands a lot of what we say to her and that might be because Lottie and I had so much to catch up on, after so many years. We would talk for hours on end sometimes, it was lovely. Lottie told me quite a bit about her mother, all that I had missed out on. She could only tell me what she knew in her short life; I still don't know what happened when I first left. And, of course, vice versa. I was able to tell her about her mother when she was young. It's been a strange set of circumstances."

"Yes, I should think it was. Anyway, you were relating your story. I'm all ears!"

After lunch, Rachel and Jan sat back with another glass of wine and Summer was still asleep, worn out from the morning activity.

"Well, I'd better start at the beginning or you might be confused. I was brought up in Bristol but my first husband, Geoff, came from Devon. I suppose it started as a kind of holiday romance. I met him when I was thirteen and he was seventeen. My parents rented a cottage in a little village in Devon and we stayed there the whole of the school summer holidays. It started platonically obviously as I was only thirteen and we used to write to each other, a lot, after I returned to Bristol. Then every year after that we would go there for the holidays and, of course, each year Geoff and I became closer in that time. Still nothing happened," Jan added for effect, with a smile.

Rachel nodded her understanding of the situation but said nothing. Jan continued.

"When I was sixteen, he moved to Bristol to be nearer to me. He gave up his job but soon found another in Bristol. It was very intense on his part but after a time I got fed up with him and kept trying to break it off because I wanted to meet other boys. Every time I told him it was over he would cry and begged me to take him back, which of course I did, not wanting to upset him. Inevitably, when I was nineteen, I became pregnant and Geoff wanted to marry me so my parents, I think, were relieved that I wasn't going to remain an unmarried mother. How shameful that was in those days. I didn't believe in abortion, which actually had only just become legal at the time."

"I remember it well. Go on." Rachel was becoming absorbed in the tale.

"We settled down to married life, firstly in a little rented flat in Bristol and then after a couple of years he persuaded me to move to Devon. He said it was the only way we were going to be able to afford a home of our own with not having to rent. Houses in Bristol were starting to become very expensive and I could see the advantage of owning our own home, with not having dead money tied up in rent. I was too young and feeble to speak my own mind so agreed in principle, even though moving away from my hometown was not really what I wanted. It was what Geoff wanted so I had to toe the line. Big mistake. So there I was in Devon, in a place where I knew no one, away from my friends and family with a young baby. He was a complete control freak and manipulator as well as being jealous and possessive. I just had to knuckle down and get on with life, such as it was. I had Steven, my second child, because I did not want Louise to be an only child but Geoff would have been happier with just one. An only child just like himself. My family were still in Bristol and I did miss them so, especially when there were family-type occasions happening, like cousins' weddings, things like that, and I was upset because I couldn't go. It was a very unhappy time for me, although my kids kept me firmly rooted and I loved them to bits. I wasn't allowed any friends. Even so, I did make one or two, but Geoff hated that. He wanted me all to himself. After making the best of a bad job, fast forward twenty-one years from first moving to Devon. We went on our first holiday without the kids, to America. It should have been a fantastic holiday, a coach tour covering many states. I was so looking forward to it."

"Oh, I love it there. Whereabouts did you go?" Rachel was becoming enraptured with Jan's story.

"We started off in Denver. It was mainly mountains, parks and canyons that we visited, around Wyoming, Montana, Nevada, Arizona, visiting so many fantastic places like Yellowstone Park, Monument Valley and the Grand Canyon. Absolutely beautiful it was. But Geoff wasn't happy at all, I've no idea why. When we went up a mountain he said he had altitude sickness but I'm pretty sure he didn't. He found so many things wrong I wondered why he was there at all. Probably because it had been my idea to go there in the first place. Everyone avoided us because of his moaning. All apart from one man who was very kind to me."

"Oh yes?" Rachel said, with a knowing wink.

"Yes!" Jan laughed, as she transported herself back, almost twenty-five years ago, to those heady times when she first met Mike. "But obviously nothing happened then. I was attracted to him, yes, but I never thought in my wildest dreams that anything would come of it. So, to cut a long story short, Mike contacted me when we got home and we met up. But he lived in Surrey and I was in Devon, such a long way away. He used to come down once a week and we would have clandestine meetings. It was very romantic. Six months later I took the biggest gamble of my life, left home and we set up together in Surrey. The kids were grown up so I thought, 'this is my time now'. Very selfish, I know, but, like they say, 'life isn't a dress rehearsal.'"

"Ain't that the truth!" Rachel interjected.

"GAN!" shouted Summer at the top of her voice from her cot indoors.

"Excuse me. She won't stop yelling until I pick her up. I'll put her on the swing; she loves that."

Jan was ever aware that she did not want to disappoint her great-grandchild and actually enjoyed all the time she spent with her. After several pushes she was mindful that she had left her guest and in the middle of her story. She took Summer down to play on her own but still within sight. She put some of her toys out on the lawn in front of them and encouraged her to play with them.

"Just play nicely on your own for a while, Summer. You could throw the ball for Sandal too; he would love that," Jan suggested, trying to placate Summer as she hurried back to Rachel.

"So sorry to abandon you like that. Summer has me just where she wants me but I don't mind; I love her to bits. We can keep an eye on her from here so she's quite safe. There's no escaping this garden!"

"Quite understandable." Rachel agreed. "Do go on. You were at the point of setting up home with Mike."

"That was a very stressful time for me, as you can imagine. Well, the long and short of it is, the kids never forgave me. I've no idea why but I think my mother-in-law might have had something to do with it. I did actually go back for a few months when Geoff was on the verge of a nervous breakdown and the kids had begged me to go back because they couldn't cope. Another big mistake! But hindsight is a wonderful thing. It wasn't what I wanted but felt it was my duty to go back to help out, but it was only temporary. Three months later I had to leave all over again. They never spoke to me again after I left for a second time."

"So your two presumably married and had kids but they never let you meet them?" Rachel guessed and Jan nodded. "That's unbelievable!"

12

"But true. At the time, I jokingly told people that I left home before the kids. They were both grown up and I had always said that if they had been younger and were still dependent on me I would never have left. I tried and tried to get them to see my side but they still never wanted anything to do with me. Maybe I didn't try hard enough to fight for them, I really don't know. All they did say to me was, 'While you're with that man there will never be a reconciliation.' Those final words have rung in my ears for years."

"That's so sad. You missed out on so much with not only your children but also not seeing your grandchildren growing up. And now they are grown-ups themselves?"

"Pretty much, yes. At the time I left Geoff, my father was disgusted with me and never wanted to meet Mike. My mother wanted to meet him but she didn't dare to until after my father died. By then my mum was in a care home because she couldn't look after herself. She had mental health problems. We used to visit her and she absolutely adored Mike. Mind you, he was a very nice man, completely different to Geoff. He was kind, romantic and charming but he also let me be myself again. It was such a relief to be with someone who liked me for who I was and didn't want to change me, although I'm sure I did change a bit, but for the better, I like to think."

"Lucky you!"

"I was very lucky indeed. When you think Mike and I hardly knew each other at first, with just meeting up for a few hours once a week for only six months. It could so easily have gone pear-shaped. He was very easy-going and I was very glad to live with someone who wasn't jealous or possessive or controlling. My brother and sister accepted him too as part of the family, which was good. It would have been awful if they had shunned me like my kids did."

"Quite. You need your family when the chips are down."

13

"I did miss the kids, wrote them many letters. I tried phoning them but they would hang up and eventually they changed their telephone numbers to stop me ringing them. I was always perplexed as to why they should behave in such a way. After all, I was their mum! I don't believe I ever did anything harmful to them to make them behave like that, apart from leaving when they were grown up. At times it was unbearable but Mike and I had twenty-three very happy years before he passed away suddenly just over two years ago. I lost six close people in quick succession so that wasn't a good time for me. Apart from my parents, who you expect to predecease you, my older sister contracted lung cancer and died a couple of years before Mike. Then a good friend from school committed suicide. Finally, my daughter, Louise, died in an horrific accident nearby here. It was going to be part of a reconciliation after Mike died. Of course, once he died my brother got involved in getting my kids back, only for Louise to have that terrible accident. A tree branch came down, right on top of her. There was nothing I could do to save her. It was the worst time of my life."

"That's tragic! How awful for you. However did you cope?" Rachel enquired.

"I've no idea. Went into overdrive, I think. I was not in a good place, that's for sure."

"Did you go to your daughter's funeral?" asked Rachel.

"Well, I wasn't invited to her wedding so I certainly wasn't going to be welcome at her funeral, knowing they would all think it was my fault," said Jan sadly.

"Not invited to her wedding? Whyever not?" Rachel asked.

"I've really no idea, still, after all this time. Nor to my son's wedding either. They really had it in for me, presumably because I left their father. Luckily for me that has all changed now. Which brings us closer to the present time. My granddaughter Lottie, Summer's mum, came to me when she was seven months pregnant. I took her in and have supported her ever since. When Louise died, Lottie was only fifteen. She went off the rails apparently. Her father had no control. She ended up pregnant and walked out. She ended up at my brother, John's house in Bristol with not a lot of money on her. John had been trying to cope with his wife, Vera who had only just been diagnosed with early-onset Alzheimer's disease so he didn't need another problem. So he brought her over to me to deal with."

"Crikey, that's quite a tall order!"

"Well, it was a surprise certainly, but as well as that, it was a distraction from my own problems. After Mike died I was not in a good place. I didn't know whether to sell the house because it was too big but I put that on the back burner while I took a trip to New Zealand and Thailand to see friends there for Christmas and New Year. They invited me soon after they heard Mike had died to help me get over the loss. They were so kind to me and said I could stay as long as I liked. The ones in New Zealand were Mike's friends first, of long standing but they have been so supportive to me, I don't know what I would have done without them. And my friend Marian in Thailand I've known since we were at school together."

"You have true friends there, by the sound of it."

"Yes. Like I say, Lottie came to me. She wasn't called Lottie before she came. She was born Charlotte but everyone called her Charlie, which she told me she always hated. She said it was a boy's name. I suggested the name Lottie and she loved it. I never asked her about the father of the baby and she has never imparted who he is. It doesn't matter these days. So different from when I was pregnant all that time ago."

"How things change," Rachel agreed.

"And how Lottie has changed too! She's a different person altogether to the one who first came to me. She was a bit of rebel who I like to think I tamed! We shared our grief and bonded immediately. Amazing really as I had never met her before. We were both feeling quite vulnerable but time has healed a little and we have helped each other with our losses. It's just like I have a daughter back."

"That's fantastic," said Rachel, with real feeling.

"It is. I can't believe all this time has gone by in the blink of an eye. Help, where does the time go?"

"I know, it's quite frightening," said Rachel, looking at her watch. "Talking about the time flying, I really must go; my husband will wonder where I've got to! Well, he knows where I am but he does worry if I'm back later than I say. Thank you so much for a lovely lunch; I've really enjoyed myself. And for the fascinating story of your life. Makes my mundane life look a real bore! Well, we must do it again, you must come over to us and you can meet Frank."

"It's been lovely – thank you for coming." Jan looked over to where Summer and Sandal were playing and called out. "Summer, come and say goodbye to Auntie Rachel."

Summer dutifully bounced over to the patio, smiling coyly all the while.

"It's been really lovely to meet you," Rachel looked directly at Summer. "One thing I meant to ask you, something I noticed as I walked around your lovely garden," she asked Jan.

"Oh, yes?" Jan put her head on one side as she wondered what was coming.

"Your owl sculpture. There's a little door around the back. Does that lead somewhere? Like the rabbit hole in *Alice in Wonderland*?" Rachel enquired.

"Oh, the door! Ah yes, I'd forgotten about the door. Well, you'd be surprised what is inside. Shall we go and see?"

Rachel nodded. Jan took Summer by the hand and together the three of them walked across the grass towards the owl.

2

Devon
Two years earlier

Dean sat in a trancelike stupor, head in hands. His wife, Louise, was Jan's daughter and he had just heard of her tragic death in Surrey. The police had just visited him with the devastating news. He could hardly believe his own ears. He was mortified that he was not there by her side to be able to help in any way. Dean knew it was his job to convey this information to his children but he was not looking forward to that. He needed another drink.

Jan's brother, John, had set himself the task of taking his niece and nephew to see their mother with the design of a reconciliation. It had been twenty-two years since Jan left the family home and her children had never forgiven her. They were both adults in their early twenties when Jan left and they refused to have anything to do with her or to let her meet her grandchildren when they came along one by one. Everything changed after Jan's second husband's untimely death only six months earlier. John had always been upset by Jan's split family so he was instrumental in trying to get the family all back together again, in harmony. Louise and Steven agreed to go with John to meet with their mother, after much persuasion and cajoling.

John lived in Bristol so it was going to be a long day for him. He was tall and balding, a family trait on the male side. He had risen early in the day to drive to Devon to pick up Louise and Steven to take them to Surrey for Jan's long-awaited reconciliation with her precious children, now in their mid-forties. The idea was that, after all was well, with a wonderful reconciliation between his sister and her children, John would then take them home, all in one day. He had worked it out as doable in one long day.

Unfortunately, it did not end well when Louise was tragically killed in a freak accident while out for a walk. Jan had thought it was a good idea to be on neutral territory while they talked and sorted things out between them. She wanted to show them the lovely area where she lived with woods and a lake but a gust of wind blew a tree branch down, onto Louise, piercing her carotid artery. There was nothing anyone could do to save her. Jan was distraught. What started out with high hopes ended with tragedy and fears for the future.

After cursory preliminary arrangements with undertakers, John brought Steven straight home. He could not believe that it was indirectly because of his actions that this tragedy had occurred. He felt totally to blame but at the same time he believed he was doing the right thing. If he had let sleeping dogs lie then this would never have happened. He left Jan in meltdown but he felt he had to get Steven away in case he blamed his mother. Poor Jan, thought John, on the verge of a fantastic reconciliation with her estranged offspring after such a long time and then this had to happen.

After fetching a can of lager from the fridge, Dean grabbed the nettle and set his children down to inform them of their tragic loss.

Dean's children were his greatest achievement after marrying the woman of his dreams. He could not believe his luck, twenty-one years ago, in gaining the attention of Louise, who was, at the time, on the rebound from her first sweetheart from school, Olly. Olly had aspirations of going to university and making something of his life, hoping to become a doctor just like his father. Louise could not wait the five years, in a long-distance relationship, for Olly to eventually qualify. She wanted some fun rather than be satisfied with the occasional phone call when Olly had the time to talk to her. Whenever he came home from university he became more and more distant and eventually the relationship found it had run its course.

Dean met Louise in the pub when she was drowning her sorrows with friends. She tried to persuade everyone that she had dumped Olly and only her close friends knew that the truth was that Olly had met someone else. Dean jumped at the chance of getting to know this beautiful young lady with long dark hair and vivacious, outgoing attitude. She was a little older than him but, after a disastrous relationship he had had with a girl from school, he had been on his own for several months and was becoming desperate. Little did he think that Louise would look twice at him so he was as surprised as anyone that she not only liked him but quite took him to her heart.

Dean had not excelled at school, scraping through with two GCSEs in art and woodwork, something in which he always had an interest. He enjoyed sport but mostly the watching rather than playing, and football was his favourite. He would go and watch the local Torquay club as much as his finances would allow.

His first job when he left school was at a local factory that made shaver parts, starting off with sweeping up the remnants from the warehouse floor. Promotion eluded him through his lack of drive and initiative. However, when some younger souls started working there, he was put up to packing, which included loading and unloading deliveries, which he enjoyed. After ten years he was promoted to warehouse assistant and then two years later to warehouse operative, where he was satisfied that he had made his mark in the world. He had aspirations of being made up to foreman or even supervisor but the company had other ideas and promoted younger, more go-ahead personnel ahead of him. He would just shrug his shoulders; what will be, will be.

He enjoyed going to the pub after work to sink a pint or two and to watch Sky football on the big screen for some relaxation before venturing home. He had very few friends, if any. He counted work colleagues as friends and they would sometimes accompany him to the pub after work. Louise would make him a meal after being at her own job in the bank. She had managed to change from her full-time duties to work part time when the children came along, with the proviso that she could go back to full time at a later stage. That stage was just about to come, since her youngest child would soon be old enough to be left on her own.

Now, however, Dean was worried because Louise's income from her part-time job would dry up completely with her recent demise. The constraints of low wages over the years were taking their toll. Dean had been looking forward to Louise being able to finance his future "Rolls Royce" imagined lifestyle when she went back to working full time again. At least it would have meant not having to worry about spending more on his beer and also to have the odd whisky chaser. They had both been looking forward to having better holidays now the two older children might not want to come with them. A family holiday for five always drained resources but just spending out for a couple plus one child would be much more doable. They had recently been looking at brochures and dreaming of going abroad for a change and to finally put the family tent away for good.

Now he was on the verge of giving his children the most devastating news they would ever hear. He gathered them around and told them straight what had happened to their mother. He felt that they were old enough to understand the implications so they must draw their own conclusions as to the next step in their lives. He would help them as much as he was able to but he had difficulties of his own to overcome.

Jake, at seventeen and a half years old and six feet, four inches, had already outgrown both his parents. A sensitive, intelligent boy who took the news as Dean would have expected, with great dignity and common sense. He mulled over the information and took time out to check his emotional state and that of his sisters, the caring boy that he was. He wanted to ease his father's pain by taking it upon himself to help out as much as he could.

He had just started his second year of A levels at the grammar school but he felt that they would have to take a back seat for the time being. University beckoned in a year's time and he had been looking forward to obtaining good grades to get into a first-class establishment. Cambridge interested him, partly because he wanted to have the opportunity to row in the Boat Race, something to which he had aspired since he was a young boy. He loved rowing; it gave him the opportunity to excel in a sport that he enjoyed: he had been rowing since he was seven. There would be plenty of time for him to knuckle down to extra work. This time at home with his family was far more serious and important.

Charlotte, or Charlie as the family called her, was the complete opposite to her brother. A bit of a rebel who did not like to conform. Aged fifteen, she was a pretty girl with long blonde hair. She was grown up for her age and was just looking forward to actually being an adult. In her own eyes she was already there. She would have to go through the motions of taking her exams, though, just to placate her father. He was determined that his children were going to do better than him but no university was ever going to grace her specifications of life. Her head had been turned, helped along by her friend, Amelia, fuelling her ambition to become famous. Girl groups had more or less began in earnest with the Spice Girls in the mid-1990s, although there had been some before that, like Bananarama and the Three Degrees. Anyway, that was a long time before the two girls had been born and they wanted a piece of the action. Except, of course, they had no idea of how to go about furthering their "careers". Charlotte had a good voice and loved to sing but did not really know how to go about "becoming famous". Her mother had tried to encourage her along the lines of more normal vocations for girls like secretarial work or nursing or teaching. Normal, that is, unless they were really ambitious and wanted to further their education to become doctors or lawyers, but this was not for Charlotte.

Daisy, eleven, the youngest, was her mother's favourite and had been a little bit spoilt. She had struggled with her weight for some time – "puppy fat", her mother used to call it. Both she and her parents had all struggled with their weight. Her older siblings, on the other hand, were tall and slim. They were much closer in age and Daisy sometimes felt a little out of place, the baby. She had been conceived after a camping holiday with a lot of drink consumed by both parents. She had been a surprise to them both as Louise had been on the pill at the time. They thought their first boy and girl had completed their family. However, Daisy came along and no more was said about it. Her long dark plaits were still in place after her mother had made them when she left earlier in the day and Daisy loved them so much. She started to cry when reality kicked in; her mother would never make her plaits ever again. Jake found comfort in cuddling Daisy, who was completely confused by her emotions as the news sunk in.

Charlotte walked out; it was her only way of coping. She hated it when people cried, even though she felt a little tear appear in her eye when she thought of the enormity of it all. Her mother was dead. How was this going to change the dynamics of family life? It was bound to change and not for the better, she thought. She walked around the block to help clear her head. She crept back into the house and went upstairs to the quiet privacy of her bedroom.

Dean found the telling to his children of their mother's death the most demanding challenge of his life. His wife would always do that sort of thing but, of course, she was not around to take it off his shoulders. He noticed their individual reactions through inebriated eyes, which helped to dissipate the trauma of his life falling apart, like a slow-motion action movie.

John dropped Steven off at home in order for him to tell Cheryl, his wife and their children the awful news of the loss of their Auntie Louise. John was also hoping that Steven would take on the task of telling his father, Geoff.

"I will do it if that helps," John said to Steven. They had driven back from Surrey in almost stunned silence. What could they say to each other? Steven had lost his older sister, someone whom he had known all his life. And now he would have to tell his father the tragic news.

"No," said Steven. "It will be better coming from me. I will go round and see him as soon as I've told my own family. I can't do it on the phone, it would be too cruel and I know he will need my support. He has his wife Lynda there with him so that should soften the blow."

Lynda met Geoff, Louise and Steven's father, only a few months after his wife, Jan left him for another man, twenty-two years earlier. He had been in a fragile state of mind at the time and not really ready for another relationship so soon after his marriage collapsed. He was still ever hopeful of his wife returning to the fold after her "fling" but he wondered if he would actually be able to forgive her. He would have to because he still loved her. Even after she had treated him so badly by leaving him to live with a man she met on holiday. *How dare she leave me*, he had kept saying to himself over and over at the time. Jan never did return to him and he always wondered why. He never thought that he had been a bad husband like Jan had inferred. *Yes, I was jealous of her friends. I only stopped her doing things for her own good. I thought I was doing the right thing. Obviously not!*

Geoff had not enjoyed good mental health and at the age of seventy-one now he was feeling insecure most of the time. He hated the thought of getting old. His depressions came and went but each time they lasted longer and longer. Lynda was his rock and he relied on her to be there for him but he was constantly worried that she would leave him like Jan did. He was careful about what he said to her and learned to bite his tongue when he was having bad thoughts.

John waited as Steven gathered his thoughts and reiterated that he was okay with telling Geoff and Lynda once he had told his wife and children. Steven had mulled over how he was going to broach the subject in telling his father but now had it in his head how he was going to overcome this difficult task.

"Okay. If you're alright with telling your dad I will go to Dean's now and see if there is anything I can do there," said John.

You've done enough! Steven felt like saying but it never came out. He knew that his Uncle John had their best interests at heart, it was not his fault that everything had gone pear-shaped.

Steven's two daughters, Milly and Poppy, were thirteen and ten, respectively. Both were blonde like their mother. Steven told the three of them together and then waited for their reactions. Cheryl put her arms around Steven. She smelled smoke on him but decided not to nag him for smoking; he probably needed a cigarette after losing his sister so tragically. He had promised her that he was not going to smoke again, especially not the type of cigarettes that he really enjoyed, the reefers. They were the ones that calmed him the most.

Poppy cried and Milly comforted her with dry eyes. She was far too grown up for tears.

"What's going to happen now?" Cheryl asked Steven.

"John is making arrangements between the coroner and the undertakers; he has it all in hand. Then the body will be brought back to Devon and I shall help Dean with the arrangements for the funeral. But first I must go over and speak to Dad. I'm not looking forward to telling him but someone has to and I've told Uncle John that I will do it."

"Do you want me to come with you?" Cheryl asked.

"No, you stay here with the girls. I think it would be better just coming from me."

Steven left the house and went, with trepidation, to see his father.

"Oh *no!*" cried Geoff when he heard the news. He crumpled onto his knees, his head in his hands. Dean and Lynda helped him up. "I... I can't believe it! Are you sure?"

"I'm quite sure. I was there! Come on, let's go and sit down." Steven was fighting back his own tears.

"I'll make some tea," said Lynda helpfully, wondering how she was going to deal with Geoff, knowing his history of depression. This was bound to drag him down, which in turn would pull her down. She had coped with his deep depressions over the years but this was different. It was bound to make him worse than usual.

"Tell me, what happened?" Geoff asked his son.

Steven went through the whole situation from start to finish from his point of view. How John had fetched himself and Louise and taken them to make it up with their mother after so many years of non-contact. Geoff knew that his own mother had made them promise on her deathbed to not have anything to do with their mother. Louise was instrumental in keeping that promise until they heard that Mike had died and John had suggested to them that they could make it up with their mother.

"We arrived at Mum's house in Surrey and she suggested we went out for a walk to be on neutral ground, rather than being in the house where John was waiting. We walked and talked but Louise had been very much on the defensive; she was there pretty much against her will. I really wanted to make it work because I missed Mum. Then all of a sudden a gust of wind tore down a tree branch and hit Louise, stabbing her in the chest area. Mum and I were a bit further away and there was absolutely nothing we could do to help her. It was awful." Steven still felt nauseous as it all came flooding back to him, over and over, as if in a dream. "The ambulance people said it was very quick as it was the carotid artery that had been speared. God, it was dreadful. I've never seen so much blood!"

As Steven was going through the story, Geoff was feeling sick and faint. He thought he would die. He quite often had feelings of suicide and with this loss of his daughter he did not know how he was going to cope. With Lynda's help he made his way to the bedroom and lay on the bed without saying another word to anyone.

Steven left then saying he had to get home. Lynda quite understood and went to sit with Geoff and watched over him. Quite soon he was in a fitful sleep.

John arrived at Dean's house to see how they were coping. The sight of Jake and Daisy on the settee both in floods of tears moved John to tears himself. He had kept himself together for the sake of Steven but now the emotions took a hold of him. Dean was sitting in the chair, head in his hands. Two empty cans of lager were on the table beside him.

"I'm so, so sorry for your loss," John said to them all. *What else can I say or do?* he thought to himself. He sat down opposite Dean and observed the scene with Jake and Daisy crying on the settee. Dean kept drinking copious amounts of lager but did not offer any to John. No one said anything and John felt slightly uncomfortable. He did wonder where Charlotte was but assumed she had taken herself off to her bedroom to cry alone.

It was getting late and he had to get home to Vera and convey the news to her too. It was going to be another couple of hours before he would arrive home. He waited around to see that they were all coping as well as could be expected. He told them that he would be the link with the coroner's office and then arrange with the undertakers for the body to be brought back to Devon with all the formalities that entailed. Then he offered to help with preparations for the funeral before taking his leave but Dean informed him that he would do it himself with Steven's help.

John took his leave after a short time and drove home to Bristol.

"Oh God, Vera, it was the worst thing I've ever had to do," John cried when he finally arrived home and told Vera. It was late and he was mentally and physically exhausted.

"Why did you take them? I can't remember." Vera had been diagnosed with early-onset Alzheimer's and this turned out to be one of her bad days. She had wandered around the house all day wondering where John was.

"I took them to see their mother, remember? Jan had lost contact with them years ago after she left Geoff, remember? They wanted nothing to do with her after she left, but after Mike died I thought it was an opportunity to get them all together again." John was trying to keep it simple but was met with a blank face. "We'll talk about it tomorrow, I'm exhausted."

Next day he rang Jan to see how she was after the disaster the day before.

"I'm trying to keep myself busy," she told him. "How did Dean take it? And the kids?"

"Oh, they're all in meltdown, as you would expect. I need to arrange things with the undertakers. I can do it all over the phone with them and then Dean and Steven are going to arrange the funeral themselves," John imparted to Jan.

"I still can't believe what happened; it's all been like a bad dream. How did Geoff take it, or didn't you see him? I would have rung him myself but I don't suppose he would want to hear from me after all this time, and with news like that I don't know how he's going to cope."

"Steven went to see him after I left. I had to get home to Vera. She's not in a good place at the moment, although she has good days as well as bad. Yesterday, no matter how many times I told her where I was going, she still asked me when I got home where I had been all day! I think she's losing the plot!"

"Oh dear, that doesn't sound good. Is she getting worse?

I know we all forget things occasionally, especially at our age, but..." Jan was concerned for her sister-in-law.

"Yes, it's getting worse gradually, but I can cope with her if I'm here. At least she's not aggressive like I've heard sometimes that happens. Apparently the doc says there is some medication she can take which halts the condition, stops it getting any worse."

Jan then felt guilty for taking John away from his wife for the day.

Early next day Charlotte left the house and met her friend Amelia after texting her. She was still reeling from the news her father had given her siblings and herself. Amelia and Charlotte were best of friends at school as well as outside of school. They were inseparable. They always met at the same place, in the bus shelter at the end of their road whether they were catching the bus or not. Their school was only one stop along the route and sometimes they walked if they wanted to save the fare.

Amelia had a big personality and was funny and beguiling with whomever she was with; she was never short of friends. She was tall, like Charlotte, but with a bigger build. She had a penchant for jewellery, the chunkier the better, which suited her large frame.

"What's up? What're we going to do? D'you wanna go shopping down the mall? There's a nice top I'd like to get but I can't really afford it. I could try and poke it up my shirt. I might get away with it. What d'you think?" Amelia asked her friend but was puzzled as to why Charlotte was so quiet. "Why the glum looks, Charlie?"

"My mum has died, that's what!" Charlotte wanted Amelia to be quiet and this piece of information certainly did the trick. Charlotte sometimes wanted Amelia to realise she was not always the most important person.

"OMG, NO!" Amelia suddenly felt out of her comfort zone with not having had to handle a situation like this before. She wanted to change the subject to make Charlotte not have to think of such bad things as the loss of a mother. "My parents are divorced and I live with my mum. I don't know what I would do if she wasn't there anymore. Live with my dad, I suppose – and his new woman. Oh, no, I've changed my mind, I'd hate that. Can't wait to be old enough to leave home. I think I'll get a job as soon as we leave school. If our dream of becoming famous doesn't work then I'd like to be a hairdresser or something like that. Or work down the mall in one of those swanky fashion houses…"

"Just shut up, will you? It's not all about you all the time, Amelia." Charlotte finally got a word in.

"Sorry. And I'm sorry you lost your mum. Do you want to talk about it? How did it happen?"

"She went to see her mother, my grandmother, in Surrey. They hadn't been in contact for absolutely years and years and then all of a sudden she decides she ought to go and see her. Maybe she wanted to get into her good books in case she was not included in the will. I don't know. I've never met my grandmother and I don't know why there was a split. Mum would never talk about it."

"So, how did she die? In a car accident on the way there?"

"No, nothing like that. According to Dad it was a freak accident: a tree branch came down on top of her and there was nothing anyone could do to save her," Charlotte started to explain and Amelia laughed, which made Charlotte cross.

"It's not bloody funny!"

"Sorry." Amelia stifled another guffaw as the thought of someone beneath a tree branch could possibly mean someone dying as a result.

"My Uncle Steven was there with her but he's as useless as

a fifth wheel on a coach! He takes drugs, y'know. Reefers. But he thinks no one knows about it, silly old fool. I reckon his wife just closes her mind to it but we all know about it."

"I've met a boy from school and he's asked me out." Amelia was desperate to change the subject from Charlotte's dead mother. It was not important to her. There were much more salient things in her life and she had been dying to tell Charlotte all about the boy she had just met.

The co-ed school was only a fifteen-minute walk away from both their houses. They often walked to school with friends, both boys and girls, but as they grew older the two friends were seeing boys as more than just friends. It was inevitable that they were all of an age to notice the difference between boys and girls. The girls were always more advanced than the boys. Charlotte herself had fancied a boy, Seb, for ages but he would not heed her hints and advances towards him. She was biding her time until he got the message. Now Charlotte was worried in case Amelia was talking about "her boy, Seb", who had asked Amelia out. She realised there was no point in pursuing the fact of her mother's death with Amelia. She was far too self-centred to be interested in that anymore.

"Oh yes? What's he called?" Charlotte enquired.

"Darren. He's really lovely and I think I shall go out with him. What d'you think? I don't think my mum will let me so I won't tell her."

"Is that wise?" Charlotte knew the answer even before she asked. Amelia had quite often made the wrong decisions so Charlotte was trying to warn her. "He's not at our school, is he?"

"No. He goes to the grammar school. He's clever. Not like you and me!"

"We're not exactly stupid! Well, I'm not!" Charlotte was indignant at Amelia's remark.

"Thanks." Amelia was miffed to think Charlotte thought she was stupid. This type of banter was not unusual between these friends and they would usually just shrug it off.

"Maybe my brother knows him," Charlotte suggested.

"I think he's only been there a couple of years and Jake is taking his A levels, right? Darren is only a bit older than me. I think he had his sixteenth birthday at the beginning of the year."

"Well, I've heard that all boys can think of at that age is sex." Charlotte had learned that from her mother and having an older brother too helped her to understand how boys' minds worked. Amelia too had an older brother but they did not discuss personal things like sex.

Charlotte got up to go and left Amelia mulling over what her next move would be with Darren. Should she see him or should she not see him? Of course she was going to see him.

Charlotte arrived home later in the day. What struck her was the silence. Yesterday had been the devastating news of her mother's death with all the crying and wailing that went with it but now it was all quiet.

Dean had helped himself to another can of lager but then thought of the bottle of whisky that was kept in the cupboard for special occasions. This was a special occasion but not the sort for which it was meant. He had always had to wrestle with keeping his weight down but it was a losing battle. He had been told that alcohol had empty calories but this time he just did not care and his wife wasn't around to nag him so he felt carte blanche to help himself. He had given up smoking for the sake of his wife's asthma but he refused to give up alcohol. It was his friend.

Geoff had a complete mental breakdown and was not able to attend his daughter's funeral. His deep depression was exacerbated when the doctor was called and he was told he might have to be admitted to hospital for his own safety. The doctor told Lynda he was worried that Geoff's symptoms were bordering on psychosis, with possible delusions, which was a certifiable condition. Lynda knew that his condition was worsening with age and this setback did not help.

Dean felt relieved when the funeral service for his wife was over. He had been in limbo for what seemed ages, having to wait for the coroner's report. How was he going to be able to rebuild his life without Louise? He knew he was going to have to cope in order to try to keep family life on an even keel. He asked his mother for help, which he was not happy to do because he thought that showed weakness, but she said to him that she would do all she could to help out. She had been widowed herself nearly two years beforehand so she had great empathy for Dean and thought it was far harder for him, as a man, to be widowed. But she was really worried about his excessive drinking. He had always been a heavy drinker, mostly beers, but now he had a penchant for the hard stuff. Anything he could lay his hands on in fact; whisky, gin or vodka were his favourite tipples. As well as lager. And plenty of it.

3

Surrey

Jan was in turmoil. The day of a wonderful reunion with her estranged children had started well but ended disastrously. Hopes of reconciliation so cruelly dashed.

She had her own way of coping with the tragic loss of her daughter. She waved goodbye to her brother and son on that fateful day and sat down and cried. She cried herself to sleep, utterly exhausted. When she woke she thought she had dreamed everything until the nightmare became reality. It was not late enough to go to bed so she just sat thinking about the day. It was weird. It had started with great expectations and her making cakes for her two estranged children who were actually adults. Both well into their forties.

She had left her first husband when Louise and Steven were twenty-three and twenty, respectively, and were still living at home. She never thought in her wildest dreams that they would behave the way they had by totally cutting her out of their lives. She really thought they would get over it after a few months and then forgive her. After all, she explained to them time and time again, it was her husband she left, not them.

Mike, her second husband, had died a few months earlier and she was still coping with her bereavement. Her children had always said that, while she was with "that man", they would having nothing to do with her. After Mike died, her brother, John, decided to intervene. He was going to bring them to see her and all those years would melt away.

Cautious excitement had followed when Jan heard of his plans that he was bringing them to see her. Was she going to manage to persuade them to finally forgive her for leaving, all those years ago? Were they going to respond in a positive way? She was certainly going to try for a full reconciliation with them.

How it had all gone so badly wrong was still beyond her comprehension. Could she have done anything else to save her daughter? She decided that she did all she could. Now she had to try and cope with two bereavements in one year.

She wondered from afar, as to how they were coping and worried for them. She was not able to contact them but wished that she could. She had been shunned in the past and then rejected so many times she was afraid, in their bereavement, that they would blame her and then reject her all over again. Her hands were tied.

She went to a drawer in the sitting room, extracted a candle, lit it and then went over to the CD player. She put on a Phil Collins CD. Her all-time favourite song, "Two Hearts", rang out loudly as she turned up the volume to lift her mood. That music made her melt as it reminded her of Mike and the ring he had given her with a tiny ruby heart on their first ever holiday together, in Thailand. It never left her little finger and she often caressed it as she thought of him. She started to feel a little better as soon as she listened to those soft melodies.

The days following the death of her daughter, Jan had feelings of extreme vulnerability. *Would she feel the same way as she would have if she had had a proper relationship with her daughter?* she wondered. She felt nothing right now but that would change, surely.

So soon after her husband's passing, at times she did not know which way to turn. Where was her life going, what was she to do? Should she move away and have a complete change? Should she stay and let her friends help her to adjust? She felt so alone.

She had wonderful friends who rallied whenever she was low. They used to call themselves the ladies who lunch, but only because that was the time of day they usually met. The Thai restaurant or the Indian were their favourites. They put the world to rights whenever they met up and Jan enjoyed these times and their company. Her friends would always lift her spirits.

She looked at herself in the mirror and what stared back at her was an older person than was familiar to her, with greyer hair where it had been quite dark when she was young. More lines on her face than she remembered. Sixty-seven years old now. Not young but certainly not old. Surely a few years left in her? *Maybe I could put a colour on my hair to lift the sallowness of my skin? I could go on a diet, lose a few pounds? Go on a fitness regime? For what? For me? Am I worth it? How do I go on from here?* She pondered all these hypothetical questions. Was she diving into a depressive state? She hoped not.

She suddenly made a decision. She ought to move. But where? She would get a valuation for the house and then make a final decision. She could move right away, abroad even. What about New Zealand? She loved it there. But she had so many friends in Clayfold, it would mean starting all over again. At her age it would be difficult to start a new life in a completely different place. And making new friends too, might be difficult.

When in doubt, do nothing. God, I feel so lonely right now, more than ever in my life.

She walked out into the garden and made a beeline for the owl sculpture. He always had a friendly face and Jan loved that.

"What should I do? Come on, give me some guidance." She felt over the trunk, which had a smooth surface since the bark had been taken off. "Should I sell the house? It is rather big for one person, don't you think? The garden is lovely but I don't know how I'm going to manage it. I shall have to get someone in and help me. What do you think?"

She stood back from the owl and waited for an answer. He just sat there atop his plinth while Jan waited. *What am I doing, talking to an inanimate object? Am I going mad?*

A few days later she had an email from Ray and Daf in New Zealand inviting her to go there and stay and with them for Christmas. Stay as long as she wanted, they said. They were going to invite her anyway after they heard of Mike's passing but as soon as they heard about Louise they were adamant that she should not be on her own. This was going to be Jan's first ever Christmas alone so being with her good friends in New Zealand seemed the easy answer.

What she really wanted to do was to combine seeing her old schoolfriend Marian, who lived in Thailand. She would understand. She was the one who helped Jan and Mike get together in the first place, all those years ago. Jan emailed her and got a reply straight away to come to Thailand. Marian would make the pain go away, Jan knew.

Jan worked out the best way. Christmas was coming all too soon and she knew that Ray and Daf wanted her to stay for that. She could stay as long as she liked, they had said. While she was there she would also like to visit her brother-in-law, Jamie. His place was not far from Ray and Daf and she hadn't seen him since her sister died over two years beforehand. Then she could visit Marian in Thailand on her way home; that would break the journey too. After all, what did she have to come back to? Selling the house? Moving away? Or what?

I will just have to bite the bullet and get on with things on my own. Steven will carry on where Louise left off, I just know it. I will try to build bridges with him when I get home. I will try and try until I succeed, she told herself strictly. *And then I hope to meet my grandchildren at long last, if I'm lucky.*

Jan's best friend, Vicky, comforted her as nobody else could. She came to Jan's side as soon as she heard of her loss. Her second loss within six months.

"How are you, my dear?" Vicky asked kindly. "Shall I make you a cup of tea? That always seems to be the cure of all ills!" She tried very hard to lighten the mood when she saw how sad Jan looked. She started to switch on the kettle even before Jan answered.

"Yes, thanks, tea will be fine. I'm fine, thanks. I just can't decide what to do. Should I sell this house and buy something smaller? Should I move away? Should I move back to my home city of Bristol? I've still got old schoolfriends there. Or should I go and live in New Zealand?"

"New Zealand? Are you mad? What will I do without you?" Vicky was joking and hurriedly explained that she was not just thinking of herself at this time. "What I mean is, I shall miss you if you go anywhere else. I really don't think you should make any hasty decisions about anything right now."

"Yes, you're right. I just don't know what I should be feeling. I don't sense the emptiness that I thought I should have, with Louise gone. Is that because we were estranged for so long and so I don't feel that I have lost anything? Even though I *have* lost her. I think I ought to be suffering because I have lost something. But I don't! Do you know what I mean?"

"That all sounds pretty normal." Vicky agreed.

"And, talking about New Zealand, my old friends there have asked me over to spend Christmas with them. I have thought it over and decided I should go. Not only that, I emailed my friend in Thailand and she has persuaded me to visit her too, on the way back. It will be quite a trip although I'm a bit apprehensive as I've never travelled on my own before."

"You'll be fine. People are doing it all the time. You are the strongest person I know. In no time, while you're there, you will forget all your troubles, I know you will."

"So, what am I going to do about the house?" asked Jan "It's too big for one person."

"Well, I refuse to let you move from Clayfold!" Vicky cried.

"I knew you'd say that! I really haven't decided anything for certain. My life is in a state of flux, as you know. Which is why I need to get away at Christmas and New Year. Even if it's just to clear my head. It was only last Christmas that Mike and I had started talking about planning a trip to Japan. It was going to be a fabulous holiday. And now look at me: a complete mess with no husband and now no daughter. And it's all my fault!"

"It's not your fault! Well, I hope your New Zealand friends will talk some sense into you. And you will come back refreshed and knowing what you want to do, I'm sure," Vicky reassured Jan.

Vicky left after two hours of talking things through. Jan went straight into the garden again, to talk to the owl. He never spoke back to her but she liked to think that he gave her comfort. She clutched at thoughts and expectations of aims for a happy life. Luckily the garden was quite secluded as she did not like the thought of someone watching her talk to the owl with the fear that they thought she was losing her mind.

"Am I doing the right thing?" she asked the owl and she swore he put his head on one side as if he was listening hard. She continued. "I'm going away to think things through. Daf and Ray have been kind enough to invite me to stay with them to take my mind off everything. Then I shall stay with Marian and she will make things right, I just know she will. When I come back, my head will be a lot clearer. I hope! If I sell up I shall have to take you with me. I can't leave you behind!" Jan swore she saw the owl smile. "I shall be away for Christmas and New Year but I will say goodbye before I go!"

The weeks dragged by and Jan left everything on hold at home for the time being. She was reticent about travelling alone because she had never done it before.

How hard can it be? People are travelling on their own all the time. Vicky told me that. Come on and get a grip! Jan told herself.

She did get a grip and pulled herself together and started packing for her holiday. She wrote her Christmas cards and prepared everything for her holiday. Soon her suitcases were packed and she set off for New Zealand post-haste.

4

Devon

As the days passed into weeks, Jake did his level best to keep his younger sisters happy, especially Daisy as she was not coping well with mourning for her mother. Her twelfth birthday was approaching fast but she was too upset to even think about it. She had joined secondary school only two months beforehand and she was one of the oldest in her year. In that short time she had made some good friends who she hoped would understand and be sympathetic towards her. Although she was now at the same school as Charlotte, Daisy did not feel like she could ask Charlotte for the help she now needed.

Jake had to tread on eggshells with Charlotte in case she flew off at him if he said a wrong word. It was getting nearer to Christmas and, as far as he could see, his father had not started to prepare anything for the festive season. Granny Kath, Dean's mother, had been helping out as she said she would as she tried to smooth the way for them with everyday eventualities.

She agreed that she would help with the shopping and would cook the dinner on Christmas Day.

"Leave it to me," she told Jake and Daisy. She was happy to keep herself busy to take her mind off her own problems. She was glad to help out and loved her grandchildren equally. She would not normally have spent Christmas Day with them because her daughter-in-law had never invited her. Now was her chance to spend more time with her beautiful grandchildren.

Charlotte's coping mechanism was shot to pieces. The only thing she could think about was going out and about with her friends and cutting herself away from the family. They only made her feel sad. Unfortunately, her new-found freedom was the beginning of her downfall.

Amelia wanted Charlotte to double date as that was the only way her mother was going to let her go out with boys. Both girls were fifteen and Amelia's mother was worried that they were becoming too grown up too soon. The girls had talked about sex and had giggled about who was going to do it first.

"Come on," Amelia persuaded Charlotte. "You know you want to do it so why does it matter who it's with?"

"Well, I want it to be with someone I fancy, that's a start, I guess," Charlotte demurred. "After that, well, who knows?"

Charlotte persuaded Seb to double date with Amelia and Darren and he was delighted. It turned out that the two boys knew each other from primary school. They all met up and went to McDonalds to start with, for an early meal. They were too young to go into a pub so they went to the local youth club and chatted all evening. Charlotte and Seb decided they wanted to be alone, away from the other two. They made their excuses and left the youth club.

"I know a place we can go," Seb told Charlotte as he held her hand and guided her along the road. He had been told about an old car that belonged to his brother's friend that was parked in the drive. He had already been given the keys and was told to post them in the letterbox when he had finished. Charlotte was a virgin and was very naïve but she was inquisitive and wanted to find out what everyone was talking about.

I can't think it is such a big deal, she told herself. Seb could not believe his luck. He guided her towards the car and opened the back door for her to climb in. It was very clumsy and awkward and quick.

After an hour or so Amelia was fed up with Darren and decided to leave and go home alone. She went to Charlotte's house the next day to ask her what happened. She was there alone and told Amelia what happened when they left.

"Did you go all the way?" Amelia was curious so it was the first thing she asked.

"You bet! It was painful at first and I think it was Seb's first time too. I'm not sure if he knew what he was doing. It only lasted a couple of minutes and then it was all over. Apparently some boys feel very tired – after all the exertion, I suppose – but Seb was okay and he walked me home afterwards."

"So, did you… enjoy it?"

"I think so. Like I say it was all over so quickly and it was a bit messy. Quite disgusting really as he asked me if I had any tissues to mop up. Luckily I had some so we used those."

"So, didn't he use a condom?"

"I don't know! S'pose not." Charlotte was non-committal. Everything else was wrong in her life; she just did not care.

Amelia wondered if she was going to be able to go through with what her friend had endured but knew if she was going to lose her virginity she did not want it to happen in an old car. Charlotte agreed and thought she would rather it was in a more comfortable place.

"It's my brother Tom's eighteenth soon and I think he's

going to persuade Mum to have a party. Will you come if he does?" asked Amelia. "It should be good and we might be able to have a drink. And… his friends are rather dishy!"

"In that case, count me in!" said Charlotte.

The party was hastily arranged for the following week on the Saturday nearest to Tom's birthday.

"I'm going out with friends," said Sue, Amelia and Tom's mother. "But I don't want you to have loads of friends in, just a few, okay? I've heard about parties that get out of hand and our place isn't that big."

"Okay, Mum. I get it. Just a few close friends, that's all," Tom agreed.

"You'll bring your friend Charlotte, won't you," Tom said to his sister.

"You like her, don't you?" Tom winked at Amelia which told her the answer. "What about Seb, the boy she's seeing at the moment?"

"Tell her to come alone." Tom made it clear to Amelia that he was wanting to get to know Charlotte better.

Charlotte arrived at the party with a present for Tom and some cans of lager to help the party go with a swing. She had taken them from her father's stash from the under-stairs cupboard. She had never really had alcohol before and she was unaware that Tom liked her. As soon as she arrived he took her to one side and gave her a glass.

"What's this?" she asked.

"Oh, it's party punch. Try it, it's just some different fruit juices," Tom lied. It was fruit juice but laced with large amounts of gin and vodka. She took a big gulp as she was thirsty. She was not sure if she liked it so she drank some more to make sure. She and Amelia were the youngest there and kept to themselves at first in the kitchen, before they were going to venture into the party to meet Tom's friends.

"And who are these two gorgeous young things?" Harry had been lurking in the vicinity of the hall, lager can in hand. He had sidled into the kitchen when he heard the girls talking to Tom. Harry was a friend of Tom's from school, slightly older than Tom: he had had his eighteenth just a few weeks ago.

"Oh, hi, Harry. This is my sister, Amelia, and her friend Charlie," said Tom, introducing them.

"Well, Tom, are you keeping them all to yourself, you sly old bugger?" Harry had already been drinking before he arrived at the party and was not thinking before he spoke.

"Hardly! This is my sister, I told you!"

"Oh, yes, you did, sorry. Oops!" Harry sniggered.

Tom kept topping up Charlotte's glass and, although she liked the taste, she was not aware of the effect it was starting to have on her. He was good to his word that there were only a few of his closest friends, about twenty in all, a mixture of girls and boys, including Amelia and Charlotte. Out of all the girls there, Tom had had his eye on Charlotte. He had met her only once before and liked what he saw. He bided his time and, when he noticed she was slurring her speech a little, he thought it might be time for him to make a move on her. Unfortunately for him, Harry decided to take her for himself behind Tom's back, while Tom was busy mingling and giving out food and drink. Amelia had briefly left the kitchen to help Tom with plates of food and, when they came back to the kitchen, Harry and Charlotte were gone. Harry had pounced on Charlotte while she was alone.

He guided her upstairs with his arm around her shoulders and into one of the three bedrooms. He didn't care whose bedroom it was because he only had one thing on his mind. She knew something was happening to her but was not quite in command of her own legs.

Harry was not sure if Charlotte was a virgin. He hoped she was. He liked virgins. He carefully unbuttoned her blouse and lay her on the bed and started to kiss her, first on the lips and then on her shoulders where her blouse fell open. When he felt there was no resistance from her, he felt under her skirt, from where he could easily remove her knickers. Charlotte was only just aware of what was happening to her.

Harry had to slap her awake, slightly disappointed that he had had such little response from her. *Maybe Tom had given her too much alcohol and she wasn't used to it. It was like making love to a corpse! Better luck next time.*

Harry helped her up off the bed and sat her down in a chair while he made the bed, as good as he found it, probably tidier. He took a quick look around before taking Charlotte by the hand and steadied her down the stairs to the kitchen.

"Coffee? I'll make us a coffee," said Harry to Charlotte but she did not answer. He made a tray of coffees, gave one to Charlotte and left her sitting at the kitchen table while he went back to Tom and their friends in the sitting room to distribute the coffees.

"Where did you get to?" asked Amelia. She had been to the toilet and when she came back to the kitchen she saw Charlotte sitting at the table with her coffee in front of her.

"Up-shtairs," Charlotte slurred, pointing her finger upwards. She did not say anymore and Amelia assumed she meant she went to the bathroom upstairs because the downstairs cloakroom was engaged. "Not feeling very well." Charlotte's head thumped down on the table.

"Come on," said Amelia. "I'm taking you home. I think you've had enough; you don't look too good." She fetched their coats and took Charlotte home on a very circuitous route as Charlotte stepped two forward and one back, her arms around Amelia. Amelia rang the doorbell and Jake answered. She pushed Charlotte into the house, happy that she was safely home, her job was done.

Harry found Tom and started goading him, giving him very graphic details of what had happened when he took Charlotte upstairs. He made sure he embellished the facts for effect. Tom was furious.

"You bastard. You must have known I was after her myself." Then more quietly he asked. "So was she a virgin?"

"Nah, don't think so. God, she was hot for me!" Harry boasted. "Best shag I've had all week," he lied.

"It's my birthday and you take the girl I was interested in, you little shit."

"Yeah! What are you going to do about it?" Harry was a good two inches taller than Tom and of a much bigger build, since playing rugby for the school team. He squared up to Tom, who could do nothing but back off.

Amelia came back into the house just as the party was beginning to break up and people were starting to leave. Harry saw Amelia and made a beeline towards her.

"Hellooo," he said, sleazily. "Where have you been all my life?" Tom heard him and went to push him out of the way. He felt he should protect his little sister from this predator.

"Get out, Harry. Go on, bugger off, you're not trying it on with my sister too."

Harry got the message and did not want a fight. He left with another girl and never looked back.

"What did you mean, Tom?" asked Amelia. "Trying it on with me?"

"You'll know soon enough when Charlotte tells you. She obviously didn't tell you tonight but she had it off with Harry this evening. I've gone right off her now; she is far too loose for my liking."

The following week Charlotte met with Seb again. He was

very kind to her as he felt sorry for her when she had told him
about her mum. They talked a lot this time and got to know
each other better. They had known each other at school but
only as friends. They went to Charlotte's house. He jumped at
the chance when she had told him that the house was going to
be empty. Daisy was having a dancing lesson after school and
Jake was always staying on at school for extra tuition and their
father was still at work.

Seb discovered where Charlotte's bedroom was and
she put up very little resistance, wanting him as much as he
wanted her.

They met up several times after that when Charlotte knew
the house would be empty, until she started to get fed up with
Seb. She cooled off when she started fancying another boy she
had met. William was taller than Seb and a little older and
more experienced. He told Charlotte that he was learning to
play the guitar.

"I'd love to play a musical instrument," Charlotte gushed.
"Would you teach me?"

"Yes, of course, I'd love to," said William.

"You can come to my house on Thursday after school. The
house will be empty so we won't be disturbed," she imparted
to William. She made it known that she liked him and he had
already taken a fancy to Charlotte.

She took William home for "guitar lessons" whenever she
knew the house was empty and they made the most of being
alone. William was a caring lover for Charlotte but it was not
long before Charlotte fell out with William and they went their
separate ways. Charlotte was becoming disillusioned with boys
and decided it might be best just to keep them as friends.

Jake and Daisy contemplated their first Christmas without
their mother. They hatched a plan to decorate the house just

the way their mother used to do with streamers and tinsel and the Christmas cards Sellotaped to ribbons that hung on the walls. They found the Christmas tree in the loft, together with all the baubles and strings of beads and the angel for the top.

"Come on, Charlie, come and help us decorate the sitting room." Jake tried to cajole Charlotte but she was not interested.

"I'm busy!" Charlotte replied.

"Have you done your Christmas shopping yet?" Daisy asked Charlotte and then waited for a reply. But Charlotte had other ideas. She completely ignored the question and shut herself in her bedroom. Daisy was not impressed with her sister's antics.

"Leave her alone," suggested Jake to Daisy. "She's still grieving in her own way." Jake was still a little miffed that he was left to sober up Charlotte after her night at Tom's eighteenth birthday party. She had obviously had alcohol even though she was underage but he knew that she was the type to experiment. He knew his sister too well.

"Well, so are we! It seems we just have to get on with it and behave like normal. It's just not fair!" Daisy complained.

"No, it isn't but what else do you suggest? I think it would be nice if you and I just try and keep the peace. Dad is grieving too and doesn't seem to want to do anything towards Christmas."

Daisy shrugged and carried on decorating the Christmas tree and Jake helped her. After a few minutes Charlotte surfaced and disappeared out of the front door, slamming it shut behind her. Jake looked out to see if he could see where she was going but he could not see which direction she went. She went to meet Amelia in order to hang out in the bus shelter as they waited for the youth club to open.

"Where shall we go?" Charlotte asked Amelia.

"My mother's out, although my brother's in the house." Amelia informed Charlotte.

Tom had aspirations of going to university next year. In fact, he was the same age as Jake and they would be going off at the same time. But probably not to the same place.

"That's okay," said Charlotte. "Let's hang out at your house. It's no good going to mine, everyone is moping about so much it's doing my head in! Got any booze?"

"I think there's some left over from Tom's party," Amelia answered. "Let's go and investigate."

Amelia and Charlotte then ran along the road to Amelia's house in anticipation of finding something alcoholic. Anything.

They heard subdued voices in a bedroom upstairs. Amelia put her finger to her lips to tell Charlotte not to make a noise. Amelia was going to investigate as to who was upstairs. She heard Tom's voice coming from his bedroom together with another male voice.

"Go on, try it…" Amelia did not recognise the voice.

"I will if you will. Where did you get it?" Tom's voice.

"A mate of mine. Well, a friend of a friend. I can't guarantee anything. They weren't that expensive. Go on then, you try it first."

Tom was a little apprehensive. Amelia could hear shuffling on the other side of the door. She did not want them to discover her there so she crept away as fast as she could down to where Charlotte was waiting in the hall. She took Charlotte by the arm to guide her quietly into the kitchen.

"Is it your mum?" Charlotte asked.

"No, it's Tom with a friend in his bedroom," Amelia affirmed.

"Oh yes?"

"What are you suggesting?"

"I'm only kidding," said Charlotte.

"What d'you want to do?" Amelia asked her friend.

"We can just hang out here, if you like." Charlotte was hoping to see Tom again. She really liked him and was hoping to get to know him better since she had split with Seb and William. She had hoped something might have happened at his party but he was too preoccupied with his other guests to notice her. Then her thoughts turned to Harry. Is that who is upstairs with Tom? She was not sure if she liked Harry since she thought he had taken advantage of her at the party, but she still was not too sure what had happened that night.

Amelia opened the kitchen cupboards, one by one, looking for something that they could drink. Something that wouldn't be missed by her mother. She found a half-empty bottle of Cointreau right at the back of one of the cupboards. She took the stopper out and sniffed at the contents.

"This smells orangey. D'you want to try it? I think it's some sort of liqueur. I'm sure my mum doesn't drink liqueurs; she's more into gin and wine."

"Okay. We'll have a go at it," Charlotte replied. She got two glasses out and held them out for Amelia to pour the liquid. "OMG, that's thick!"

"It is rather!" Amelia giggled. "Well, we'll just try a little to start with. It'll either be disgusting or okay. It's got two chances. If it's disgusting we will just put it back and if it's okay we can polish it off and no one will be any the wiser. One thing though: it's bound to have some alcohol in it!"

"That's true!" They giggled in unison.

They both decided that it was not like any other drink they had tried. They both liked the orangey flavour but they weren't sure about the consistency, being used to drinks that flowed like water. They emptied the bottle into both glasses and then they heard footsteps on the stairs. They downed the last few drops in one gulp.

"Quick, hide the bottle," Amelia said to Charlotte as she was closest to the bottle. Charlotte slid it into the nearest cupboard, under the sink. They both started to giggle as Tom and his friend Mark arrived in the kitchen.

"What's going on here then?" enquired Tom of his sister.

"Nothing!" Amelia tried to sound as innocent as she could.

"Guilty as charged!" Tom announced. "You two are tipsy!"

"Of course we aren't." Amelia suddenly felt sober as she did not want her brother to tell their mother she had been drinking. "Are we?" She nudged Charlotte for confirmation.

"Of course not!" Charlotte could only just contain a little snigger.

"This is my friend Mark." Mark did a little wave to the two girls. "We want you two to try these." Mark produced four little white tablets, on the palm of his hand and proffered them towards Amelia and Charlotte. Tom was still miffed that Charlotte went with Harry at his party and wanted to get back at her. He had fancied her but not anymore.

"What are they?" Amelia asked her brother.

"Never mind what they are. You might feel quite relaxed and happy afterwards."

"Happy pills? Let me at 'em," Charlotte said bravely.

Tom and Mark stood by and watched the two girls take the pills then waited. They exchanged glances and Mark winked knowingly at Tom.

"I don't feel happy yet!" said Amelia impatiently. "And why aren't you two taking them? Don't you want to feel happy?"

"We've already tried them earlier. We just wanted to see if they worked on girls. We know they work on boys," said Mark, starting to get impatient.

He did not have to wait too long when a few minutes went by and he could see the pupils in the girls' eyes were starting to become dilated. Charlotte stood up and went towards Tom, looking him straight in the eye before she tripped up on a chair leg and ended up in his arms.

"Come to me, not to him," said Mark sharply to Charlotte, taking her by the arm. He guided her through the kitchen door towards the stairs and she felt her knees starting to wobble. He caught her before she fell and started carrying her upstairs.

"What's going on?" Amelia asked her brother.

"Nothing! It's really affected Charlie. Are you okay?"

"I'm fine. Charlie had more to drink than me."

"So you were drinking? I thought you were. What did you find? I was sure there wasn't much left in the house after my party."

Amelia opened the cupboard under the sink and showed him the empty bottle. Just as he was looking at it they heard the front door open.

"Hello? Anyone in?" said Sue, Amelia and Tom's mother. She saw two feet disappearing quickly upstairs, stumbling on the last stair and then a hefty thud as Mark dropped Charlotte on the landing floor.

"What's going on? Who's that? Tom? Amelia?"

"Hi, Mum," said Tom, appearing nonchalantly from the kitchen. "You're back early. We're in the kitchen." He wanted to distract her from what was happening upstairs. Too late.

"Not early enough it appears! Who is upstairs?" Sue asked sharply.

Amelia stayed in the kitchen and stashed the bottle away in her rucksack before going out into the hall. Her mother folded her arms and tapped her foot as she waited for an explanation.

"What's going on? You're all looking somewhat guilty! Someone is upstairs but no one is giving me any answers."

"Give me a chance," said Tom. "It's just Mark. Come down Mark," he called upstairs.

Mark thumped his feet down the stairs, gave Tom a dirty look and then disappeared through the front door without saying anything to anyone.

"Charming! Some friend he is," said Sue as she made her way towards the kitchen just as Charlotte started down the stairs, very slowly and carefully, her knees almost buckling under her.

A text came through just then on Tom's phone. He took it out of his pocket and looked at the message. It was from Mark with three little words. "You owe me!" He put it back in his pocket.

Amelia went to Charlotte's aid when she saw her. She helped her down the rest of the stairs, put her coat over her shoulders, grabbed her own and went out through the front door.

"See you later," Amelia called to her mother. She did not want her giving Charlotte the third degree and having Charlotte tell her about the booze they found.

"Come on, let's get you home for Christmas." Although there were several days left before Christmas Day, Amelia wanted her friend to be safe so she escorted her all the way home. This was becoming a habit, she thought to herself. Normally they would have gone their separate ways but Amelia felt responsible for Charlotte after her own brother had given them the pills. She still had no idea what they were and she made a mental note to ask Tom when her mum was not in earshot. She felt okay herself but it had definitely affected Charlotte, and not in a good way.

"Where've you been?" asked Jake as soon as Charlotte arrived through the front door. Amelia made a quick exit as soon as she knew her friend was safely indoors.

"None of your business." Charlotte disappeared upstairs to her bedroom. She was still feeling very woozy and unsteady.

Without undressing, she climbed straight into her bed to sleep off the effects of the pill and the alcohol. She soon fell into a deep sleep.

"Oh, leave her. She's in one of her moods, I expect. Probably the time of the month," Daisy said to her brother.

Daisy and Jake had finished the decorations, the tree and the lights and they stood back in admiration of their handiwork.

"I wish Mum was here to see what we've achieved," Jake said to Daisy.

"Or even Dad! He hardly spends any time at home now, always down the pub." Jake pondered on life since his mother passed away. He was starting to feel like he was the only adult in the house with responsibilities.

Daisy went to bed and Jake started packing away the decorations they did not use and started thinking of how Christmas was going to pan out without their mother to see to everything. But that was a few days away; no need to worry about that now. Maybe his father would do the right thing and help out. Jake knew that Granny Kath was going to help with shopping and cooking and to spend Christmas Day with them. In fact, it had been agreed that she would stay for several days, for which he was grateful for the help. He shrugged and went to bed hoping and praying that their Christmas was not going to turn into a disaster.

On Christmas Eve, Dean was buying drinks in the pub for anyone who would talk to him. He was feeling lonely and he tried desperately to make new friends.

"Cheers." Dean's new "friends" raised their glasses to him. "Merry Christmas."

He bought drinks for people as they came in the door so they felt they should stay with him at least while the drinks lasted. He had nothing in common with them apart from being drinking buddies. They returned the favour and bought him a drink in return but they did not stop too long to talk with him. They found him abrasive and annoying, especially after several beers.

It was starting to get late when his "friends" had to go home and left Dean to his own devices. But he did not feel like going home yet. What was there to go home for? No wife. Three children with whom he felt he had lost touch lately.

Dean was starting to sway and Keith, the landlord, was getting worried.

At the youth club on the same night Amelia and Charlotte were talking with their friends at a Christmas party. There was no alcohol provided but Amelia had persuaded Tom to get them some.

"I felt dreadful after those pills Tom gave us. What were they?" asked Charlotte.

"I don't really know; he wouldn't say. I felt okay but you were really out of it."

"That's cos I've got a small frame, d'you think?"

"Probably. Anyway, this should cheer you up." Amelia brought out some cans of lager, cider and a half bottle of gin with some tonics. She had to hide them or everyone else would want some of their stash. Amelia plied Charlotte throughout the evening and then with Tom's help they took her home. It was late and Jake and Daisy were already in bed, although their father was still nowhere to be seen. They had no idea where he was. Once inside the house they tried to be quiet as they put Charlotte to bed and then crept silently out of the house and back to their own home.

"No more drink for you, me ol' china," Keith, a Londoner, told Dean. "Go home to your family, now, there's a good chap. Merry Christmas."

Dean got the message, emptied his glass and put it on the bar. Unfortunately, it missed the bar and dropped to the floor.

"Oops, sorry," said Dean, stifling a giggle. He did not mean to drop the glass but saw the funny side of everything when he had too much to drink. He started to feel tired but knew he must make it home. He walked home: only three roads away but with his swaying it took him longer than normal. One step forward, two steps back. It was well after midnight when he tried to find his front door keys in his pocket.

"Oh, where the hell are they?" he asked himself. He searched every pocket and eventually found them, then searched for the keyhole. He fell into the door and stumbled on the step, just saving himself from falling to the floor.

"Ssh!" he told himself and then laughed as he tried to shut the door really quietly. The lock clicked. He told the lock to be quiet and put his finger up to his mouth.

The whole house was in darkness and quiet. Everyone had gone to bed. There was no one to greet him home. He went into the kitchen to see if there might be a little nightcap in there. He found a nearly-empty whisky bottle in the kitchen cupboard and emptied it straight into his mouth. No point making more washing up.

He left his shoes in the hall and staggered upstairs as quietly as he could manage. He started to undress himself and left a piece of clothing every three stairs. By the time he was at the top he was on his hands and knees and naked. He looked at the closed doors before him, opened one and went inside. He climbed straight into bed and, in his drunken stupor, imagined his wife was already there waiting for him. He fondled her before he dropped into a deep sleep.

In his inebriated state he dreamed of making love to the world's beauties including Cheryl Cole and Nicole Scherzinger, the tall dusky beautiful singer famous for dating

Lewis Hamilton. Cheryl left her husband for Dean and then fought Nicole for his affections. In his last dream he cuddled up to Charlie Dimmock, the garden makeover woman who really caught his attention. He loved her humungous breasts, just like those that belonged to his wife.

At 5am the next morning the effects of last night's alcohol had just about dissipated from Dean's body. Still moved with emotion, re-enacting making love over and over with Charlie Dimmock and fondling her great mammaries. He loved big breasts.

He slowly awakened from his dream and Charlie Dimmock disappeared as he opened one eye. The first thing he saw was a photo of Charlie on the wall. But not Charlie Dimmock. It was a picture of his own daughter Charlie, with his wife, Louise, in happier times when she was alive. He looked at the unfamiliar bedroom surroundings and realisation came to the fore. But both Charlies had disappeared. He looked under the duvet and saw his naked body.

Oh my God! This is Charlie's bedroom! I've been making love to my daughter all night! What must she think of me?

5

The taxi picked up Jan and took her to Heathrow, where she checked in with no trouble. The gate was full but she found a seat, a single seat with many other people milling about.

"That's the advantage of travelling alone, only needing one seat," Jan said bravely to the woman next to her. Jan thought about the last time she travelled, which had been with Mike. She had never ever been on a plane on her own before and this had been a daunting prospect. She was determined not to spoil the occasion, especially as the end result was going to be so enjoyable when she meets up with her friends.

"I'm on my own too! First time ever. My husband refused to come with me. I'm visiting my daughter and son-in-law in Melbourne. They've just had their first baby, my first grandchild. I'm so excited so I'm not thinking about travelling alone, disconcerting as it seemed to start with."

"I agree. That's wonderful." Jan was caught up in this lady's enthusiasm. "Are you staying for Christmas?"

"I wish I could but my husband wants me back in time to cook his Christmas dinner! So it's just a fleeting visit this time. What about you?"

"Yes, I'm staying with friends in New Zealand for

Christmas and New Year and then I'm seeing an old schoolfriend in Bangkok after that. On my way home. I shall be away for about seven weeks."

"Oh, lucky you, I wish I could stay longer."

Jan wished her all the best as they were called to board the plane. They were stopping off in Dubai but Jan never saw the woman again.

Jan learned from Mike many years before that long-haul flights can be managed by just switching off. He had travelled abroad many times during his working life and, of course, they had travelled far and wide while they were together. She made herself as comfortable as she could next to the window and started to relax and "switch off". This was short-lived as she saw a large woman wobbling down the aisle looking at the seat numbers. Jan kept her fingers crossed that she wasn't coming to sit next to her. The woman kept going and Jan was relieved until she then saw a young woman with a baby. *Oh, no, that's probably worse if the baby cries!*

The stewardess came to help the young woman find her seat: nowhere near Jan, much to her relief. It was a bulkhead seat, which is usually reserved for families with a baby where a drop-down cot is provided by the airline.

Jan watched two of the latest films on the journey but she couldn't tell what they were about. Her mind was in turmoil as to her predicament but she tried not to let anything spoil her holiday with Ray and Daf. At the back of her mind niggled her last conversation with Vicky. Should she stay or should she go? Should she sell the house? Move away? Buy something smaller? She was determined to forget about all that for the time being.

Ray picked her up from Auckland airport and Jan felt better as soon as she saw him standing there with his smiling face. They went to the car park but the car was not where he left it.

"Oh no! It can't have been stolen in that short time, surely," Ray complained. He paced up and down while Jan stood there dumbfounded. She was tired after the long journey and just wanted to relax.

"Are you sure it was this car park?" Jan tried tentatively. She did not want to make him feel stupid, as if he was looking in the wrong place. "What is the registration number? I could look as well."

He tutted as if that were a silly idea but he told her the number as well as the colour and type of car. Jan trotted off to another car park a little further away, walking down the rows of cars. One by one she scrutinised each car.

"Found it!" she shouted at the top of her voice over to where Ray was still looking in the wrong place. He looked very sheepish as he came over to his car. He opened the boot to put in the suitcase but it was completely full of his golfing things – bag, irons, woods plus other things that Daf had put there. They had both forgotten to clear it out.

"Oh dear. I'm not at all organised today, am I? Never mind, your suitcase can go on the back seat."

"That's fine. Don't worry about it. I'm just glad to be here. Thank you so much for inviting me. That's just what I need."

"It's our complete pleasure. Just a pity Mike isn't with us anymore."

Ray drove home and the two of them talked and talked. Daf had stayed home to prepare for the festivities and do the cooking in preparation for Jan's stay. Ray told Jan that Daf had made arrangements for them after the festive period to go away for a few days. He knew that she had booked for them a farm-stay on the Coromandel for a few days. There was also a big secret to which he was not privy but Daf would tell them when she was ready. He was also prepared to take them on a few day trips out. He wondered if Daf might have booked to go down to South Island to stay with their daughter and family but he thought that might be put on hold until Daf had asked Jan what she thought. He was very vague but Jan appreciated that they both thought enough of her to think of things to do to keep her mind occupied.

Daf gave Jan a big bear hug when they arrived.

"It's fantastic to be here again after all this time. Thank you so much for inviting me," Jan said again, but to Daf this time.

"It's been far too long."

"Yes, it's been a while, hasn't it?"

"Have you been looking after yourself since Mike died?" Daf asked kindly. "It must be difficult readjusting to life without him. And, of course, we were so sorry to hear about your daughter. That was an unkind blow, just as you were about to reconcile with both your children."

"Yes, it was. I've been at sixes and sevens ever since. I haven't known from one day to the next what I'm going to do. I keep on changing my mind. One day I think I will move away from Clayfold but then I have so many friends there now. And where would I go? Back to my home city of Bristol? It's been such a long time ago that I left there I hardly know anyone there, only my brother and a few old schoolfriends. I could go back to Devon, where my grandchildren live, and try to set up some sort of relationship with them but I don't know them. And they don't know me. I would dearly love to at least meet them. Hopefully my son and son-in-law won't still keep me from meeting them. But I just don't know. I think it was my daughter who was the driving force in not letting me meet them."

"That was very cruel, I have to say. Sorry, but I think that was completely out of order. It's not as if you did anything wrong apart from leave your husband. What was the matter with them?" Daf asked.

"Don't ask me! I really have no idea why they have been that way all these years. Hopefully things might change from now on. Anyway, let's just enjoy our time together and not think of anything else right now. I will decide when I get home what the next move will be. But that is a long way off."

Jan unpacked her things and settled into Ray and Daf's family routine and she was soon forgetting her own problems back at home. Daf told Jan of her plans of what they could do and Jan was delighted to be organised and not have to think for herself. She could stay as long as she liked but in four weeks' time her flight was booked to Thailand to stay with her old friend Marian. This arrangement was opened-ended as Marian, too, had said for Jan to stay as long as she liked.

Christmas was a very happy affair, with Daf and Ray's friends and family coming and going. Jan met a lot of their different friends as well as Daf's cousins. Her family was large and she enjoyed entertaining them all at Christmas. It was very different to what Christmas would be at home, Jan thought. She would just be on her own, although she had her own friends who would rally and see that she would be okay. No family to speak of, though.

On Boxing Day Daf had a surprise for Jan, which she was keeping very close to her chest. All she knew was that something was going to happen but in her wildest dreams she had no idea what it could be.

After breakfast the doorbell rang and Daf rushed to answer and let in the person standing on the doorstep. It was Mike's son, Richard. Jan had met him a few times but she had not seen him for a couple of years. Richard lived in Australia and could not make it for Christmas Day but this was the earliest he could come. He also explained that the flights were so cheap on Boxing Day he could not resist taking one.

Daf dragged Richard into the sitting room, where Jan and Ray were relaxing. Even Ray was surprised. Both he and Daf were Richard's godparents. Daf had kept it from Ray just in case Richard could not come at the last moment but she had been hoping he could, all the time since she had arranged it with him.

"Hi, guys!" said Richard nonchalantly as he put his head around the door.

Jan was so pleased to see him; he looked so like his father, she did a double take.

"Christmas just gets better and better," said Jan, giving Richard a hug.

"I'm so sorry I wasn't able to come to Dad's funeral. I think of him often, you know. He's my role model, even though our lives have been completely different." Richard lived in a commune in Byron Bay, living hand to mouth but very happy. Most days he would help out the farmer with bringing in the cows for milking and chopping logs. In exchange the farmer let him live in a yurt on his large homestead, where he lived alone, happy to let the days go by playing his guitar and surfing.

A few years beforehand he had married the girl of his dreams. They had been together for six blissful years before they decided to get married. Only some close friends were invited to their wedding, which had taken place on a beach in Melbourne. Six months later, when Jan and Mike were visiting, Richard told them that his marriage was over. He said that they wanted different things out of life and he could see them going in separate directions. She was thirty-six and decided she wanted babies, and soon. He was adamant that he did not want children. Mike wondered at the time why they hadn't sorted out what they wanted before they got married. Richard had been alone ever since.

Richard fitted into family life with Ray and Daf as he had done many times in the past. His close family, his mother and sister, still lived in England so Ray and Daf were the nearest family he had, even though they were several hours away by plane. He stayed for three happy days before venturing back home to Australia. He promised to visit Jan next time he was over in England when he saw his mum. Jan did not know it but that turned out to be sooner rather than later. Richard was planning on a trip to see his mother in a few weeks' time but he did not tell Jan in case his plans went awry at the last moment.

After the festivities had died down, Daf told Jan that she had arranged for them to go up north to the Bay of Islands. She loved arranging things and Jan was very happy about that and went along with whatever was organised.

"We have some friends who want to meet you," said Daf. "They run a motel business in Paihia. Do you remember, it was the first place we took you to when you and Mike came the first time? That was the first time we met you. That must be about twenty years ago! Where does the time go?"

"Oh, yes," agreed Jan. "It really is beautiful up there. It's been years since I've been there. I remember going to that kauri museum and we bought a clock made from ancient swamp kauri that was over 30,000 years old! It's graced our mantelpiece ever since we got it home. I love it."

Over the four weeks there was never a dull moment. They went to stay at their friends' motel for a few days in the Bay of Islands. From there they went right to the north of North Island, to the very remote Cape Reinga, where two oceans meet. They drove along Ninety Mile Beach and saw many pohutukawa trees, the bright-red New Zealand Christmas trees in the wild. They revisited places that they had been to with Mike, reminiscing and talking about him, feeling his presence all the while and missing him at the same time.

After being home for a few days' rest they were off again to the Coromandel, where Daf had booked a farm-stay. From there they also visited Napier with its art deco buildings and the Hawkes Bay wine-growing area. Hot Water Beach, too, where you can dig your own spa pool and lie in the hot water but you have to be careful not to burn your feet on the water coming up through the sand.

Jan took a day off from being in the company of Ray and Daf to go and visit Jamie, her brother-in-law, on Waiheke Island. She had not seen him since her sister Clare had died, nearly three years before. They used to live half the year in England and the other half in New Zealand, which enabled them to never to worry about buying winter clothes. Now Jamie was doing the same but on his own. He had taken half of Clare's ashes after the funeral, which he then buried in the garden of their second home.

He picked Jan up from the ferry and took her back to his bach. She knew that baches are an iconic part of the country's history and culture, made for holiday living. Jamie and Clare had bought the land with beautiful views and had it built about twelve years before. They had had some fantastic holidays where they enjoyed yachting, swimming, making friends and having parties. Jan and Mike had visited them once, just before Clare was diagnosed with lung cancer. It all brought back sad memories for Jan. The sight of Jamie soon cheered her up.

"Hi," he called cheerily. He came over to give her a big bear hug.

"It's lovely to see you. How are you? You're looking well," said Jan, genuinely pleased to see Jamie so upbeat. The last time she saw him he was so sad, naturally.

"Never better, thanks. I'm so sorry not to be able to come to Mike's funeral but I was packing up here at the time," Jamie explained. He had rung Jan at the time but he was not good at keeping in touch, this being the first time they had spoken since then.

"I do understand, don't worry. The distances are too big so I never expected you to come," said Jan, kindly, and Jamie was relieved to hear those words.

"You won't recognise the bach." He changed the subject. "I've put on an extension. Just as well, with all the people that visit. Got a surprise for you too!"

"Oh yes?" Jan was curious. "Good or bad?"

"I'll let you make up your own mind."

They chatted as he drove along the lanes to his second home. He had already been there two months. As he pulled up in the car, Jan noticed straight away the shrine to her sister at the bottom of the garden, where he had buried half of his wife's ashes. The other half were back in England, in a humanist cemetery.

"This is really lovely; you've done a superb job – well done!" Jan called to Jamie.

"Thank you. Now I've another surprise for you," said Jamie, walking down the path to where Jan stood. Behind him jumped Kara, his daughter: Jan's niece.

"Surprise!" Kara cried, smiling at Jan and going over to give her a hug.

"This day just gets better and better," Jan said to them both. "How long have you been here?" she asked Kara.

"Came out for Christmas. I couldn't let Dad have Christmas on his own. Josh is coming out here soon too, I think. But you never know with him!"

Kara continued to tell Jan news of Josh, her brother, as well as her own news. Jan felt very much out of touch with her sister's family since her passing. They exchanged news and Jamie and Kara commiserated with the news of Louise's demise.

They spent the day reminiscing and the time went by all too quickly. Jan went back on the last ferry and Daf came to pick her up.

"It's amazing that I've been able to catch up with my own family all the way out here! I'm so glad you persuaded me to make the journey," Jan said to Daf on the short drive home. "You are true friends."

"It's not over yet. I've just booked tickets to go and see Kiri and her family in Nelson. They are really looking forward to meeting you again."

Kiri was Daf and Ray's only daughter and they doted on her and wished she lived nearer. She had three young boys and sometimes Daf would go down on her own to look after them to enable Kiri and her husband to get away for a break.

Off they set for the visit to Nelson, near part of the Marlborough wine-growing area in the north of South Island. Nelson was named after Horatio Nelson and is the largest town on South Island and the geographical centre of New Zealand.

Jan knew Kiri from her first visit with Mike many years before when Kiri was a teenager. Kiri had moved away from Auckland when she married and loved living in the country. Her husband worked in the wine industry so Nelson was very well located.

Jan loved meeting Kiri's husband and their three boys and could see how much Daf missed them all, although she travelled south quite often to visit them.

After spending a few days in Nelson they travelled back to Auckland and Jan made preparations to leave. She would soon be seeing her old schoolfriend Marian in Bangkok.

"Thank you so much for having me; it's been terrific fun. I feel so much better than when I arrived. And it was lovely to see Richard again. It will be lovely to see him again whenever he comes over and visits me. I hope he does. I know it won't be the same for him without Mike there but I would make him welcome, like a son." Jan hugged Ray and Daf.

"Don't be a stranger," said Ray kindly to Jan. She knew exactly what he meant and very much appreciated all that they had done for her. She had almost forgotten her troubles back at home.

"I won't. You could always come over to UK and visit me!"

6

Charlotte had risen from her bed as soon as she realised it was her father who had snuck in beside her at gone midnight. He was asleep as soon as his head hit the pillow. Sleepily she made her way in the darkness along the landing to the laundry cupboard. She picked up the spare duvet and pillow set and crept downstairs to sleep on the sofa. She was feeling the worse for wear herself but had already been asleep for two hours so the alcohol in her body had dissipated somewhat. She was compos mentis enough to know that her father should not be in her bed. She would deal with that in the morning. *How embarrassing! What on earth would I say to him? He must have had far too much to drink, probably more than me. What a Christmas this is. I do miss my mum.* She then drifted off into a dreamless sleep.

In the morning Dean came around, very slowly. He opened one eye and then closed it again. He opened both eyes and looked around the bedroom dazedly. He saw pictures on the wall he did not recognise. Then he realised he was not in his own bed. He could not remember much of the day before but he did remember fondling his wife. But it could not have been his wife! She was gone. And he was in his daughter's bed. *Oh*

*NO! I didn't, did I? Oh hell, I can't remember anything. It was
all so real, I can't have dreamed making love to Louise so it must
have really happened. But to Charlie instead! Oh Christ, how am
I going to face her now?*

Jake called out from downstairs.

"Granny Kath is here!"

"You get taller every time I see you, Jake. How tall are you
now?"

"Last time I checked I was six-four. But apparently I can
still grow for another year or so."

"Heavens! Of course, you get that from your mother's side
of the family. Certainly not from our side!" Kath was only five
feet, three inches and Dean was just four inches taller than
her. "Have you got a girlfriend yet? A tall, handsome boy like
you? They should be falling at your feet."

"No Gran, I'm too busy with my studies to worry about
things like that now."

Kath had arrived early with a half-cooked turkey ready
to go in the oven. Then she went out to her car to fetch all
the vegetables, a Christmas pudding and a small suitcase, plus
presents for all. She was prepared for a few days, sleeping on
the sofa, which she did not mind. She knew the family was
still in turmoil since Louise's passing and so made allowances
for every eventuality. She felt needed, which was something
she had not felt for a very long time.

"Merry Christmas, everyone!" she called out to the whole
household. "Here, Jake, you seem to be the only one up. I'll
put the turkey in the oven and then we can do the vegetables
together. I'll show you. It'll be fun." She looked around the
kitchen to find boards and knives for the two of them to peel
sprouts, carrots and potatoes ready for a sumptuous meal to
celebrate this day.

"I can cook, Gran! Mum showed me years ago and she

taught me more recently when she knew I would be going off to uni next year. But you're right, I've never done a turkey before so it will be good to see how it's done properly."

Charlotte heard the commotion in the kitchen from her temporary bed in the sitting room. She rose from the sofa and crept softly upstairs to the bathroom where she could shower in peace.

Dean heard that his mother had arrived and, shaking his head awake, fell out of Charlotte's bed and crawled out like the guilty worm that he felt. He stood up and peeped around the door to see the coast was clear, went quietly across the landing and into his own bedroom and en suite, where he could shower his feelings away. He felt he would not be able to look Charlotte in the eye. *What must she think of me? What's she going to say? Will she spill the beans and announce it to everyone? How am I going to deal with that?*

He showered and dressed and decided to confront his demons with bravado and deny anything happened, like a fearless lion. He was hoping that Charlotte will not mention it to the whole household. *How could she? She is just as much to blame!* he blindly told himself.

Charlotte finished her ablutions but was worried that if she went to her bedroom her father would still be there. She wrapped a towel around herself, cautiously unlocked the door and vacated the bathroom. She saw her bedroom door was open and was relieved when she peeped in to see that he had gone. She closed her bedroom door behind her and quickly dressed. She did not want to be with him alone upstairs so she went downstairs to see her grandmother.

Daisy wakened and, as like every day since her mother died, she looked up at the wall of her bedroom to see the family photo of happier times. *Christmas Day! I can't bear it without my mum! How will I cope? I shall have to show happiness*

73

when I'm not that happy. How will I get through today? She stayed in bed as she heard someone go into the bathroom and waited. She listened out for the unlocking of the bathroom door, which meant it was empty, then charged over to grab it. It was like that most days with sharing with her siblings; at least her parents had their own bathroom.

"Granny Kath! Merry Christmas," Charlotte said airily to her grandmother. She was putting on a braver face than she actually felt. The alcohol she had consumed the night before was giving her a headache, which she tried to ignore.

"Merry Christmas to you too, Charlie. How are you?" Kath went over to give her granddaughter a kiss.

Kath had been widowed for nearly two years and had really hoped to be invited to look after the family this Christmas. There was no way she would have been invited had Louise still been alive. They did not see eye to eye and consciously avoided one another. Here she was in Louise's kitchen and she felt she had the last laugh. *Louise would be turning in her grave if she saw me now, in her kitchen!* In her mid-sixties, Kath was a big woman, rather matronly with long grey hair, which she always pushed up into a bun to keep it tidy. *Last year Christmas was so lonely for me when I had not long lost George, my darling hubby.*

"I'm fine, thanks," Charlotte lied but smiled to her grandmother to hide how she was really feeling. "Nice to see you." Charlotte felt grateful to Kath that she was taking over where her mother left off and so she herself would not have to do too much work in the kitchen, which she hated. Charlotte was not domesticated at all despite her mother's best efforts of trying to train her in cooking, like she did with Jake. Jake took to it like a duck to water but Charlotte baulked at every opportunity.

Kath pointed and said, "Have a look in that bag over there.

Can you put the presents under the tree for me?" Charlotte did as she was told and came back to the kitchen.

"Do you want to help Jake and I in the kitchen?" Kath asked Charlotte.

"Not really, I'm a bit busy at the moment." Charlotte replied.

"Oh, come on, Charlie, you can't be busy today." Jake was exasperated with Charlotte as she had done nothing towards Christmas but he did not want to drop her in trouble with their grandmother.

"Well, don't worry, dear, we've nearly finished anyway. There will be plenty of work to do later so I'll put you down for that, shall I?" Kath said to a disappearing Charlotte.

Charlotte did not answer but went back upstairs to meet her father coming down. They both ignored each other in embarrassment, not knowing where to look but both knowing they must not make eye contact.

Charlotte shut herself in her bedroom and busied herself with finishing off wrapping some presents before taking them downstairs to go under the tree. She waited until the very last minute before she thought she might be missed. She hated the thought of confronting her father, wondering if she should say anything to him regarding last night. *He must know that he slept in my bed. What was he thinking? I'll play it cool and see what he says, if anything.*

Daisy finished getting ready for the day and went downstairs. She had already wrapped her presents and they had been ensconced under the tree for some days. She and Charlotte met on the landing and went down together, Charlotte with her arms full of presents.

"Drink, anyone?" Dean said to whoever was listening. His mother shot him a sideways glance as if to say, *This early?*

"No? Just for me then!" Dean went to the fridge and pulled out his first lager of the day.

"Are you going to help in any way, dear?" Kath asked him kindly. She would deal with his drinking on another day. It was Christmas, after all, and excess was what was expected.

"Of course. What would you like me to do, Mum?" Dean was ever mindful not to get on the wrong side of his mother. "Shall I lay the table? I see everything is going well in the kitchen. Jake, are you helping your gran?"

"Yes, Dad. We've done all the preparations before anyone else got up. Now it's all cooking nicely. Gran's shown me a lot. It'll help me when I get to uni. Mum showed me how to cook when I was fifteen but Christmas dinner is another thing altogether."

Daisy arrived in the kitchen.

"Hello, my fave gran!" said Daisy as she gave Kath a big hug. "Did you get me what I asked for for Christmas?"

"Daisy! You don't ask questions like that!" her father scolded her.

Daisy had asked her grandmother if she could have a puppy for Christmas. Her long ambition since she had been five was to be able to work with animals after a visit to the zoo. She had photos of all kinds of weird and wonderful animals and she loved them all. But most of all for now she desperately wanted to have a dog of her own. Kath had thought long and hard about it and decided that now was not a good time. Who would look after it when they were all at work and school? Kath started to explain why she had not come up with the goods.

"I do think, at this time, that it is not a good idea for you to have a dog. Who would look after it?" She wanted to say, *who would look after it now your mum's not here* but she did not want to remind them again of their loss.

"Me, of course!" Daisy butted in before Kath even had time to say any more.

"I was going to go on to say that a puppy is all very well but you all need to be on board to look after it, feed it, take it for walks etc. There is much, much more to it than playing with it. As they say in the ads, a dog is not just for Christmas. And they become very expensive: not just food but vet's bills too."

"Oh Gran, I know all of that!" said a tearful Daisy as she stomped out of the kitchen.

"Oh dear, I'm not the granny of the day today, am I?"

"Don't worry, Mum, she'll come around," said Dean to his mother.

Kath went off in search of Daisy to placate her with the present she had bought her. It was the most gorgeous soft toy dog which barked when his nose was tweaked. She found her in the sitting room by the Christmas tree staring at the fairy lights.

"This is the worst Christmas ever!" Daisy said when she saw her gran come into the room. Kath went over to give her a big hug for she was ever mindful that the whole family were still grieving.

"Would you like your present now?" Kath asked Daisy.

Daisy just sat there and said nothing. She was not happy. Nothing would take the place of a real puppy. It was all she had ever wanted. She had so looked forward to having it on Christmas Day; nothing else mattered. She sat and sulked before she finally opened her mouth.

"I bet my other granny would have given me what I wanted," she whispered. "I've never been allowed to meet her but I bet she is kinder."

Kath found Daisy's present and offered it to her. She heard what Daisy said but chose to ignore it, knowing what a sulky spoilt brat her mother had turned her into. Daisy took it but she did not open it at first. Curiosity got the better of her and she eventually opened her present from her favourite grandmother. Of course, she was the only grandmother that she knew so she had to be the favourite but probably not today until she saw what was inside her present.

"Thank you, Granny Kath," said Daisy, not forgetting her manners, which her mother instilled into her at an early age. Kath smiled just as Dean, Jake and Charlotte came into the room.

"Are we all going to open our presents now? Not just Daisy," said Charlotte, rather annoyed at her little sister's antics.

Daisy looked again at her toy doggy and showed her father.

"If you tweak his nose he gives a little bark," Kath told Daisy and Daisy smiled when she tweaked his nose and they all laughed. Situation diffused.

"Daisy wanted a real dog and she's got a toy. Boo hoo!" Charlotte teased Daisy. "When she grows up she wants a job at the zoo, mucking out all the stinky animals! I can't think of anything more yucky."

"Well, at least it would be a proper job, better than trying to be famous by singing or being part of a girl band. How silly is that!" Daisy poked her tongue out at Charlotte.

"Now, now girls, that's enough of that. Dean, are you going to take control here?" Kath asked her son, who had helped himself to another lager.

"I'm having nothing to do with it." Dean settled himself into an armchair, keeping eye contact with Charlotte to a minimum.

They all exchanged their presents and family life was like normal again, if only for a short time. The children couldn't help feeling that something was missing. Of course, it was their mother but Granny Kath had very easily slipped into place instead. They had never had Christmas with Granny Kath before and they were starting to enjoy themselves in her capable company. Dean especially appreciated his mother filling the gap and taking over where his wife left off.

Jake was disappointed when he opened his present from his father. His mother had promised him driving lessons ever since he turned seventeen earlier in the year but they had never materialised. He thought that his father might have remembered and given them to him for Christmas instead.

He had received a letter on his seventeenth birthday from the grandmother he had never met, his mother's mother, who was estranged from them. She had sent him a small cheque plus a promise of a large amount of money, which she had saved up for him every birthday since he had been born. This plus enough driving lessons to enable him to pass his test. He had been ecstatic to receive the letter but Louise sent back the cheque to her mother and told her not to harass her son in a letter. Jake thought that was going a bit far. He could have done with that money. Louise had promised at the time that she would make it up to him and offered to teach him to drive herself and also give him professional lessons. It never happened.

Dean was not able to give Jake lessons because he himself had never bothered to learn to drive. He caught the bus everywhere as it was a very good service with a bus stop just down the road. When he met Louise she could drive so he never saw the point. Louise's mum, Jan, had taught both Louise and Steven as soon as they were seventeen, just like Jan's parents had taught her.

Louise's car was looking forlorn, still sitting in the carport where she had left it. Jake had been eyeing it up for himself. If he could learn to drive he would be able to use it, if he could afford to run it. The tax and insurance had run out but he was looking forward to having some lessons to start the journey and be able to drive. Maybe he should contact his grandmother Jan, who gave him the original offer of lessons.

But what would she think of him after his mother wrote her that awful message not to harass him? He would leave it for the time being, at least until Christmas was over. In the new year he made a mental note to contact his grandmother, whom he had never been allowed to meet. The telephone rang, which brought him back to the present.

"Uncle Steven and Auntie Cheryl have just rung. They've invited us over for tea," Jake imparted to the rest of the family. "That'll be nice, won't it? Gran, you're invited too."

"They've never done that before. Do we have to go?" Charlotte complained.

"Maybe they thought it would be nice for a change as a family to get together for Christmas, especially this Christmas since we are without your mum," Dean said.

"Well, you can go if you like. I want to stay here, on my own if need be." Charlotte informed the assembled company.

"Spoilsport!" Daisy interjected.

"Just let her be." Dean was rather glad that he would not have to be in Charlotte's company in case she blurted out about his misdemeanours in front of everybody. It would be too embarrassing.

"I shall go and see Amelia. They have a much smaller family than ours and she asked me if I would pop round. So I will. I won't be on my own."

Christmas lunch was served with all the trimmings. Kath showed Jake how to carve the turkey just like her beloved husband had used to carve.

After lunch they went in Kath's car to Steven and Cheryl's house. Steven had also invited his father, Geoff, and stepmother, Lynda, who had been on their own for Christmas.

"Well, this is nice," said Kath as they poured out of her car. She had never been to Steven's house before. She was starting to feel a part of this family and not before time.

"Welcome," said Steven as he opened the front door to his little terraced house. "It'll be a bit of a squash but it'll be fun. Daisy, go on upstairs and find the girls; they're looking forward to playing with their cousin. It happens so rarely and yet we live so close."

Daisy duly ran upstairs to find Milly and Poppy in their shared bedroom sitting on their beds playing games on their phones. Milly looked up and tutted at the distraction. Poppy, being nearer in age to Daisy, just a year younger, was glad to see Daisy.

"Oh, hello?" said Poppy as Daisy arrived in her cousins' bedroom. "How're you? Merry Christmas."

"I'm good. Merry Christmas," Daisy said to them both.

"Yeah, you too!" said Milly, being far too old to have anything to do with younger people. She then turned her back on Daisy and Poppy, faced the wall and carried on with her game.

"Come and see what I've had for Christmas," Poppy started enthusiastically, showing Daisy a set of hair chalk pens and a glitter tattoo outfit. They proceeded to do each other's hair and give each other outrageous tattoos.

Meanwhile, downstairs the grown-ups, including Jake, were starting to get together and waiting for Geoff and Lynda to arrive.

"How's your dad now?" Dean enquired of Steven, well aware that he took Louise's death very badly.

"Not brilliant but, considering what he was like three months ago when Louise died, he's doing much better," Steven replied to Dean. Dean thought that was odd; it was he himself who had had the biggest loss, his wife.

Geoff and Lynda arrived soon afterwards and exchanged cards, plus presents for the children. They had agreed long ago not to buy presents for the adults as it was getting too expensive.

"Good. I'll make the tea now," said Cheryl.

"Are the girls upstairs?" asked Lynda and Cheryl nodded. "I'll go up and see them and take them their presents,"

"You get taller every time I see you," said Geoff to Jake. Jake smiled; he was getting used to these inane words from older people. It was as if they said it just for something to say.

Geoff made an effort for the sake of the family but he was not happy. All he could think about was the loss of his daughter, some three months ago. That and the thought that had bugged him since before Louise died. That was the thought that the mother of his children was now on her own, widowed. Should he go after his first love? Should he forget his marriage and try and make contact with Jan?

7

Charlotte ran down the road as soon as the others left in Kath's car. She could not wait to get out of the house away from her family and see Amelia.

"Hello, Merry Christmas," Amelia said to her friend as she opened the door.

"Yeah, you too." Charlotte was out of breath as she gave Amelia a big hug and a little present. "I'm so glad to get out of the house! They're doing my head in with all their false jollity." Charlotte was dying to tell Amelia all about what happened after they said their goodbyes the night before.

"Oh, thank you very much, can I open it now?"

"Of course. Hope you like it, it's only little. I picked it up at the market."

Amelia opened the present and was surprised and delighted. It was something that she had admired when they went shopping together a week or two earlier. It was a frog bottle opener. Charlotte knew that Amelia collected frogs in all shapes and sizes and this was a little different.

"Oh, it's fab, I love it. Do you want your pressie now?"

"Of course!" said Charlotte and Amelia turned on her heels to fetch it from under the Christmas tree and came straight back. It was a bottle of perfume also purchased from the market on the stall that sold fake perfume as well as other cheap products. Charlotte pulled the paper off in seconds.

"Oh, I haven't got this one, thank you. Shall we try it out? I think it's the one that smells like Opium." Charlotte hugged her friend. "What shall we do now? The youth club won't be open."

"I guess we'll have to stay here with Mum and Tom," Amelia conceded.

"Yeah, okay. Can we just go to your bedroom first? I've got something to tell you and I don't want anyone else to hear."

Amelia was intrigued and led Charlotte upstairs to her bedroom.

"What is it?" Amelia was impatient to hear what Charlotte had to tell her. She thought it might be some juicy gossip about their friends.

"My father got into my bed last night!"

"What?" Amelia cried, rather too loudly for Charlotte's liking, in case anyone else might hear. "Oh, yuk, that's disgusting. What did you do?"

"Well, he stumbled into bed at gone midnight and woke me up when he started to come over to my side. I lay there for a while wondering what to do. He started snoring straight away so I went downstairs and slept on the sofa. What a cheek, don't you think? I haven't spoken to him about it, don't even know if he realised it was my bed. He must have drunk too much as usual."

"Oh well, best forget about it, I expect he has." Amelia was dismissive of this news as she wanted to create a drama of her own. "Tom's got a girlfriend! He's never had a serious relationship before. His friend Mark got one so he had to have one too. They're plonkers. I dread to think what their girlfriends are like. I shall probably meet Tom's later. He's invited her over. What're you doing later?"

"I'm not sure. They've all gone over to my uncle's place for tea. I ducked out of going but I suppose I shall have to go home to spend an evening of 'fun and games' with them. Can't wait!" Charlotte said sarcastically.

"I thought I heard the doorbell," said Tom as the girls arrived in the kitchen, where Tom was pouring himself a drink. "Where did you two get to?" he asked them. Tom smiled at Charlotte and went over to give her a Christmas kiss under the mistletoe. After the news that he now had a girlfriend, she thought his Christmas kiss gave her mixed messages, as she really liked him.

"We just went upstairs to give each other our presents," Amelia lied.

"Come and have some tea and cake." Sue beckoned to them all. "You can put that bottle away, Tom, it's too early for alcohol. When is your girlfriend coming over?"

"Not quite sure, Mum. But she's not my *girlfriend*. She's just a friend."

Tea at Steven and Cheryl's consisted of home-made Christmas cake and a cup of tea.

"Just what the doctor ordered." Kath tried to make polite conversation. "This is delicious cake, Cheryl. Did you make it yourself?'

"Thank you, yes I did. It's my grandmother's old recipe passed down through the generations. My mother always made it and now it's up to me, I guess. Then I shall pass it on to my girls. On that subject, Steven, where are they? It seems awfully quiet upstairs."

"I checked on them just now; they're fine. Best leave them playing while they're enjoying their Christmas presents. It's nice for them to have their cousins over: they see so little of one another; anyone would think they lived the other end of the country!"

"That's how Mum used to like it," Jake piped up. "She always just wanted us to be on our own at Christmas. This is the first Christmas that Granny Kath has spent with us."

Kath smiled through her frustration, still smarting from all those years she had been left out of her family's celebrations at Christmas, all because of her daughter-in-law. She was determined not to let that spoil this first Christmas with them and hoping it wouldn't be the last.

Dean sounded out Steven to see if there was a lager instead of tea. He was feeling like a top-up of alcohol but tried not to let his mother hear. His guilt was getting the better of him. *What if Charlotte lets the cat out of the bag about what happened last night while she's out with her friends? I feel so guilty.*

"How're your studies coming along, Jake?" asked Steven.

"They've taken a bit of a back seat since Mum died. There's just been so much going on, and now Christmas. I'm going to buckle down in the new year; I must get to uni later on this year, come hell or high water. If I don't get the grades I need, God forbid, I think I might take a year off and go travelling. It's what all my mates are going to do. And I want to learn to drive too. I shall be eighteen in a couple of weeks. Mum said she would teach me but that never happened. Her car is in the drive and I'd like to learn so I can perhaps use it if Dad gives his permission." Jake looked hopefully over at his father, who just shrugged his shoulders.

"If you can afford to run it. Just don't ask me to teach you!" Dean slurred.

"I wasn't. You can't drive anyway!" Jake was annoyed with his father for being such a wastrel, in his view. His mother was much more go-ahead and with-it. Why did she end up with a man like this?

The girls came down from upstairs to see what everyone was doing.

"Would you like some Christmas cake, girls?" asked Cheryl, knowing her own girls did not like Christmas cake but she could not exclude them and it would give Daisy a chance to have some. Cheryl felt sure that no one would have made a cake at Dean's house.

"Oh, yuk!" Poppy and Milly said in unison. "Isn't there anything else?" Milly asked. "I'll have some if you take the fruit out," Poppy added. The adults laughed at the thought of fruit cake with no fruit.

"You can have a biscuit if you like. Daisy, would you like some Christmas cake?" Cheryl asked, kindly.

Daisy started to look a little shy but nodded at the same time. Cheryl put a large piece of cake on a plate and placed it on the table. She had always been quite strict that children should eat at the table so there would be no crumbs trampled into the carpet. The grown-ups, however, were all eating their cake at the coffee table, sitting in comfort.

"This is so lovely to have all my family together. I don't think this has ever happened before, has it?" asked Geoff. He was well aware that one was missing, his daughter, Louise. He wondered if he would ever get over her loss. He tried very hard to be happy but he felt his insides were churning up.

Steven looked out of the window; snow had been forecast but it had not made an appearance until now. He had been keeping a look out all day.

"It's just started to snow! Come on, let's go and have a look. Girls? You haven't seen snow before; now's your chance," said Steven, making a beeline for the door.

The three girls rushed out to see the snow. The Devon winters of late had been very mild but this winter was threatening to be the coldest in twenty years.

"Well, that's us gone," said Geoff. "Come on, Lynda, get your coat. We don't want to be snarled up in traffic with people who can't drive properly in snow."

"Thanks for having us," Lynda hugged Cheryl and Steven.

Kath suggested they ought to make a move too. She drove her family home to Dean's house after thanking Steven and Cheryl.

Charlotte was already home after being at her friend's house for the afternoon.

"Shall we play games this evening?" Jake suggested. Charlotte made groaning noises but Daisy went enthusiastically to the cupboard to find the board games and cards.

"Count me out," said Dean, reaching into the fridge for another lager.

Christmas and New Year came and went and Kath was utterly exhausted. She was glad to help out but did not realise just how much work would be involved. She had forgotten what it took to cook for a family and thought that they would help out a bit more. Jake had done the most and Kath was thankful for that.

She put the key in her front door and was greeted with a cold blast of air. She thought she had left the heating on low so she was puzzled as to why it was so cold. There was a definite draught coming from somewhere.

She arrived in the kitchen to find the back door ajar and a windowpane smashed.

Oh no, thought Kath. *I wonder, if someone has broken in, are they still here? I'd better call the police. No good worrying Dean at this early stage; I'll tell him after the police have been.*

Kath called the police and then tentatively looked around the house, calling out all the while to let them know she was there. She left the back door open in case there was a burglar still in the house so they could have an easy escape. She had heard of people trapping burglars and then ended up the worse for wear where they were attacked.

In each room she looked, there was more and more chaos. Drawers were pulled out and the contents scattered on the floor in nearly every room. But it was quiet. That was a good thing, surely.

After what seemed to her a very long time, the police arrived. One police car together with a man and a woman arrived on the doorstep. It was not quite what she was expecting. She thought they would come up the road with sirens blazing at full pelt with three or four police cars. What happened next was completely underwhelming for her. She invited them in and showed them each room in a mess.

"Well, Mrs Dubbin, it looks like whoever was here has gone now."

"I can see that for myself!" Kath was just a little annoyed with them telling her exactly what she already knew. "Now, what are you going to do about catching them?"

"Have you discovered what is missing, if anything?"

"I've hardly had time to look through and decide what is missing, have I?"

"Then we cannot easily establish if it was a burglary, can we?"

"No, I suppose not. I'll have a look around."

"Here's my card, Mrs Dubbin. Please contact me when you know what is missing. We'll take it from there. Good day to you."

Kath saw the two to the door and then started to clear up the broken glass in the kitchen. As she swept up the glass she noticed yellow crumbs in among the glass. She swept the kitchen floor and on closer inspection she saw what looked like bits of cereal. She always kept the cereals in a cupboard and one box of honey nut cornflakes was empty, but put back quite neatly in the cupboard.

She scrutinised each room in turn to see if she could discover anything else missing, something of value. She particularly looked in her jewellery drawer but found nothing was missing at all. She looked around her bedroom and found that her bed was not as tidy as she had left it. She pulled back the cover and discovered that the sheets were dirty and the blankets in disarray and the smell made her turn her head away and gag.

"It looks like the person who broke into my house came in for a sleep and some food." Kath told the police on the phone the same day. "My bed is in a disgusting state so I'm about to strip it off and put all the bedclothes in the wash, unless you want them as evidence. I'm going to have to fumigate my bed before I can sleep in it; I shall have to sleep in the spare bedroom until such a time as it feels right to go back, if at all. I feel so violated but I know it could have been worse," Kath admitted to the police on the phone. "I can't see that anything is missing apart from some food."

"Thank you; we won't need your bedclothes. It sounds as if a homeless person has used your house if they knew you were away. There is no way we can discover who it could have been. The only thing we could recommend is that you put in a burglar alarm. That would probably deter them in future. Thank you for letting us know. We will probably close our files immediately. There is no way we could prosecute a homeless person even if we knew who it was. I have to tell you actually that we are not allowed to call these people homeless anymore so we now refer to them as 'rough sleepers.'"

"Well, thanks for your time; sorry to have bothered you." Kath was still a little miffed that they weren't taking her seriously and were not going to take it further. "Rough sleepers?" she muttered under her breath. "They were always homeless; same thing really. Why do they always have to change things? It all means the same."

Kath had ideas of buying herself a new bed at some stage and this forced her hand. She promised herself that she would look around the after-Christmas sales and she wouldn't bother Dean. He had enough to cope with.

8

Sitting on the plane to Bangkok, Jan was mulling over all that had happened over Christmas. Meeting up with Richard was the pièce de résistance. He was so like his father in mannerisms, it was uncanny. Weird, really, as his parents divorced when Richard was only two years old.

His mother remarried within a couple of years and he was forced to change his surname to that of his stepfather. They moved to Derbyshire which he always hated. So much so that he could not wait to emigrate as soon as he was old enough. First of all to New Zealand and then to Australia.

His sister, Sonia, had a baby girl when she was seventeen and stayed at home where her mother looked after her and the baby. Sonia became pregnant again but her stepfather made her have a termination. He was so fed up with his wife pandering to her daughter and granddaughter, he started having affairs which was like a ticking time bomb. It was only a matter of time before an explosion would split them apart.

Sonia left home when she was nineteen but left her mother to look after the baby, who was now a toddler. She looked around to see if she could capture a man who would be suitable as a father for her baby. She had every intention of going back to take the child but time and her living arrangements were not suitable for a small child. She lived in a squat with some friends for a short time and then fell in with a drug dealer who would think nothing of abusing her both mentally and physically.

Eventually she took herself away from the abuse and went home. After nearly three years away with little or no contact with her daughter, they were like strangers. Her mother tried really hard to make her daughter take responsibility for her child.

Marian fetched Jan from the airport and took her back to her house. They had not really had much face-to-face contact since they attended school. Marian went to a different college from Jan and then she left England soon afterwards to set up home with Kai. Jan missed her so much. Their main contact had been airmail letters and then emails latterly. Her black hair, which was her natural colour, was now bottle blonde, which Jan thought really suited her.

"Blondes have more fun, according to Marilyn Monroe!" Marian told Jan and they both laughed. "Actually I was getting very grey so decided to find some solace in a bottle. Most of my friends are very envious of my blonde look. For some reason they are afraid to use a hair colour." Marian's friends were mostly of Thai origin, apart from her old friends from school, of whom there were only two left, Jan and Sally. Sally frequently went to Thailand and loved it there. She would have liked to have met up with Jan again but it was not possible for her this time as she had family commitments.

They were now in their late sixties. Marian's skin had always been very pale. Having lived in a sunny country for most of her life, she always managed to keep her skin light by either wearing a wide-brimmed hat or by mostly only going out at night.

She met her future husband, Kai, when they were at college together in Bristol in the late 60s. She was eighteen and he was nineteen. It was love at first sight and they became inseparable. He was there to learn English and economics. His family owned a thriving business in Bangkok and he was expected to go back to take over the family business and work alongside his brothers. Instead of going back alone, he acquired a pregnant wife, Marian.

As soon as she arrived in Thailand in the early 70s, she was expected to work in an office within the family business. She had a maid to care for her children as they came along. She had two boys and then a girl. She always felt she had missed out on her children because she was forced to work in the office. She also went to night school to learn the language as it was expected that she converse in their language rather than her own. She found it very difficult to learn at first and it took her four gruelling years to learn to speak fluent Thai.

Her life with Kai would have been enviable to most people because they were very wealthy. Marian had confided in Jan in the past that her life was hard at times, despite their wealth. Kai was sometimes a very difficult man to live with but she had no option but to put up with his behaviour. A few years ago Marian wanted to leave Kai but he told her that she could walk away but she would never see her children again and he would not give her a penny. She knew when she first went to live in Thailand that the law was very much on the man's side. "A man's world", Marian always quoted. That infuriated her. She was starting to make decisions of her own as she wanted desperately to live in Australia rather than Thailand and she was planning on telling Jan her plans when the time was right.

"So, you didn't go to Louise's funeral?" asked Marian.

"No, I couldn't. It would have been too painful. And, anyway, they would not have wanted me there. I bet they blame me for her death. If she hadn't come to see me, none of this would have happened."

"And you would still be having no contact with them," said Marian. "I've never understood their mentality. You are their mum. Blood is thicker than water."

"No, there would still be no contact. Or rather, they would have no contact with me. I would, like a shot. It's the main sadness in my life. Just because I left my husband I've had to miss out on my family. It's just not fair."

"Nothing in life is fair. Don't you think that I've missed out on things by not living in England? I know I shall never go back there to live. At least you live there. How did you get on over Christmas with your friends?" Marian wanted to change the subject of the past as it was upsetting her.

"I had a lovely time in New Zealand, thank you. It was great to meet up with Ray and Daf again and also my brother-in-law, Jamie. Now I'm getting closer to getting back home, I'm starting to get worried about decisions I'm going to have to make," Jan told her friend.

"I did say you could stay here as long as you like," Marian said kindly.

"Yes, I know you did, but I have to face going home and getting back to some sort of normality. I was hoping to discuss my options with you."

"Of course! But we can have some fun as well! We've seen precious little of each other all these years," said Marian. "I think at our time of life, we should be able to enjoy it."

"Yes, of course, I agree. Are you retired yet? I retired when I was fifty-two because Mike's pension was very good, luckily, and that was how we were able to travel a lot."

"I have sort of semi-retired but Kai still insists he will work until he drops! Silly man. There's more to life than work, don't you agree?"

"I certainly do. You can't take it with you, you know!"

The last time Jan saw Marian, fleetingly, had been at Mike's funeral, several months earlier. It was such a lovely surprise to see her there in the church; it made the sadness of the occasion dissipate for Jan just a little. Then, with losing her daughter just six months after losing her husband, Jan felt at the end of her tether.

"We have seen little of each other over the years..." said Jan, but never finished her sentence.

"And I'm going to make up for it now, while you're here. I get so few opportunities to get back to England these days and you don't come here as often as I would like, even though I've given you countless invitations in the past!"

"You can't make me feel any worse than I already do. You know it was impossible when I was with Geoff. He flatly refused to come and there was no way he would have let me come on my own."

Jan's first husband, Geoff, had refused point blank to visit Marian in Thailand. As soon as she left him to be with Mike, the love of her life, it was the first place her took her.

"So, what are these plans you talked of?" asked Marian.

"I don't know if I can stay at the house now. It's too big. Well, the garden is big. The house is too, now I'm on my own. What do I want with four bedrooms?"

"For when I come with my entourage, of course!"

"I reckon you would rather stay in a hotel, wouldn't you? Anyway, the options are to sell the house and buy something smaller. To sell the house and move away. Back to Bristol, maybe. My brother is still there although he is always busy. There are one or two girls left from school still there who I could get back in touch with."

"Yes, but what do you have in common with them now?"

"I don't know. Nothing, probably. I always felt Bristol was

my home, even though I left when I was twenty-two. That was because Geoff forced me to move. God, I was so stupid when I was young, I can hardly believe how it has shaped my whole life. I should never have married Geoff. I suppose I should have had an abortion but I didn't believe in them. So I told myself at the time. I might have a different opinion now." Jan pondered all that she had told Marian. She felt that was the most honest she had ever been with herself, or anyone, in fact.

"You would have married someone from Bristol and you would still be there now. That means you would not have met Mike. And I thought you liked it in Surrey?"

"I do! I've got such fabulous friends there and there is always so much to do. I love being so near London, we were always popping over to go to the theatre or sightseeing."

"Well, I think you've answered your own question."

"I guess so."

They talked and talked like they had never done before. Kai had kept a low profile as he knew it was important to Marian that she wanted to help Jan with any decision-making that was needed. Like the good friends they were, they could carry on where they left off as if there had not been all that time in-between.

They reminisced about their school days and about how their lives had taken completely different turns from each other. Marian had followed her love to Thailand when she was in her early twenties. Her choice entirely. Whereas Jan was forced into marrying the man who deliberately made her pregnant to up his status within the community.

"That Geoff, I never did like him," said Marian, honestly.

"There must have been something there that I liked, I can't really remember. I know I just felt trapped with him, especially once I got pregnant. There was no escape then. But I think that was what he wanted all along. I wanted to play the field and go out with other boys but whenever I tried to break it off with him he would cry and make me feel awful. God, I wish I could have been braver. I was so young and stupid." Jan felt silly admitting this person was herself but even she didn't recognise herself from all that time ago. It seemed like a lifetime away. It was a lifetime away, nearly fifty years ago.

"Don't say that. You were far from stupid, at school, anyway. I always envied your marks and intelligence. My mum always teased me that you were cleverer than me."

"Really? I didn't think she liked me!" Jan mused.

"Oh, yes, she did in her own way. She just didn't show it. Her Irish way, I suppose."

Marian was itching to tell Jan her own plans for her future. She didn't even know if her husband would agree to what she wanted. She did not want to divorce Kai but she wanted desperately to live in Australia, with or without him. She had always hated Bangkok even though she had put up with it for so many years. Their two sons could carry on in the family business with Kai and she could go with their daughter, Cathy, to live in their second home on the Gold Coast in Queensland. Marian knew in her heart of hearts that Kai would hate to leave his beloved homeland. He liked visiting their second home, but only for a holiday.

Cathy had already met a boy, Karl, while on her travels in Australia in her gap year. It was a whirlwind romance and now they were very much in love. Karl moved temporarily to Bangkok to be with Cathy but he did not like it there. Marian was hoping that in time they would marry and she knew that Cathy would be on board with living in Australia. She would certainly go wherever Karl was.

Marian had so many ideas in her head she was bursting to tell Jan but, first, she wanted Jan to have it clear in her mind what she was going to do with her own life.

Marian took Jan and showed her all around her favourite places where she liked to go. Jan met nearly all of Marian's extended family, of whom there were many people of all ages, sizes and colours. It seemed that Marian and Jan towered over most of them, as they were of Thai origin and not very tall. Kai was about the same height as Marian so he was also taller than most of his family. His father had four wives and twenty-seven children in all. Kai was number three brother but was brought up by his father's second wife because his mother had died just after giving birth to him.

"What does Kai think about your idea of living in Australia?" asked Jan.

"I have only just mooted the idea to him. If he knows it's what I want, I think he will go along with it," said Marian, with fingers crossed. Jan smiled, knowing that Marian usually had her own way.

Jan stayed for three happy, relaxing weeks with her friend and by that time she was ready to go home and face whatever was going to happen, having been helped to make decisions.

She arrived home to a garden in much disarray, with the owl looking forlorn and needing attention. There had been a fresh snowfall and the owl looked like he had acquired a white cap.

After unpacking and seeing to the washing, she went out into the snow to see the owl.

"I've missed you, you know," she told the owl. She put her hands on the trunk and smoothed her hands over the hard surface, feeling around the sculpture and smiling. "Yes, you're overdue for the decking oil. I'll get some when it gets a bit warmer and pretty you up, I promise."

She arranged to have a set of gardeners to come in and clear all the old fallen leaves and dead plants, pruning all bushes that had overgrown since the warm autumn. Nothing much had been done in the last nine months since Mike died and the whole garden was looking very sorry for itself. Jan reckoned if the house was going to be sold it all needed to be "shipshape and Bristol fashion".

Jan had at last made a decision on her next move. Being a Libran, it was not easy and she could easily change her mind again.

9

The children went back to school after the Christmas period. They tried really hard to concentrate on their studies but were still suffering from the loss of their mother. Daisy moped about the house as she was still disappointed at not getting a little puppy for Christmas. She was determined she would have one when she was older and was more able to look after an animal in her care. She would save up her pocket money and eventually she would get what she wanted.

She decided for the time being that she wanted to learn to cook. Jake was able to cook and indeed, lately, cooked most of the meals for the family. He had been taught by his mother and he enjoyed the experience. He was able to give Daisy some lessons on providing a meal from virtually nothing. Leftovers were made into tasty snacks. Dean never learned to cook, believing it to be the wife's duty to cook for her husband and family. He occasionally felt guilty that he was not able to provide food from the kitchen so he would treat his children to a takeaway and left it at that. He actually felt hard done by that his wife had left him, not that she had a choice.

Charlotte took her turn with Jake and Daisy to do the food shopping, taking the responsibility away from their father, as long as he gave them money. She tended to buy ready meals until Jake told her off, saying they were too expensive. He promised to teach her to cook but she had no interest in doing such things as mundane cooking. Her mind was on other much more important things like going out and about with her friends.

Jake started to think about his driving lessons and wondered how he could go about contacting his grandmother in Surrey. When no one was in the house he started to look for his mother's address book. That would be a good place to start to find out where she lived.

He was aware he must now get back to his A level studies in earnest, in order to be able to go to university later in the year. They had been on the back burner since his mother had died in the autumn and time was going on faster than he would like. Maybe he would have to wait regarding the driving lessons after all. He really must concentrate on getting good grades in a few months' time. Luckily, he had always been ahead of his friends at school but at this time he felt he was somewhat lagging behind.

His eighteenth birthday in mid-January came and went without any fuss. His mother would probably have given him a party or at least something to which he could celebrate. Dean gave him a card with some money in it. He never asked Jake what he wanted. Dean was not used to buying presents; he had always left that to his wife in the past, but now he knew that he would have to take responsibility for buying presents for his children. *What a chore*, he thought to himself. *Just give them money, then they can buy what they like.*

It was Daisy who piped up to her dad that she thought he could do more for Jake's special birthday. She wanted to say how disappointed she was at Christmas when he gave them some money rather than a personal present but she tried to understand how he was feeling. It was the first time he had to deal with anything so awful so she made allowances for him.

"Dad?" started little Daisy. "You are aware that it's Jake's special birthday? His eighteenth!"

"Course I am! I'm not stupid!" said Dean in his inimitable way. He did feel stupid at times and with all his children becoming teenagers he felt ever more so as they were starting to overtake him in the intelligence stakes.

"Leave it, Daisy," Jake warned his sister. He did not want his father to feel bad.

"No, she's right," Dean admitted. "I'll take you down the pub later and buy you your first proper drink. How's that? You like beer?" Dean knew that Jake had had the odd drink at home and possibly while out with his friends.

"I don't know about proper beer from the pub but I've tried a lager that I found in the fridge once." Jake wasn't going to admit he had tried lager more than once plus other alcoholic drinks. "Yes, I think I like it but prefer a glass of white wine, if I'm honest."

"That's okay. We'll go down the pub later and I'll introduce you to beer – a proper man's drink." Dean tried to hide his disappointment that his only son might prefer wine to his own preferred tipple but he would take him out and show him what proper men, like himself, drank. Louise had always intimated that she preferred men who drank wine or spirits but had to accept that her husband liked only beer, although he liked a whisky chaser at times, when finances were favourable.

Charlotte felt a little nauseous one morning so she waited until the others had left for school and her father to work. She rang her friend Amelia to tell the school she wouldn't be in and asked if she could go to her house after school.

"I'm late!" Charlotte whispered to Amelia when she came

to the house. As soon as they got to her bedroom she closed the door, not wanting any prying ears listening.

"How late are you?" enquired Amelia of her friend.

"About three or four weeks," Charlotte replied. "I don't really know, I don't take any notice of it usually but I've felt a bit icky the last couple of mornings. And look! My bras have suddenly got too small or my boobs have got bigger!"

"I had noticed but didn't like to say. I thought that maybe someone might have put your bras on an extra hot wash so they might have shrunk that way. I wasn't sure who was doing the washing these days but guessed that your mum used to do it but now someone might not know what they're doing."

"I've looked up on the internet for signs of pregnancy and those three things are the exact signs. What on earth am I going to do?" asked Charlotte.

"You never took precautions, did you? You know, when you went with Seb that first time."

"No, we didn't, nor the time after." Charlotte never mentioned the fact that she thought back to the time of Tom's eighteenth birthday party when his friend, Harry, took Charlotte upstairs to his mother's bedroom. She was positive that he might not have worn a condom but in her drunken stupor she really had no idea. She knew she was being irresponsible but that was how she was feeling at the time of her mother's death. She wanted to die herself.

Amelia's mother called up from downstairs. The girls duly went down and promised each other to talk about this subject later.

They all sat down to a high tea and the girls gave each other knowing glances. Amelia started to worry about her friend. *What if she was pregnant?* Amelia dismissed the thought. She herself had never been regular with her periods so she thought Charlotte might have exaggerated her condition.

Charlotte looked for more signs over the next few days that she might be pregnant. She eventually bought a pregnancy kit from the chemist and it took her a long time to actually use it. She decided to try it out when she was with her friend; even let Amelia look at it for her. She waited a few more days before she asked Amelia to come to her house after school one day when no one else would be there.

Amelia was puzzled by Charlotte's secrecy. She wouldn't tell Amelia why she had been invited to her house. Then Charlotte produced the pregnancy kit.

"OMG! Is that what I think it is? Do you really think you're pregnant?" asked Amelia.

"Well, we'll soon see, won't we?" said a defiant Charlotte.

She proceeded to the bathroom and Amelia waited outside for what seemed an eternity. Charlotte sat on the side of the bath and read the instructions word for word.

"Hurry up, will you? I need to go now!" Amelia informed her friend.

Charlotte emerged from the bathroom holding the offending stick as if it were something quite noxious. Amelia rushed past her, ignoring the stick. Charlotte waited for Amelia's return before she looked at the stick so they could look at it together.

"Sorry about that," Amelia apologised. "Let's have a look."

Charlotte turned the stick over to show the window. Both girls jumped with surprise but it confirmed Charlotte's suspicions. Amelia had thought all along that Charlotte was being a drama queen but now she knew she had not been telling lies.

"Oh!" This was all Amelia could think of to say to her friend. She racked her brains for something else to say and eventually thought of, "What're you going to do?"

Charlotte shrugged her shoulders. She decided to ignore

it for the time being but knew in her heart of hearts that she could not hide from it forever. At some point she will start to show a bump and only then would she admit to herself her predicament.

"God knows! Just carry on as normal, I guess. There's plenty of time; it's months away yet." Not even thinking that eventually she would need to tell her family and have medical check-ups. She was far too young to think rationally. "Maybe it's a mistake and will go away."

She was kidding only herself.

Jake eventually found his mother's address book after much searching when no one else was in the house. He did not want to cause alarm but he really wanted to be able to contact his grandmother to first of all apologise for not getting in contact before. He had received a letter from his grandmother in Surrey when it was his seventeenth birthday. She had sent him a very kind letter, together with a cheque for £50 and offered to buy him driving lessons. She also told him that she had a nest egg saved for him, and had added to it ever since he was born. Of course, as she was never allowed to meet her grandchildren, she could only do what she could from afar.

Jake never understood why his mother had refused to let him meet his grandmother, something about her leaving them a long time ago. He believed that it had all happened when his mother and uncle were young and still dependent on her but then he found out that his mother was aged twenty-four and her brother, Steven was twenty, so they were both grown up. Why would they not want to meet with their mother ever again? It just didn't make sense. He was not allowed to answer the letter his grandmother sent him. Instead, his mother sent a nasty letter back to his grandmother, returning the cheque that was meant for Jake. He confided in his older sibling, Charlotte.

"Remember when our grandmother from Surrey sent me a letter and a cheque on my seventeenth birthday?"

"Yes, I do," Charlotte said, distractedly. "Mum took it off you and sorted it out, didn't she?"

"Yes, she did, but not to my satisfaction. I didn't get anything out of it, not even the £50 which was meant for me! Our grandmother in Surrey promised me driving lessons but I never got them, nor my nest egg she talked about. I don't know how much it is but she said she had put money away for me ever since I was born, on every birthday and Christmas. So it could be quite a bit by now. D'you think I should ask her now for the driving lessons and apologise for Mum's letter? I wonder if she would understand. Should I try it?"

"Go for it," Charlotte said to Jake. "If you think that she will give you driving lessons and that's what you really want." Charlotte had other things on her mind and could not waste time on things that did not concern her and so were not important to her. She wondered what Jake would say to her if she told him she was pregnant. Would he be supportive? Certainly she felt her father would be furious with her. When should she tell? She would be sixteen soon so she could leave school but how would she be able to support a baby? What was she to do?

"I don't know if I have time for driving lessons now. I just wanted to contact our grandmother to tell her how sorry I was that Mum sent back her cheque and maybe she'll send me another one. I could certainly do with it." Jake was talking to himself by now because Charlotte had disappeared out of the room.

10

"Your owl sculpture is quite magnificent," said the estate agent to Jan as he stepped back in admiration, almost falling over the low stone wall on the rockery behind him.

"Thank you," mused Jan wistfully. She couldn't help thinking about the day, five years ago, that she and her late husband, Mike, had arranged for the carving to be done. Their garden had five very tall oak trees but as they lived next door to a woodland they had been told to expect to get honey fungus in their plants.

Their tree surgeon friend, Les, had been keeping an eye on all the trees in their garden ever since they had moved there sixteen years before. Honey fungus was quite evil in that it spread underground, taking plants by surprise, killing them one by one. The nearest oak tree to the house, which was about sixty feet away, succumbed to the fungus and needed to be cut down.

"It will be too dangerous if I leave it up any longer; I wouldn't feel safe as it's such a tall tree," Les had said. "I will take it down ASAP but, you know, it would make a lovely sculpture; it's in an ideal position with a view from the house. It would be a pity not to do something unusual with what is left of the tree. I can take it down to ten feet, and then you can arrange for it to be done. I'll give you some names of people I know who would make a good job."

"That's absolutely marvellous; what a great idea," Mike had said. "We'll do it."

In the weeks that followed Les had taken the tree down and Nicolas, a very experienced wood carver, had arrived with his six chainsaws, ranging in size from huge to quite minute. They had talked about what he could achieve and he had showed them his portfolio and then agreed on what they wanted.

"It will take about three days to complete," Nicolas had told Jan and Mike.

They had all agreed on an owl sitting at the top. All the bark would come off and Nicholas would sculpt oak leaves and acorns into the side.

"I can do whatever you like but could I make a suggestion?"

"Of course," Jan and Mike had said in unison.

"Well, I can sculpt, and have done before, a little nest of three baby owls – Sarah, Percy and Bill. Do you know the story of the three baby owls?"

"No, I don't," Jan had said, curious.

"Well, you can look it up on the internet. It's something that people with grandchildren tend to want. I can also add a back door; your tree has just the right shape for this."

"That sounds fantastic, thank you." Jan had pondered the thought of her grandchildren as she had done when she heard about them coming along, one by one, over the years. Always her brother or sister had let her know about all five grandchildren. But she had still not met any of them. This was the great sadness of her life.

Mike had spent many hours tending that big garden and had refused to get a gardener in to help him. It used to take him over three hours just to mow the lawn. Apart from the oak trees, there had been big shrubs, plus he had liked to grow flowers in pots for the patio. One year he had so many pots, Jan told everyone they had a "potio".

Jan would ring a bell when it was mealtimes and sometimes it would be the only time they would spend together in the summer. They would have their mid-morning coffee at the table on the patio and admire all their lovely flowers. When they moved there they had agreed that his domain was the garden and Jan looked after the house.

Since Mike's demise nearly a year ago, Jan had found it increasingly difficult to keep up with the house and the garden so she employed a part-time gardener who helped her to keep everything under control.

"I'm so glad it's still looking this good. My husband used to oil it every year and it came up really lovely," said Jan to the estate agent of the owl sculpture. *I will have to do it again if I stay here,* Jan thought to herself but not letting on to the estate agent her thoughts.

He had already looked around the house; the garden was the pièce de résistance. Everyone Jan knew loved the garden as soon as they saw it and said it had the "wow" factor. And the owl was the icing on the cake.

"I know this will sell very quickly and I know someone who is looking for just such a property in this location. They will be delighted." The agent was starting to get his phone out of his pocket.

"Hang on just a minute," cried Jan, surprised by the finality of it all. "I haven't definitely decided to sell. I only wanted you to give me a valuation today."

The agent looked disappointed when he thought of his commission disappearing out of sight. He shuffled his feet and started to write something down on a piece of paper. He gave the paper to Jan.

"I will go back to the office and write up the valuation properly but this is just so you know today what you can expect to get for your house. And also that people will be queuing up for it. It's really lovely."

"Thank you." Jan was surprised at the valuation. It was a pleasant surprise but she still was not sure what she was going to do. She would mull it over and not do anything in a hurry.

"Don't forget, spring is the best time to sell your house and it's only just around the corner, not long now."

"Thank you," Jan said again. "I will definitely let you know in the next week or so." She wanted to leave it vague because she really did not know what to do.

She saw the estate agent to the door and went outside to the owl.

"Well? What should I do? Should I stay or should I go? That sounds like the words of a song! Not sure what song. Come on! Give me some inspiration."

Jan went indoors to make herself a cup of coffee then went back outside again.

"Have you made a decision yet? Wink once for me to go and blink both eyes for me to stay."

She was certain she saw the owl blink. *That means you want me to stay!*

"Is that your final word? Hark at me talking to a piece of wood! I might as well be talking to myself. Oh, hang on, that's exactly what I am doing! Silly me. I need to get a life, that's what I need. And I need to give you a good clean and oiling and I will, I promise, soon."

It was still winter as far as Jan was concerned and still feeling the cold, even though the estate agent was convinced that spring was just around the corner. The doorbell rang just at that minute and Jan was glad of an interruption to her thoughts. It was her friend Vicky.

"Hi, do come in and save me from talking to myself," said Jan.

"That's the first sign of madness, you know," Vicky said, smiling.

"Yes, and the second sign is hair on the palm of your hand."

Vicky started to stare at her hand.

"Gotcha! Ha ha! That's the third sign, looking for it!" Jan was feeling smug that she had conned her friend, but in a nice way.

"Oh, very funny. I just came over to see how you are. I noticed an estate agent's car in the drive. Are you seriously thinking of selling up? I do sincerely hope *not!*"

"I really can't make up my mind. Where would I go? I love this place. I love this house but maybe there are too many memories here. Some quite sad. Mike and I bought it and it was just right but now it's too big for one person and the garden really is too much for me to cope with it, even though I've got that nice gardener chap who comes part time. I don't know if that will be enough once everything starts to grow again in the spring. There is just no let-up. I need to oil the owl now so he won't crack up. In fact, I was just about to do it when you arrived."

It had been over nine months since her husband Mike had passed away but to Jan it seemed longer. Much longer. She missed him so much. Vicky and her husband missed him too but was aware of how much they would have to support Jan. They were truly good friends. Jan had made many friends in Clayfold so she would miss them all if she moved away.

"Well, I know what that's like! To crack up." Vicky thought she had cracked a huge joke but Jan was not in the mood for laughing.

"It's okay for you, you're not unsettled like I am. You have a lovely husband who looks after you. I used to, but not anymore. I've been so lonely this last year," Jan told Vicky sadly. "I know it might sound daft but, with Louise gone just a few months ago, I can reconcile myself to that fact. I think I must have grieved a long time ago when she refused to see me or have anything to do with me so I can't miss her any more than I did before. It's really strange that I feel so unconnected to her. So I don't really miss her because I never had her in the first place. Do you know what I mean?"

"I… I think I do." Vicky was slightly puzzled but she tried hard to understand. "Well, we will have to see what we can do. Leave it with me."

Vicky went away with ideas in her head. Jan was puzzled but left it at that and started to clean the owl.

Vicky came back an hour later. Jan answered the door as she was wiping the remnants of the decking oil off her hands. She was slightly annoyed at having the break off in the middle of the job.

"So soon!" Jan exclaimed sarcastically, but smiling all the while to show her friend she was joking. "To what do I owe the pleasure this time?"

"Well, I've been thinking," Vicky demurred.

"Careful! That could be dangerous you know!" Jan was feeling more herself than she did earlier. Vicky carried on, ignoring the comments.

"We haven't had a dinner party lately. You know we are famous for our good dinner parties and Gerry has suggested we have one."

"How does that affect me? I don't have a plus-one anymore," Jan said sorrowfully, but not meaning to sound down.

"Well, you can come, can't you? It will cheer you up, I'm sure. Try and make this winter a bit shorter."

"Oh, yes, I'd like to do that. It's been a long time that I've done anything nice like that. Apart from my holiday, of course. I think I've been in the doldrums lately."

Vicky wanted to bring the subject back to her potential dinner party which she was itching to arrange. "So, are you okay for Monday week, coming to us for dinner?"

"Oh, go on then. I've not got anything nice to wear so you'll have to take me as I am," said Jan, slightly puzzled as to why it would be on a Monday night when it was usually a Friday or Saturday but she didn't query it with Vicky.

"Great. I'll get on and organise it."

Vicky had in mind to invite some people who had become friends since they moved to the village about two years ago. They owned a very popular local Italian restaurant that Vicky and Gerry frequented. Little Italy was the name of the restaurant and Giovanni and Rosa Lina ran it like a well-oiled machine. Monday nights were their night off as the restaurant was closed and so that was the reason Vicky had decided to make her dinner party on a Monday night.

Jan finished off cleaning the owl and when she finished she stepped down from the ladder and took a step back to admire her handiwork.

"My, you're looking beautiful again, aren't you?" she asked the owl hypothetically. "That's better isn't it? I can't possibly leave you now, can I?" Jan was determined to talk herself into staying and not selling, although she was still unsure. She looked around the back at the door which she had all but forgotten about. She opened the door to see that all was okay inside, in case there was attention needed in there. There were a few cobwebs but otherwise it was quite clean. Then she had an idea.

11

Dean tried to put to the back of his mind the awful time over Christmas when he thought he had made love to his own daughter, when he was too drunk to know what he was doing. He was so ashamed he kept a low profile whenever Charlotte was around the house. He was surprised that she was non-committal about the whole sorry episode. He hoped that maybe she had had too much to drink too and could not remember anything. He sincerely hoped that was the case. He was in too much turmoil to wonder why his fifteen-year-old daughter might have had too much to drink. She was vastly underage after all.

The pressures of work were getting to Dean, at the factory where he worked as a warehouse operative. His bosses were starting to query why his work was not finished by the end of each day. Was it something to do with his absences from his post when work was piling up? His leaves of absence occurred at odd times throughout the day but he never went anywhere outside the factory. He would spend time in the toilets or in the passageway around the back of the factory, where no one else would go. He would sit for long periods of time just contemplating his situation, sometimes regarding the death of his wife and, at other times, the worry of his growing family and how he was going to cope. Of course, the worst worry now for him was Charlotte. The guilt, he felt, was eating away at him.

His work colleagues covered for him in the early days of his bereavement but after several months they were starting to get fed up with doing their own work as well as his. He took advantage of their kindness but now they were starting to refuse to take on extra work for no extra pay.

"Look, Dean," said Dave, the under-manager on the factory floor. "The bosses are starting to notice your absences. I'm really sorry, mate, but you're going to have to step up and start knuckling down to do your own work. We can't cover for you anymore. Okay?"

"Yeah, I suppose you're right. You'll still come to the pub with me after work and let me buy you a drink?"

"Course I will. We're all good, aren't we? You didn't mind me saying?"

"Of course, that's fine. See you later. Must get back to work now!"

Dean was disenamoured with working in the factory but knew in his hearts of hearts that he would not be capable of working anywhere else. He was too lazy to try anything else so felt trapped with this job as he knew he would not be able to climb the ladder to promotion. He was always being overtaken by younger and more ambitious men in the factory.

I'll just have to stick with what I know, Dean told himself. *After all, warehouse operative is four up from where I started all those years ago so that is good going. Now, what am I going to do about Charlie? She seems to be ignoring me lately or am I just imagining it? Maybe I'm ignoring her! She's not my little girl anymore. Hardly surprising after what I did to her! I was hoping to sweep the whole sorry episode under the carpet. Should*

I reprimand her for drinking too much? Like the pot calling the kettle black! And it was Christmas.

Charlotte's sixteenth birthday was only a week away but no one said anything. *Should she remind them?* she wondered. *Why not?*

"What're you giving me for my birthday?" Charlotte announced at breakfast time when the whole family were gathered on a weekday morning. Dean pretended not to hear and started to read an old newspaper he found on the spare chair. The chair that his wife would have sat on, had she been there. Breakfast used to be a sociable occasion when Louise was alive as she would make sure her brood communicated at least at one meal a day.

"Oh yes," Jake mumbled first, through a mouthful of cornflakes. "We hadn't forgotten, you know." He himself actually had not forgotten because he knew it was almost exactly four weeks after his own birthday. He knew his father had forgotten. He was astute enough to be able to read his father's mind and he knew how distracted he had been since his wife had died, understandably. But lately he seemed worse than when it first happened. Daisy just raised her eyebrows when she realised she had not remembered her sister's birthday.

"What d'you want for your birthday, Charlie?" Daisy asked. "Some make-up? I could run to a lipstick; what colour are you into these days?"

"Must get to work." Dean got up and almost ran from the room. It was rare that they would all have breakfast at the same time these days. Louise would have turned in her grave. Dean had arrived downstairs first, hoping to be finished by the time the children arrived. He made his toast and coffee and was just finishing the last mouthful of coffee when Charlotte dropped the birthday word. He couldn't ignore it but then he couldn't bring himself to ask her what she wanted. He decided he would get her a card and put some money in it and that would have to do.

"What's up with him?" said Charlotte to her siblings as Dean disappeared from the room.

"He must be late, I guess," Jake made allowances for his father but in reality he did not really know what was up with his father. He put it down to still being in mourning. Other mealtimes were very disjointed lately. Dean preferred to take his dinner plate into the sitting room so he could catch up on TV programmes he had recorded. He liked most sport and recorded whatever they cared to show. Snooker and football were his favourites. He loved films and waited until they showed new films on the television but he would also watch old films, sometimes over and over, especially the classics. As they were not the sort of films the children enjoyed, they never joined him there, preferring to stay in the kitchen, eating as fast as they could so they could spend time in their bedrooms, either playing games on their mobile phones or doing their homework. Dean never had to remind them to do their homework because it had been instilled into them at an early age by their mother.

"Thank you, Daisy, for asking what I'd like for my birthday," Charlotte tried to get her birthday back into the conversation in case anyone forgot. "Yes, I'd like some make-up. A new lippy would be good, probably a paler one than I usually have."

"And what can I get you?" Jake asked. "If Daisy's getting you a lipstick, shall I get you some other make up?" He really did not know what sixteen-year-old girls wanted but was willing to get whatever she liked.

"Yes, okay." Charlotte knew that neither Daisy nor Jake had a lot of money to spare so presents were just token gestures. "A nice smoky grey eye-shadow or even a mascara: my old one is running a bit dry. Thank you."

"Okay. And what shall I get Dad to get for you? You say what you want and I'll have a word with him. He obviously didn't hear what you said," Jake said kindly.

"I thought I had said it loud enough!" Charlotte complained. "I don't know what's up with him lately; he's behaving very strangely."

"Well, I guess grief does funny things to people so they react in different ways. Maybe it's just his way of coping. We ought to cut him some slack and then he'll come around, I'm sure." Jake, ever the peacemaker.

"Well, we're all still grieving for Mum!" Daisy piped up. "I miss her terribly."

Jake went to give Daisy a cuddle as he noticed the wobble in her voice.

"I know," he said. "We all do. But unfortunately there's nothing we can do to bring her back so we just have to get on with it, I'm afraid."

The siblings got themselves off to school. Daisy walked with her friend Lucy while Charlotte went to call for Amelia and the conversation soon turned to babies.

"I'm not going to discuss it!" Charlotte cut Amelia dead as soon as she mentioned the B word.

"Well, you're going to have to think about it sooner or later. It won't just go away, no matter how much you think it will." Amelia felt a little put out that she was only trying to help her friend.

"Come on or we'll be late." Charlotte changed the subject and she started quickening her step.

"You've never worried about that before!" Amelia laughed as they ran down the street.

"Happy Birthday, Charlie," chimed Jake and Daisy together as they pushed their way into her bedroom on the morning of Charlotte's sixteenth birthday. They gave her their presents, all nicely wrapped in pretty pink sparkly paper.

"Oh, thank you," Charlotte said, still bleary-eyed from sleep. She was normally a morning person but she had been up in the night being sick, which was unusual for her. She had also noticed some pains in her chest, mostly after eating. When she looked it up on the internet she found that pregnancy could cause heartburn, which seemed very similar to the pains she was getting.

They all went down to breakfast together and found their father had had his breakfast and left for work already. He had placed an envelope for Charlotte on the table.

"Well, he could have waited and wished me a happy birthday!" Charlotte moaned. "He has been behaving very funny lately."

"Must be your imagination," said Jake. "I've found him the same as normal. He's never been good at conversation at the best of times."

"He's still grieving, don't forget." Daisy put in her twopenn'orth. "I shouldn't worry about it. Look, he hasn't forgotten your birthday; he's left a card for you."

Charlotte picked up the envelope and shook it. She took a knife from the cutlery drawer and slit it open. Out popped two crisp £20 notes. She looked in the envelope but there was nothing else in there.

"He couldn't even be bothered to buy me a card!" complained Charlotte, feeling very disappointed. "Yes, I know he's still grieving, but so are we all!"

"Don't forget, when it was my birthday it was just after Mum died and I didn't get anything!" Daisy reminded her siblings. "I didn't like to bring it up because it was just after the funeral and everyone's thoughts were on that. I didn't mind because I didn't want to make a fuss when there were more important things to worry about."

Nobody said anything else. It was left that Daisy felt a little aggrieved that no one had remembered her birthday and Charlotte's birthday was all but skated over by her father. He had not forgotten, though, because he had given her £40, albeit without a card. He would have left things like that to his wife so it was alien to actually go out and buy a card for his daughter.

"What did you get for your birthday?" Amelia was the first to greet Charlotte after her family, when they met before going off to school.

"Daisy and Jake gave me some make up which I wanted and Dad gave me some money but no card! I don't know what Granny Kath will be giving me. The post hadn't arrived by the time I left home but I know she won't forget. And Uncle Steven and Auntie Cheryl and my cousins. I know they won't have forgotten." The thought of more presents later lightened her mood.

They chatted about Charlotte's meagre presents, plus how she would spend the money from her father and the time went by quickly as they soon arrived at school. Charlotte was on the verge of telling Amelia about the pains she had been experiencing and being sick in the night. She thought better of it as she knew she would go on about the pregnancy and Charlotte did not want anyone at school hearing that word and putting two and two together. She knew in her heart of hearts that she ought to go to the doctor to seek advice but she kept putting it to the back of her mind as if the whole thing would go away of its own accord.

After work Dean came home earlier than usual because he had gone in early. His hours were flexible as his company had old-fashioned clocking-in procedures. As long as the employees were there for the majority of the middle of the day, their hours could adjust at the beginning and the end of the day provided they completed their weekly contractual hours by the end of the working week.

It was quite peaceful in the house on his own and he enjoyed that. The children would soon be home and that quiet time would pass all too quickly. He put on the kettle to make a cup of tea and switched on the TV in the kitchen. It was a nature programme so he made up his mind that he would watch it with a cup of tea and maybe a biscuit. He kept a comfortable armchair at one end of the kitchen for just such times as these.

Ah, this is lovely. Nice and quiet and a good cup of strong tea with a chocolate biscuit while watching an interesting prog. What else could a man ask for?

Before long, Dean was fast asleep in his chair and dreaming of rowing a canoe in a far-off country but he could not make out where it was but it was really hot, maybe the jungle. He was confused because he was by himself but he knew he was on a mission to get somewhere and the more he rowed the less headway he was making. He was going backwards! He saw some natives on the banks of the river and they were fishing. Somehow he knew they were fishing for piranha and suddenly his whole canoe was full to the brim with piranha fish, writhing and biting. He had to get out but knew not how.

His arms and legs started thrashing about and he awoke to the sound of a crash. He opened his eyes and realised with relief that he had been dreaming and that there were no piranha fish. No boat either. Just a smashed teacup on the floor several feet from where he sat.

Cor, that was a close shave! What a relief. I'm glad not to be in that predicament.

He looked at his watch and saw that he had only been asleep for a matter of minutes. He carried on watching the programme. He was so comfortable in his armchair that he felt his eyelids getting heavy again. The television sound was quite low and hypnotic and Dean started to drift off to sleep again. This time he was making passionate love to his wife. Again it was set in a country that he did not know. They were in a mud hut; it was very hot and he was sweating profusely. Louise was panting and enjoying every minute of her husband's lovemaking, even though she too was sweating. They tried different positions and eventually they both climaxed together. It was heavenly.

Dean was startled awake with Charlotte's face very close to his own. She had arrived home from school first and wondered why there was broken crockery on the floor. She had to check that her father was not dead too, like her mother.

"Oh my God!" Dean jumped out of the chair and ran upstairs. He didn't know where to hide and Charlotte was most perplexed.

"Sorry, Dad!" Charlotte called after him. "I didn't mean to frighten you. I just wanted to thank you for my birthday money."

Dean heard what she said but did not reply. He closed the door of his bedroom and lay on his bed, his heart pumping rather too quickly for his liking.

Daisy came home next and asked Charlotte why there was a broken cup on the floor.

"Dad's home and he must have dropped it. He's behaving very funny," Charlotte told Daisy. They both went upstairs to change out of their school uniforms.

"Hello," called Jake as he came through the front door. Silence. He went into the kitchen to find a mess on the floor, which puzzled him. He knew someone must be home so he called out again.

Charlotte flew downstairs and went straight out of the front door. She had changed her school clothes and was going to go and meet her friend and some boys for after-school fun.

"Hello?" Jake called again. This time Daisy came downstairs and said hello to Jake.

"What on earth's going on?" Jake asked Daisy. "It's like a madhouse here. The TV's on and no one is watching it. There's broken crockery on the floor. Charlotte's rushed out and said nothing."

"She's a law unto herself," Daisy told Jake, like a person of much older years. "I think Dad's home too but I haven't seen him. He's shut himself away in his bedroom."

12

Jan busied herself in the garden, always coming back to have a chat with the owl. She never thought any more about the impending dinner party at her friends' house the following Monday.

"Well, what d'you think?" Jan asked the owl. "I suppose I should go to the dinner party, although I've nothing to wear and I shan't be very good company. This last year has been torture, all on my own. But I must bite the bullet and get on with it. I think I've made a momentous decision at long last. I'm going to stay put, for the time being, anyway. I know the house is a bit big for one person and the garden is too big but with help I think I shall manage. I do hope you're pleased with me?" Jan stood looking at the owl and hoped for some sort of recognition but he just sat there atop his oak tree home. She thought he was looking a lot better for a clean.

Jan finished in the garden and started on cleaning the house top to bottom, keeping herself busy. It was the only way she could keep from moping about and feeling sorry for herself. This was going to be the year that would be happier than last year but then no year could possibly be worse than last year, losing not only her beloved husband but also her daughter. Jan was waiting for the time when she could properly grieve for Louise but she still felt nothing but emptiness. She had felt empty for a long time since the estrangement of her children but at least she knew Louise was alive and well. Now she was gone but Jan did not feel any different.

Shopping was not Jan's favourite pastime but essential if she was going to be able to wear something nice to her friends' dinner party, which was fast approaching. They always liked to dress up and expected everyone else to as well. She decided to go to Kingston, where the shops were a lot smarter than the shops in her village. She spent the least amount of time browsing around one or two of the better shops and found a lovely matching skirt and top in bright colours that she thought she would be able to wear again as it was not too formal. She loved colours, quite often being drawn to the purples and pinks, being her favourite colours.

As most things had taken a back seat since she lost Mike, she had never imagined life without him. Now it was a different story and she would just have to get on with things on her own. She could get back to joining the local U3A groups, where there was a whole host of things to do and which she had enjoyed in the past. Her usual bridge partner, Hazel, had all but dropped Jan. Not thinking that she would ever return to bridge, Hazel had asked around and found a new partner and seemed happy enough to carry on with the new person. Jan thought that was fair enough and she would just have to ask around and let it be known she is back on the market again and find a new partner.

Other U3A groups did not need a partner so she was able to fit back into those groups again. She was welcomed back with open arms in many of the groups and then she realised just how many friends she had.

"I'm so pleased I made the effort," she told Liz at pétanque one day. Liz gave Jan a little hug.

"We have all missed you, you know. How are you now? I know it's been a difficult year for you," Liz asked out of genuine interest.

"Oh, you know, I'm getting there, gradually. I did think of moving away but then stopped myself when I realised I had such good friends here," Jan said, looking Liz straight in the eye. Liz blushed slightly but was pleased with what she heard and glad she made the effort to talk to Jan where other people had avoided her for not really knowing what to say.

Then, one by one, different people came over to say hello to Jan and to tell her how much they had missed her. She hadn't played at all since Mike died. They used to play matches together against other teams and usually did quite well. There were going to be lots of things that made Jan think about Mike. Everything in her house reminded her of him but in a way that was comforting. Nearly all of their ornaments and pictures they had chosen together in some far-flung country. Every time she dusted them she had thoughts of happier times.

The Monday of the dinner party arrived and Jan started dreading the thought of going there alone. She had never in her life gone to a dinner party alone. She took herself off to the shops to buy some nice flowers for Vicky and then busied herself for the rest of the day but the evening was approaching fast, just as she knew it would. The more she dreaded things, the quicker they came into being.

She had a shower and put on her new clothes. She had lost a little bit of weight in the last few months when she couldn't be bothered to cook just for herself. She would end up with a bowl of soup instead of having a proper meal. She knew that tonight there would be a big meal and she then started to dread the thought of that.

Vicky and Gerry's house was only a couple of roads away so Jan decided to walk. She took her slippers as she would normally have done when going to a friend's house but she changed her mind as she arrived at the front door. *I can't go putting my old slippers on in front of people I don't know. What was I thinking?*

At the front door she hesitated and wanted to run away. A car drew up outside and people were getting out. There was no escape so she rang the doorbell.

"Darling, do come in," Gerry was as animated as usual. "You're looking as lovely as ever." He gave her a huge peck on the cheek as he took her coat and ushered her into the sitting room, all in one smooth movement. Jan was relieved to see that she was the first to arrive. She put her slippers discreetly away in her oversized handbag. Just in time. She heard the doorbell ring and Gerry excused himself.

"Vicky will be in in a minute. She's just putting the finishing touches in the dining room. You know what a perfectionist she is. I'll just open the door and get you a drink in a minute." Jan nodded and he went to open the front door. She still had the flowers in her hand so she went into the dining room to give them to Vicky.

"Oh, thank you, they are gorgeous. I'll get a vase but I haven't got time to arrange them. Just doing last minute things in here."

"Can I do anything to help? I could arrange them for you if you like." With one sweep of the hand, Jan took them back off Vicky and went into the kitchen to find a vase, put water in and unpack the flowers. They arranged themselves once the string came off. Jan took a step back to see that she was satisfied that they looked well arranged. She heard a commotion in the hallway as guests were arriving. She took herself back to the sitting room, avoiding the hallway, with vase in hand and put the flowers on the mantelpiece.

Gerry was doing his job as host as he always did, with panache and cleverly over the top. Jan could hear lots of mumblings and laughter. She guessed that whoever had arrived had not been to the house before. They were making remarks about all sorts of paintings that were in the hall and Jan heard Gerry explaining about each one in infinite detail.

Next she heard Vicky's voice and so as not to let Gerry get over enthusiastic with their guests, Vicky tried to take over.

"Do come in and meet our very good friend, Jan."

A woman arrived in the sitting room first, followed closely by, Jan assumed, her husband. They were a handsome couple in their late thirties or early forties. Very smartly dressed, the man in a smart, silver grey suit with a colourful tie and the woman wore, Jan noticed, as she would call them, "killer heels". Her pretty peach organdie layered dress had all the hallmarks of a designer, rather than something off the peg. Jan started to feel quite dowdy next to these beautiful young people.

Before Vicky could formally introduce them, the woman went straight over to Jan.

"Oh, how wonderful to meet you," Rosa Lina held out her hand to Jan. Jan could not quite place the accent. "My name is Rosa Lina. This is Giovanni, my husband. We have heard so much about you; it's a great pleasure to meet you."

Giovanni went forward to meet Jan and took her hand and kissed it. Jan blushed a little but accepted that was his way. With a name like Giovanni she could only assume he was Italian. And maybe Rosa Lina was too: certainly not an English name. Jan was stuck for words but Gerry came to the rescue.

"First things first. What would you like to drink?" He aimed the question at the new guests and Jan was happy with that as she felt quite awkward, like a fish out of water. She would be perfectly okay with whatever Gerry gave her; as a Libran she hated making decisions. She would much rather just have a drink placed in her hand.

"Prosecco?" Gerry suggested before they had even had a chance to think.

"Perfecto." Giovanni could not think of anything better than a drink from his home country. Gerry sidled off into the kitchen to get the bottle out of the fridge and prepare their drinks. He took out the best cut glass champagne flutes from the cupboard and placed them on a non-slip tray.

"Lovely," said Vicky. "Now, do please sit. Anywhere you like." She noticed that Jan had sat herself on one end of the settee. Giovanni took the opportunity to sit next to her and Rose Lina sat at the other end, while Vicky went to help Gerry with the drinks.

"I don't know how much Vicky has told you about us but we run the local Italian restaurant called Little Italy in the High Street." Rosa Lina began to explain. "We've not been there very long but the business is doing quite well. We decided to come here because there was no Italian restaurant here. I think we made the right decision; it's a lovely village."

"Oh, yes, I know the restaurant. I'm afraid I haven't had a chance to come but I certainly will try you out one day. I've been a little distracted this last year and have been too busy to socialise at all, I'm afraid. Italian food used to be my husband's favourite but he died last year. He would probably have been your first customer."

Gerry came in balancing the tray of glasses, with Vicky following behind him with a tray of nibbles.

"My goodness, you look like Hear no Evil, See no Evil, Speak no Evil! The three of you all on one sofa. There's plenty of other chairs, you know," said Gerry and Vicky cast him a knowing look, but said nothing.

"We're okay, thanks," said Jan, trying to sound cooler than she was feeling. She was hoping the food would not be too long. She had not had much to eat that day and with Prosecco on an empty stomach she was hoping not to make a spectacle of herself. She was not usually a big drinker of alcohol but she told herself she would pace herself and just sip. She was starting to feel hot: probably a hot flush, she told herself, although she hoped that she could take Vicky aside and ask her to turn the heating down. It was difficult because Vicky was flitting in and out of the kitchen and perched on a dining chair for just a few minutes at a time.

Gerry handed out the drinks and left two glasses on the tray after everyone in the room had had theirs. Jan was not sure that she noticed glances between Rosa Lina and Gerry. And then Giovanni chipped in too, winking at Gerry. All without saying anything.

What on earth is going on? thought Jan. *I'm going to have to say something; we can't just sit here in silence. And where's Vicky got to? I must go and ask her to turn the heating down or I'm afraid I'll faint.*

"Excuse me, please." Jan got up to go to the kitchen just as Vicky was entering the room.

"Ah, Jan," said Vicky, but Jan took her by the arm and steered her back into the kitchen.

"What on earth is going on?" Jan asked.

"Nothing!" Vicky sounded guilty.

"Please can you turn the heating down? I feel a bit faint and hot."

"Oh dear, yes, you do look a bit flushed." Vicky went to turn the thermostat down straight away. "Gerry must have turned it up, I agree it is a bit warm."

While they were talking in the kitchen, Jan could hear the cloakroom door open and shut. Then she could hear a sudden rush of talking and laughter coming from the sitting room.

"Look, I'm really sorry but it's supposed to be a big surprise for you. Rosa Lina's dad is over from Italy and he's helping out in the restaurant. I think it could be a permanent arrangement now. It was Gerry who cooked up the idea that you two could have a chat. He's not match-making at all but I think Giovanni might have had a hand in this too, with Gerry. Maybe hoping that Rosa Lina's dad could get hitched again. He's a widower. They might try and push you two together."

Jan was horrified.

"Mike's only been gone less than a year and you think I'm going to be interested in some old Italian man?"

"Please don't be cross with me. It's not quite like that. I think he was widowed last year too. Look, just play along and enjoy the evening. Nothing can come of it, I know. It was just Gerry being Gerry. Thinking that two and two could make five. Something like that!"

Vicky cajoled Jan into returning to the sitting room. As the two of them came back into the room, Jan was aware of the set up and was now more prepared. As she surveyed the room, she saw the three men standing in one corner, looking at a large bottle that Gerry was holding. Rosa Lina was still sitting at one end of the settee, watching the men. As Jan and Vicky arrived in the room the men stopped talking. For a moment there was an awkward, stony silence. Vicky ushered Jan over to the men and broke the silence.

"Jan, I'd like you to meet Agostino, Rosa Lina's father," Vicky began.

"Halo. I am vary please to meet you," the new man said, proffering his hand. "But, please, call me Tino. All my friends do."

Jan noticed the lilt in his voice. She always had a soft spot for an accent and found it a very attractive trait.

"I'm pleased to meet you too." Jan felt happier now she knew what all the secrecy was about. She made a decision to play along, especially as Vicky had told her that nothing would come of it. When Jan put out her hand, he shook it very firmly. She was glad he didn't kiss it like Giovanni had.

"Right, now the formalities are over, let's all sit down," Gerry was glad that Jan seemed okay with the situation. He had worried that she would blame him for bringing a single chap to the party and getting the wrong idea, or maybe even the right idea as he was hoping. Rosa Lina was watching everything from the comfort of the settee, unaware of what the men were thinking.

"Come, Jan, come and sit down." Rosa Lina patted Jan's seat at the other end of the settee from where she was seated.

Jan went back to where she had left her bag. She was surprised when Giovanni proffered his middle seat to Tino. Tino sat down between his daughter and Jan. Giovanni sat in an armchair and Gerry and Vicky sat in chairs around, making a circle. There was another awkward silence for a short time until Vicky spoke.

"Nibbles?" Vicky handed around two dishes, one with special olives from Italy, which she had managed to buy from the market. The other dish contained cashew nuts. Everyone dived in and Gerry starting firing questions at Tino. They had only met once before. He was genuinely interested in the family and how the business worked.

"How long are you over here for?"

"I am really not sure. As long as they need me, I think." Tino replied.

"You can stay as long as you like. We are very pleased to have you help out in the restaurant," Giovanni interjected.

Rosa Lina nodded at that. She was very happy to be able to keep an eye on her father; to have him help out too, that was a bonus.

"I have nothing to return to Italy for, not now," Tino said sadly. He had a little tear in his eye, which he wiped away. "Only my son," he added. By way of explanation to Jan, Rosa Lina took it upon herself to explain the situation.

"My mother died last year," she began. "It was a tragic time for all of us but especially traumatic for Father. I felt really bad because our restaurant was quite new and needed a lot of our time and effort to make it a success. So I was not able to give father the attention he needed. Being in another country made it very difficult."

"I'm so sorry to hear about your mother." Jan felt a genuine empathy, having had losses herself last year. "Your wife." This was aimed at Tino.

"Thank you." Rosa Lina also brushed away a tear. It was all still so raw, for all of them.

Niceties and explanations over, Vicky was anxious to get on to happier times. She made one more visit to the kitchen and then came back to announce that the meal was ready. She had decided to prepare a very English dish, roast lamb with all the trimmings with blackberry and apple crumble for pudding. Even though she loved Italian food, she was not prepared to compete with the experts in Italian cuisine.

Jan was anxious that she was going to be put next to Tino at the dinner table and she was not wrong. And not disappointed either. He made good conversation as his English was better than she expected. She tried to make out his age and put him at a little younger than herself. She put Rosa Lina at about thirty-eight or thirty-nine or even early forties, and Giovanni probably a little older than her. Giovanni talked like an old man with funny old-fashioned ways. She liked him; in fact, she liked the whole family and enjoyed the evening more than she had expected. The conversation flowed as well as the drink and Jan was glad not to be driving home that night. Jan was surprised to see her glass topped up by Gerry, more times than she cared to mention.

"The time has flown by." Jan surprised herself when she looked at her watch and saw that it was getting late. She was pleased that Tino did not throw himself at her. Why would he? He was still grieving for his wife. And she was still grieving for Mike. It was all still very raw.

"We must do this again. It's been fun," said Gerry, aware that this family could not be late as they would be back to work next day. It was okay for him and Vicky and Jan as they were all retired. They were putting on their coats in the hall.

"Shall we give you a lift home?" asked Giovanni of Jan.

"Oh, no, I'm fine, thanks. I don't live very far away. It will be nice to walk off that lovely meal," Jan replied to Giovanni. "Thank you very much for a lovely evening," to Gerry and Vicky this time. "Goodbye," to everyone.

Jan walked along the road and she noticed a black Mercedes go by with people waving. She waved back and they were gone.

13

Dean managed to avoid Charlotte for the best part of every day. She did not really notice as she had far more important things on her mind. But she knew that one day she would have to tell her father, and also her siblings, that she was expecting a baby.

She decided to go to the doctor after several weeks of the knowledge after buying the pregnancy kit from a chemist. She still could hardly believe it until her doctor confirmed her worst fears.

"You have left it too late for a possible termination," the doctor told her. "By the look on your face, you don't seem too happy about the situation," he asked tentatively.

"It's just that I don't know how to go about telling my dad. He's been really off with me lately; it's as if he already knows."

"Probably best to let him know as soon as possible in that case. You're due about mid-August, I reckon, if you've given me the right dates."

After a brief examination Charlotte left the doctor's surgery with his words ringing in her ears. She went to call for Amelia to tell her what he had said.

"You just kept ignoring it whenever I mentioned it. Did you think it was just going to go away?" Amelia could not help but think that Charlotte was being totally ignorant about something so important. Amelia felt that she was more grown up in so many ways and she would never have acted in this irresponsible way.

"Oh, I don't know! Let's go and meet the boys and forget about it. It's still a long way off." The last thing that Charlotte wanted to think about or talk about was a baby.

"Only a few months away, if it's due in August!" said Amelia, trying to be sensible and hoping it would rub off on her friend. She might have imagined it but she was sure she noticed a little bump starting to appear. A baby bump. And four and a half months to go to B-day. Halfway there.

"Yeah, like I say, ages yet."

Charlotte and Amelia went to meet Seb and Oliver from school. Charlotte had a history with Seb; in fact, he could be the father of her unborn baby. They had unprotected sex a few times at the very beginning. After Seb she had been with William and also Amelia's brother's friend on one occasion. All within just a few weeks of each other, so any one of them could be the father. Charlotte was not going to hold any one of them responsible and didn't care which one it was. None of the relationships lasted and they just became friends latterly.

"But when are you going to tell your dad?" Amelia asked Charlotte when they were alone again. "And, of course, the burning question – who is the father?"

"Oh, I've no idea, stop hassling me! I'll tell Dad when the time is right. I hardly ever see him these days; he's always busy doing something in the shed or he works late or he's in the pub. It's nothing to do with him, anyway. And, as to the father of my unborn child, I don't think I want any of them in our lives. I'm sixteen now and I shall leave school soon."

"NO! What about your education? Qualifications and things like that?"

"Stuff it, I don't care. I shall bring up my baby so I won't need any fancy education, will I?"

This was news to Amelia. She had no idea that Charlotte was thinking of leaving school. She was starting to get really worried now.

"But Charlie... what are you going to live on?" Amelia persisted.

"I dunno. Benefits, I guess. Other people do it, why shouldn't I?"

"But that's horrible. You need some support. Would your dad let you still live at home? He's a bit old-fashioned about things like that, from what you've told me."

"Dunno that either! I don't see why not: it's my home; it just means one more mouth to feed. Look, there's plenty of time to think about all this so stop worrying, will you? I'm not."

Amelia left it at that and went home to tell her mother. To get some idea of what a parent thinks about the situation.

"Well, dear, you can't do any more than you've done. You've tried to persuade her to tell her dad. From what I know of him he's not going to take it well. And to leave school at a critical time in her life, she'll have no qualifications if she wants a job later on."

"No, of course not. I've said all that to her. We've got our exams coming up in the summer and I suppose she thinks she won't pass them so she will leave before even taking them." Amelia mulled over the situation. *God, I'm glad I'm not in the same position as Charlie. I know we talked about starting a girl group but that was all pie in the sky. I know now that "being famous" just doesn't happen to girls like us.*

Easter was fast approaching and Charlotte decided to tell her family when they all got together on Easter Sunday. She would give her father a nice egg with dark chocolate which was his favourite, and then drop the bombshell to him first before telling her siblings.

Her plan was to finish her education at the end of the spring term, only a week away, and then just not turn up for the summer term.

"Have you changed your mind?" Amelia asked Charlotte.

"About what?"

"You know, about leaving school and that."

"How can I bring up a baby and still go to school? Get real! I've made a decision, though, about telling my dad. I'm going to butter him up with a nice chocolate Easter egg and tell him then."

"How will he take it, d'you think?"

"Dunno. Don't really care what he thinks. I've got used to the idea now of being a mum to my baby now I'm starting to show."

"Oh, yes, is that it?" Amelia started prodding Charlotte's tummy.

"Get off! Yes, it is. Are you jealous?"

"God NO. Whatever made you think that?" Amelia was horrified at the idea of having a baby to look after. "I never want kids."

"Well, you'd better be more careful than I was, then. I thought you'd like the idea of never having to go to school again. That's what appeals to me."

"Me? No. My mum told me I should get good grades if I want a good job."

"Well, I haven't got a mum to guide me and I don't think Dad cares too much. His education was a bit hit-and-miss, apparently, so he tells us. Maybe he only said that to make us knuckle down but Jake is the only one to take any notice. Not sure about Daisy, maybe she'll do okay in the end if she doesn't take after me. I suppose I've always been a bit of a rebel."

Charlotte bought her father the best Easter egg with dark chocolate that she could afford. She was nervous on Easter Sunday when she gave it to him. She waited until her siblings were not in the same room as her father. They were in the kitchen cooking a special Sunday lunch. She knew that they would be too busy for at least half an hour so she took the opportunity to catch her father in the sitting room. She closed the door and hoped he did not disappear before she had told him her news, like he had had a habit of doing lately.

"What's this, Charlie?" said Dean as he took and started to unwrap his Easter egg. "Oh, wow, that's a lovely one, that is. Thank you very much. I haven't got any Easter eggs for anyone. It was always your mother's job to provide things like that." Then he felt embarrassed that he hadn't bothered buying his children Easter eggs.

Dean had been starting to feel less guilty since the episode at Christmas when he had found himself in his daughter's bed and he had hoped that she had all but forgotten what happened. Until now.

"Dad?" Charlotte began.

"What is it now? I've said thank you and I've explained I haven't bought any eggs. I'll have a look in the shops later and see if there are any in the sale. They're bound to have a sale of the eggs they haven't sold and I'll buy you one each."

"Never mind about that now. I've got something to tell you." Charlotte was itching to get it off her chest and she had told herself that Easter was going to be the time, as there were only just over four months to go before B-day. Every day she thought she was showing more and more and so she covered up with baggy jumpers. She just *had* to tell him. Today. She could not put off the evil moment any longer.

"What is it?" Dean saw the look of terror on his daughter's face. "Has something happened?"

"Well, yes and no. Most of it has already happened but the main event will happen in a few months' time."

"You're talking in riddles, girl. What are you on about?"

"Oh, for heaven's sake! I'm pregnant!" Charlotte almost shouted.

"What?" Dean was transported straight back to Christmas. It was all he could do to stop himself saying, "Is it mine?" He took one look at her and ran out of the room.

"Dad? Dad?" Charlotte called after him.

Dean ran up to his bedroom, two steps at a time. He jumped on the bed and curled himself into a ball and started punching the pillow. His mind was working overtime. *Oh fuck! What am I going to do now? It's mine, I just know it is.*

"What's all this shouting?" Jake came into the room, where Charlotte was staring at the door. It was as if her father had disappeared in a trail of dust.

"It's Dad. I've just told him that I'm pregnant and he ran upstairs! He didn't shout at me or anything!" said Charlotte, quite relieved but still worried about his reaction.

"Well, maybe I should. What were you thinking? Are you going to get rid of it?" Jake took the news in his stride, calm as ever, but quietly seething inside, wondering what his sister was going to do next. Nothing surprised him with Charlotte these days.

"It's too late; I'm over four months gone!" Charlotte was not going to tell her brother exactly when it was due.

"Oh *no!*" Jake could hardly contain his disappointment in his sister. He was quiet for a moment, looking at his fingers, which puzzled Charlotte. "Is that about the time that Mum died?"

"I guess it must be, yes."

"Do you know who the father is? You didn't have a boyfriend then."

"Well, I did actually." Charlotte was not going to go into details with her brother. Her first sexual experience was with Seb, a boy from school. "Anyway, it's got nothing to do with you. Or anyone. It's my body so I shall do what I like! So there!"

"But how are you going to bring up a child? Have you actually thought this through?" Jake was starting to get exasperated. "Where are going to live? Here?"

"Yes, why not? You'd help me wouldn't you, dear brother?" Charlotte tried to wheedle her way into his good books but she could tell from his face that he was not prepared to play ball.

"Why should I? How can I? If I go to uni later this year, which I fully intend to do, then I can't help you bring up your child, can I?"

"I guess I'll have to do it all by myself then. I expect Dad will help out when he's calmed down a bit."

"He might chuck you out! You know he sometimes has old-fashioned views on some things, doesn't he?"

Daisy was wondering where everyone was as she felt that she was doing all the work in the kitchen for Sunday lunch. She arrived in the sitting room just as Jake was telling Charlotte that their dad might chuck her out.

"Why is Dad going to chuck you out, Charlie?" asked Daisy.

"Well, I suppose you'll know soon enough so I may as well tell you now, Daisy. I'm expecting a baby."

"Oh, that's fab news! What're you going to call it? Do you know if it's a boy or a girl? I shall be an auntie, won't I? I've never been an auntie before," Daisy said excitedly. "Where's the father of your baby? You never mentioned who the father is.

What did Dad say? Was he cross? Did he say you ought to get married, stuff like that, that's what fathers say, isn't it?"

"Shut up, will you?" Charlotte was getting exasperated. "I've only just told Dad and he disappeared upstairs. So he hasn't said anything. I'm just waiting for him to cool down and then we can discuss it. Not that there's much to discuss. I'm having it and that's that!"

Jake went back to the kitchen to serve up the lunch, shaking his head as he went. Daisy followed him to help with dishing up the vegetables while Jake carved the meat.

"Charlie?" began Jake as she followed him into the kitchen. "Can you lay the table and then go and get Dad to come and eat lunch? Just tread carefully, that's all I advise. I think he could be at breaking point. I don't know how much more he can take after losing Mum last year."

Charlotte put the mats on the table and then the cutlery, all in slow motion. She was dreading facing her father again after the last reaction from him. Then she heard the front door crash shut. She went to look out of the window to see Dean walking in a fast pace down the road. He was not quite running but his head was down as if to start a marathon. Jake rushed over to the window too.

"He's gone out! I don't believe it, just when lunch is ready. Typical!" said an indignant Jake. Charlotte was quietly relieved but worried for the fireworks that would go off when he returned, presumably the worse for drink. She only assumed that the place he was making for was the pub. And she was right.

The three siblings settled down for their special Easter lunch on their own when it was ready and when they realised that their father was not going to join them. They enjoyed roast lamb with all the trimmings. Jake had become an expert cook since his mother's passing and he actually enjoyed trying out new recipes as well as tried and tested ones that his mother had taught him. He thought the more he practised on his family the better he would be able to feed himself when away at university later in the year. He enjoyed starting to teach Daisy too and she was a good student, learning every aspect of cooking for several people or just for one.

Dean arrived at his local and rushed straight to the bar where the affable landlord, Keith, greeted him. A large Cockney-born man with thinning hair, he got out of London as soon as he possibly could at the age of twenty-five and had been running the Black Swan with his wife for the last eighteen years. He had been disillusioned with life in London after his parents both died when he was a young adult in his early twenties. He had put a pin on a map and decided to settle in Devon. He met his wife, Deirdre, almost as soon as he arrived. She was a local through and through and had Devon in her blood. Dean, at forty-four, was only slightly older than Keith and they had a good, friendly relationship that went no further than the pub.

"Hiya, Dean, me ol' china, how're you doin'? You're lookin' like you dropped a shilling and picked up sixpence!" Keith had an array of sayings and this was one of his favourites.

"Pint, please, Keith," Dean said dolefully. "I… I can't really tell you. It's the family. And I'll have a whisky chaser with that pint, thanks," was all Dean could manage.

"Oh, it'll all come out in the wash, I'm sure," ever-cheerful Keith replied with another of his puns as he put Dean's pint on the bar and went to get the whisky.

"I'll have a packet of pork scratchings too, thanks, I'm a bit hungry. The kids are cooking Sunday lunch but I'm not feeling like eating with them today."

"Whyever not?" Keith scratched his head in wonderment.

Dean decided not to go into details with Keith so he bottled up his feelings until closing time and several beers later, when he staggered home slowly, dreading the fallout of the situation at home with Charlotte.

14

Jan woke up on the morning after the dinner party with the mother of all headaches. She crept tentatively to the bathroom and looked in the medicine cabinet for something for the pain. She could hardly see without her reading glasses but she saw what looked like paracetamols on the shelf, reached out and took the bottle. As she became more aware and awake she decided to hunt for her glasses to make sure of what she was going to take. Wincing with the pain, she soon found her glasses and carefully put them on. As she squinted at the bottle she discovered that they were about two years out of date but there was nothing else so she prised open the bottle. They looked okay so she swallowed two pills with water left over after cleaning her teeth.

That'll teach me for drinking too much last night! I just can't take it so much as I used to. Jan scolded herself for overindulging. As she became older she was less and less likely to drink a lot but would sometimes go for a soft drink instead. Gerry, as usual, had been heavy-handed with the alcohol, being the generous person he was, and Jan did not say no when she probably should have.

It was getting quite late and she made herself a cup of coffee to wake herself up before showering and dressing for the day. She had a small breakfast, well aware that she had had quite a big meal only a few hours before. When her headache had gone, she had decided that today she would prune the roses as she had been told the best time to prune roses was St Patrick's Day, which was a few days ago. It was not a day for the gardener to come because he came on Thursdays and Fridays, so she had free rein in the garden. She enjoyed days like this, otherwise she felt it not prudent to be in the garden when the gardener came because she was afraid that he would think she was interfering. Obviously she would see him when he first arrived to let him know what she wanted but then she would leave him to do what was necessary and busy herself indoors.

The rose bushes in the front garden were all but fully pruned when Jan heard footsteps on the pea shingle in the drive. It was her friend Vicky.

"Hiya," Vicky called to Jan as soon as she spied her. Jan took off her gardening gloves and gave Vicky a hug. "How are you after last night? Not too hung over?"

"Not at all," Jan lied. "If you remember, it wasn't me who was drinking rather too much!" She decided not to mention the headache she had earlier.

"What are you suggesting?" Vicky did not wait for a reply to her question as she knew that she had had far too much to drink but that was fairly normal for her; she never knew when to stop. She continued with anticipation. "I'm dying to know what you thought of Tino."

"He seems a very nice man, kind and thoughtful, I thought. Why d'you ask?" she said, innocently. She knew exactly why Vicky asked and she was not disappointed when Vicky replied.

"Do you fancy him?" Vicky waded in with both feet. She just could not wait to ask the question even though Gerry had told her not to. It was typical of her, so impatient.

"I think 'fancy' is going a bit far! I've only just met the poor chap and he's only just been widowed last year, same as me."

"Seeing any similarities?"

"Oh, Vicky, you're not suggesting…?" Jan was horrified to think that Vicky was hoping it was going to go anywhere. "Come and have a cup of coffee."

They went inside and sat in the kitchen. Jan liked to sit in the kitchen on squashy stools by the breakfast bar with a lovely view of the back garden and the prominent feature of the owl sculpture. Jan loved the owl and would go and talk to it most days but not when the gardener was there, in case he thought she was losing her mind by talking to an inanimate object. To Jan, though, the owl was very real and reminded her so much of Mike. He had had a lot of input when they first had the sculpture made.

"I'll have a black coffee and no sugar, please," Vicky said to Jan.

"But you usually have it white with sugar!"

"I know, but today I'm having it different. I'm cutting down on the calories, hence no sugar. Well, maybe just a little. And I think I might be dairy intolerant."

"Well, that's a new one on me. When did you get it checked?"

"I haven't! Anyway, enough of me. I want you to tell me all your thoughts on how you think the evening went."

"I thought it went very well. Have you heard from them? Did they enjoy themselves?"

"I haven't heard from them as yet. I expect they are busy with opening the restaurant today. Tuesdays they do a special luncheon to try and get the punters in as it's always quiet at the beginning of the week. We should go sometime; it sounds a really nice menu, a good deal."

"Yes, okay, I'm up for that. But not today. Maybe next week. Or the week after." Jan was not going to commit herself to anything, especially as she knew that Vicky's ulterior motive was to try and match-make her with Tino.

"You're on." Vicky had to console herself that Jan was not going to want to talk anymore about the Italians. She knew Jan well enough that that was the end of the conversation, on which she herself was dying to carry on.

Jan thought no more about the Italians after Vicky left. Later in the morning, on checking her emails, she found one from Mike's son, Richard. He was coming over soon and wanted to visit her. He would stay with her for a few days before going up to Derbyshire to visit his mother and his sister, Sonia, and her brood of five children. He used to come over from where he lived in Australia every four or five years but Jan was not expecting to see him again quite so soon. Their relationship was good but Jan thought he only came to see them because Mike was his dad. Mike and his first wife had their two children but divorced when the children were quite young. Sonia had wanted nothing to do with Mike after the divorce but Richard always wanted a relationship with his dad from the beginning and maintained it after adulthood by visiting them whenever he came over from Australia.

Jan was delighted to reply to Richard's email in the affirmative. She would pick him up from Heathrow in a week's time. Richard always did things last minute so she was not at all surprised that he did not give her much notice. Luckily she had nothing much else on, but even if she did she would have cancelled so as to have time for Richard, whom she really liked. She had met his sister only once before but felt she was completely different to Richard. She estranged herself from Mike from an early age, when her parents first divorced. However, when she had her first baby she had contacted Mike out of the blue after years of non-contact and that was the one time that Jan had met her. When Jan worked out how long ago that was, she realised it was probably about eighteen years ago. That would mean that Sonia's firstborn would be about the same age as Jake, Jan's first grandchild.

Jan often thought about her own family. How sad she was when she realised how long the estrangement had been, well over twenty-two years now. She had still never met any of her grandchildren, even though she felt she was very close to meeting them when Louise and Steven agreed to meet her last year. This was when Louise had a terrible accident and was killed by a tree branch falling on her. Jan was devastated to lose her daughter in this way. She often had pensive moments but felt she just had to get on with her life as she felt that the rest of her family would blame her for Louise losing her life in the way that she did.

They are never going to want to know me now. At least having never met them I don't know what they are like. I guess they are pretty much all grown up now. I know Jake is over eighteen. I wonder if he ever actually read my letter to him when it was his seventeenth birthday last year. Maybe Louise snatched it from him once she knew it was from me. I really don't know what I've done to make them hate me so much. At least Richard can't hate me but then he's not related to me, except by marriage to his father, of course.

Jan went out to talk to the owl as she was feeling quite down. She always became quite depressed when she thought of her family growing up without her. She knew it was of her own volition by leaving but felt it unfair that they ostracised her the way that they did. She felt rejected, more now that she was on her own after losing her beloved Mike.

"Richard is coming to see me in a week's time, isn't that lovely?" Jan began to tell the owl. "I never thought he would want to come here without Mike being here. I will make him very welcome and then he will want to come again, I hope."

The owl sat there atop his tree home and said nothing, as usual. Jan was not disappointed because she was well aware it was an inanimate object but it comforted her to be able to talk to it sometimes, even pour her heart out.

Jan picked up Richard the following week from Heathrow early in the morning and took him home.

"I expect you're tired or did you manage to sleep on the plane?" Jan made polite conversation. She wanted to make Richard as welcome as possible under the circumstances.

"I had about forty winks but there was a baby crying for most of the flight – it seemed to be, anyway; maybe I imagined it. I'm not used to babies, they're a bloody nuisance, especially on planes. I would love to be able to sleep in a proper bed and not upright. If that's okay with you, I could have a couple of hours and then I shall feel more human."

Richard took himself with his rucksack and guitar to the spare bedroom, which he had occupied a few times before. Jan busied herself until he surfaced again, all the better for some quality sleep.

"I expect you're hungry." Jan had been baking as well as preparing all the meals they would have over the next few days. She did not realise how much she had missed cooking for two instead of just for herself. It was mid-morning so she was not sure what meals he had had on the plane.

"Wonderful." Richard helped himself to a rock cake. "Just like Mum used to make!" he said, wiping crumbs from his lips. "My mum was a fair dinkum cook and used to bake cakes like this and flapjacks too. If I remember rightly, Dad never liked flapjacks, did he?" His Aussie twang came through on certain words.

"No. It was one of the first things I cooked for him and it upset me when he turned his nose up. When we first got together, we didn't actually know each very well. We had only met six months before we started living together! I used to make flapjacks for my kids almost every week and they loved them. So did I. It was a bit of a shock when Mike said he hated them. I think he hated all things to do with oats; he would never have porridge. In fact, he hated all cereals too because he didn't like milk. I found it very difficult to know what he did like. It must have been very boring because he only liked white bread and I liked brown. So he only ever had bread or toast for breakfast. Or sometimes hot cross buns." Jan did not want to make it sound like a complaint against Richard's father; it was just an observation.

"Well, I like everything. You can cook me a full English if you like! No, only kidding. I like any cereal or porridge or brown toast."

"You are very easy-going, then. I like that. Well, now you've had your elevenses cake, can I make you tea or coffee? Then we will start proper food at lunchtime."

"That sounds great. Coffee, please. I don't drink tea. And I don't touch alcohol."

They sat down in the sitting room and chatted, reminiscing about Mike and all their memories of things that had happened in the past. Most of their memories with Mike were separate so they each took turns of telling the other little anecdotes and the time went by so quickly.

"Did I tell you that some Aussie publishers have now agreed to publish one of my novels?" Richard asked Jan.

"Oh, how exciting, you must be thrilled. Wow, you will be a published author."

"Well, in a way I already am with my travelogues. They are doing rather well. So things are looking up at long last.

You and Dad travelled at lot. Where was your favourite place?"

"There are so many! Loved South America. Peru with Machu Picchu. And Chile. We had an extension from Chile to the very remote Easter Island – you know, with those statues? They're called Moai, which are very old. The locals there are very superstitious with stories of legends and spirits. Do you know they still don't know how they made those Moai, let alone how they transported them many miles around to different places on the island or how they got them up onto the plinths, and I'm talking hundreds of years ago. It is such a small island, but so interesting.

"Was it a bit like the Stonehenge stones, where they trundled them along on logs?"

"I guess so. They just don't know, it's a real mystery. We did a tour of Iceland. Most people stop off there on cruises and say they've done Iceland but they never get into the interior to see the wonderful waterfalls and glaciers. We've met such interesting people on our travels, some of which we are still friendly with. We went to South Africa and although it was a beautiful country, especially Cape Town, it turned out to be quite dangerous, with the people, you know? We had an incident in Durban whereby two of our party were in a supposedly safe area but some thugs robbed them at knifepoint. We had been told this might happen but we never thought it would; we just thought they were warning us to be vigilant. Mike and I had a feeling at one place, can't remember the town but I think we strayed a road too far and there were a lot of young men giving each other a kind of look. We immediately turned on our heels and fled as quickly as we could without running and making it look obvious!"

"Crikey, I bet that put the wind up you," said Richard.

"It certainly did. We did China a long time ago and I bet it's changed a lot since then. I remember walking along the Bund in Shanghai; it was so lovely and quiet and now I hear the place has grown to twice the size it was twenty years ago when we went. It's full of skyscrapers now but there was only a handful when we were there. And there were hardly any cars: everyone went around on bikes. I bet that's a lot different now. We enjoyed seeing the Terracotta Army in Xian and we did a Yangtse cruise from Wuhan to Chongxing before the dam was built. That was an extraordinary sight, it was the biggest project in the world at that time with about 25,000 people working on it at any one time, so we were told. It seems unreal now. I loved India and, of course, Australia and New Zealand."

"Which do you prefer between those two?" Richard enquired curiously.

"Ah now, that's a good question. We loved visiting New Zealand, seeing friends and staying with my sister and her husband when they were there. Seeing Ray and Daf, of course. We have been to both places several times but I do like Australia, probably more. It is so diverse, with its coastal regions, where most people live, and then there is the interior, the Outback, which is so different to anywhere else. We pretty much did all of Australia after Mike retired and we were able to spend a lot of time away, sometimes three months at a time. We have friends in Melbourne so we were able to go to the tennis there a few times, which was great fun."

"Oh, Dad loved his tennis, didn't he? Did you ever play?" Richard was curious.

"I played tennis from the age of five. My grandparents had a court in their garden and the whole family played. They put a racquet in my hand and that was it, I was hooked! I wasn't as good as my sister, though. She was very competitive but then I was too! I played right up until a couple of years ago. I had to give it up because my back was playing me up. I did miss it, and still do. Did you ever play?"

"Oh, I did a bit at school but cricket was my game. Dad loved cricket too. Neither of us were keen on football and we never understood the rules of rugby! Sorry, I interrupted you. You were going to tell me more about why you liked Aus best." Richard loved being regaled of stories of his favourite place on earth and never tired of them.

"Your dad's favourite place in Aus was Perth and I have to say I liked it there too. Once we did back to back tours, first in Tasmania, all around the island. I have a friend there too, someone from school, who we met up with a few times. After the tour of Tassie we flew to Perth and toured all around that area, down to Esperance and Albany, the Margaret River wine-growing area and then up as far as Shark Bay and Monkey Mia, the preservation area, which is where you can feed the dolphins. And the Pinnacles Desert region and the mining area, not forgetting Broome, where the pearls are famous. It got up to fifty degrees C at one point – phew, was it hot! I bought an ice lolly and went outside with it but it almost disappeared straight away! I had to go back into the air-conditioned shop to eat it! We went to the diamond mines at Kimberley in the north and flew to the Bungle Bungles and ended up in Darwin. Oh, we had some fab times, Mike and I. On another trip when we toured down the eastern seaboard, my greatest excitement was snorkelling on the Great Barrier Reef. Mike could never see the interest but then he couldn't swim so he missed out on a lot. There are just too many places to mention really."

"So I see! You did travel the world, didn't you? Okay, so where was your all-time fave place?"

"Well, as you know, we got married in Sri Lanka, so that has got to be one of my favourite places, it's really lovely there.

But we actually met in America. It was a place called Artists' Point in Yellowstone Park. It's really beautiful there. We got married exactly six years to the day after we met. We went back a few years later and it was very romantic. So I shall have to say that that was the place that changed my life forever so it has to be my all-time favourite place. Of course, my kids wouldn't agree because it was the time I left my husband and my kids never forgave me. Your dad was very supportive and helped me through the trauma. I think I thought at the time that the kids would come back to me but they never did. It was a very difficult time for me."

"Yes, I can imagine." Richard sympathised. He could only just remember when his mother and father split up when he was very young, only three years old.

"We went back to Sri Lanka ten years after our wedding and we stayed at the same hotel." Jan wanted to change the subject of how her children treated her when she left, focusing on the happier times. "They remembered us and also some of the locals who had shared our wedding cake! It was five years after the tsunami that devastated the island and it was all looking incredibly sad. They really need tourism to take off again but it took them a long time to rebuild after the tragic tsunami had claimed so many lives."

"That's one of the places I'd like to visit," said Richard.

"Yes, you must. They definitely need more people to go there to inject money into their economy. It's a very poor country indeed. Your father was a very romantic man. Do you take after him?" Jan enquired.

"Hardly! I don't get much chance these days." Richard had tried marriage a few years before. He and his girlfriend set up home and were together for six years before tying the knot. Richard did not want children and had made it clear from the start but his wife felt her body clock ticking and eventually they split up, both having different ideas. Richard described the situation as two people together but being worlds apart in the future. He put both his hands together and raised them gradually parting to indicate what he meant. He asked Jan more about her first marriage to Geoff.

"We met when I was thirteen and he was seventeen. My parents took a rented cottage in Devon for the summer holidays. Geoff lived opposite with his mother, who had recently been widowed. I can't say it was love at first sight, although I think it might have been for Geoff. Because I was only thirteen, my parents did not give their permission for us to date. I think I was curious as to why someone was interested in me as whenever we met he sounded me out and wanted to talk to me rather than anyone else. I think I was flattered to have so much attention. When I went home to Bristol after that first holiday, we wrote letters to each other. From my point of view, it was more like having a pen pal. The following year my parents rented the same cottage and Geoff really upped his game and went for me in a big way."

"What did he do?" asked Richard, fascinated. He never knew Jan that well because they had only ever met occasionally and then for such short visits. And always there were other people around. Jan felt this time together with Richard alone was so valuable; they really got to know each other better.

"Oh, he was always asking me out, mostly to the pub, which was only just down the road from where he lived. My parents allowed me to go but only when they were going to be in the pub themselves, as chaperones. Geoff knew he was not allowed to buy me alcohol and also my father made sure he never took me pillion on his motorbike. It was something my father felt strongly about, even though Geoff never asked me, but I made it known that I would have liked to. Actually it was not long after that that he got his first car, after he passed his driving test."

"Were you able to get a quiet moment to yourselves?" Richard was tempted to say *Nudge, Nudge, Wink, Wink!* but kept his naughty thoughts to himself.

"Not really, no." Jan knew what Richard was thinking but ignored it. "I was only fourteen and only just allowed into the pub legally but I could only have soft drinks. Geoff liked beer but he also sometimes had a rum and blackcurrant, which I tried and really liked. Occasionally he bought me one but not when my parents were looking. Very daring we were in those days! When you think what the kids drink these days. We were very innocent in those days, you know."

"Yes, I do know," Richard agreed. "The kids are supposed to show ID cards when they are under eighteen but they get forged ones and get away with it. What else did you get up to?"

"We played darts and he taught me a card game called euchre. It was a great game and I loved it. So we were always with other people even if it wasn't my parents. Geoff's mum would sometimes join us too. She was a funny old stick, never really took to her. I think she had a chip on her shoulder. She only had the one child. In fact, they were a very small family, not like my own. Her sister only had one child, who also only had one child, and when he grew up he married but they never had any kids at all. I don't think Geoff's mum liked that I came from a bigger family. It was me who insisted on not having an only child, so at least my second child was planned because the first certainly wasn't!"

Richard knew that Jan and Geoff got married because there was a baby on the way when Jan was nineteen. He also knew most of the background of how she and Mike got together after meeting on holiday in America. Mike had been with his second wife and Jan was with Geoff. She had not been happy for several years with Geoff but never looked for a way out of her marriage. Not until Mike showed her that he wanted to be with her and offered her a way out, which she grabbed with both hands.

"I'm really glad not to have any offspring; they only cause heartache," said Richard. Jan agreed up to a point, although she felt that his views were a little pessimistic.

"Well, my kids were my pride and joy when they were young. They never gave me any problems either when they were little or as teenagers. It was only when I left their father that they became so vindictive. I don't suppose I'll be the first to be with the wrong partner and I won't be the last. It was a very difficult time for me, but I have no regrets."

"No, you should never have regrets. I don't intend to have any and that's that." Richard ended the conversation. He got up and took himself to his bedroom, where he picked up his guitar and starting playing bluesy music, his favourite. It was his way of relaxing.

As he was not able to go to his father's funeral last year, much to his dismay, he wanted Jan to take him to his last resting place at some stage during his visit. She and Mike had bought a plot at the local humanist graveyard, where trees were planted in memory of loved ones. Then when she dies they could be together once again. She was very happy to take Richard there as it was a very peaceful, beautiful area especially at this time of year as a lot of the trees were in spring blossom, colours of white and pale pink. She did not tell Richard that she also kept some of Mike's ashes at home, so she could feel near to him.

The three days that he was with Jan went by in a flash. They talked a lot about Mike and travel abroad until it was time that Jan took him to the station for his train to Derbyshire to meet up with his mother and sister.

"Don't leave it so long. It's been lovely to see you again," said Jan, hugging the nearest thing she had to a son.

Richard waved from the station door and was gone.

15

Easter was glossed over while Dean was in meltdown over Charlotte's baby. He found himself at the pub at every available opportunity. The publican, Keith, had a good way with listening and Dean appreciated this.

"Wotcha, me old cock," said Keith in his inimitable way, as Dean walked in. He greeted all his customers in this way unless they were newcomers. "How's things with you?"

"Oh, don't ask!" Dean huffed. "It just gets more and more difficult these days, without Louise. I don't know how she managed, I really don't. Pint, please, when you're ready."

Keith was already pouring the pint before Dean asked. Keith carefully put the drink down on the bar and Dean sipped some before taking it over to a table. He was happy to be by himself as usual. His work colleagues would sometimes have a swift half on their way home and Dean usually tried to persuade them to stay but they never did, usually saying they had to get home or there would be "hell to pay" from their wives. They were a little more careful with their words since Dean lost Louise but they still made an excuse not to stay.

It was not long before Dean was up to the bar again for another pint.

"What's occurring these days?" asked Keith, making polite conversation. He had noticed Dean looking glummer than usual over at the table in the corner. Dean was in two minds to tell Keith what had been on his mind since Easter when Charlotte dropped her bombshell. A trouble shared is a trouble halved as the saying goes. He decided he would ask Keith's considered opinion. He would understand, thought Dean, although he was not going to tell Keith the whole truth.

"My daughter's pregnant. She's only fifteen. No, actually she's just sixteen. She's too far gone to have an abortion, apparently. Now she's refusing to go back to school."

"Oh dear, that's not good, is it?" Keith mulled it over for a few seconds. "That means she had sex when she was fifteen and that's against the law. You should get whoever did it banged up for having sex with an underage girl. That's my view. What d'you think?"

Dean had decided he was definitely not going to tell Keith what happened at Christmas; he was too ashamed. He knew that he might probably lose his one friend that he could confide in if he told him that it was he who slept with Charlotte. He was afraid that he would be marked as a paedophile if he told anyone so he would definitely keep that fact a secret. He had been surprised that Charlotte had not castigated him for his actions but maybe she had been too drunk to know. All he could do was hope.

"Maybe she gave her consent, I don't know," Dean continued.

"It makes no difference. As far as I know, you could go after the boy who made her pregnant and get him put away. Make him pay for his actions."

Dean thought this through and decided this action would stir up a hornet's nest and then it would all come out that it was he who made her pregnant.

"Thanks, Keith. I'll see if I can get it out of her but she's been in a funny mood since Easter when she announced everything. I would rather she went back to school but she says, now she's sixteen, she's entitled to leave. I can't force her, can I?"

"Well, she was still only fifteen when she got pregnant so you must ask her who did the dirty deed. Get him put away." This was Keith's only answer and Dean was not happy. He mulled it over and left the pub with his head hung low.

In the following days he made the decision that he could not be around her anymore. He kept out of the way of all of his children but it was getting increasingly difficult since Charlotte had announced she was not going back to school for the summer term. Dean hated confrontations so he asked Jake to be the go-between. Dean's alcohol intake was out of control and Jake was getting worried about him.

"Tell her," Dean began to tell Jake. "She's not having her baby here. She's going to have to find somewhere else to have it. I am serious about this. She got herself into this mess so she must take the consequences." Jake had little choice but to see Charlotte and pass on his father's message.

"Look Charlie," Jake began, "Dad reckons you're going to have to go. He can't bear to have you around anymore. He's not going to tell you himself but he's asked me to tell you."

"What? Where am I supposed to go? On the streets? I thought family were supposed to be supportive! That's not fair." Charlotte complained.

"What about trying Uncle Steven? Maybe you could stay there for a while, until things settle down a bit. I'm sure Dad might change his mind once the baby has arrived. His first grandchild."

"Will you ask him for me?" said Charlotte hopefully.

"I can do without this, you know. It's your mess; you sort it out yourself." Jake left it at that. This summer term was important to him, with his A levels coming up. He knew he was falling short in his grades. Charlotte started to cry. Her hormones were all over the place. Jake tried to ignore her and eventually went out, leaving Charlotte in the house alone. Dean had retreated to the pub and Daisy had gone out to meet her friend Lucy. Charlotte stormed around the house in a bad mood. She lay on her bed for a while but soon became fed up with that. She started to play games on her phone but could not concentrate.

How can I ask Uncle Steven? He won't understand; we hardly ever see him. Auntie Cheryl might be a bit more sympathetic so I suppose I could ask her. That's what I'll do.

Straightaway, while the phone was in her hand, she called Cheryl.

"Hello?" Cheryl said cheerily.

"Hello, Auntie Cheryl, it's Charlotte here. I... I've got something I want to discuss with you." She left a long pause as if she was going to continue and Cheryl waited but in the end Cheryl was curious and had to say something.

"What is it, Charlotte? Are you in trouble?"

"Trouble? Me? Oh no! Well, not trouble exactly. Why would you think that?"

"Well, because you don't usually ring just for a chat so I guessed there was something wrong or something specific you wanted to say. Would you rather speak to Uncle Steven?"

"Oh no! It's more woman talk." Charlotte wanted to sound grown up, as if she were a woman already, instead of just sounding like a silly teenager.

"Okay." Cheryl was starting to feel as if she was going to have to drag it out of her niece. "So, what can I do for you? How can I be of assistance?"

"Well," Charlotte began. "I'm not sure where I can start." Still prevaricating.

"At the beginning?" Cheryl suggested. Cheryl felt sorry for Charlotte since she lost her mother and thought that probably this was the sort of thing that Louise would have dealt with. Poor Charlotte, she thought, she hasn't got a mum to go to so she was the next best thing. But what could it be? "Come on, you can tell me, I won't bite!"

"No, I know. It's really difficult. You have daughters."

"Yes, I do."

"Well, what would you do if they got into trouble?"

"I would help them out of course. Come on, spit it out. I'll help you as much as I can but I can't help if you don't tell me what is wrong." Cheryl was starting to get a little impatient. She had been in the middle of baking and needed to get back to the kitchen.

"I'm pregnant!" Charlotte suddenly blurted out, surprising herself and Cheryl too. Cheryl waited while she digested the information.

"Oh… Okay." Cheryl began slowly, thinking on her feet. "Are you sure? How far gone are you? A couple of months? Have you looked into having an abortion?"

"It's too late for that and Dad's kicking me out!" The drama queen coming out in Charlotte. "What am I going to do? Can I stay with you?" There. It was out. She's asked now and all Charlotte waited for was for Cheryl to take the pain away and say it would all be alright in the end.

"Crikey! I don't think your Uncle Steven would say yes to that," said Cheryl. "Our own children are growing up and as soon as they leave home we are off travelling. In fact, we have already started making travel plans. We've been tied down for long enough. Sorry, but *no can do!*" Cheryl felt bad at letting her down but she felt it was the only way. Being cruel to be kind.

"Well, thanks for nothing!" Charlotte slammed the phone down.

She stormed round to Amelia's house but found she was out. Her brother, Tom, was in and he already knew her secret from when he had overheard Amelia telling their mother about Charlotte.

"Come in," said Tom. When Charlotte was hesitant he continued, "I don't bite…! Well, I might," he teased her when he saw her take a step towards the front door.

"I've only come to see Amelia."

"Well, it looks like I'll have to do until she gets back." Tom was a couple of years older than Amelia and Charlotte and liked to think of himself as a man of the world, even though he had never been away from home, let alone as much as possessed a passport.

"Cup of tea while you wait?" he proffered. He already had a cup in his hand, as if he were going to give it straight to her.

"I'm fine, thank you."

"I know you're fine but does that mean yes or no to a cup of tea?" he inquired.

"No, thank you. Will Amelia be long, d'you think?"

"Oh, I've no idea with that one. She could be hours or she could be home any minute. Care to come and sit with me instead. I've got a free half hour before I get back to my studying."

Charlotte felt it polite to ask him about his studies and his imminent A levels, the same as Jake. They were not at the same school and they only knew each other through Charlotte and Amelia. They chatted more easily about school and their friends until Amelia came rushing in the front door. Charlotte was relieved not to have any more small talk with Tom as the subject matter of their conversation was beginning to dry up.

"Hi," said Charlotte from the sitting room, getting up to greet her friend.

"Oh, hello," said Amelia, surprised to see Charlotte in her house. "Did we arrange to meet here? I didn't forget, did I?"

"No, we hadn't made an arrangement. I just thought I'd come and see you, that's all."

"Come upstairs." It was a command from Amelia and Charlotte dutifully followed her upstairs. "What were you and Tom talking about? You looked quite guilty!"

"I'm not guilty of anything. We were only talking about school and things."

"Did you tell him about the baby? How is your father taking it?"

"He just ignores me now. I told him about it at Easter and he's completely blanked me ever since! Can you believe that?"

"I think you're showing more and more every time I see you." Amelia was back at school and so they did not see each other every day. "What on earth are you going to do?"

"Dad says I must go!"

"Go? Go where?"

"I've no idea. Can I stay here with you?" Charlotte was hopeful.

"I don't think Mum would allow that. Besides we haven't got room for another person, let alone a baby as well."

"I don't think a baby would take up much space."

"It's not that. It's everything else that goes with it. I really don't think you've thought this through, have you? In a few months you will be giving birth to a real live person so you must be more prepared for it."

"I hadn't thought of it like that. Yes, a real live thing. A baby. A person. Oh help, what am I going to do?" Realisation at last dawning on Charlotte that she alone would have to be responsible for another human being. It was okay talking about it but having it come closer to home she was starting to panic.

"I'll help you as much as I can but I'm not sure what you

would want me to do. I can't do that much what with school and that. Mum wouldn't let me anyway."

Charlotte felt totally rejected. No one was prepared to help her and she did not know how to help herself. She went home and packed some clothes in a rucksack. She was just raiding her piggy bank when she heard the key turn in the front door. It was Daisy.

"Hi," Daisy called out. She heard nothing so called out again, louder. "Hi!"

"Hiya," called Charlotte from her bedroom while hastily looking through drawers to see what she had missed. Daisy rushed upstairs to tell her sister all about the day she had had. She was very excited after meeting her favourite pop star, who had been opening a store in town.

"Guess who I've just met and got her autograph?" Daisy was slightly out of breath. She had been with her friends in the local shopping centre where they hung around for ages when they knew that Victoria Beckham had been booked to open the new Primark store. Everyone around was really surprised that Primark had managed to secure a star like Posh Spice. When Daisy managed to push her way to the front where Victoria was talking to the crowd, she asked her for her autograph. Someone next to Daisy asked Victoria how come she would come to a small town in the South West to open a Primark store. Her answer was an eye opener.

"I'm always pleased to open Primark stores wherever they are. I'm hoping to be the face of Primark; it's such a successful company and I love their clothes. It's my intention to have a range of my own in every store." This was to the surprise of everyone who heard her say this, including Daisy.

Daisy was relating all this to Charlotte, who was not really listening, all the time as Daisy was coming upstairs. Through tears Charlotte was packing to leave home and nothing or nobody was going to stop her. Eventually Daisy arrived at Charlotte's bedroom.

"What are you doing?" asked a puffed Daisy, asking the obvious when seeing clothes all over Charlotte's bed and her rucksack half full. "Where are you going? On holiday?" she had half forgotten about the baby. Nothing had been said in front of her since the time at Easter when Charlotte announced she was pregnant. Daisy had been pleased at the time but knowing her sister to be such a drama queen, she did not think she was serious or in fact that it was even true that she was expecting a baby. She had forgotten the whole episode at Easter.

"No one wants me or my baby!" Charlotte announced through her tears.

"I do!" said Daisy, really surprised by her sister's words and actions.

"Well, it's too late! I'm going and that's that. Please say goodbye to Dad. I've not seen him at all since I told him. Whenever I would come into a room he would disappear. It's like he can't bear the sight of me. Now Jake tells me that Dad says I've got to go but I've no idea where to."

"Oh, that's not true! Is it?" Daisy was doubtful but then started to try to think back and thought it probably was true. "Where are you going to go?"

"I don't know. I've not got much money, maybe someone will feel sorry for me and take me in." Charlotte was not sure what she was saying. She hoped that if she went, that would show she was serious about keeping her baby.

"Oh, like reverse psychology? I've heard about that. Well, good luck with that. Once Dad gets something into his head, I remember Mum saying how stubborn he can be. Were you hoping he would take you back?" asked Daisy, really afraid for her sister.

"No! I don't care what he does. He doesn't love me. I used to be Daddy's girl. That is, until you came along!"

"That's not my fault!" said an indignant Daisy. "If you're determined to go then at least wait until Jake comes back. He is the voice of reason and can talk Dad around, I'm sure."

"I don't want him to talk Dad around. I've made up my mind. Now, if you don't mind, I want to finish packing and go."

"But go where?"

"I don't know. I shall sleep rough if I have to. The world is my oyster, as they say. I'll text you when I've had the baby and let you know but you must promise not to tell anyone else."

"Don't be silly. At least Jake will want to know. And Dad, I expect," said Daisy doubtfully. "Let me at least give you some money. I've quite a bit saved. It will help you along to start with." Daisy did not wait for Charlotte to say if she would take money from her. She went straight to her bedroom and opened her moneybox. She had been saving for some rollerblades, together with helmet and pads, and had nearly enough for them but she decided that this was far more important. She took £48 out of the box and gave the money to Charlotte.

"I can't take your money! You're saving that for your rollerblades and everything. You've told us enough times that you were so looking forward to go rollerblading."

Daisy carefully folded the money and put it in a pocket in Charlotte's rucksack.

"I don't care about them. I want you to be safe. I know it's not very much—"

"It's plenty." Charlotte cut her short. "Thank you. I've got some too so I shall be alright. For a while, anyway." Daisy did not know how much Charlotte had and she was not going to tell Daisy that she already had £50.

Daisy could do no more but to watch as her sister finished

packing hurriedly. Charlotte wanted to go before anyone else arrived home.

Charlotte gave Daisy a quick hug and set off with no idea where she was going to go.

16

Jan had a text from Richard saying he had met up with his mum and all was well and thanking her for having him to stay. She was so pleased to be able to do something nice for him and wished she had a better relationship with his sister, Sonia. In her heart of hearts, Jan knew that would never be because Sonia never wanted anything to do with her father when he was alive so she why would it be any different with her. She was just thankful she had a good rapport with Richard.

She thought about her short time with Richard and the things he asked her about travel. She decided she would write up her own travelogue, including all the places she had been to with Mike. She had mentioned a few countries to Richard but by no means all of the places she had enjoyed visiting in all of the continents of the world, apart from Antarctica. She and Mike had talked about visiting there but decided against it, preferring warmer climes.

She took her time and researched all the places they had visited and kept a log on her computer. This filled an empty space in her time and she enjoyed reminiscing about the places they had enjoyed. Looking through all the photos stored on her computer brought back such happy memories and now she had the time to add the photos to her travelogue. It was a long and laborious job so she dipped in and out as it was going to be a long time before it was actually going to be completed.

She filled her time with reading books and pottering around the house and garden but with no idea of what lay ahead. She still thought about her family and wondered how they were coping without Louise. Should she contact them? She thought not as the thought of more rejection, like she had had over the years, was abhorrent to her.

The phone rang and Jan went to answer it. It was her brother, John. They rang each other very rarely and usually only when something needed to be done. They would never ring for just a chat.

"Hi, Jan, how are you?" said John cheerfully.

"Oh, you know, not too bad, keeping busy. Just had Richard, Mike's son, to stay for a few days and he's given me an idea about making a travelogue about all the places that Mike and I went to. I did keep a journal so it would be easy enough to make more of it and put the photos to the places. Keep me out of mischief! I should have done it years ago. The more I think about it, the more I'm looking forward to it. In some ways it keeps the memory of Mike alive at the same time. I do miss him so much."

"Yes, I expect you do. That's a jolly good idea. You'll still keep travelling, won't you? You enjoyed it a lot I seem to remember."

"Oh, yes, hopefully, but travelling alone doesn't have the same appeal as sharing the experience with someone. Maybe I should try and find a travelling companion! How about you?"

"I'm afraid not, sis. Not while Vera is the way she is. She's losing the plot these days!" Vera was diagnosed with early-onset dementia in her mid-sixties. She was just a little forgetful at first but in the last nine months she had deteriorated quite significantly. "In fact, I was going to ask you a favour on that score," John said hopefully.

"Oh? What can I do for you?" Jan replied, always ready to help out.

"Well," began John, not quite knowing how to ask a very big question but deciding in the end it was best to just dive in and ask. "I was wondering if you could have Vera for a couple of nights. I've got an important meeting up in London and I'd really like to go. I could drop her off to you on the way and then pick her up on the way back. How does that sound to you?" John had his fingers crossed. He knew very well if he told his sister it was important then she would be loath to say no.

But, in fact, it was not important at all. It was a "jolly" that one of his single friends had arranged that would mean lots of drinking would be involved. He had not been to one before, being happy with their set of friends in Bristol. He had heard all about the London set but never before wanted to get involved. Now, though, with caring for Vera twenty-four hours a day, he was getting tired of being at home with her. Their friends were gradually dropping off, making excuses not to meet up and he was feeling let down. He needed a break from her and to have some enjoyment. It was only going to be one night. One hell of a night he had been led to believe and he was looking forward to it.

He reckoned that if he asked Jan to have Vera for two nights that would give him some leeway and a little breathing space to get over drinking too much. Then the drive home would be safer and he would not have to worry if, in fact, he had too much to drink. He had been promised a bed by his friend who arranged this get-together and, if the drinking spilled over into the next day, then so be it. He would have another night to get over it, get sobered up enough to drive home after picking up Vera on the way. He had it all worked out in his mind. He had never asked Jan for this kind of favour before because he had never needed to, but this time he really hoped she could help out.

"Oh," said Jan, quite surprised. "Yes, I guess so. It'll be nice to see Vera again after all this time." She last saw Vera after Mike's funeral, when she had been extremely kind to Jan, almost exactly a year ago, so Jan was very happy to return the favour. John held back in telling her how bad she had become lately with her dementia and so Jan was unaware of what to expect.

They made the arrangements for a week later and Jan started to get the house ready for her guest.

John and Vera arrived at the appointed time and Jan welcomed them both in. He brought in her overnight bag and her medication, which he gave to Jan, with instructions. She had not seen them for ages and wanted to catch up with news but she could see John was itching to get away.

He waited until Vera had sat down in Jan's sitting room and kissed the top of her head but being very careful not to say "goodbye" as he went out to his car, without making too much fuss. Jan was surprised to see his car disappear down the drive and out of sight. He had already told her the time he would be back two days later and so she just thought he was in a hurry. She waved goodbye to him but he was already gone.

"Well, Vera, how about a cup of tea?" Jan asked kindly.

"Yes, I'd like a cup of tea, thank you." Vera started looking around the sitting room. "Where's Mike?" she asked.

Jan wondered how to answer this question. *Has she forgotten he died last year? Maybe I should just tell her how it is. Tell her he died*, she told herself.

"Oh… yes. Mike passed away. Do you remember how kind you were to me after he died?" Jan asked.

"No! I didn't know he died! John never told me. He never tells me anything, you know!"

"Oh, well." Jan began. "Mike died last year."

"Oh, maybe I mean Geoff. How is Geoff? What's he doing with himself these days?"

"I really don't know what he's doing. I never see him," Jan said, confusing herself now. *Surely she knows we parted over twenty years ago! I'll just have to humour her*, thought Jan.

"Never see him? Why not? Surely you must see him. And the children? Where are they. Are they coming in for tea?"

"Oh, yes, I was just going to make a cup of tea. Would you like to come in the kitchen and help me? We can chat in there while I make the tea."

"No, I'll stay here if you don't mind." Vera was not going to be budged from her comfortable armchair.

Jan went into the kitchen wondering how she was going to answer the incessant questions. She decided that as she didn't see Vera very often she would just see how it went and look after her for the two days as she had promised John. It was the least she could do for her only brother and let him have a couple of days off.

John drove himself to London to meet up with Andrew and Simon, chums from college whom he had not seen in years. *Would they still get on?* he wondered. There had been an awful lot of water under the bridge in all the years that had passed. John felt that they might not have very much in common anymore. People change in time and, whereas they used to go drinking in the local pub, John's habits had changed significantly especially since Vera's condition had worsened. He would console himself with buying beer in the supermarket and drinking at home. He hoped that he wasn't wasting his time with trying to rekindle his youth by meeting up with pals from a dim and distant past.

Andrew was single after one disastrous and short marriage when he was in his twenties but since then he had been free and single and enjoying life to the full. Sometimes he felt a little lonely as all his friends were still married or had been married a couple of times with children. He had no children.

Simon was married to his second wife and, like John, had left his wife behind to enable him to regain some lost time. Although he was twenty-five years into his second marriage, Simon had been having marital problems for a second time in his life and wanted some freedom and time to talk things through with old friends. He had four children, two with his first wife and one with his second. His fourth was a short liaison between the two marriages with a girl almost half his age. That relationship was doomed to failure right from the start as he wanted to settle down again after his first marriage ended but the young lady in question was a party girl. She liked the idea at first of dating an older man until he became too serious and then it was too late as she found herself pregnant. He asked her to marry him many times but she refused. As a good practising Catholic girl, she did not believe in abortion, or rather her faith did not allow it, so she went ahead with having the baby. Her parents supported her and she lived at home with her child while Simon supported his child financially.

John arrived at Andrew's in time for supper. Andrew was a good cook and liked to experiment, his signature dish always ending up with some type of curry with pilau rice, his favourite.

"Hello, mate," Andrew greeted John. They shook hands very formally. They were brought up to shake hands with the men and kiss the women very lightly on the cheek. They had both winced when seeing younger men not only shaking hands but hugging each other, as well as kissing women on both cheeks and sometimes three times, like the French.

"This is great," John said. "Freedom at last. Mmm, I think I can smell a curry? Just like the old days."

"Yes, but I've cooked it myself this time. Not like when we always used to get a takeaway curry on Friday nights! This is a proper curry. And pilau rice, my fave."

"I remember that. And poppadums?" asked John.

"I'm afraid I'm all out of them, forgot to put them on my shopping list, sorry."

"What about mango chutney?"

"Oh, you can't have a curry without mango chutney, of course I've got that," Andrew retorted. They both laughed. Not that anything said was particularly funny. Except the situation in which they found themselves. Slightly awkward. Christmas cards year after year and never meeting up until now, twenty-five years since they last met at their old friend Simon's wedding.

"This is great," John felt relieved that he had arrived and was happy that Andrew had not changed all that much. "When is Simon coming?"

"I think he shouldn't be too long now. Let's not wait for him. A beer?"

"Now you're talking, I thought you'd never ask!" John teased.

Andrew went into the kitchen and came back with two cans of lager. Their chat was slightly stilted until they talked over old times and it got much easier as the alcohol helped to make them relax. The doorbell interrupted their chat and Andrew went to answer the door.

"What a godawful journey I've had," shouted Simon as his initial greeting to Andrew. "It's taken me an hour to go about two miles! Bloody London. What d'you want to live in a place with traffic that doesn't move? Up North it's not that like at all! Sorry, just got to let off a bit of steam now and again. Hello, me old mucker." Simon pumped Andrew's hand and barged past him into his flat as if he owned the place. Andrew could do no more than follow him.

"John!" Simon put out his hand for John to shake. "It's been far too long. What happened to your hair?" John had hoped no one would mention his baldness but of course his old mates would be bound to notice. Andrew could do no more than just stare in wonderment at the whirlwind of Simon's entry.

"Well, at least I can't go grey like you two," John retaliated, smiling. He wondered if this was going to be the order of the evening, with insults flying. But he was pleased that it seemed to be a fairly relaxed atmosphere as Andrew put a beer in Simon's hand.

"This'll calm you down," Andrew said, as he proffered the can to Simon and they all sat down together on odd chairs in the sitting room. It was a typical bachelor pad and both John and Simon wondered what their accommodation would be like in the sleeping arrangements department. Andrew had said he could put them both up for a night or two so they did not think anything more until they arrived. The flat had two bedrooms, one of which of course belonged to Andrew himself.

When Andrew eventually got around to showing them the apartment, they realised they would be sleeping in the same room, one in a bed and one on a mattress on the floor.

"You can take the mattress into the sitting room if you prefer to sleep alone; you'll have to sort it out between you. There's only one bathroom so we'll have to take it in turns but that's okay, I've had four staying here in the past and we managed – just."

John and Simon looked at each other, both wondering if the other was going to consent to sleeping on the mattress, letting his friend have the bed.

"We'll draw straws, shall we?" suggested John.

"Haven't got any straws," Andrew announced. They're not allowed anymore since the plastics scandal. Got to do your bit to save the environment."

"I hope we're not going to talk about saving the environment or, even worse, Brexit! Can't stand politics," Simon huffed. "No, I'll take the bed, save my bad back. You okay with that, John?"

"Guess I'll have to be," John said in a low voice. "No, that's okay, I don't mind, really. You take the bed the first night and I'll take it the second, how does that sound?"

"I'm not staying two nights!" Simon was adamant.

"Well, that's that sorted then," said Andrew, as he disappeared into the kitchen to get the supper ready. "You guys still eat curry?" This was directed at Simon as John had already made his opinion clear regarding curry. Andrew was still talking but more loudly this time from the kitchen. "All these years have gone by and actually we hardly know each other now. That's very sad. Happily married, you two, and you've almost forgotten about me, free and single. It ain't what it's cracked up to be, I can assure you!"

"Huh! Happily married, you say?" Simon snorted. "Hardly. Twenty-five years of hard slog. Couldn't wait to get out the house. Tomorrow night I'm on a promise so it'll be bye-bye to you boys. Yes, John you can have my bed."

"Thanks. I've been very happy with Vera for over forty-five years. That is, until she got full-blown dementia last year. It's bordering on Alzheimer's except I don't really know the difference. She's being very difficult lately. I've dumped her on my sister just so I can meet up with you lot. And to have a break, of course."

"I remember your sister! Jan?" Andrew's eyes lit up as he came back with another beer in his hand. "Wow, she was gorgeous. I missed out there big time." Andrew was getting animated. "Is she still married to that bloke, Gerald or Geoff? God, what a plonker he was, never did like him. They had to get married, didn't they?"

"Yes, Geoff, that was a long time ago. Again, about forty-five years ago, or more, probably. No, they had their silver wedding anniversary and had a holiday in America to celebrate and she met someone else." John explained. "Turns out he was the love of her life until he died last year. He was only seventy. Sudden heart attack or something like that."

"Crikey. That's a bit tough. So is she free and single now? I'll give her a bell if you give me her number."

"No, you won't!" John warned Andrew. "She's still grieving and anyway she never liked you, she told me. Thought you were too brash and a typical bachelor. She goes for the gentler sort, like Mike. He was a good chap, actually. I liked him. Not that we saw each other that much, what with her living in Surrey and me in Bristol. She's had a really tough time with her kids. They never forgave her for leaving and the rift just got wider and wider. They never made up until last year just after Mike died. I got them together and then her daughter, my niece, had a terrible accident and died. Then poor Jan was blamed all over again. It was all so tragic; I do feel for her. But I think she's gradually picking up the pieces and getting on with her life. I was sorry to have to drop Vera on her but I had no option if I was going to make it here. Just needed a break really and you filled the gap."

"Oh, thanks. Nice to be just a stopgap, to feel wanted! Love you too!" Andrew retorted, feeling a little hurt but at the same time he thought he knew what John meant.

"Sorry. It came out all wrong. I've got a bottle of wine in the car; I'll go and get it."

John was glad to get out. He was starting to think it was

a big mistake to come. His old mates were just so different to him. They seemed so childish, like they had never grown up, Andrew in particular. He went to the car to retrieve the bottle of wine plus his overnight bag. It looked like he was going to be on the settee so he was preparing to have a bad back by the morning. Maybe plenty of alcohol would numb the process.

Jan made Vera a cup of tea and they sat chatting about nothing in particular until Vera started asking questions again.

"Is John out in the car? His tea will be cold if he doesn't come in soon."

"John's gone away." Jan tentatively tried Vera with this piece of information and waited for the explosion.

"What! How can he have gone away? When is he coming to take me home?"

"Soon," Jan tried to smooth the waters, noticing how agitated Vera was becoming.

17

Cheryl spoke to Steven when he came home and told him of the phone conversation she had had with Charlotte.

"Oh, God. If that ever happens to one of ours I should go mental."

"Let's hope it doesn't then." Cheryl was ever mindful that Steven would be far less understanding than she herself would be to situations as they arose. He was like his father in the way he dealt with difficulties. "Well, what can we do to help her? It looks like Dean is throwing her out sooner rather than later."

"He can't do that to his own daughter!" Steven was furious to think that his niece might resort to sleeping rough.

"That's what I thought but it looks that way. Can you at least talk to him and see what exactly is going on there?"

"I don't think I should interfere," said Steven and Cheryl was not surprised by his reaction. In fact, she made a bet with herself that he would say those exact words. She was ready with a quick retort.

Men, Cheryl said to herself, *you can read them like a book!*

"Of course you must!" she said out loud. "We can't leave it. It looks like she might run away and have the baby God knows where. She did ask if she can come here…"

"Let me stop you right there." Steven was starting to get the gist of what might be occurring. Another baby in the house when his two girls were getting to the stage to be more independent was not his idea of fun.

"Don't worry, I said no. But I did feel bad about it," said Cheryl.

"She's not our responsibility!"

"No, I know she's not, but I can't help feeling we ought to help in some way."

Charlotte left the house, with Daisy waving her off, crying on the doorstep. Charlotte walked slowly down the road, trying to decide where to go. She got as far as the bus stop and wondered about getting on a bus, seeing how far it would take her. She sat down at the bus stop and let three buses go by while she racked her brains.

I could try my granddad and his wife, Lynda. I'm not sure if there is a bus that goes to where they live; they're quite far away in the country. And anyway, she wouldn't want me even if he was prepared to help. What about Grandma Kath? I've not seen her since Christmas. I wonder if anyone has told her about my predicament. But I bet she'll judge me or, worse, send me back. I can't go back now and Dad will be relieved that I've gone. I'll try Amelia again and appeal to her better nature.

She got up from the hard bench in the bus stop and for the first time felt a little kick from within. It surprised her so much that she felt a little emotional as a tear slid down her cheek. When she arrived at Amelia's house, her mother, Sue, opened the door. She was not at all surprised to see Charlotte as Amelia had told her she had asked to stay.

"Dad's kicked me out," Charlotte announced, still with a tear on her face. "I've nowhere else to go."

"Well, you'd better come in. We can put you up for a couple

of nights but I'm sorry, you'll have to find somewhere else to go after that. Have you tried your uncle and aunt?"

"They don't want me either. Nobody wants me." Charlotte hung her head and another tear appeared in her eye.

"Come on, don't be sad. I'll try and get you the help you need."

"Thank you."

Daisy went indoors after seeing Charlotte walk slowly down the road with her head hung low. She felt she must do something. The only person she could think of to speak to was Uncle Steven or, better still, Auntie Cheryl.

"Hello." Steven answered the phone in a gruff tone. Daisy was disappointed that Cheryl had not answered, instead of Steven.

"Charlie's gone!" Daisy blurted out, without any introductions. "She's going to have a baby so Dad's kicked her out." She decided to ignore his tone of voice and just go for it and if needs be she would throw in some crying; that usually did it for men, she thought. "I don't know where she's going and I don't think she knows either."

"Oh no, that's all we need. I'll go and search for her, don't worry, Daisy. I'll try and keep her safe." Steven relented in his views. He could not let a member of his family down.

He hung up and went to his car, calling out to Cheryl to stay by the phone in case Daisy rang again. Or Charlotte. He had no idea where to start looking for his niece but he started by going to her house. He trawled the streets around the house and then gradually trawled further out, like a fan. He spent two hours searching, going up one street and down another.

Charlotte was oblivious to the trouble she was causing in her wake. She had only gone a short distance, just a stone's throw away, to Amelia's house.

Sue showed her to the spare room, which was nothing more than a dumping ground. The single bed was piled high with boxes and photo albums, which she systematically started clearing onto the floor.

"I've been meaning to put these photos into albums for years. Just another job which has gone by the board. Let's get you settled in here, but only for a couple of nights, remember."

"Yes, I know and thank you." Charlotte helped with putting boxes on the floor. She put her rucksack on the bed and started to cry.

"Come on, now, don't cry," Sue consoled Charlotte. "We need to have a plan of action. Do you know where are you going to go? Have you tried anywhere yet?" Sue decided that she would sit down with Charlotte and have a heart to heart with her. See what was going on in her head.

"I've really no idea."

"Have you tried your grandmother, Kath, or your granddad, Geoff?" Sue asked.

"No! I don't want them involved."

"What about your uncle and aunt? Surely they would help out?"

"I tried them but no go there. Look, no one wants me! I'm just a liability. I'll walk the streets until someone takes me in. How does that sound?"

"Not good, I'm afraid. I can't let you do that. Shall I ring them and ask them?"

"Good luck with that!" Charlotte felt defeated.

"Well, I can try. What's their number?" Sue was starting to get exasperated with Charlotte's negativity.

Charlotte gave Sue the number for Uncle Steven and she went off to use the telephone. Meanwhile, Charlotte made herself as comfortable as she could on the spare bed, surrounded by old photos on the floor. She wondered about going for a shower and, when Sue did not come back for some time, Charlotte started getting undressed. She found the bathroom across the landing and put the lock across. She stepped into the shower and languished in the warm water as it cascaded over her body. She thought she knew every inch of her body but suddenly she discovered new lumps and bumps. Her breasts had grown but she did not know why. She had wondered why her bras had not fitted her lately; she assumed they had shrunk in the wash. As it slowly dawned on her she realised that this must be to do with the baby growing inside her.

A bang on the door awakened her daydreams.

"Charlotte? Are you in there? What are you doing?" called Sue from behind the door.

"Just having a quick shower," Charlotte replied. "I'll be out in a minute." She stepped out of the shower, dried herself and wrapped the towel around her as she unlocked the door.

"I've been talking to your Uncle Steven. He's only just come back from looking for you, all around, apparently. He was glad I rang as now he knows you are safe. He was really worried when he heard you had left home."

"Does that mean I can go and live with them?" Charlotte asked hopefully. "I know I'm not really welcome here."

"That's not true; you are always welcome to visit Amelia. We just haven't got room for you to stay long term. Your uncle says you can stay with them but only for a little while, maybe a few days, maybe longer, I don't know. That doesn't really solve your problem of where you will go long term. Why don't you just make it up with your dad and I'm sure he will see you right. He won't want to see you on the streets, will he?"

"He doesn't care about me! I can't go back now. I'll be really good with my Uncle Steven and Auntie Cheryl – they won't know I'm there."

"I think they will! Anyway, he is coming to get you tomorrow at 9am so make sure you're ready and be good and be as helpful as you can."

"Thank you, I will."

Amelia called up from downstairs as she heard voices, floating down the stairs in hushed tones. She recognised her mother's voice but was puzzled as to whom she was talking.

"Hello, I'm home. Is tea ready? I'm starving."

"We have a guest and so I haven't started preparing anything yet but I'm on it," Sue began as she descended the stairs. "Come up and say hello to our visitor."

Amelia took two steps at a time and arrived on the landing in seconds, curious as to who their visitor might be. Charlotte peeped around her bedroom door and smiled.

"Oh, it's you! That's a surprise. Mum had said you weren't able to stay. Did she change her mind?"

"Well, I think she took pity on me..."

That evening Amelia and Charlotte stayed up late in Amelia's bedroom talking. They talked over how things were going to change and Amelia told Charlotte how much she missed her at school. Charlotte confided that she was scared witless as to what the future held for her and her baby. She could not think any further than actually having the baby.

"And what about all our talks of being a girl group, like Little Mix or the even more successful girl band the Spice Girls?" Amelia was quick to remind Charlotte of their aspirations of becoming famous one day.

"Well, we didn't exactly practise our singing or anything, did we? I suppose we were too interested in boys to think anything further," Charlotte demurred.

"Huh! You were!" Amelia was indignant.

"Well, okay, I was, but I thought you were too."

"I might have been interested but not so much as to get myself pregnant."

"Charming!" Charlotte was furious that her best friend could say such a thing and she stormed out of Amelia's bedroom and slammed the door. She huffed herself into the spare room, which was only going to be for one night now, instead of two. Then she would be whisked off by Uncle Steven to stay with his family. She wondered what her cousins were going to make of her and her predicament.

She undressed and slipped into bed without venturing out to the bathroom. She did not want another confrontation with Amelia on the landing so she stayed in her room until morning. She tossed and turned in bed but could not sleep for hours. Eventually she drifted off and dreamed of prams and nappies but not of a baby. She tried really hard to see if she could see a baby because she wanted to see what he looked like, who he looked like. She was certain she was going to have a boy baby and she was going to call him Jet.

The following day Steven and Cheryl called to take Charlotte home to their house. As she opened her car door she noticed Steven gave Cheryl a look that she did not quite understand. He looked annoyed but then when he noticed Charlotte looking at him he forced a smile.

"Come on, Charlie, get in," he said to Charlotte as he threw her rucksack into the boot of the car.

"I must go and say goodbye." Charlotte rushed back indoors to see Sue and thank her for having her but she had already left for work. She helped out on a Saturday at the local post office. Charlotte saw Amelia in the kitchen making her breakfast and hated leaving under a cloud. She wanted to make it up with her friend but decided to leave it at that. If

Amelia wasn't going to come out to say goodbye, then neither was Charlotte. She closed the front door quietly and crept away.

18

John, Andrew and Simon reminisced well into the first night and eventually went to their beds around 2am after a lot of alcohol had been consumed.

John awoke at 6am in desperate need for the bathroom. He rolled out of the mattress onto the floor and just managed to stand up, staggering for the first few steps. He looked over at Simon, who was still asleep in the one bed. He crept over to the door, opened it quietly and saw the bathroom door was shut with peculiar noises coming from inside. He realised it was Andrew being sick. He waited in the semi-darkness and eventually Andrew came out.

"Oh, you made me jump!" Andrew said to a bleary-eyed John.

"Are you okay?" John was concerned for his friend. "Got a dicky tummy?"

"Probably the curry. It was a bit stronger than usual. I was trying to impress last night with a hot madras but actually my stomach can't take the strong flavours nowadays."

"Yes, it was a bit hot but I liked it, very tasty, I thought. Simon is still asleep. Do you want me to make you a cup of tea or anything?" John asked.

"No, thanks. I'm going back to bed, it's too early. You make one for yourself, though, if that's what you want. Help yourself." Andrew was feeling the worse for wear with a bad stomach ache. He had more often than not been sick after an evening of overindulgence, not only the curry but probably too many beers and then some whisky chasers to finish off the evening.

John made himself a cup of tea and decided to go into the sitting room rather than back to his mattress on the floor, which he actually found more comfortable than he expected and he was pleased with that. He found a newspaper from the day before and after rooting around for his glasses he proceeded to read yesterday's news.

Simon woke up and sleepily looked around the unfamiliar room until he realised where he was. He saw John's mattress was empty and had a slight pang of guilt as he had had a good night's sleep. Then he remembered what he had on for later today. He was going to meet up with an old girlfriend, and who knew how that was going to pan out? He hoped he was going to be able to persuade her that he was the best thing since sliced bread and then get her into bed – somewhere – he knew not where but something would turn up, he was sure. The thoughts of that put him in a good mood, although he knew it would be short-lived as he would have to go home to his wife tomorrow.

"Hiya," Simon said good-naturedly to John, who was still reading the old newspaper.

"Oh, hi," John replied as he looked over his glasses. "Cup of tea?" he offered.

"Or a hair of the dog?" Simon thought that that sounded more cool, although these days a cup of tea was more welcome. He had decided he would not ask John if he slept well for fear of hearing his friend moan about a bad back after sleeping on the mattress.

"Thought I heard voices," Andrew interrupted the conversation. "Breakfast anyone?"

They started planning their day over breakfast. They all had different ideas and Simon was keen to get away soon after lunch for his assignation. In the end they just sat chatting over coffee, talking over old times and the time soon disappeared. Andrew made them some soup and sandwiches for lunch and then Simon made his excuses to get away early.

"That was awkward," John said to Andrew after Simon's departure. "I thought that we were just a stopgap when he told me before we went to sleep last night that he's going to meet up with an old girlfriend today. I think he used us so he could tell his wife he was with us. Which he was, of course, albeit only one day instead of two. I think his day today is more important to him."

"Oh, well, as long as he enjoys himself. We all deserve a bit of enjoyment in our later years, don't you think?" said Andrew, wistfully.

"Of course." John was thoughtful, thinking of times gone by and their racing towards old age at a much faster rate than he expected or wanted, which made him sad.

After Simon's departure, John and Andrew went out for a walk in the park nearby. It had rained and was wet underfoot but the sun peeped over the clouds and it turned out a nice day. It was springtime and the bluebells were showing their beautiful blue carpet under the trees. Summer was just around the corner, getting warmer day by day.

"This is my favourite time of year with all the bluebells, although my favourite flowers are the daffodils, but they are over now," John imparted to Andrew. "Vera and I always said we liked the springtime, knowing summer is just around the corner."

"Hark at you! Ever the family man! Did Vera make you say that? She always had you under her thumb." Andrew felt slightly jealous that he himself had no one with which to share his life.

"Never! I'm the man about the house, always have been and don't let anyone tell you different. Vera and I were always on an even footing although I'd like to think I was the more superior being, like a man should be." John felt slightly miffed that Andrew would think that Vera wore the trousers. "Anyway, these days she doesn't even know what day it is – I have to make all the decisions for her as well as myself. It's just as well I'm retired now but it hasn't panned out quite as I imagined with having to look after her. Not only look after her but look out for her and make sure she doesn't do anything stupid like leave the gas on, for instance, or leaving a tap on. So for her own safety I have to be alert all the time. It's a nightmare. I'm so glad to have these days away – like a mini break."

"Glad I've been of assistance in that department. Is she really that bad? Surely she should be in a home if she's that bad?" Andrew asked as sincerely as he could muster, although he couldn't imagine what it was like to care for someone else, having only himself to look after.

"I don't know how bad is bad. The doctors reckon they will let me know when it's time to let someone else look after her. These homes are really expensive, over a grand a week, sometimes. The better ones are nearer fifteen hundred."

"What? That's ridiculous! Who can afford that? Especially if they live on into their eighties or nineties, which a lot of people reach these days. That would cost hundreds of thousands of pounds, wouldn't it?" Andrew said, aghast and secretly glad that he didn't have to make the decision for which his friend so obviously had.

"Which is why I'm doing the work myself while I can. I call it 'work' because that is what it is. Every day I have to consider her needs before by own, making sure she takes her medication and thinking for her. Thinking for both of us. It's very wearing, I can tell you."

They walked back to the apartment when the sun went in again and the rain threatened.

"What's on tonight?" John asked, pleased to be able to think of something other than Vera but at the same time knowing the time was getting near to when this day would end and he would soon be back to full-time care. "Is there a plan?"

"Well, we could go down the pub. There's a new act on tonight, some sort of comedy open mike act, I think. Or there might be a quiz or it might be karaoke – you like?"

"Like a quiz but can't stand karaoke," John retorted. "You'd never get me up singing. It's just an excuse for people to show off; none of them can sing a note. They tried that at our local but it was the kiss of death. The publican soon learned his lesson and never did it again; he must have lost a lot of money as people just stayed away."

"Yeah, s'pose you're right. I'm not that keen either, although I don't really take any notice as the pub is usually buzzing with noise, so the caterwauling would have to be really loud to make anyone notice. We can just sit in a corner and see who is there. Some mates usually come in; I'd like you to meet them."

Jan felt exhausted after two days with Vera. After John left, she became a little agitated and kept asking for him. In the evening they watched programmes that Jan knew Vera liked so that kept her occupied and happy. After getting ready for bed, Vera started asking for John again.

"He'll be here when he's ready. He's had to go and visit some friends up in London," Jan explained.

"I don't understand that. He always takes me with him. Why couldn't I go with him?"

Jan did not have the heart to say her brother needed a break from her.

"He's got some business to deal with," she lied.

Jan heard Vera singing and talking to herself in her bedroom. At least she sounded happy, thought Jan. Jan dropped off to sleep but was awakened by a heart-chilling scream in the middle of the night. She jumped out of bed and rushed in to Vera who had fallen out of the bed and was disorientated.

Jan slept with one eye open for the rest of the night. *God, I've got two nights of this!* Jan thought.

In the morning Jan went into Vera's bedroom.

"Are you okay?" Jan asked.

"Of course I'm okay! Where's my early cuppa? And where's John?" Vera was starting to get flustered. "He always wakes me with my early cuppa!"

"He'll be here tomorrow morning. When you're ready to get up, do you want me to help you in the shower?" Jan asked kindly.

"Of course I don't!" Vera was indignant. "Do you think I'm a child? I'm not your daughter, you know!"

"Yes, I do know that; I was just trying to be helpful. If you can manage on your own, that's fine."

Vera went into the bathroom and Jan heard splashing so she took the opportunity to make the bed. She found the sheets were wet – soaked, in fact. She took them all off including the under-sheets and found the mattress was also very wet.

John could have warned me! I'll just have to make do and try and dry the mattress, I haven't got time to buy a new one. I'll lay towels over the mattress to soak up the wet. I've got a plastic sheet somewhere. Don't want that happening again tonight.

Jan proceeded with finding the plastic sheet and making

up the bed, putting the sheets in the washing machine and all before Vera came out of the bathroom.

She jollied her along as best she could and included her in everything she was doing. The garden was the saviour as Vera loved Jan's garden. She started to get the garden furniture out of the summer house and was glad of a little warmer weather to enable them to sit out.

"I've got some lettuce plugs, which I bought at the garden centre. They need pricking out – would you like to help me?" Jan offered Vera.

"Oh *no*! I can't get my hands dirty. John would tell me off. He always tells me off if I get dirty and he has to wash me."

"Well, he's not here. I could wash your hands for you."

"I said no and I meant it." Vera was adamant.

Jan was unsure whether to go ahead and plant the lettuces while leaving Vera sitting in the garden on her own. The vegetable patch was around the side of the house and out of sight from where the patio seats were. Vera started nodding off so Jan made a stealthy escape as the lettuce plants had started to wilt and needed to be planted in the ground as soon as possible.

One by one the lettuce plugs were lovingly planted by Jan, just like Mike used to do. There were more than she expected in the box but she had visions of lovely salads, which she loved. The last one went in and Jan stood up to ease her back. She had forgotten about Vera briefly as she immersed herself in the planting.

I'll just pick some rhubarb while I'm here. Oh, yes, Vera! I must ask her if she likes rhubarb. Jan often talked to herself when she was deep in thought.

As she rounded the corner and expected to see Vera still asleep, she saw the empty garden chair. Maybe she had just gone inside to the loo. Jan went into the kitchen, where she saw her electric kettle on the stove with full gas on underneath. The plastic was starting to melt and then it suddenly collapsed in front of her with a whoosh of water, quelling the gas flames and flooding the well of the hob, overflowing onto the floor.

Jan kept calm and first of all turned off the gas. She began to mop up the water on the floor and decided to leave the melted plastic until it had cooled down. She left the water on the hob and went in search of Vera.

"Vera?" Jan called out. No answer. "Vera, where are you?" she called louder.

The whole house was silent. Jan began to panic. She searched every room but Vera had disappeared.

"This is ridiculous; where can she be?" Jan was now starting to worry. "VERA!" There was no way Vera could not hear that. Not a sound anywhere in the house.

Vera's coat was still on the hook in the hall. *She can't have gone out without her coat. Oh, God, she could have gone out, couldn't she?*

Jan opened the front door to look in the front garden but went back for her keys and her coat. She would just have to go and search for her. What would John say to her if she has lost Vera!

John was not thinking of Vera at all. It turned out that there was a quiz on at the pub so John was in his element. He loved pub quizzes. He and Andrew palled up with a couple of Andrew's drinking mates and won the quiz easily by a couple of points.

"That was a good evening," John said to Andrew as they walked home to Andrew's flat.

"Never enjoyed myself so much. We wouldn't have won without your knowledge of geography and history. And so many sport questions! Well done! How on earth do you know so much?" Andrew asked.

"I've been doing quizzes for some time now and it's surprising how much you learn from them, as long as you've got a good memory."

"I'll let you know when the next one's on so you can come and join us."

"Sorry mate. If I was nearby I'd love to but over 100 miles away is just too far, unfortunately."

As they went in the front door Andrew offered John a nightcap. "A little whisky to help you sleep? Or something else?"

"I really mustn't. I've got to pick up Vera tomorrow morning. I'm hoping to sleep off this evening's booze so it won't register if I get stopped and breathalysed. I feel okay now so hopefully I will be alright by the morning if I lay off any more."

"When did you get so boring? If you get stopped and breathalysed? They only do that at Christmas, don't they?" Andrew had not driven for years, happy to have given up his car as it was so easy with transport in London on buses and the underground.

"I really don't know. I just don't want to take the chance of losing my licence. Vera lost her licence a few months back when she drove down a one-way street the wrong way. She very nearly ran over a mother and child in a buggy who weren't looking to see if a car might be going the wrong way! She saw them at the last moment and crashed into a lamp post. The police were called and Vera swore blind she hadn't done anything wrong. Anyway, there were plenty of eyewitnesses who testified against her so she didn't have a leg to stand on. So they took away her licence, for good they said."

"Oh dear, naughty Vera!" Andrew laughed.

"It's no laughing matter. I have to take her everywhere now. She has lost her independence and that means she is either stuck at home with me or I take her out with me in case she does something stupid to herself. I don't get a minute to myself; we are together twenty-four seven . And that really is not a good thing. It's doing my head in, I can tell you!"

Jan searched for Vera, first of all in the garden, calling her name every few seconds. Jan soon established that she was not only not in the house but not in the garden either. Jan ran down the road looking in people's front gardens.

She can't have gone far. Could she? Should I go back and call the police? They would have a better chance of finding her. Oh hell! What will John say?

Jan scanned the streets around her house and then went further afield until she arrived at the local shops. She went into one and enquired after describing Vera if they had seen her. Nothing. Then the next shop. Nothing again. She went into all the shops but Vera had not been seen. At the end of the row of shops was a restaurant. It was Little Italy, the Italian restaurant run by Rosa Lina and Giovanni.

Jan went inside and saw there were people having coffee. Jan recognised Rosa Lina from Vicky and Gerry's party a few weeks ago.

"Ah, hello, Jan?" Rosa Lina welcomed Jan. "You have decided to join us at last? I have a table here for you. Coffee? A cappuccino, maybe? On the house, of course."

"That's very kind. I'm so sorry but I haven't come in for a coffee." Then Jan decided that sounded rude so she quickly explained that she had lost her sister-in-law and she was out looking for her. "I thought she might have come in here," Jan explained. "She was wanting a cup of coffee and put the kettle on but then went out. I should have been looking after her and I failed!"

Jan started to tell Rosa Lina about Vera's mental state and also what she was wearing from what Jan could remember. She knew she did not have her coat. She looked around the restaurant at all the people's faces but they became a blur through her eyes, which were starting to water as she became upset at not finding Vera.

"I haven't seen her," Rosa Lina said. "But then I haven't been here that long; I've been to the shops."

Just then there was an almighty crash coming from the back of the restaurant in the kitchen.

"Oops!" Jan said with a slight smile. "I'll leave you to it; it sounds like you might have some clearing up to do! I'm so sorry to have bothered you." Jan quickly went out of the door and back down the High Street to carry on with her search.

Back in the restaurant, chaos was reigning. Giovanni appeared at the kitchen door with what looked like blood on his hands just as Rosa Lina approached in haste.

"What on earth happened?" said Rosa Lina.

"Rosa, just come in here and help me please." Giovanni was trying to keep as calm as he could muster in front of their customers enjoying their coffee, but they were also concerned as to the commotion going on at the back of the restaurant which was usually a place of serenity.

Rosa Lina rushed towards the kitchen and Giovanni stood aside in the doorway to let her through. In front of her she could see the floor covered with broken crockery interspersed with the remains of what looked like pasta, tomato and pepperoni pieces all mixed together. Giovanni pushed her so he could shut the door behind them.

"For God's sake, Rosa! Who is that?" Giovanni pointed to a woman bent over the sink with her hands under the tap. "She came into my kitchen and just took over. Then she opened the oven door with a tea towel and took out my creation! My manicotti. Mamma mia! Of course it was too hot and she dropped it but never said a word. She's broken my best casserole; I'll never be able to replace that!" His head was in his hands in desperation, leaving bits of pasta and tomato on his face like something out of a comic strip.

"Never mind your casserole dish. I'd better go and see to her first." Rosa Lina picked her way around the mess and hastily went to the sink to see what injuries the woman had. Giovanni felt miffed that Rosa Lina felt nothing for his favourite ceramic Dutch oven, which he had originally bought in Italy and had carefully packed after nurturing it for years. He started picking up the pieces again but they were too hot. He was glad that the redness on his hands was just the tomato sauce he had lovingly prepared earlier and not blood. Although he felt his blood pressure was rising and all because of this woman. Who the hell did she think she was, coming into his kitchen and interfering?

Rosa Lina arrived at the sink, where the woman was bent over the sink with cold water running over her hands.

"Hello?" Rosa Lina said kindly. "Can I help you?"

"Not at all," Vera said indignantly. "That man made me drop the dish; it's his fault! He shouted at me and now I've burnt my hands and they hurt like hell. The cold water is helping."

"But what are you doing here?" Rosa Lina asked, then seeing what the woman was wearing and recognising Jan's description of her sister-in-law.

"I'm helping out, of course. You asked me to but I'm not coming here again." Vera dried her hands and starting walking towards the door.

"Is your name Vera?" asked Rosa Lina.

"So you do know her!" Giovanni looked up from the floor where he was attempting to mop up the mess. "What were you thinking, asking her to help?"

"I didn't!" Rosa Lina said quietly to Giovanni and making faces at him to try and make him aware she was doing what she could to ameliorate the situation.

"Oh, yes you did!" Vera had heard Rosa Lina. Vera tutted and waltzed through the kitchen door, into the restaurant.

"I'm not coming here again," Vera announced in a loud voice to the customers enjoying their coffee. She found a full cup of coffee waiting to be delivered and decided she would have it for herself. She picked it up and started drinking it while she was standing.

"Honestly, I never asked her to help but I think I know who she is." Rosa Lina started explaining to Giovanni. "Jan came in just now asking if I had seen her sister-in-law, Vera. She is suffering from Alzheimer's and Jan was beside herself with worry because she had gone walkabout. Jan described her to me. I must ring Vicky and ask for Jan's phone number so I can contact her and she can come and collect her. You must go in and try and stall her while I call Vicky, okay?"

"Do I have to?" Giovanni asked resignedly, knowing he must do this as it was the only way of getting rid of her once and for all. He knew he didn't want her to come back here – ever.

Rosa Lina phoned Vicky and told her the circumstances of her call. Vicky was very helpful and not only offered to speak to Jan but would drive down and pick up Vera herself if Jan was not home yet.

Jan had looked in all the shops again after visiting the restaurant but decided to go home again in case Vera appeared. She was at Vicky's road when she saw her coming out of her driveway. Vicky had called Jan's number but no one answered so she was just about to fetch Vera herself. She was relieved to see Jan and drove over to her.

"I've lost my sister-in-law, Vera!" Jan said to her friend.

"I know!"

Jan looked puzzled.

"Get in," Vicky commanded. "I'll explain on the way."

When they got to the restaurant Vera was sitting calmly with a cup of coffee in front of her. Jan was so relieved to see her safe and well. Rosa Lina did not have the heart to tell Jan about the kitchen incident, although Giovanni was still seething. They were both glad that Jan had come for Vera and hopeful that they would not see her again.

"They didn't want my help after all!" Vera complained to Jan when they got home. Jan was puzzled but left it at that. "It was a nice coffee, though; that was kind of them to give me that and I didn't have to pay for it. Even better." Jan made a mental note to settle up with them at a later stage.

Vera went into the kitchen and was faced with an almighty mess. The second kitchen mess in one day and both caused by her. She did not remember putting the plastic electric kettle on the gas stove and turning the gas on full before going out.

"Oh, would you look at this? What have you done here?" Vera tutted.

Jan contained her anger as she felt sorry for Vera. It was not her fault she had Alzheimer's and she was sure she would not wish it on her worst enemy.

Jan cleared up the now cold plastic of the electric kettle, which was like a gnarled fist with odd shards of petrified plastic poking in odd directions. She made a mental note to buy a new kettle but in the meantime boiled water for their tea in a saucepan.

The rest of the day Jan did not take her eyes off Vera. They went out for a long walk in the afternoon as Jan wanted to make sure she slept through the night without waking. She made sure the front and back doors were locked tighter than usual. She hid the keys in a secure place known only to her. The alarm was set for downstairs only so they could walk about upstairs but as soon as anyone went downstairs the alarm would start. Jan felt happy that Vera would not be able to get out again. Only a few more hours before John came to pick her up, as he was due about mid-morning.

"Where's my John?" These were the first words spoken by Vera when Jan took her a cup of early morning tea.

John arrived in time for coffee. Jan was very thankful. She never told John about what had happened and he wondered why Jan was boiling water in a saucepan but never asked for fear of an answer he did not want to hear.

19

Charlotte unpacked her meagre amount of clothes in another spare room, the box room in Steven and Cheryl's house. Her cousins, Milly and Poppy, still shared a room, neither of them wanting the little box room that Charlotte was now inhabiting.

Milly had been starting to think that now she was fourteen she needed time away from her little eleven-year-old sister. They got on really well but there were times when they both wanted their own space. But the box room was just too small so they persevered with each other in their large, prettily decorated pink bedroom. Lines were drawn and they knew when to keep out of each other's way.

There was a knock on the door of the box room and Charlotte went to open it. Milly was standing there with a cup of tea for Charlotte.

"Mum's made this for you.," said Milly, handing her cousin the mug. "Don't know if it's what you drink but it's a start, isn't it?" Milly felt awkward, this almost-stranger in her midst. They were only two years apart in age and yet they hardly knew each other, only spending an hour or two together at family gatherings or Christmas. They did not live that far apart and yet they knew so little of what the other liked or was like.

"Oh, thank you so much," Charlotte gushed, taking hold of the hot mug. She was determined to make herself liked and would try as hard as she could to be nice, although she was feeling as if she could inwardly scream.

"What's it like to be pregnant?" Milly asked curiously.

"Oh, you know, it's not as bad as people make out."

"But what happens when the baby comes out? There's not room for you and it here! When's it due?"

"About two or three months, I think."

"Crikey, that's not long. Mum says you're not going to go back to school, is that right?"

"Yeah. Thought I'd just bum around till it's born. Although of course I will help out around the house. Is there anything that needs doing?" Charlotte was forcing herself, finding it really hard but this was the start of her trying to sound helpful.

"Nah, don't think so. Mum has it all under control, I think. I could ask her, if you like. Shall I ask her?"

"Okay, but only if you want to, thanks. I'll be down in a minute."

Milly went downstairs to ask her mother if there was anything that Charlotte could help with. Being a Saturday they were all in the house and Steven looked up from the newspaper.

"She can go and mow the lawn and do some weeding, if she likes."

"Just to give you a rest? I think not!" Cheryl retorted.

"No, Dad, I think she meant help around the house." Milly was hopeful that her mum could give Charlotte the jobs that she herself hated, like emptying the dishwasher or hoovering the bedrooms or, worse still, dusting. What a godawful thankless task that was!

"I know!" Steven had a brainwave. "She can wash my car. That'll save me time."

"Time for what?" Cheryl enquired.

"Well, you know, time for other jobs. She can wash the car and I can check the oil and see whatever else it might need."

"Ready for you to take me out later, you mean?" Cheryl laughed. "Shopping."

That dreaded word.

"You know I don't like shopping. That's a woman's job!" said Steven, knowing full well those words would annoy her so he added, "Only kidding!"

"Oh, really. But you like to eat and drink all the things that come out of a supermarket. We always go together on the weekend and you like to choose special things you like. That's what you always say, anyway." Cheryl always hated it if anyone said that something is a woman's job but she held her tongue this time. She knew he was not really kidding.

"Only to keep you sweet, my sweet. Actually I can't think of anything more boring than shopping."

"I like shopping!" Milly interjected.

"Yes, but only when it's for clothes or handbags or shoes for you!" Steven had become used to being around an all-woman household. "What about the shopping for necessities like food?"

"I'll come with you. Give Uncle Steven a break." Charlotte arrived in the kitchen having heard some of the conversation. "I don't mind food shopping. I used to go with Mum."

Silence ensued as they all thought about her mum, Louise.

"Of course, I prefer clothes shopping," Charlotte continued, to try and break the silence. "All my clothes seem to have shrunk in the wash! Let's face it, I just love shopping!"

"Let's all go," Cheryl decided at last. "Go and get your sister, Mils, and we'll go in about half an hour, okay?"

"Don't call me Mils. You know I don't like it." Milly told her mother off.

"Just like I don't like people calling me Charlie," Charlotte confirmed.

"That's agreed then! Milly and Charlotte," Cheryl averred. "Go and get Poppy and we'll do the shopping and then get a hot dog for lunch, okay?"

Steven's ears pricked up at the thought of a hot dog. With all the trimmings. Onions, chilli sauce and mustard. His mouth was watering already.

"I don't like hot dogs," Charlotte piped up, even though she wasn't sure if she had ever had one. "They don't sound very nice. Hot dogs. Ugh, that sounds horrid. Do they really cook stray dogs?"

To this everyone laughed out loud heartily, which made Charlotte embarrassed.

"They're sausages, silly," Milly told Charlotte as she disappeared upstairs to get her sister.

"Mmm, I like hot dogs." Charlotte announced as they arrived back at the house after shopping and having lunch.

"It's amazing that you've never had them before. Did you really think they were made from dogs?" Milly asked Charlotte.

"Course not! I was only kidding," Charlotte lied. She liked to think of herself as worldly wise. After all, she was pregnant and proud of it.

Charlotte went to her bedroom and shut herself in for the afternoon. She put her headphones on and listened to her music as she lounged on her bed.

"D'you think she's depressed?" Cheryl asked Steven. "Our girls don't just shut themselves away like that."

"Maybe she's tired. We're going to have to discuss things long term with her. You know she can't stop here forever."

"Of course not, I know," Cheryl agreed. "I wonder if we should speak to Dean. See what's really going on there."

"That'll be like opening a can of worms. Charlie seems adamant she's not going back there so we can't force her."

"She's only sixteen; she can't know what's best for her at that age. Can she?" Cheryl asked the hypothetical question to which she knew there was no answer. "Shall we have a word with your dad? He might come up with something."

"Well, you can try but he's getting old now; he won't want to know," Steven demurred.

"What? Won't want to know what's happening to his own granddaughter? I think you underestimate him. He's the one person who might be able to help – after all, he knows all about things like this: he got his girlfriend pregnant a long time ago!"

"Hey, that's my mum you're talking about!"

"I know. But that doesn't change history, does it? It happened. And where is she now? Banished. And all because she wanted a better life for herself. Or different, anyway; after twenty-five years of marriage maybe she wanted something different. I know it was mostly Louise who didn't want anything to do with her but you followed her lead. All that time ago. Do you ever wonder about her?" Cheryl had always been confused by Louise and Steven's attitude towards their mother.

"Course I do," Steven said defensively and trying to change the subject back to Charlotte. "Look, this is getting us nowhere. We'll see how madam is and talk it through with her. It's no good making decisions for her."

"Look, speak to Dean," Cheryl reiterated. "He's her father and so he should be making decisions about her, not us."

"Okay, okay, I'll give him a ring."

Steven rang Dean and Daisy answered.

"How is Charlie?" Daisy sounded worried as soon as she heard Steven's voice. Charlotte had already texted her to say where she was staying as Daisy had asked her to.

"Oh, she's okay, thanks. Is your dad there? Just wanted him to know that Charlotte is with us…"

"We know!" said Daisy sarcastically. "Dad's down the pub but he's said he's washed his hands of her! Whatever that means!"

"I was going to continue to say that she is with us but she can't stay here indefinitely."

"Okay, I'll tell him. Is that all?" Daisy hung up without waiting for a reply. She was in the middle of baking some scones and did not want to be sidelined. Whenever she was concentrating on something, anything, she hated to be disturbed. She almost did not pick up the phone but she thought it might have been her friend, for whom she would not have minded an interruption.

"Who was that on the phone?" Jake had been studying in his bedroom. He found peace in his bedroom but he had been studying for some hours and came out for a break when he heard the phone ring.

"If you had answered it you would know by now!"

"Don't be so cheeky to your elders. Why are you behaving like your sister?" Jake knew that Daisy would be wound up by that remark. That would teach her a lesson.

"It was Uncle Steven, telling us that Charlotte was there and that she couldn't stay indefinitely."

"Well, Dad was adamant that he won't have her back here. Did you tell him that?"

"Yep."

"Is she okay?"

"Dunno. Look, I'm trying to bake scones and with all these interruptions they won't get done. Leave me alone." Daisy pointed to the door.

"Women!" Jake tutted as he left the kitchen.

The next day, Sunday, Cheryl was up early in readiness for

the battle to try to get anyone to go to church with her. Every Sunday was the same and she was not holding out much hope that their new guest would be any different to her own family. Cheryl's parents had always been good churchgoers and she followed suit. She tried in vain to get Steven interested when they first married but failed. She took the girls when they were younger but, now they were older and could decide for themselves, they said they no longer wanted to attend. She felt a failure in that department but resigned herself to go alone, although she felt she would try with Charlotte.

"Charlotte?" Cheryl knocked on Charlotte's door. Nothing. "Charlotte? Are you awake?" She looked at her watch and thought maybe it was too early. She tried again half an hour later but had no response. So she went to church alone.

Charlotte was awake but she was keeping her head down in case there were jobs to be done. She was unaware that she was expected to go to church. Not that she had ever been to a church so would not have known what to expect. She had always dreamed of a having a big white wedding in a church or better still a cathedral but now in her condition her thoughts of any sort of wedding were waning. She really had no idea of her next move or how the baby was going to affect her whole life or even where she was going to be when she gave birth. She was ever optimistic that something would turn up. Someone would come good but she knew it wasn't going to be at the only home she knew, with her own family supporting her. She was sad about that, of course.

She heard Cheryl go out and then she heard the girls and Steven going to the bathroom in turn. She decided she would wait until the coast was clear then she would go and have a shower.

When Cheryl returned from church mid-morning everyone was dressed and ready for the day. Except for

Charlotte. She was still languishing in the shower and taking her time.

"Hello, everyone," Cheryl called out. "Who is going to help me cook lunch?"

No one came forward to offer so she decided to delegate jobs for everyone. That was the only way things were going to get done.

"Steven, please can you peel the potatoes?" Cheryl found this was the safest job for him. How could he get that wrong? "And when you've done that I want you to have a heart to heart with Charlotte. Where is she, by the way?"

"I know!" Poppy piped up. "I know Charlie's in the shower. I saw her creep in there when we had all finished in the bathroom. But she's been in there ages!"

"Good, thank you, Poppy. You know she wants to be called Charlotte, don't you? And I want you to lay the table. Please use the best cutlery for a change. It's no good just leaving it to use for best. We've had it for years and hardly used it. And, Milly, I want you to help me with the cooking. Maybe you could do a nice pudding. What about a pineapple upside-down pudding? You're really good at those."

Everyone went about their chores and Steven mulled over in his head what he was going to say to Charlotte. He would be very diplomatic and suggest different things to her.

Charlotte eventually came downstairs when she thought the main jobs would be done and lunch would be nearly ready.

"Hello," she said cheerily. "Everyone okay? Is there anything I can do?" she offered half-heartedly.

"No, that's okay, Charlotte," Cheryl said kindly. "Lunch will be in about half an hour so Uncle Steven wants to have a word with you before that."

Steven glared at Cheryl and opened the door to the sitting

room and beckoned Charlotte to enter. He closed the door behind her.

"Now," he started. "Have a seat and we'll have a little chat."

Charlotte crossed her arms defensively and sat in a nearby easy chair.

"Do you know where you are going to have this baby of yours?" Steven asked.

"No!"

"Well, you know we don't have room for you here, don't you?"

"So you say. But there seems plenty of room, if you ask me." Charlotte was being deliberately belligerent and arrogant. She was not going to be pushed around by her uncle. Or by anyone for that matter.

"Have you been to the doctor? Do you know when the baby is due?"

"Yes. More or less."

Charlotte's one-word answers were beginning to annoy Steven. It was bad enough being in a household with three women, let alone four. At least he had control over his own children but he had no control over this one and he knew he was losing the battle. He had a light-bulb moment as he thought he was almost convinced of a solution.

"Look, I'm not an unreasonable man and I obviously know the circumstances are not ideal but you have to meet me halfway here."

Charlotte started to cry. They were genuine tears as emotions were running high but she also made the tears last longer than normal. Steven was sympathetic but stoic.

"I'm going to make a couple of suggestions and at the end you're going to have to make a choice. A decision. Okay?"

Charlotte nodded through all her tears. She blew her nose

and wiped her tears. She was aware her uncle was only trying to help her.

"May I suggest you make it up with your father?"

"No way to that one! I'm never going back there. He was horrible to me. Anyway, he doesn't want me or to have anything to do with me or my baby."

"Okay, no to that one. What about seeing if you can stay with Grandpa Geoff and Lynda? They wouldn't want to see you out on the streets." Steven was trying hard to be reasonable.

"I don't like her. She's a bitch! And, anyway, he's not been well and gets depressed. That's all I need." Charlotte harrumphed.

"What about asking your father's mother, Kath? She's nice, isn't she?"

"Yes, she's nice but she's only got a small flat and will say the same as you. There's no room at the inn!"

Steven only had one more solution up his sleeve but he was not going to tell her just yet. He needed to make a few phone calls.

"Well, okay. We will leave it for now but I will think of something, trust me."

"Is that it?" Charlotte said rudely.

"For now, yes, you can go and see if there is anything in the kitchen that needs doing."

Charlotte left the sitting room and went upstairs to speak to Amelia. She felt that she was her only ally since they made up almost as soon as they fell out. Charlotte had rung her and apologised for her hissy fit when they were last together. When she got to her bedroom and saw that her phone only had a little battery life she decided to text her instead.

Cheryl heard Charlotte go upstairs and went up too. She knocked on her door. Charlotte got up off her bed, opened the door gingerly and peeped out.

"Charlotte," began Cheryl, "I just wanted to talk to you."

"Oh, not you too! I've just had it in both ears from Uncle Steven!"

"No, not about what he spoke of. I heard you say yesterday that your clothes had shrunk and I wanted to help you out a bit."

Charlotte thought she meant she would give her her old clothes and she turned her nose up before Cheryl could explain further.

"Tomorrow we will all be at work and school. What about going back to school?"

"No way. I've already left. I'm sixteen so I can leave school legally."

"But you have no qualifications." Cheryl was not going to bring exams into the conversation but it just slipped out. "What I was actually going to say to you was: would you like to go and buy some new clothes tomorrow? I expect you will need some in a bigger size. I don't really think your clothes shrank in the wash; you've actually grown out of them so you're bound to need new ones. Look, I can see your jeans are very tight and that can't be doing the baby any good, can it?"

"No, s'pose not," Charlotte agreed. "But I don't have much money for new clothes so I'll just have to make do."

"Don't tell Uncle Steven but I'm going to give you some money to buy yourself some proper maternity clothes. Are you okay to go on your own or would you like me come with you to help you? I could see you in my lunch hour tomorrow."

"I expect I can manage," Charlotte said grudgingly and also wondering how much Cheryl was going to give her.

Cheryl went to her bedroom and came back to Charlotte with £100 in £20 notes. Charlottes' eyes lit up and she had thoughts of a new handbag and shoes. But before Cheryl gave Charlotte the money she had stipulations. She saw the slight smile on Charlotte's lips and had seen that look before. She was not going to be hoodwinked. The money was for bigger clothes, nothing else.

"Now," she began, "this is only for new clothes and I shall want to see the receipts."

Charlotte felt a slight disappointment but she knew in her heart of hearts she needed bigger clothes. Maybe now was the time she had to grow up and do as she was told.

"You can thank me, if you like," said Cheryl, rather underwhelmed by her niece's aloofness. Charlotte felt embarrassed and got up off the bed to give Cheryl a hug.

"Thank you," Charlotte said at last.

Steven saw there was still time before lunch so he rang his Uncle John in Bristol to see if he had any ideas. He crossed his fingers as he dialled the number.

"Hello, Uncle John, how are you? Steven here."

"Ah, long time no hear. How are things with you?" said John, pleased to get a call.

After all the niceties and asking after Vera, Steven began the long explanation of Charlotte's problem, which systematically had become his problem. He was hoping John would be able to have a solution. Steven knew that John would not want to take care of her as well as Vera. Steven was not able to ask his own mother because of the estrangement for over twenty years but he hoped that she would take pity on Charlotte, but only if John would be able to ask her. John was the only one in contact with his sister but he said he would wait a while before he asked her. Jan had never met any of her grandchildren and this might be a good opportunity for her to do so. Steven knew she was living in Surrey and on her own now since her husband had died. Maybe she would be lonely and would want to look after a bolshie sixteen-year-old who was about to give birth…

20

Jan went to the shops to buy a new kettle and also called in to the Italian restaurant to pay for Vera's coffee and apologise for any misunderstanding. She was still unaware of the catastrophe that Vera had caused in the kitchen.

Giovanni was a little cold towards Jan but Rosa Lina saved the awkwardness by offering her a cappuccino. She sat herself down with Jan and they chatted for some time. Jan proffered cash but Rosa Lina would not take any money for Vera's or her own coffee. She explained to Jan that her father was due back from a little holiday in Italy and that when he got back he would be pleased to see Jan. He had talked about her after Vicky and Gerry's party a few weeks before and she was still reeling from Vicky's suggestion that maybe some spark was there, although Jan thought it must have been in Vicky's imagination. Nevertheless, Jan blushed a little as she remembered Tino. She really liked him but she dared not think about him in that way for she was still grieving Mike. After all, it was only just over a year ago that he died. *How long is a suitable time for bereavement?* she wondered. She was sure that Mike would have given his blessing and would rather she be happy after he had gone. Nothing had been said when he was alive but then he had died so suddenly. Jan decided to put Tino out of her head completely to concentrate on more pressing matters.

After coffee she went home with her newly purchased kettle, which was much smarter than her old one. It was made of glass and had a blue light to show it was in the boiling mode. She was rather pleased to get rid of that nasty old plastic kettle. *Thank you, Vera!*

The next day it was lovely and sunny so she busied herself in the garden, pruning bushes and planting tomato plants as well as watering in the lettuce plants. They were looking much perkier than when she planted them.

After a long day of hard work she came in at teatime and was ready for a nice cup of tea. There was a message on the answerphone so she pressed the button to listen to who had rung her. It was Rosa Lina offering her a job! *A job at my time of life?*

She drank her tea and mulled over the job offer. *I wonder what sort of job. I used to do waitressing and I might have told them that, I can't remember. If it's part time I reckon I could do that. Actually I'd really like that. I'll ring her right back.*

"Hello, Rosa Lina, it's Jan here. I've thought about your offer and would like to know more. I could be interested."

"Wonderful. Come down whenever you want and we'll talk about what it entails. It's only a case of going through the motions to see what you would like to do."

Next day Jan donned some smart clothes and went to the restaurant when she knew it would not be too busy. Rosa Lina was so pleased to see her and explained that her father had been due back the next day but he had been delayed. Nothing serious but her brother wanted Tino to help out with his business there, just temporarily for a couple of weeks or maybe more, if needed. He was glad to help out his son in his engineering business but sad he was letting his daughter down with the restaurant work, just when it was starting to pick up after the winter lull.

"We can do without him but not for too long. We held out as long as we could but now we know he will be longer away we could really do with your help. Almost as soon as you left, I had a call from him. I know secretly that he prefers helping out at my brother's because he's always liked working on engines and he's very good at it. He's always tinkering about under his bonnet or with our car, which is quite old; there is always something needing to be done."

"Oh, men always like to know how things work! How can I help you? In the kitchen? I don't think I would do so well with cooking but I can prepare vegetables and I could do waitressing and any other odd jobs. When would you like me to start?"

"Right away, if possible! Not with cooking, no, but maybe preparation of the vegetables sometimes, plus waiting on the tables when it gets busy. And any odd jobs which I will show you, as and when." Rosa Lina looked desperate so Jan felt she should help her out, especially as she had been so good with Vera.

"What? Today?" Jan asked. They had not talked about wages but Jan knew that they would pay her what was fair. She was just glad to be able to help out and it gave her something to do.

"Yes, please! Thank you so much." Jan had not said yes but she had nodded and so Rosa Lina took that as affirmative. "I'll go and get you an apron." Rosa Lina could not believe her luck. She never thought Jan would say yes. "Can you start with filling all the salt cellars with salt and the pepper grinders with peppercorns? I'll show you where everything is. This really is very kind of you to step in. We will see you okay and, of course, you are welcome to have a meal after working. Will twenty hours a week be about right for you?"

"Perfect. I was hoping you wouldn't want me full time. And it is only until Tino gets back?"

"Yes, yes, of course. Although, if it works out well, you might want to stay on?"

"Well, we'll see how it goes. Okay?" Jan was unsure.

Jan prepped vegetables for Giovanni and waited tables when it got busy to help Rosa Lina out and then had a meal afterwards but not until mid-afternoon.

"Thank you again for helping us out; we are truly grateful, aren't we, Giovanni?" Rosa Lina said when they sat down together, quite exhausted. Giovanni put plates of food down in front of the women. He had made a creamy tagliatelle carbonara, one of Jan's favourites.

"Oh, yes, we really are very grateful to you," Giovanni averred. He took Jan's hand and kissed it and smiled, the business with Vera all but forgotten. He had ordered himself a new Dutch oven but this time it was made of cast iron to replace the ceramic one, which had been more vulnerable to breakage.

"You really are a very good cook, Giovanni. This is delicious," said Jan, enjoying every mouthful. She did not realise how hungry she was after working through the lunch hour.

Jan was in her element and surprised herself as to how much she enjoyed working at the restaurant. It was variable: sometimes she was in the kitchen and sometimes she was sweeping floors or cleaning tables, as well as waiting on tables. There was always music on low, which made her heart sing and left her with a feeling of elated happiness. She felt this was going to give her a new lease of life, something she needed since she had felt so lonely since Mike had died.

Jan arrived home utterly exhausted. She had not done manual work like that for some years and yet somehow she took to it like a duck to water. Rosa Lina had given her a timetable of the times when they would most likely need her and sometimes it was in the evening, especially on a Saturday evening, when they were at their busiest. Jan was happy to work on a Saturday evening as it would make the weekend shorter and sometimes she would see her friends and even serve them. She made good tips when she worked in the evening, better than in the daytime.

She had no other commitments, nobody else to see to, only social occasions with friends, which seemed to occur less and less these days. Otherwise there were U3A classes, which she enjoyed, but they were starting to come to an end for the summer so she would have more spare time on her hands.

Tino eventually returned after about three weeks. They were all glad to see him back and he was surprised to see Jan working there.

"I'm only helping out; you have nothing to fear. I'm not going to take your job!" Jan thought she would be on the defensive before he said anything to her.

"Don't mind me. I'm really glad you were able to step in. Thank you," said Tino, kindly.

Jan was not aware that Giovanni and Rosa Lina had not told Tino that she was working there. They said he must stay in Italy as long as he was needed there and that they now had some help, but not who it was.

"I helped my son all I could and now he is managing okay without me." Tino regaled them all over dinner of the work he had had to do in Italy.

John psyched himself up to telephone Jan and give her the good news that she would finally be able to meet one of her grandchildren, albeit in strange circumstances. Jan was surprised when John dropped the bombshell but delighted all at the same time. She also had mixed feelings.

"How can I look after Charlotte? And how come you are asking me and not Dean?"

"Dean's a mess. He is not capable of anything! He has kicked her out and she is staying with Steven and Cheryl at the moment. They haven't really got room for her and especially not after the baby is born. Steven and I talked it over and we thought of you."

"Thanks! And I suppose Steven didn't think to ask me himself? Am I still persona non grata as far as he is concerned? Until, that is, I can be useful to him. Is that it?"

"No. I think he wanted me to ask you because he is embarrassed that this estrangement has gone on too long and he doesn't know how to break it. So, is it okay with you? It should only be a temporary arrangement. Until Dean sees sense and has her back."

"You know as well as anyone I would do anything to meet my grandchildren. All this nonsense has gone on long enough so I would think Steven is right to be embarrassed. Of course I want to help out and I'd be delighted to have Charlotte to stay. I will make her as welcome as I can. But, if this is foisted on her, what does she feel about staying with an old woman like me?"

"I really don't think she's got much choice," said John resignedly.

It was left that John would be bringing Charlotte to Jan in a week or two. John was taking Vera away for a well-earned break.

Jan felt a ball of excitement in the pit of her stomach as she started to prepare mentally to meet one of her grandchildren for the first time. A pregnant one at that. Jan knew she would cope with whatever was thrown at her and was starting to get enthusiastic at the prospect.

One day Tino came in with a bouquet of flowers.

"Whose birthday is it?" Jan asked him when he came into the restaurant for his shift.

Tino looked a little shifty and just a tad embarrassed.

"Beautiful flowers for beautiful lady," he said but then just put the flowers on a table. His English was not as perfected as Rosa Lina's or Giovanni's but then he had not lived in England for as long as they had.

"Oh, who is the lucky lady?" said Jan as she brushed past him to go to the kitchen to help prepare the vegetables for the day. They were a bit behind and she was anxious to get on with her work.

Tino arrived in the kitchen holding the bouquet and said again. "Beautiful flowers for beautiful lady."

"Come on, Tino," said Giovanni. "Put them down and get on with some work."

Tino felt a bit dejected. He wanted to give Jan the flowers but then felt a little embarrassed. Instead he fetched a vase, put them in and started arranging them. Then he gave the vase to Rosa Lina with a smile.

At the end of the day Jan went home and the Italians finished clearing up before finally getting home and closing the door behind them.

As they arrived home they reverted to their native tongue. It was as if a switch was turned on as soon as they set foot in their own home, away from strangers.

"Another good day with lots of customers. We make a pretty good team, don't we?" said Giovanni to Rosa Lina and Tino.

"We certainly do," Rosa Lina agreed.

"Yes, we do." Tino agreed too but he had something pressing on his mind. "I want to ask you two something. Is that okay?"

"Of course, Father, go ahead," said Rosa Lina. "I'll put the kettle on and we'll have a nice hot drink before we go to bed. We can talk before we retire. What is on your mind?"

"I like Jan!" Tino blurted straight out. He could not keep it to himself any longer nor could he wait until they were having their hot drinks.

"Well, that's obvious!" laughed Giovanni.

"Oh no! Not too obvious, I hope!" Tino felt mortified. "That is what I wanted to tell you. But I also wanted to ask you of your thoughts on this. What should I do?"

"It's a bit sudden, is it not? I mean, Mum has only been gone a year." Rosa Lina felt a little miffed that her father would have forgotten about her mother so easily. "Maybe you should wait a bit longer. Have you said anything to Jan?" Rosa Lina was hoping to put her father off, for several months at least.

"No, of course not. But I liked her from the moment I put my eyes on her. At Vicky and Gerry's party. She is a widow and I am a widower. That is a connection to start with. I mean, we both lost our partners last year. Surely I deserve a little happiness in my latter years. We are not getting any younger, are we?" said Tino sadly.

"You go for it, Tino," Giovanni made light of the situation but Rosa Lina glared at him. She had made the drinks but all the time she was looking at her father. He did look sad. *Maybe he does deserve some happiness*, she thought.

"It's alright for you to say that, Giovanni, but I think he should wait a little while longer. And, if he still feels the same about Jan, then, well, he will have my blessing."

Tino went to bed with his daughter's words ringing in his ears. He slept fitfully that night and dreamed that he was at sea. All at sea because he did not like the sea and shunned the idea of a cruise when his wife had suggested it a few years ago. He loved his wife but now she was gone and he was still alive. Barely alive, he thought to himself. Living to work at his daughter's business and also helping out his son occasionally. But he was retired and needed female company in his life. He was lonely.

He woke in the morning thinking of his wife. He remembered his dream of being on a cruise with her. She very much dominated his dreams and he did not know why. Then he thought of Jan. A totally different type of woman. Independent, not needy like his wife. Exciting to be with, whereas his wife had sometimes been boring. Maybe he had made her boring. Jan always came into the restaurant with a smile on her face and lit up the place. His wife had had a furrowed brow, which he had put down to her scowling a little too much. He hated that he was comparing the two. Maybe he should make a list. No, he won't because he knew who would come off worst. He was biased and that was not fair on either of them.

He left his thoughts and dressed. Another day in the restaurant, working hard. But today he was looking forward to going to work, partly because he would meet up with Jan again. He would play it cool and see how it went. He would look at her from afar and get to know her that way. Then after a while Rosa Lina might not be so against the two of them being together.

A week went by and Tino was sure that Jan was flirting with him. Maybe she liked him as much as he fancied her. Maybe she was playing it cool and found a little harmless flirting was okay. Tino was starting to get frustrated and wanted to tell her how he felt but held back.

Late on Saturday night after all the diners had left, Jan dropped a bombshell.

"I'm afraid I can't work for you anymore. I've loved working here but I have my granddaughter coming to live with me. I'm not sure for how long but I have to give her my undivided attention. I've never met her before and she is a teenager so it will be a challenge. Her mum, my daughter, died last year so she is in a bad place at the moment." She never mentioned that Charlotte was heavily pregnant.

The Italians were all very surprised and upset to hear this news.

"We will miss you," said Rosa Lina. Giovanni and Tino nodded. "Maybe when she goes home you will help us out again?"

"Yes, for sure. I've really loved it here. It's given me a new lease of life. But you understand I have to do the best for my family now. The rift was so huge and now I have the chance to make it much smaller. You do understand?"

"Of course," they all chorused and nodded. Tino went to give Jan a hug but as he took her in his arms he did not want to let go.

21

The grass was getting longer by the day. Dean used to help Louise in the garden but he never had much interest in gardening. It was always his job to mow the lawn. It was only a small patch of grass and only took twenty minutes at the most.

"The garden is getting a bit out of hand. Look how long the grass is! Who's going to cut it?" Dean asked nobody in particular. It was the weekend. Jobs around the house were waiting to be done and Dean was hoping that someone was going to offer.

"You are!" Jake and Daisy said in unison, then both laughed out loud. They had shouted it out from different rooms. They were doing their schoolwork and did not want to be interrupted. Jake was also revising for his theory driving test, which was the next day.

"I've passed!" Jake announced the next day after his test. "I got ninety per cent."

"That's great, son, well done. When is your proper test?" Dean asked.

"It's in about six weeks' time. Of course, I should already be able to drive by now if Mum hadn't tried to scupper my chances last year when my grandmother offered me driving lessons on my seventeenth birthday!"

"I don't know anything about that," said Dean. "Enlighten me."

"Don't you remember when it was my seventeenth birthday and I got that card and letter from Granny in Surrey. Mum took it off me and wouldn't let me reply or thank her. It was a cheque for £50, plus she said there was a nest egg that she had saved up for me ever since I was born, so much a year. She didn't say how much it was but she wanted to meet me so she could give it to me. It sounded like it could have been quite a substantial amount. She also said she would pay for driving lessons until I passed my test. Her father had done the same for her and actually gave her a car when she passed her test. I don't remember much more because Mum took it off me and hid it away. Then a few weeks later I got another letter delivered to me at school. Mum found out about that one too and took it off me. I think she replied to it herself and sent the cheque back too! I could have done with that £50 but I wasn't allowed to keep it. Mum said she would pay me £50 herself but it never materialised!"

"Well, that's all news to me. She never told me about any of that. Do you think those letters are somewhere in the house? They could be salted away in all the paperwork that still needs looking into, with the bills etc. Your mum used to pay all the bills and since it's been left to me they are all in a bit of a pickle, I'm afraid."

"Dad! You've been paying the bills, haven't you?"

"Yes. Sort of. The ones I know about," said Dean, sheepishly.

"We're not going to be made homeless, are we, cos you've not paid the mortgage?"

"What do you know about mortgages?" asked Dean indignantly.

"I know enough, thank you very much," Jake affirmed.

"Let's not worry Daisy about trivialities."

"Trivialities! The mortgage is hardly trivial. We don't want to be made homeless, do we? Come on, Dad, d'you want to show me what you've been doing? Or not been doing, as the case may be? I just assumed you would carry on where Mum left off."

Jake followed Dean upstairs to where Louise used to do the bills in their bedroom. The computer was there, unused since Louise died. Dean had never bothered to learn how to use it.

"Looking at these bank statements, it looks like the mortgage is paid by direct debit. Is that right?" Jake asked his father. Dean shrugged.

"I guess so. We'd've heard by now from the mortgage company, wouldn't we? All I know is my money gets paid into the joint account and the bills get paid. I take out what I need for my beer and for food, of course."

"The mortgage seems incredibly low; is it right?"

"As far as I know, why?"

"Well, I would have thought it should be much more than this."

"Your mum sorted it out at the time. We put down a good amount as a deposit through your mum's good financial wizardry! I know her mum used to save the money Louise gave her for her keep all that time ago when she lived at home. Then she gave it all back to her to put towards buying a house."

"That was astute of her."

"Yes, it was one of her better judgements. Also, your mum inherited some money from her grandparents when they died and I suppose she put that to good use too. Apparently they were heavily into property and made quite a bit. We would never have been able to afford a house like this otherwise, with an en suite, which your mum always had her eye on. She knew I wasn't a big earner so I reckon she thought she would reduce the mortgage as a way of saving."

"Look, Dad, do you want me to sort out the rest of these bills for you? I can take a look and see that they are all in order. Like you say, we would have heard by now if there was anything else to pay." Dean looked blank. "I could have a look at changing the provider of services like the gas and electric. I know you can save quite a bit that way. But you can't expect me to do it for you forever, though. We're nearly halfway through the year now. Actually, it looks on the surface that Mum left it all in good shape, lucky for you, but you must take control yourself…"

Dean preferred to pay for things by cash, which was why Louise had most of the bills set up with the bank to pay by direct debit. Jake had a look through and made some minor alterations and then handed it back to Dean.

"All in good order now, Dad. Over to you."

"I'm going to take you to your Great Uncle John's in Bristol," Steven announced to Charlotte after phone calls back and forth with John and John arranging it with Jan. "And then he's going to drive you to stay with your grandmother in Surrey for a while. Maybe just until you have the baby. Then you'll be back in no time at all and I expect your dad will have calmed down by then. It's probably just a case of him accepting that you are a grown woman. I'll have a word with him while you're gone and see if I can get him to see sense."

Jan had agreed to take in her oldest granddaughter and she was looking forward to meeting her. She was also hoping to meet the rest of the family at some stage too but at the moment she was happy to be able to step up and help out after John explained the situation to her.

"But why can't you take me?" Charlotte complained to Steven.

"You know about the separation between your mum and I with our mother, your grandmother, when she left us over twenty years ago?"

"Yes, of course I do. Mum wouldn't stop banging on about it. She hated her but I never really knew why. Then all of a sudden you both went to see her and that's when Mum died." Charlotte was near to tears thinking of her mum. "I thought you had made up with her," she said to Steven.

"Well, we had, sort of. But I don't feel ready to see her again just yet. I feel embarrassed that we ignored her all those years, if you must know. She wrote us letters and tried to explain to us why she left. She also sent us parcels, which we returned unopened. I don't really think she has forgiven us for being so mean to her."

"She sounds kind. I need someone to be kind to me," said Charlotte, wistfully.

"And you know it's only temporary. Once your dad gets his head around all this I'm sure he will accept it. Then you will be back with the family in no time."

"I doubt it! Anyway, I'm prepared to give it a try as I know you don't have room for me here and it appears no one else does either. Does Gran have a big house?"

"It's huge! Like a mansion! And there is only her in it so there will be plenty of room for you and the baby. I really think she is looking forward to seeing you." Steven was not at all sure about his last statement; he was just guessing as it had been John who had set up all the arrangements.

"Can't wait," Charlotte said sarcastically, feeling as if she was just being pushed from pillar to post, by her own family.

"Well, you'll have to wait actually because Uncle John is going away. You are safe here until then, though."

The move was set for the following month, on a Saturday, when Steven was not working. During the week Charlotte bided her time while the others were at work and school. Cheryl set her some tasks around the house and she begrudgingly did some of them. The rest of the time she hung around the shops but all her contemporaries were at school so she soon became bored. She did however enjoy spending all the money that Cheryl had given her. She bought clothes a size or two larger for herself, plus some baby clothes from the market, but she did not have the same enthusiasm as she did for her own clothes. She had no idea what size to buy for the baby and was completely perplexed by the whole situation.

One day, when Cheryl came home from work, Charlotte showed her all the purchases with receipts. Cheryl was very impressed by her honesty.

"Is this all you have for the baby?" Cheryl said when she looked at two baby tops in blue plus a rattle. The tops looked far too big for a newborn baby.

"I didn't know what to buy. I thought I'd better start buying stuff for the baby but I had no idea what colour and what size. I thought blue because it's going to be a boy."

"Is it? Are you sure? Have you had a test?"

"No. It's fifty-fifty but I know it's going to be a boy and I'm going to call him Jet."

"Oh, okay." Cheryl was not totally convinced, reckoning that it was wishful thinking on Charlotte's part. "I'm going to suggest something now and I want you to think about it."

"What's that?" Charlotte was worried in case there was more housework to be done. It was not her favourite pastime.

"I have some baby clothes, left over from when the girls were babies. They are second-hand but they're good quality and in very good condition. There is a selection of colours but mostly white because that goes for both sexes. I want you to have them. It will give you a good start. If you say yes, I will dig them out of the attic. Please say yes because I'd like you to have them and also they will stay within the family. They are all different sizes and you would be able to sort through and see what you want. I can help you if you like."

Charlotte was not sure if she should accept them or not but she thanked Cheryl and they went to the attic together to rummage in two trunks full of baby clothes. They came out with two carrier bags full. Charlotte decided to leave the pink clothes behind. Cheryl made a face behind Charlotte but accepted that she must know what she wants.

"What about nappies?" Cheryl asked. "I have terry towelling ones if you would like them."

"My baby's gonna have disposable ones." Charlotte was adamant.

"But they are very expensive, you know. How are you going to afford them?"

"I'll probably steal some from the hospital, I expect." Cheryl was surprised by her dishonesty, especially since she showed her honesty with the receipts of how she had spent the money. She really was an anomaly.

"They are very bulky. I don't think you'll get away with very many. Anyway, I wish you well and you will keep in touch, won't you?"

"Course I will. I'll send you a photo of Jet. Not sure if he'll have jet-black hair but I hope so."

Cheryl was worried that she was sending off this vulnerable girl into the sunset to a place she knew nothing about. To stay with a person she had never met. She also felt that Charlotte did not really know what she was letting herself in for.

However, the Saturday of the move finally came and Charlotte packed her belongings and went off to Bristol with Steven. Cheryl, Milly and Poppy waved her off.

"I'm glad that sulky bitch has gone," said Milly.

"Milly! That's not very kind." Cheryl was horrified to hear her daughter speak like this. She was always such a kind girl.

"Yes, well, you know she stole my favourite top?" Milly moped.

"No, I didn't know that; are you sure? There are still some things in the wash that you haven't had back yet so don't be too quick to judge. I'll go and look for you."

"And she never helped out with anything in the house," Poppy piped up, not to be outdone in the dissing of Charlotte. "She always came in when all the jobs had been done. I'm sure she timed it that way."

"Wow, you two have quite got it in for your cousin. Let's just settle back into our family routine as soon as your father gets home. It was a little blip and I'm sure we wish Charlotte and her baby well." Cheryl knew she was talking to herself as the girls were looking at their phones and had started texting their friends.

"We will be there in no time." Steven tried to make polite conversation with Charlotte as he drove along the M5 towards Bristol. "John is expecting us around lunchtime but we will stop off for a cup of coffee at a service station and I need to get petrol."

Charlotte said very little. Mostly they drove along in silence.

As Steven put petrol in the car at the service station, Charlotte needed to go to the toilet. She climbed out of the car like an old woman. It was the first time her bump had hindered her and she felt the baby kick. She did not like the feeling and ignored it.

"I'm going to the loo," she announced to Steven. "Shall I meet you in the café?"

Ah, she does have a tongue in her head, thought Steven.

"Yes, that's fine. See you there." Steven forced a smile.

"Cappuccino, please," said Charlotte when she arrived at the café. "With chocolate."

"Shall we have a snack, Charlotte? I fancy some of that coffee and walnut cake? It looks lovely, doesn't it?"

Charlotte pointed to the scones and Steven went to pay. They sat in silence but Steven felt he had to make small talk and asked Charlotte questions that he reckoned would make her have to talk to him.

"Do you have any money?" he asked.

"Why? Do I have to pay you for my keep and for petrol for driving me?"

"No, of course not! Don't be silly. I just wanted to make sure you are okay for money. If you like I can lend you some. Or give you some, I mean."

"I've got a bit. Not much."

"Okay. I know, I'll go over there to the ATM machine and get you some. It will give you a good start with your great-grandmother. You could buy her some flowers or something for having you."

"I didn't buy Auntie Cheryl or you anything for having me. Are you saying I should've done that?"

"No, of course that's not what I'm saying." Steven left the table and went to the ATM. He came back and gave Charlotte £100. "There you are."

"I'm not a charity, you know!" Charlotte felt indignant instead of grateful.

"No, I know you're not. I just wanted to give you a good start. You are going to have a lot of expenses with the baby."

"Thanks," said Charlotte as she quickly put the money away into her bag.

"Shall we go?" *Get this final leg over with. Deposit her with*

John and then I can get home and forget about her. God, she's hard work! If I'm honest, the last four weeks have been absolute hell!

An hour later they arrived at John and Vera's house.

John came out to greet them as he saw the car draw up in the driveway.

"Hello," he said as he opened Charlotte's door.

"Hi, Uncle John," Steven said as he came around to the other side of the car.

"Oh, please, can we drop the uncle bit? We are all adults now!" Steven was not sure whether to call him John or Uncle John. He was always Uncle John to him and so it felt awkward to just call him John.

"I'm sure we can… John." With that they shook hands and then hugged.

Charlotte got out of the car. She waited for the inevitable kiss on the cheek, which she hated. Or a hug was even worse.

True to form, John kissed her on the cheek. Charlotte wiped it away on her sleeve and stood there waiting for the invitation to go indoors.

"Come on in. Vera is waiting for you," said John enthusiastically. "And lunch is nearly ready."

"Vera?" John called as he went inside followed by Steven and Charlotte. "Vera! Come and say hello." John looked in the kitchen and then the dining room and then the sitting room. Vera eventually appeared from upstairs.

"What's all the fuss?" she said to John. "Oh, hello, who are you?" She looked at Steven and Charlotte as if they were strangers that John had brought in off the street. They were too embarrassed to say anything. Best to wait for John to explain.

"Remember Steven and Charlie? They have come here for lunch. And we are going to drive Charlie to see Jan. Remember? I told you earlier," John said kindly to Vera.

"No, I don't remember. Well, never mind. They're here now." Vera ignored them and only spoke to John. The only face with which she was familiar. Charlotte glared at John for calling her Charlie. She thought it was a waste of time telling him she is Charlotte now, not Charlie.

"Hello, Vera." Steven went to give her a kiss on the cheek but she backed away.

"Well, never mind," said John. "Come on in. I've laid lunch in the dining room. That room is little used these days and I think it's not quite warm enough to sit outside."

Their dining room used to be at the heart of their social life. Their friends would come, sometimes six or eight. Around the dining table they would put the world to rights. Sometimes they hosted parties for up to forty of their friends. But gradually their friends either stopped coming and made excuses or John felt embarrassed to ask them for fear of rejection. He knew the reason why they would make excuses but then maybe they were not true friends. Only one or two couples who were true friends stayed in contact. But even they visited less and less frequently.

Vera sat at the table and waited for her lunch with her arms folded. John dutifully brought in soup, salad, cold cuts and rolls for them to help themselves. Charlotte ate a little soup and a roll but she was not keen on salad. Then John brought in some cake.

"I baked a cake earlier and want you to try it. It's a lemon drizzle cake. I've never made it before. I always bought it from the shop but it looked easy enough with the recipe I found on the internet."

They all had a slice and remarked how good it was.

"Well, that was a lovely lunch, thank you very much." Steven stood up to take his leave. "I must go now so I don't get back too late. You be a good girl now, with your grandmother, Charlotte."

"I will," said Charlotte as demurely as she could muster.

John saw Steven to the door and waited until he drove down the street, waving all the time. He got back in the dining room just as Charlotte was starting to clear the table.

"Don't worry about that now. We ought to get going," he said to Charlotte. And then he took Vera by the hand and steered her towards the cloakroom. He was not going to have any accidents in his new Jaguar.

He took Vera's coat and put it on the back seat at the same time as helping her to the front seat. Charlotte climbed in the back with her bags and sat quietly.

John put on his favourite music as it helped him to concentrate on long journeys. He reckoned it would take them the best part of two hours to get to Surrey. They wouldn't be home until the evening. He did not mind as he liked his new car and enjoyed driving.

They pulled up to Jan's house almost exactly two hours later, after an uneventful journey.

Charlotte was starting to get nervous at the first meeting with her maternal grandmother. *How would they be together? Would she like her?* she wondered.

John got out of the car first and rang the doorbell.

22

Jan answered the door. She was all prepared for the visit and gave John a hug. Vera and Charlotte stayed where they were. They were waiting for the call to get out and for Charlotte to meet Jan. John rushed over to the car and opened both front and rear car doors.

"Hello." Jan smiled. A little nervous to be meeting her granddaughter for the first time ever and she was almost a grown woman. And very pregnant, to boot.

"Hello," said Charlotte tentatively. "It's nice to meet you at last." She almost curtsied as if she were being presented to the queen. She thought better of it and half-smiled instead.

"Likewise," said Jan and gave Charlotte a big hug. Jan could almost feel a tear in her eye, which she resisted. She had told herself earlier she was *not* going to cry.

"Let me do the honours properly," said John. "Grandma, this is Charlie – Charlie, this is Grandma. Or would you like to be called Grandmother? Or Gran? Or Nan? Heavens, I don't know!"

"Gran will do fine," said Jan, sparing John's awkwardness at having to introduce Jan to her own granddaughter.

"And, while we're at it, I'm not Charlie anymore. I'm

Charlotte. Charlie is a boy's name and I've always hated it. Not that keen on Charlotte either, if I'm honest."

"Oh, okay," John and Jan chanted together.

"Are we going in or what?" said Vera, impatiently. She had been standing by the car watching the charade of Jan and Charlotte eyeballing each other.

"Of course," said Jan. "Get your stuff and I'll show you around."

Charlotte fetched her bags and dropped them in the hall.

"Cor, Uncle Steven said you had a mansion! It's not that big, is it?" Charlotte piped up.

"Well," Jan was taken aback by that remark. "It's not a mansion, no. Whatever gave him that idea? But I do have four bedrooms and there is only me here. I did think of downsizing a few months ago but decided against it, luckily."

Jan showed them around downstairs first and then out into the large garden. She was very proud of the owl sculpture and took them over to show them. Charlotte took particular interest in it and wanted to know all about it. It was carved five years before by a man who had six chainsaws of different sizes and he took three days to complete the sculpture.

"Have a look around the back. There's a door. What do you think is inside?" Jan asked Charlotte.

"I don't know. What?"

"Well, not a lot actually. The door has proper hinges and opens but there is only a small space inside." Jan was not prepared to say exactly what was behind that door.

Jan showed them the rest of the garden and didn't want to boast about it but someone she knew likened it to a small parkland with beautiful specimen plants. Plus the kitchen garden around the side of the house. John and Vera had seen it all before but they made out it was the first time they had seen it to show interest and to help Charlotte settle in.

Jan decided on showing Charlotte the rest of the house later, when John and Vera had gone. First of all she was making tea and decided it was warm enough to sit out for the first time in the year.

"Wow, this garden never ceases to amaze me," John crooned. "I wish I had this garden! It's lovely, isn't it, Vera?"

"If you say so, dear. I'm just parched and waiting for my cuppa! You told me we would get a cup of tea when we arrived." Vera's patience was wearing thinner by the minute.

"Okay," said Jan. "I'll make the tea and you go and sit down and I will bring it all out for you. I made some cakes and scones."

Charlotte was taking it all in. She thought the house and the garden were lovely and she was surprised how much she liked her grandmother. She was very natural, down to earth and motherly.

Jan arrived with the tea on a tray and they all sat around the garden table drinking tea and eating the cakes that Jan had baked earlier in the day.

"Are you two going to stay the night?" she asked John and Vera. "I've made up all the beds just in case you wanted to."

"Must get back," said John, aware that Vera was not comfortable being away from her own familiar surroundings. Albeit he left her with Jan when he went to meet his friends but in hindsight he realised that this was probably a mistake and decided he would never be able to leave her again. "It's best you two get to know each other."

"Okay, if that's what you want." Jan was silently relieved.

John opened the car door and Vera climbed in. He came back to Charlotte and gave her a sealed envelope.

"Thank you," she said, slightly puzzled.

With that, John drove away and Jan waved them off. Charlotte went back into the house and opened the envelope.

"He's given me some money! That was kind of him," said

Charlotte. "You can have it for having me to stay." She held out her hand to Jan.

"Oh, no, he gave it to you. You keep it. You're going to need it when the baby comes along. There's another thing we need to clear up," said Jan.

Oh no, here we go. She's going to ask who the father is, I just know it! That's all grown-ups want to know. Well, I'm not telling her; she can ask all she likes, thought Charlotte.

Jan continued. "You said you weren't keen on your name. I want you to feel comfortable here and make it like your own home. So what would you like me to call you? Charlotte is your given name and your siblings called you Charlie, which you said you don't like. What about Lottie? That is a derivative of Charlotte, I believe." Charlotte was much relieved that the "father of the baby" was not mentioned.

"Oh, yes, I love it. Lottie. It has a nice ring to it." Charlotte perked up at this idea. She had a feeling she was going to like it here.

"That's that sorted then. Come on upstairs and you can choose which bedroom you would like. Sorry if you were expecting a mansion but I do have three bedrooms from which you can choose. I thought maybe you would like this one as it is almost the same size as mine so you can also have the baby in with you." Jan showed her to the room she hoped Lottie would like. It was her favourite, next to her own bedroom. Then she showed her the other, slightly smaller bedrooms. "There is enough room for a proper full-size cot when he or she gets older."

Lottie felt a little coy about choosing a room. She wondered what Jan meant when she mentioned a proper full-size cot for when the baby gets older. She was not going to be staying that long so it would not apply. However, she really took to the bigger bedroom, which had one wall behind the bed, decorated with pretty pink and purple wallpaper with tiny flowers, green leaves and little bluebirds dotted here and there. The other walls were painted white. The bedspread matched the wallpaper and the plain carpet was the colour of bluebells, a very soft lilac blue.

"This room is beautiful," said Lottie to Jan. She put her bags on the bed then sat down on the bed and started to cry. Her emotions were running high and she just loved the sight of her new bedroom so much, it brought tears to her eyes. Jan went over to comfort her, putting her hand gently on Lottie's arm.

"What is it?" said Jan, softly. "I know, it's all a bit much, isn't it? What with the baby's birth imminent and coming to a strange place and meeting me for the first time. All too much, I expect," she reiterated. She wanted to show Lottie empathy and understanding.

"It's not that," Lottie tried to explain. "It took me by surprise but… I love it here, already. I love this room; it is exactly how I would have decorated it."

"That's nice to know." Jan wanted to take Lottie in her arms and give her a cuddle. Something she had not ever been able to do before now. She did not want to appear needy so she just smiled at Lottie. There would be plenty of time for cuddles later on, thought Jan.

Lottie noticed three soft toys lined up on the bed: a penguin, a rabbit and a teddy bear. She recognised them but was instantly puzzled as to why they should be in this house. She dived into one of her bags and brought out her favourite cuddly toy, which was identical to the one in the middle on the bed. Jan smiled when she saw the bunny in Lottie's arms but thought she had better explain to her how all three came to be here.

"When I left my first husband (your grandfather Geoff), both your mother and Uncle Steven were grown up. It was a very difficult time for them to come to terms without their mother, i.e. me. They were so incensed with my leaving that they wanted nothing more to do with me. I thought at the time that they would come around but it was never to be. They tried to be as nasty as they could to me and told me that, if ever they had any children, I would never ever meet them. They were both unmarried at the time I left."

"Oh!" Lottie was shocked at hearing that. "They obviously wanted to hurt you like you had hurt them by leaving them?"

"Yes, I guess so. They wanted to get back at me, I suppose. Anyway, it was quite a few years later, about six years after I left, that first of all Jake arrived and I heard about his birth through my family. I think my sister told me. At around that same time, my father died. I went to his funeral in Bristol, on my own because my father never wanted to meet Mike so Mike thought it was not right that he should attend a funeral of someone he had never met. And he was scared also of any repercussions from your mum or Uncle Steven because they had threatened him when we first got together. Luckily we lived far enough away and we didn't tell them where we lived at first because we were scared of what they might do. They had made threats, you see."

"OMG! I never knew any of this." Lottie sat on the bed with her mouth getting wider and wider.

Jan sat down beside Lottie on the bed. She picked up the penguin and started to cuddle him but at the same time feeling a little sad as she continued her story.

"I thought at the time that your mum might bring Jake to the funeral and I would be able to meet him but she was true to her word and she left him behind to be looked after by a friend. She was very cool towards me at the wake, which we had in my father's favourite pub in Bristol. I had bought a toy penguin and was hoping to give it to Jake myself, but as he wasn't there I gave it to your mum to give to him. I was surprised she took it actually because all presents that I had sent them previously, to your mum and Uncle Steven, were returned to me unopened. So I was pleased that she took the penguin to give to Jake. But I didn't know at the time if she was actually going to give it to him."

"Just like this one here?" Lottie touched the penguin, still in Jan's arms. "I recognise it! Jake keeps it on his windowsill. I don't remember him ever playing with it so it is in just as good condition as this one. So did you buy two?"

"Not at first, no. When I thought about it and realised that your mum meant what she said about me never meeting my grandchildren, it dawned on me that I might never meet you and that saddened me no end. So I went out and bought an identical penguin just so I could imagine him playing with it. It was the nearest thing I could do to get close. Then, when you came along about two years later, I bought two of these rabbits and sent one to you. You were obviously too young to realise where it came from. Then I did the same for Daisy but with a teddy." Lottie picked up the distinctive pink teddy and scrutinised it, agreeing it was an exact replica of Daisy's.

"Daisy loves her teddy and takes him to bed every night. She called him Cuddles! I call my bunny Flopsy and he goes everywhere with me – as you can see!" Lottie took out a rather grubby rabbit from her bag.

"Of course, I did the same for Steven's two girls, as well. I am really so glad to meet you at last, Lottie. Too much time has gone by but I'm sure we will have time to make up for it." Jan said, sadly. Too many years had disappeared but now at last, after much sadness for both of them, with the loss of Louise, they are together.

"Me too… Gran." Lottie reflected. "Oh!" the baby kicked and she instinctively put her hand on her tummy area.

"Did the baby kick?' asked Jan. Lottie nodded. Jan was prepared now to ask the question she had been aching to ask but wanted to wait until the subject came up. "When is it due?"

"About six weeks, I think," Lottie answered as she totted up on her fingers. "Yes, about mid-August he's due." Jan noticed Lottie said "he" rather than "it" but guessed it was just a slip of the tongue unless, of course, she did know the sex of her baby. *Had she had a scan?* Jan wondered. She decided to ask her that question another time.

"Okay, then we have quite a few preparations to make. Maybe we should make a list of things you need before the baby arrives. Have you got anything at all prepared for baby?"

"Auntie Cheryl gave me some of her old baby clothes and they are in here." Lottie took the bag and emptied it onto the bed. Jan had a quick look through and made a decision.

"They look nice; that was kind of her. It was lucky she kept them and was able to give them to you. It'll be a good start. We will need a pram and nappies but we have plenty of time to go shopping. I have an idea though and will run it past you now. I know someone who has an old pram. We could borrow that and that would be one less expense."

Lottie took in everything Jan said and accepted the fact that there might be quite a lot of things needed for a new baby. She was beginning to realise that just the things she bought recently were not nearly enough.

"Let's get to know each other before we worry about baby," Jan said kindly. "Come on, let's go downstairs and we can talk over supper."

Lottie noticed that in nearly every room of the house were photos. When she took a closer look she realised a lot of them were of herself and her siblings when they were younger. Jan noticed her looking and wanted to explain.

"Your Uncle John and Auntie Vera used to send me loads

of photos after they used to meet up with you. Not so much recently since Vera became ill."

"What *is* the matter with her? She seems very strange these days. She can't seem to remember anything Uncle John tells her and she always seems so bad tempered."

"That's the Alzheimer's, I'm afraid. I think your Uncle John is finding it very tiring. He is looking a bit haggard these days. I'm really worried about him but there is nothing much I can do. I had Vera a few weeks ago to stay for two nights and she went AWOL. Luckily I found her and then I had to lock her in! It is very wearing having to look after someone with this condition."

"Oh dear. Yes, I suppose it must be. What was my mum like when she was a girl, before she met Dad, that is?"

"Oh, that's an easy question! She was the best daughter anyone could wish to have. She was like a best friend, really. She was no trouble at all, right from when she was born. She was beautiful and bright, a real joy to be with."

"Then why did you leave her?" Lottie was puzzled, Jan could see it in her face.

"Is that what she told you?" Jan felt horrified that anyone would think she could leave behind such a lovely person. "I had no choice if I was going to get out of an abusive marriage. You probably don't know but your grandfather Geoff was not a nice person. I stuck with him for twenty-five years and then just by chance, and luck really, I met Mike on a holiday we went to in the USA and we – Mike and I – just clicked. It was the hardest decision I had ever made or ever want to make again. I didn't know Mike very well but, six months after our first meeting, I was up in Surrey living with a man I actually hardly knew. After we first met on that holiday he used to come down to Devon from where he lived in Surrey, once a week, and we would meet up clandestinely."

"OMG, that's a long word, what does that mean?" Lottie was intrigued and enjoyed drinking in the whole story.

"It just means on the quiet. It was very exciting. I couldn't let anyone else know because if it got back to my husband there would be hell to pay. He would have been so mad he would have locked me up, I'm sure of it. I had to be really careful that he didn't find out. Mike and I decided we wanted to be together and so planned it for a few months later. I was so lucky to have met such a lovely man who was going to take me away from all my troubles."

"Couldn't you have taken your children with you?" asked Lottie.

"No, not really. They were both grown up by then, both over twenty. If they had still been young then I would have. They both had jobs and also a boyfriend and girlfriend and they still lived at home. I always made a joke of it that I left home before the kids did!"

"Was he really that bad, your husband, Granddad Geoff?"

"Well, yes. I don't want to go into detail but right from the moment we got married he abused me and controlled me. I put up with it for years. I don't mean he beat me up. He was far too clever for that. It was mental abuse, pure and simple, I can see that now. He was a control freak, wanted everything his way. He was a very jealous and possessive man. He didn't like it if I made friends with anyone and heaven forbid if I ever talked to another man. It was pretty awful, I can tell you. My life wasn't my own; I was always on tenterhooks as to know what sort of mood he was in. As soon as I saw an out I took it, grabbed it with both hands and Mike was the one to give me that opportunity. I know I was very lucky to find him. Not that I went looking, I can assure you. I was always faithful to Geoff. Until Mike, that is!"

"What was he like, as a person. Mike, I mean?"

"He was kind and generous and romantic. We got on really well and as time went by we became more and more comfortable with each other. Like an old pair of socks! He was my soul mate and I was his, I think, until he died, that is. Just over a year ago now."

"What did he die of?"

"Oh, heart mainly. There were several underlying health problems he suffered with; he was only seventy-one. His father, and his father before him, never made old bones either."

"What does that mean?" Lottie was puzzled to hear this expression she had never heard before.

"It just means they never got to a ripe old age. I think his father was only sixty-four when he died. His mother made it to eighty-six, though. I met her a few times when we first got together but she died within the year. She seemed a nice old lady, very kind; maybe that's where Mike got it from. He was an only child and his parents were quite old when they had him."

Lottie never stopped asking questions until it was bedtime. Jan answered, as honestly as she could, all the questions that were put to her. She had questions of her own but she reckoned they could wait until another day. She was exhausted. And happy.

23

Dean came home from work, bypassing the pub for the first time for months. Jake was preparing their supper and Daisy was in her bedroom doing end-of-term schoolwork.

"Hi, Dad, you're home early! Supper won't be for a while."

"I thought I might as well come home and save some money. The prices have gone up yet again. What's for supper?"

"Spag bol," Jake replied.

"Oh, not again! Can't we have something different?"

"Yes, of course, if you're prepared to cook it! Isn't it about time you learned to cook, Dad?"

"Can't cook, won't cook, as the saying goes." Dean thought that was a clever remark and laughed.

"Then you'll starve! Mum used to say everyone should learn to feed themselves. And that includes you." Jake was indignant and annoyed at his father's ignorance.

Dean picked up the newspaper and pretended not to hear Jake's retort.

"How are your exams going?" Dean tried to change the subject.

"I never thought you were interested in my A levels, Dad! You've never asked before. I finished the last one weeks ago. I've worked really hard for the last few months, all this year in fact, in case you hadn't noticed. So I can get to uni in September."

"Which uni?" Dean asked. "You said before that you were keen on Cambridge?"

"Don't know yet; depends on my results." Jake was surprised and pleased that his father was taking an interest in his future. Something that had never happened before. "I'm quite keen on Bristol as well. I'm not sure if I'm cut out for Cambridge. I'm probably not good enough. I had a lot to make up for last autumn when I took so much time off. D'you remember, when Mum died?"

"Not good enough?" Dean ignored Jake's last remark. "Of course you are, son. And Daisy too. Both good candidates for Cambridge, or Oxford, by my reckoning."

"Which one did you attend, Dad?"

"Don't try and be clever with me, son! You know perfectly well I wasn't able to go to university. I had to go out to work to pay for my keep. My father was ill for most of my life, ever since I could remember, and my mother never encouraged education like we have tried to do with you lot. It fell on deaf ears with Charlie but you and Daisy are on the way up. Where is Daisy, anyway? Is she home?"

"Yes, she is. By the way, have you heard from Charlie?" Jake asked tentatively.

"Charlie who?"

"Your daughter!" Jake was getting exasperated with his father *Charlie who*, indeed!

"No, why should I? I've no idea where she is or what she's doing and, frankly, I don't give a damn. That's from the film *Gone with the Wind*. Not a lot of people know that. And that's taken from another film, said by Michael Caine. Not sure what film, actually. Oh, I know! I've remembered! It was from *Educating Rita*, a marvellous film, have you seen it?" Dean was desperately hoping to change the subject away from Charlotte but Jake brought it back into the conversation.

"I don't know why you're taking this attitude with Charlie. Anyway, for your information she's gone to stay with her grandmother."

"What? My mother?"

"No, not your mother, your wife's mother. My mum's mum. Uncle Steven's mum. Oh, for heaven's sake, you know who I'm talking about! As we've never met her I've no idea what we would call her."

"Oh, her! The one your mum kept on about how much she hated her. I only met her a couple of times and she seemed okay to me. But then she left and all hell broke loose with your mum. That all happened a long time before you kids came along." Dean kept trying to change the subject of Charlotte but Jake made sure it kept coming right back.

"Well, anyway. Charlie. She's gone to stay with our grandmother in Surrey because it appeared no one wanted to take the responsibility of bringing up her baby."

"And why should they?"

"We sent her away and now before we know it she has left Devon. God knows when we will see her again. For your information, she went to stay with Amelia for a short time and then to Uncle Steven for a while. He cooked up the idea with Uncle John that she should stay with our grandmother in Surrey."

"How do you know all this?" Dean asked.

"Daisy is in constant touch with Charlie and I get the occasional text from her. I think she is hoping to come back here once she's had the baby."

"I don't think that's a very good idea."

"Look, I don't know what your problem is with her. Lots of girls her age have babies out of wedlock. It's a bit old-fashioned to castigate her in this day and age." Jake was trying to keep calm but he could not understand why his father was behaving this way.

"It's not that. I know they do, but this is different." *I can't tell my own son that his sister is having her father's baby, I just can't. What would he think of me? Charlie obviously hasn't told anybody either. I bet she is just as ashamed as I am.*

Daisy popped her head around the door.

"Supper ready yet?"

"Nearly. Go and wash your hands," said Jake.

"God, you sound just like your mother," Dean said to Jake.

"Well, someone around here has to be the adult!" Jake retorted. "By the way, I thought I would get a job for the summer holidays. It will help towards my driving lessons and I can save a bit towards going to uni."

"Go for it, son. The more that is brought into the house the better. It won't be such a drain on me then, will it? Do you want to start paying rent too?" Dean asked hopefully.

"No!" Jake said indignantly. "You know I don't like to come to you for money. I just thought it would help out if I can pay for a few things myself. Like my driving lessons."

"What are you going to do, Jake? For a job, I mean," asked Daisy.

"I don't know. I've been looking in the paper and also at the ads in shop windows. I reckon I could turn my hand to anything," said Jake.

The family of three tucked into Jake's spaghetti bolognese, his signature dish. Louise had taught him all she knew and he was so glad she did. Dean was not interested in learning to cook and Daisy was happy to let Jake take the reins in that department. He had an idea that he would teach Daisy in the summer holidays because once he had gone to university at the end of September he was afraid his father and sister would not be able to feed themselves. Unless Charlotte was back, Daisy would have to cook for their father so Jake wanted to teach her everything he knew.

Dean put his knife and fork together and decided he was thirsty. A drink in the pub was very tempting and might be on the cards after all.

"That was a particularly good spag bol! What did you do different this time?" asked Dean.

"Ah good, glad you noticed," said Jake. "I actually started to cook it yesterday. Warmed it up today. Some things are better for standing. Take note for when you start to cook, Dad. Cook the mince with onions the day before…"

"What? It has to cook all that time? Surely it doesn't take that long, does it?" Dean was horrified that it should take twenty-four hours to cook a meal.

"Hang on, I haven't finished! Cook the mince with the onions and then turn it off, put the lid on and leave it. Then the next day, only half an hour or so before you want to eat, add the tinned tomatoes, tomato puree, flavourings like basil and rosemary, whatever you have in the cupboard, and crumble in a stock cube. You can even add baked beans as well, if you like. No two spag bols are the same because you can put in different seasonings. You can even put in red wine, although we haven't got any, so I didn't."

"Pity; that would have made it, I reckon," said Dean, still thinking that he was getting short of alcohol in his body.

"Well, when *you* make it, make sure you buy a bottle of red wine and Bob's your uncle." Jake was determined he would get his father cooking. Failing that he will teach Daisy.

"Talking of alcohol…" Dean began.

"We weren't, were we?" Jake wondered when the subject would raise its ugly head.

"Shall we go down the pub together? I could buy you a pint."

"I thought you weren't going there because the prices had gone up!"

"Well, I've changed my mind. Okay? Are you coming?" Dean asked Jake.

"I'm busy." Jake did not like the idea of drinking with his father in the pub. "I've got a driving lesson first thing tomorrow so I must bone up on the Highway Code. Then after my lesson I'm going off to find myself a job," Jake announced.

Dean shrugged his shoulders and walked to the pub which gave him a ready thirst. He was greeted by Keith in his usual way.

"Hiya, Dean, me ol' china, how're you doin' today? Missed you earlier. I thought you had forgotten me!"

"No way. Just thought I'd do something different for a change and have my meal first. I see your prices have gone up again."

"All in line with inflation, I'm afraid, old chap. I think you'll find my prices are very competitive. I'm cheaper than some other pubs in the area. I've checked."

"I believe you," said Dean, but he had other things on his mind. "They're trying to get me to take up cooking! Me! I ask you! Can you see me at the kitchen sink peeling spuds and then sweating me cobs off over a hot oven or stove, whatever you call it?" Keith laughed at the thought of Dean cooking himself a meal. Although, the more he thought about it, with his kids leaving home, he would have to get his act together and start making meals for himself eventually.

"Lots of men do the cooking these days, Deano. In fact, it's more macho than it used to be. Look at Jamie Oliver and that Gordon Whatshisname." Keith thought about it for a while and then came up trumps. "Ramsay. They're all at it and making a mint. An absolute fortune they make just with cooking stuff."

"Well, they're welcome to it. It's not for me." Dean resigned himself to not cooking.

"How are you going to feed yourself when young Daisy leaves home? That will come around sooner than you think. You should give it a go. You never know, you might enjoy it."

"I'll get by. I'd just have to come to you after work, have my pint and a meal too. Then I can go home, put my feet up for the evening and watch the tele. Perfect!"

Jake put himself about the next day to see what sort of a job he could try for. He saw an advert near the beach, put there by the Council. They needed someone for the summer holidays, taking out deck chairs at the beginning of the day and then putting them away every evening. He also had the chance to help out in the café nearby.

"I've found just the job, Dad," Jake told Dean and Daisy that evening. "I've got to go down early in the morning. I've got to unlock the deckchairs and put several out on the beach in readiness for when the attendant arrives. He is there all day and takes the money for the deck chairs."

"Do people still sit on deck chairs?" Dean enquired.

"I suppose they must do. People who come for the day from away. Maybe they would come on the train from somewhere inland to come and sit on the beach. If they're old they wouldn't want to actually sit *on* the beach so they would hire a deck chair instead for the day. Then I've also had the promise of some work in the café on the beach."

"What sort of work?" Dean asked.

"I don't know. Clearing tables or washing up. I could do that quite easily and the money is good. Well, it's the minimum wage but it's better than nothing."

"Well done, Jake," Daisy was impressed. "I'm going to take a holiday job when I'm old enough so I can save some money."

"What do you want to save money for?" Jake was curious.

"I don't know! Anything. Everything!"

24

Jan helped Lottie with registering at her doctor's surgery and made an appointment so they would be right on track and ready for the birth. Jan assumed correctly that Lottie had not done very much in preparation and she wanted no problems to arise when the time came. The doctor confirmed Lottie's dates, that the baby was due approximately in the middle of August. Six weeks to go.

Lottie settled into living with her grandmother much more easily than she expected. It was not the type of relationship that she thought it was going to be; it was more like a mother with a daughter. Jan had been careful to make sure Lottie was comfortable and told her she should make herself at home at all times.

Over the following days and weeks Jan asked Lottie questions about Louise and the family and Lottie asked Jan questions. Loads of questions, wanting and expecting honest answers.

"How does your father feel about you coming here to stay with me?" Jan asked innocently.

"Dad? Oh, he doesn't care about me. He has been funny ever since Christmas. So that is way before I told him I was pregnant. Maybe he is still grieving for Mum? I don't know. Maybe he can't handle being the adult when we are all becoming adult. Jake has been really good and Daisy too. They know I'm here but whether they've told Dad, I've no idea. Don't care either. If he wants to be so strange then they are welcome to coping with him. All I know is he kicked me out and, as far as he knows, I could be living on the streets, so that just shows he doesn't care about me. Uncle John told me it was 'middle child' syndrome." Jan laughed at that remark.

"Oh, he would say that! He was between my sister and me. Clare, being the eldest, was our father's favourite and I was my mum's fave. John was no one's favourite! Or so the joke went. We always pulled his leg about it and obviously he has taken it to heart. I know – you should never have favourites. But it was true. In a way, I guess my daughter was my favourite because she was first. Even though she was unplanned and I had to get married. I was only nineteen when I got married and twenty when I had Louise."

"Not sixteen like me, then? With no marriage in sight! Who would want me now? A slapper who's got up the duff."

"No one is calling you that. You were just unlucky, that's all." Jan was careful not to ask the question of who the father might be. Did Lottie know? Did she sleep around? It did not matter to Jan. The main thing was that Lottie was safe and well and happy.

Jan went to her bedroom and came back with a silver locket with an "L" engraved on the front. She gave it to Lottie.

"Oh, did you have this made especially for me? Thank you, it's lovely." Lottie looked it over and wondered when she would ever wear it. It was not to her taste but she did not want to hurt her grandmother's feelings.

"No. I found it a long time ago when I was sorting through some old jewellery. It belonged to your mother from when she was christened. I sent her a load of things which belonged to her after I left but when she knew it was from me she just returned everything unopened. I don't know why, I guess it was a way of trying to hurt me back. Hurt me like I hurt them when I left." Jan was becoming tearful as she thought of the hurt of receiving back parcels unopened.

"What was it like when you first left? Was it very exciting to be with a new man after twenty-five years married to another? Didn't you think of the fallout of what you left behind? I mean, did you think they were just going to carry on without you and not get upset?"

"It was exciting, yes, but, my God, it was a difficult time, I can tell you. There is never an ideal time to leave home. I thought it would be easier than it actually was. Of course, I hoped they wouldn't be too upset. I took a huge gamble on Mike. I lost just about everything but then I gained the love of a man and a life which was so much better than the life I left behind. I think I was very selfish, yes, but doing something for myself for a change without a thought for them was quite upsetting and yet exciting. I think I thought at the time that they, the kids I mean, would come around in the end. My husband, your grandfather Geoff, was very upset and made himself ill. The kids saw this and, of course, blamed me. I take full responsibility. But, like my friends all told me at the time, life is not a dress rehearsal. You have to grab chances with both hands, otherwise you would sink. And I felt my life was sinking, the way it was going with my husband. He never wanted to go anywhere or do anything. I was becoming a right old doormat. A drudge. Everything was mundane and boring."

"And yet you say you met Mike in America? You were on holiday. Surely Granddad Geoff went to America with you?"

"Yes, of course he did. But it was my idea that we went there. I had a job to persuade him that we should take better holidays once the kids were grown up. They both had their respective partners and they didn't want to go on family holidays with boring parents anymore. And I didn't blame them. I remember when I was their age, younger in fact, I couldn't wait to go on holiday with my boyfriend. Trouble was, it got me into trouble. Geoff was my first boyfriend and, although we got on well, I'd known him since I was thirteen. When I was about fifteen, I met another boy called Geoff, from a school nearby. He rang me one day and my father answered. He thought it No 1 Geoff and started chatting to him. But it was No 2 Geoff and he wondered what on earth was going on. My father actually liked No 1 Geoff and, although my parents didn't agree at first, because I was only thirteen when I met him, they accepted him, especially when his father died. I think Geoff No 1 thought of my father as his father. He was only eighteen when his father died."

"So what happened to No 2 Geoff?"

"Not a lot! No 1 Geoff found out. I think my father let it out one day. Geoff was furious. Then he became upset and cried and begged me to take him back. After that he was very jealous if I even spoke to another boy. He didn't like my friends either. When we used to go out say, for a drink, we would never meet up with other people. He didn't really have any friends, none that I can think of anyway. I remember when I first left, he went around to all my friends asking where I was and if they had heard from me."

"So you did have friends?"

"I made sure I did, yes. I had friends at the tennis club and where I played badminton. It was a battle with him to let me play. Everything was a battle with him. When the kids went to school, I thought it would be nice to go back to work. He didn't want me to do that. I got my own way in the end with work and playing tennis and badminton. I told him how bored

I was, with just being at home. He was at work and thought he was doing his bit. Which was good, of course, but I needed other adult company and to get my brain in working gear and I wanted to contribute to the finances too. The kids never went without but that was because of my clever budgeting. My parents used to give me a cheque for my birthday and Christmas and I would never spend it on myself. There was always something that the kids needed so I made sure they were alright before I bought anything for myself. Geoff relented in the end and let me go out to work part time as long as I was home when the kids got home, he stipulated. Which was fair enough as they always came first."

"Did you threaten to leave him, then? Is that why he came around in the end?"

"No, of course not. I was too scared. Once he told me, if I ever left him, the world would not be big enough for me to hide in! Can you believe that? And that was a long time before I did leave. We hadn't been married that long and he was saying things like that to me!"

"He sounds a tyrant!" Lottie could hardly believe what she was hearing.

"It was so different with Mike. Mike was very sociable and liked us both to have friends of either sex. He loved to chat to women as well as men and was so totally different to Geoff. We went on holidays with friends and had a really good social life in general. We had dinner parties two or three times a month and so then had lots of invitations back, to dinner parties, barbecues and all sorts. It was then that I realised what I had missed out on all those years I had been with Geoff. He hated any sort of party. And if I saw, say, a famous good looking man on TV that I liked the look of, I could never mention I liked them because he would become jealous and depressed even though he must have known nothing would come of it. My life was just a drudge from start to finish in my first marriage. Obviously my kids never saw that side of it. I never regretted having my kids but I just wished I'd had them with Mike and then we wouldn't be having this conversation now."

"Maybe Mum just thought you wanted a fling with someone else to start with. To have sex with someone else because you met Granddad at such a young age? And then as time went by she realised it was permanent and that you weren't coming home. It all happened way before I was born so I only got the gist of it all when I was older. She never said very much, just that you weren't around. I guess Dad knows more because he was there at the time it all kicked off. Are you glad you did what you did or do you have regrets?"

"You should never have regrets! I just feel I was so lucky to have met Mike when I did. I took the biggest gamble of my life. I could so easily have walked away from him. But I just knew in my heart of hearts that, rightly or wrongly, it was what I wanted. Did you know that, after a couple of months into my relationship with Mike, both your mum and Uncle Steven begged me to come home because they couldn't cope with their father? They told me he was pining for me and that he had said he would mend his ways. He didn't beg me; they did. It wasn't what I wanted but I did go back to try again. It was okay to start with but then things began to go back to how they were with his jealousy raising its ugly head. Geoff was on the verge of a nervous breakdown and kept begging me not to go away again. But I could see there was no future in the relationship. It was dead. I was beginning to resent him. I wanted to be with Mike. I had had a taste of freedom and Mike was the only person who was going to make it happen so I had to make plans to leave all over again. That was the straw that broke the camel's back."

"They never forgave you after that?" Lottie asked.

"No. Thinking back, I should have done it years before but I didn't fancy leaving Geoff just to be on my own and I couldn't have afforded to do that anyway. I know it sounds contradictory but we actually got on most of the time as long as I toed the line, kept my head down and didn't come up above the parapet." Lottie was starting to frown. She did not understand, although she accepted the gist of what Jan was saying. "Also, when I went back, they confiscated my passport to make sure I didn't go away again. I seem to remember looking for it and luckily I eventually found it in a drawer in Steven's bedroom under some clothes. The other thing that Steven did was to rip a ring off my finger. It was when he discovered that Mike had given it to me. It was a heart-shaped ruby, Mike's birthstone. We bought it on our first holiday we had when we first got together, in Thailand. Mike thought it was a nice idea to take me to Thailand, where my friend from school moved to when she first got married. We met up with her and she met Mike for the first time. She loved him and was so pleased for me that I had made the break away from Geoff. She never did like him she said, although I never knew that."

"You say you sent presents and they came back unopened. Did you write them letters too?" asked Lottie.

"I wrote so many letters to them, I lost count. Every week to start with but then when I heard nothing in return from them I found it difficult to know what to say, apart from repeating myself. I tried ringing them too but they didn't want to speak to me. In the end they changed their phone numbers to stop me ringing them! As time went on and their babies started arriving I guess I must have got the message that they really didn't want anything to do with me anymore. That's when I stopped sending so many letters. I still sent them birthday and Christmas cards, though, for several years."

"That's so sad."

"More than you can ever imagine. But that is all history now. Now you are here and ready to bring another human being into this world. We need to make preparations. There's not that long to go."

Jan helped Lottie make lists of things she would need and they went shopping. Jan wanted to give to Lottie as much, if not more, than she would have given her over the years. She would not let Lottie pay for anything and Lottie felt embarrassed as she could see how much was totted up.

"I can only guide you and suggest things to buy but I don't want to take over. This is your baby so you must choose what you want."

In the baby shop they had a trolley full of baby clothes for newborns including onesies and sleepers, nappies, feeding bottles and sterilising equipment, rattles and toys.

"You must let me pay for something!" Lottie said.

"You put your purse away. It's the least I can do to help you out."

In the shopping centre, Lottie left Jan in one of the shops where Jan was browsing some shoes she had her eye on. Lottie went to buy some flowers and came back with a big bouquet for Jan.

"These are for you as a thank you for having me," said Lottie cheerfully.

"Oh, aren't they lovely? Thank you so much, but you mustn't spend your money on me. I know just where they will go and we can both enjoy them together." That made Lottie smile. She had always loved flowers. She was the one who used to help Louise in the garden. None of the others offered and Dean would occasionally mow the lawn when Louise asked him. Lottie wondered who would be tending the garden while she was not there.

"I love your garden and especially the owl; that makes a proper feature in the centre."

"Thanks," said Jan, pleased that she appreciated her garden. "You know that there is more than just the owl on the top? Around the trunk, there are oak leaves and acorns, a back door and a nest of three baby owls, all on one tree! Do you know the story of the three baby owls, Sarah, Percy and Bill?"

"Yes, but only vaguely. What is the full story?"

"The three baby owls woke up one morning and their mother had gone. They waited and waited and got hungrier and hungrier. Day and night they waited. They were beginning to think she was never coming back and were thinking she had been eaten by a fox or some other nasty thing had befallen her." Jan was beginning to wonder if she should ever have started this story as it was too close to home for Charlotte and she was looking alarmed.

"I know what it's like to not have a mum!" said Charlotte, sadly.

"Well, don't forget it's a children's story. Mum came back, eventually, with food for them and it was happy ever after."

"Yes, well, that's a fairy tale, not like real life."

"No, you're right." Jan thought she had better change the subject and wished she had never mentioned about the three baby owls. "When I am feeling sad, I talk to the owl. Anyone seeing me must think I'm mad but he gives me good advice, honestly. He told me not to move away from here. Well, not told me exactly. I gave him two options; I told him to blink once for not going and twice for going. I swear I only saw him blink once!"

"Yes, well…" Lottie was not so sure. "I love gardening. Maybe I could help out in your garden?"

"That would be lovely but it would have to be very light work. We can't have you digging the vegetable patch in your condition! No, seriously, if you are keen to keep me company and at the same time doing some pruning that would be fantastic. We can keep each other company and the time will go much faster."

Lottie was pleased to be of some use. She hated housework but always loved the garden. She felt she could even take it up as a vocation.

"I love all those gardening shows with Alan Titchmarsh and Monty Don. I wanted to be like Charlie Dimmock but without the big boobs!" Lottie laughed. "She's probably more famous for her boobs than her gardening but at least she is famous for something. I wanted to be famous. My friend Amelia and I wanted to be like the Spice Girls, although they're a bit old now. Maybe like Little Mix, even though the Spice Girls are probably more famous. It was never going to be, though; we weren't in the right place at the right time. It doesn't happen to people living in Devon; we were too far away from all the action. Now I'm here, this is closer to London. Do you think I should go for an audition? I can sing, you know."

"I think we had better just concentrate on the baby for now, don't you think?" Jan was amused with Lottie's ambitions. At least she had ambitions. Some children her age have no idea what they want to do.

"Yeah, I suppose you're right. I can't wait now; it's getting really uncomfortable. Some clothes I bought only a few weeks ago are getting so tight. I think the baby has had a growth spurt and my tummy is groaning under the strain!"

"Do you want to go shopping again? I can get you a larger size. We can't have you uncomfortable in the last few weeks. Or I can go on my own if you don't want to come."

"I'd better come and try them on. I shall only buy one pair of jeans. There's no point in buying any more as there's only four weeks to go."

"What about a dress?" Jan was not sure if Lottie wore dresses as she always seemed to be in jeans. "A dress might be more comfortable as it is getting warmer now."

Lottie quite liked the idea of a cool dress. They went shopping and Jan steered Lottie towards the maternity shop. She was not sure how Lottie would take that as she had fixed ideas, so Jan was not going to push her own ideas. However, once in the shop Lottie looked through the maternity dresses and picked out a pretty one with pink and purple flowers. She tried it on and smiled to Jan.

"This is perfect. It is so comfortable." Charlotte felt really happy for the first time in months.

The following two weeks they busied themselves with final preparations for the baby, getting everything together. Jan helped all she could without interfering and let Lottie take centre stage.

One day as they were planting some cottage garden flower seeds that Lottie liked the look of. Lottie suddenly bent double and almost fell over. Jan helped her over to a garden chair. The pain had been getting worse but Lottie had been so engrossed in the planting that she ignored the slight pains at first.

Jan knew the signs of labour and counted between contractions. They were far apart to begin with but then when they became about three minutes apart she told Lottie to get her bag.

"But it's too early!" complained Lottie. "It's not due for another two weeks!"

"Never mind about that. Let's go and get you checked out."

Jan drove Lottie to the hospital. Lottie was in pain but also telling anyone who would listen that it was too early.

The nurses took Lottie into a side ward to check that she was, in fact, in labour.

"Yep, it's coming," one young nurse announced. "Come on, we'll get you settled in. Are you staying with her, Mum?" she asked Jan.

Jan was taken aback by the nurse calling her "Mum". However, she did not correct her as it sounded good, even though it was not strictly correct. She had not been called "Mum" in such a long time and even "Gran" was still very new to her.

"Do you want me to stay?" Jan asked Lottie.

"Yes, please stay with me. It's what Mum would have done, I'm sure. Hold my hand. Are you sure it's coming now? It's too early, I've got another two weeks to go!"

It was not long before Jan saw the midwives in action. She could not really remember what it was like when she herself gave birth for the first time. She was very young but not as young as Lottie. Jan was twenty when she had Louise, a beautiful baby with lots of dark hair. She loved her from the moment she was born. She waited three years before she had her second baby, Steven. Jan was reminiscing and in a world of her own until she heard screams.

"You've got a beautiful baby girl!"

25

"A baby girl!" announced Daisy to Jake and Dean. "Charlie has just texted me. She says it was premature but she's doing well. She hasn't got a name for her yet." Daisy was reading out the text and telling her brother and father as she was reading.

"That's wonderful," said Jake. "A girl! I thought she was having a boy, at least that was what she told me."

Dean kept very quiet and said nothing. Jake and Daisy looked at him and waited for him to say something. He was totting up in his mind as to how premature the baby could have been. His baby. It was at Christmas that he had had too much to drink and made love to his own daughter. He felt thoroughly disgusted with himself but he could not let his other two children know what he was thinking. So this is the first week of August so the baby must be about six or seven weeks premature. He did not want to ask too many questions.

"I'm going for a drink," said Dean. "Wet the baby's head," he added. He could not wait to get out of the house. He could talk to Keith, the barman, about anything and everything but he could not talk to his children. At least not about something that had been on his mind for months.

Jake and Daisy looked at each other but could not tell what their father was thinking.

"What's got into him?" asked Daisy.

"Maybe he doesn't like the idea of becoming a grandparent. Makes him feel old, probably. He'll come around, I'm sure, and then hopefully we can get Charlie back here to where she belongs." Jake felt optimistic that all would come right in the end. He did not like the family having to be split apart.

"When are you taking your driving test?" asked Daisy.

"What's with all the questions?" Jake enquired.

"Well, as soon as you pass your test we could go to Surrey and pay them a visit. That would surprise them! D'you think Dad would come too? He should meet his first grandchild, don't you think? Changing the subject, I'm sure Charlie thought she was going to have a boy. Now it turns out it's a girl! She only had boys' names, as far as I know. I hope she's not too disappointed that she's had a girl." Daisy was still pondering the fact that Charlotte had had a baby girl.

"I really don't know. I can't think at the moment, there's too much going on. I can only think of one thing at a time. Not like you women, who can multitask! I don't know how you do it."

"It's easy. You just have to put your mind to it. Okay, first things first. When is your driving test?" asked Daisy.

"I'm taking the test next week," said Jake. "I have to take time off from my job but it's only a couple of hours. I can make up the time later. I'm really enjoying it."

"Okay, great. When will you get the results for your A levels?"

"Soon after my driving test. Actually, it could be the same day, I'm not sure."

"Okay. When can we go and visit Charlie and the baby?"

"I really don't know. What's with the twenty questions? I'm hoping Dad will let me use Mum's car. It's been sitting on the drive for the last eight or nine months. I don't know if he has kept up with the insurance or what sort of state it's in. I must check with him. I've gone through all the other bills with him but he's not very good with paperwork. Mum used to do all that."

"D'you think Dad will give you the car if you pass your test?" Daisy was hopeful.

"I very much doubt it. He'll probably want me to take him down the pub. I could ask I suppose."

"Yes, yes, ask him. I'll ask him too. Then you can take me to school and pick me up!"

"Only until I go to uni at the end of September."

"That's if they take you! What happens if you fail all your exams?"

"If my grades aren't good enough I suppose no one will take me and then I'll have to go back to school for another year. If they'll take me back. Failing isn't an option so I'm not even thinking about it."

"Hiya, Dean, me ol' china, how're you doin'? Not looking too happy at the moment. Pint is it?" Keith was in his usual jovial mood.

"Yes, a pint and whisky chaser, thanks." Dean was a man of few words at the best of times. Keith knew this but he always tried to cheer up his customers. He had a lot of time for Dean, partly because he was one of his best customers.

"What's occurring?" Keith lay the pint on the bar and went to fetch the whisky chaser.

"My daughter has just had a baby."

"That's grand. Well, for you 'tis grand. 'Cos that makes you a grandfather! Get it? Ha ha!" Keith loved his own jokes. "Could you tell your face that you're happy?"

"I'm in no mood for jokes." Dean took his drinks and walked to his usual table in the corner of the bar. No one else was in because it was too early for most of Keith's customers. Dean liked it that way and no one would bother him or be too loud. Or, worse, put the juke box on.

It was quiet for most of the evening, being early in the week. Keith went to sit at Dean's table with a pint for himself and another one for Dean.

"I wasn't going to have anymore!" complained Dean. "Unless it's on the house, of course!" he said hopefully.

"Of course!" Keith smiled. "Cheers."

"Cheers." Dean took a couple of sips. He was feeling a little inebriated but not drunk. He enjoyed the feeling because then it blocked out all other senses and thoughts. Thoughts of being a grandfather. Or, rather, being a father again. How was he going to be able to talk it through with anyone? He was feeling maudlin but did not know whether it was wise to open up to Keith.

"So what is bothering you, mate? It's not so bad being a grandfather, is it? What is the baby, a boy or girl?" asked Keith, carefully. He was unaware of what was bothering Dean and did not want to interfere.

"Girl."

"Oh, lovely. Have you seen her yet?"

"No. My daughter's gone to live with her grandmother in Surrey. Just as well, really."

"Oh? Why is that?" Keith was not sure how far to push Dean with questions. Maybe he should just let Dean open up when he's ready.

"Well, because I kicked her out! I'm not proud of my actions but there you are."

"Oh." Keith did not know what else to say. Dean continued, just as Keith had hoped.

"What would you say if I told you that the child is mine?" There, it was out there now. Dean felt relieved, as if a huge boulder on his shoulders had been lifted.

"What could I possibly say?" Keith could think of nothing else to say at that precise moment in time.

"You could tell me what a bloody fool I've been. It happened last Christmas."

"But you say she's just had the baby? Christmas wasn't nine months ago, you know! Are you sure it's yours?"

"Positive. It was premature, which is why it isn't nine months. They insisted on telling me it was premature but how could they know to tell me that? I'm sure they know."

"Who knows?"

"My other kids. Obviously the mother of my child knows but she has been very off with me lately. All this year in fact. I have kept out of her way to avoid embarrassment for both our sakes. Then when she decided to tell me at Easter and say she wasn't going back to school, I said she must go."

"You told her to go?"

"Not exactly. I got my son to tell her. I'm such a coward, you see. Such an idiot. How am I going to live with myself? Such shame I've brought on myself and the family." Dean had sobered up slightly by now, with the worry. He felt better telling someone about the situation. He knew Keith was such a gossip but he asked that he told no one.

"I can keep schtum," Keith lied. "Your secret is safe with me. And if there is anything else you want to tell me or if I can help in any way just let me know. How about a coffee now? We can carry on talking if you wish?" Most of the customers had left. Keith went to the bar to make two coffees before awaiting Dean's answer. He wanted Dean to open up some more so was happy to keep open even though all his other customers had gone home. It was not too late, only just 11pm, but Dean had been there almost since the pub opened. Dean was not a fast drinker but he was steady. He had to take control of the finances and could not afford to knock back the drinks like some people he had seen taking drink after drink in a short time. He had been known for keeping a pint going for an hour or two.

Keith came back with the coffees.

"So who else knows? Your son and other daughter?"

"Hell *no*! Only the one with the baby. I bet she hates me right now. I'm sure she wouldn't have told anyone else. She must be feeling shame herself right now."

"Why didn't she have an abortion at the time?" Keith enquired.

"I've no idea! She said she didn't believe in abortions. She is still so young and now lumbered with a baby. She's gone to live with my ex-mother-in-law, my wife's mother. They were estranged so I bet she is loving this now. Nothing I could have done; it was taken out of my hands. No one asked me what I thought. It doesn't matter now anyway. With Louise gone I guess the animosity she felt towards her mother died with her. I expect Steven, her brother, will be going cap in hand and making it up with her too. Good luck to him."

"But what have you got against her? Your ex mother-in-law?"

"Nothing, really. It was a big part of Louise's life that she was determined to cut her out and I just went along with it. I didn't see that she did anything wrong apart from leave her husband after twenty-five years. Louise and Steven were still living at home and I bet they were annoyed that she left them to their own devices to look after their father. They told her at the time she left that, while she was with 'that man', there would never be a reconciliation and, if they ever had children, she would never meet them."

"That's harsh!" Keith was flabbergasted on hearing this.

"Well, it's how they felt at the time. She sent them loads of letters and presents but they sent all gifts back and gave nothing, like letters, in return. They changed their phone numbers too so she couldn't contact them. The last contact she had, as far as I knew, was last year on Jake's seventeenth birthday. She sent him a card, a cheque for £50 and a letter promising all sorts of things, money and driving lessons etc., etc. In the end Louise sent her a stinking letter back telling her *not* to contact her son or harass any of us ever again. Jake fumed at the time because he could have done with the money. And the driving lessons. He is only now just learning to drive but he's saying that if he had taken up his grandmother's offer he would be driving by now."

Keith had never known Dean to be as verbose and animated as he was this evening.

"I'm sure it will all come out in the wash," said Keith. "Do you want another coffee?"

"I'm fine, thanks."

"I know you're fine but do you want a coffee? Help sober you up a bit. You can stay a while longer, if you like. I've only got to clear up a bit. It's been a quiet night."

"Is that because your prices have gone up?" Dean enquired.

"Probably. It sometimes goes like that and then suddenly people forget what the price used to be. But I've got to make a living, you know. And I don't give away free coffees to just anyone, you know!"

"Oh, go on then. Seeing as it's already made, don't want to see it go to waste!"

"Did you think any more about learning to cook, Deano?" Keith asked, pouring out another cup of coffee plus one for himself.

"Can't cook, won't cook!" said Dean, thinking that to be so clever; he decided that he was going to make that into his slogan.

26

"But I thought I was going to have a little boy!" Lottie almost complained, almost childlike herself. She sounded so disappointed that Jan went over to cuddle her. "I was going to call him Jet! Now what am I going to do?"

"Things don't always pan out the way you expect them to." Jan tried to keep Lottie calm. "Don't be too disheartened, will you? Now you'll have to think up some new names! I can help you if you like. I'll get a book and we can look through them together. It's an exciting time for you both and I am so privileged to share it with you. There's no hurry to register the birth. I think you have six weeks." But Lottie was not listening.

"Are you sure it's a girl?" Lottie drowsily asked one of the nurses as she came back from weighing the baby.

The midwife brought the baby, wrapped in a blue cotton blanket, over to Lottie which made her ever hopeful. She took the tiny mite as if she was made of china. Lottie looked her over but made no facial expression.

"Are you sure it's a girl?" Lottie asked again.

"Sure, you can see for yourself," the nurse replied in an Irish lilt. She started to unwrap the blanket until the baby was almost bare. She was hoping that Lottie would say "stop" but she did not until the baby was completely nude.

"Oh! I see. Well, I can't call her Jet, can I?"

"That's a boy's name!"

"I know! I thought I was having a boy," said Lottie.

"Who told you that? The doctor?"

"No. I just guessed, that's all."

"It's always a fifty-fifty shot. Do you want to know what she weighs?" asked the nurse and Jan nodded but Lottie was still dazed. "She is just over two point four kilos."

"What's that in old money?" Jan could never get her head around kilos but wanted to know in good old-fashioned pounds and ounces.

"That is about five pounds, five ounces. Not bad for being a little early. And because she is over five pounds you can go home. But it would be best you stay the night as it's getting late, is that alright with you?" Lottie nodded. "Then we can show you how to feed the baby and check all is okay with her."

Jan went home and Lottie stayed in hospital with the cot by her bedside. When the baby cried the nurse came in to help her feed.

"Are you going to try the breast, dear?" asked the nurse, kindly.

"Not likely! No, definitely not. I don't want my boobs to sag like my mum's did. She blamed us kids on her big saggy boobs!"

"Okay, I'll go and fetch a bottle. We keep them ready in the fridge and warm them up. I won't be two ticks and I'll be back to show you how best to feed baby."

Jan came back the next day but Lottie was not dressed. She had not had much sleep. She kept waking up when other babies cried and she had pain in her breasts. The nurse had explained that that was her milk and that it would dry up in a few days. When she was not feeding, Lottie would look in the cot at her baby's fair hair and watch her sleeping.

"When you are ready to go we will have all the paperwork ready and you'll be good to go. Are you staying at home with your mother?"

"My mother is dead! This is my gran," said Lottie indignantly.

"Oh, sure, I'm so sorry." The Irish nurse looked a little embarrassed and Lottie then felt bad about what she had said.

"It's not your fault!" Lottie started to get dressed. She was groggy but she knew she would be able to sleep it off once she got home. At least, that was what she hoped.

The nurse carried the baby out to the car where the carrycot was waiting on the back seat, secured by straps. Jan was not taking any chances. She remembered back to when she had her first child and Geoff came and picked them up from the hospital. The carrycot was on the back seat but there were no restraining belts and it was before the seat belt law was enforced. Such a long time ago but Jan remembered it so clearly, almost fifty years ago.

They arrived home and Jan helped Lottie out of the car and then reached in for the carrycot. It was a second-hand carrycot she had borrowed from a friend. Between Jan and her friend, they decided that, because the baby only really used a carrycot for such a short time, it was not worth buying one.

"You go in, Lottie, and I'll bring baby. You must be exhausted. Do you know, when I had my first baby, I was in hospital for ten days."

"Ten days? Whatever for? What a waste of time." Lottie was horrified at the thought of spending such a long time in hospital when you weren't actually ill.

"That's just what they used to do back then. It was 1969! So nearly fifty years ago now! Wow," Jan reflected. "Where has all that time gone?" She was speaking to herself because Lottie had gone upstairs. Jan turned around and realised Lottie was nowhere to be seen. Jan put the carrycot carefully on the sofa in the sitting room. The front doorbell made her jump.

"Hello," said Vicky. "I spotted you from my window and thought you might be back with baby? Can I say hello?"

Vicky had met Lottie several times on her many visits to Jan. Jan enjoyed Vicky's company and they were very good friends. Jan was worried as to whether Lottie would mind but she had gone upstairs and it was quiet. Maybe she had gone to bed; she seemed very tired.

"They don't keep them in hospital very long these days, do they?" Vicky reiterated what Jan had said to Lottie not more than ten minutes earlier. "Is she okay? Mother, I mean. Oh, and baby of course!"

"They are just fine. Lottie is tired, which is to be expected. Come and see the baby," Jan said conspiratorially. "I'm sure Lottie won't mind. Baby is asleep but is due a feed very soon. Lottie has said she doesn't want to breastfeed as she says it might make her boobs sag!"

"Well, she's got a point there, look at mine!" Vicky laughed as she pushed her chest forward.

"Well, mine too if it comes to that! Anyway, we have dried milk and I must make up some bottles. Come and help me when you've finished crooning over the baby," said Jan as she disappeared into the kitchen.

Vicky peered into the carrycot just as baby was starting to wake up. She opened her eyes and let out a bloodcurdling cry. Vicky jumped back. She rushed into the kitchen.

"I think you're going to need those bottles sooner than you thought," said Vicky.

"It won't hurt to let her cry for a bit. Trouble is, I don't know if Lottie wants me to feed her or if she wants to do it herself. We'll have to see. If she comes down, she can feed her. Otherwise I'll just get on with it."

As Jan had the baby on her lap and was giving her the bottle, Vicky loved to watch. When it was all over and Jan had the baby on her shoulder to bring up wind, Jan could see that Vicky was itching to tell her something.

"I've got some news myself," said Vicky.

"Oh, God, you're not pregnant, are you?" Jan laughed.

"Me? Heavens no, whatever next? No, we've just booked a cruise, Gerry and I. In fact, we have actually booked two cruises. It wasn't quite two for the price of one but the second one was heavily discounted."

"What happens if you don't like the first one? You've never been on a cruise before! How do you know you're going to enjoy it? I didn't think Gerry liked boats. I thought he got seasick."

"Well, he does but there are pills he can take. I'm so excited. The first one is to the Caribbean, around all the islands. We go in September. It was a real bargain," said Vicky excitedly.

"Oh, just in time for the hurricane season!" said Jan, smiling that she was able to impart something about weather conditions. She had travelled a lot with Mike so she knew the places to go and the best times.

"What? They never told us that!" shouted Vicky.

"Of course they didn't. Did you not wonder why it was a bargain?"

"Oh, hell! D'you think I should cancel it?"

"It's up to you but actually it might be okay. When do you go?"

"At the end of September and come back mid-October."

"It might all be over by then. I think the worst time is about mid-August to mid-September but don't quote me on that. You could look it up but it is quite common knowledge that the hurricanes are always in the autumn time. What size ship is it?" Jan questioned.

"Oh, it's quite small. Gerry didn't like the idea of a huge one with about 5,000 passengers with all that milling about; he hates crowds. Which is why we've gone for something quite small. About 1,000 passengers, I think.

"So it will bob about much more than a larger ship, which is obviously heavier!"

"Oh, you're just trying to frighten me now!"

"No, I'm not. I just want you to have the best time. Mike never wanted to cruise; he didn't like the water and he got seasick. And he couldn't swim. Actually we did go on a small cruise around the islands in Croatia once. I loved it but it did get very rough. We were holed up on one of the islands for twenty-four hours because there were fifteen-foot waves outside. When we did venture out it was still very rough and they were trying to serve us soup, which got slopped about! Mike didn't eat very much and went to the cabin to lie down – he felt awful, I remember. After that he said never again! But I really enjoyed it; in fact, the rougher the better for me. I was brought up on boats from a young age."

"You're lucky then. I don't know if I suffer seasickness but we know Gerry does. We just thought it would be a different sort of holiday, something to try."

"Take plenty of seasick pills then, enough for both of you. You'll love it, I'm sure," said Jan enthusiastically. "Where and when is the second one you have booked for?"

"Oh, that's next year in March. That one is far more exotic, to the Far East. We fly to Singapore and pick up the ship there. We go to loads of places, too many to mention, partly because I've forgotten! Oh, yes, the main one I'm really excited about is Japan."

"That sounds fantastic; you'll love it, I'm sure. I wish I could go on holiday, but not on my own. I do miss Mike so much."

"Loads of single women go cruising. They go to pick up rich widowers!"

"Not for me, I'm afraid."

The baby was starting to go to sleep, content with her feed and being winded on Jan's shoulder. Lottie arrived a little bleary-eyed.

"I've fed and burped her," said Jan. "Would you like to put her back in her carrycot?"

"Oh! Thank you, yes I will." Lottie was thankful that Jan had fed her baby as she was still not confident in doing it herself. She was worried in case she would not take enough milk but Gran seemed to know what she was doing. Jan was ever mindful not to take over; in her eyes she was just helping out. Helping out a vulnerable girl who knows little about anything. She reminded her of herself when she gave birth to Louise. She had been so inexperienced in life and, on reflection now, she wondered how she ever coped. She had no help from anyone so she just had to get on with it, with words from her parents ringing in her ears: "You made your bed; you lie in it."

Vicky decided it was time to take her leave.

"Do let me know if you would like me to babysit if you two need a break. I shall be more than happy to help out. I love babies."

"Oh, thank you. We might take you up on that offer but not until we have got to know her ourselves. We must decide on a name for her too," said Jan, looking at Lottie for approval of her words. Lottie nodded and smiled in agreement. Vicky took her leave and let herself out of the front door.

"Shall we have a look in the shops and get a name book?" suggested Jan to Lottie.

"If you don't mind, that will be fun finding a name for her," Lottie agreed. "Or we could just look on the internet."

"I'm old-fashioned when it comes to books or internet! I love books. We have to go out in any case to get some fresh air for ourselves as well as baby."

Jan let Lottie do the work with putting the carrycot in the car, ever mindful not to take over. It was Lottie's baby and Gran was only there for guidance and help when needed. They went to the shops and came back with a name book and had fun reading through the strange names that were used these days. Strange to Jan, anyway. The old-fashioned names were coming back but also some new ones that Jan did not agree with and she hoped that Lottie would be wise in choosing the right name.

"What about Adalyn or Aurora? Or Apple, what about that? Gwyneth Paltrow called her daughter Apple, didn't she?" asked Lottie and Jan nodded. "Evie? Or Ivy? Or Esme? Those are old-fashioned names, aren't they?" Jan nodded again. She was not sure about any of those names.

"I know!" Lottie became animated. Jan was alarmed at her enthusiasm. "Lola! Or even better – Zola!"

"Yes, why not? It's quite pretty. I prefer Lola."

"Pretty? I don't really want pretty."

"Oh! Why not?" Jan asked.

"Well, not pretty-pretty, in other words sickly. No, I want something that will actually say something. Make a mark."

"Oh, okay."

"Celeste, Venus or Olivia?" Lottie suggested again. "Roxy, Lexi or Ava: they are unusual names, aren't they?" Lottie was going through the pages but not sticking to any order of the alphabet.

"They sure are, but would you want her to stick out at school with her unusual name? Sometimes the teacher remembers the naughty children by their unusual names, partly because there is usually only one of them. If there were several of the same name it would be more difficult for the teacher to remember which is which."

"Anna, Adrienne, Alexandra?" Lottie had gone back to the beginning of the book. "Oh, I don't know. Amelia! Ha, I can't call her that."

"Why not? That's a nice name."

"My best friend is called Amelia. We fell out a while back because she didn't agree with what I was doing. I think she was jealous of me. Anyway, we made up by text and now we are texting most days now she's left school. I don't know if she's going back to school to take her A levels. There's an awful lot of work and I'm not sure she's up to it. Well, that's up to her I suppose."

"What about your education?" Jan tentatively asked. She did not want to upset Lottie but she did wonder if she would want to go back to school to finish her schooling as she left rather early and without any exams to her name."

"No, I don't think so. Had enough of that. Learning stuff. That's a mug's game if you ask me!" Jan did not want to push the subject so she picked up the book and suggested a few other names instead. She would address Lottie's education at a later date.

"What about Isabella or Emma? Or Sophie or Sophia? They are really pretty names, aren't they? Or Scarlett or Ruby? I like them."

"There are just too many to choose from; I feel exhausted just thinking," said Lottie.

"We'll leave it for now and go back to it later," said Jan kindly. "You would want it to be right and not to rush it and there is plenty of time to decide. Shall we have lunch in the garden? It really is such a lovely day, so warm and summery."

"That's it!" called Lottie.

"What?"

"Summer! That's what she'll be called. I've decided. Summer... Summer... yes, I love it."

"That's it then, wonderful. You have chosen well. It really suits her. Summer, yes I love it too."

27

"I've passed my A levels with good grades!" shouted Jake to anyone who was listening. He was waiting by the front door as he had seen the postman in the street.

"Well done!" Daisy was just coming down the stairs. "Where is Dad? Has he gone to work already?"

"I think so. He's not in his bedroom, I had a look earlier. Is this going to be my most perfect day ever? I'm taking my driving test in two hours' time. Wish me luck."

"You don't need it; you'll smash it. I do hope so. Then when I go back to school you can take me!"

"That's if Dad lets me use the car. I haven't dared broach the subject yet. I was waiting till I passed my test before I ask him."

"So later on today you will be asking him, yeah?" Daisy said hopefully.

"Yeah," Jake copied Daisy.

"If he does," Daisy began tentatively, "can we go and visit Charlie and Summer? And Gran too, of course. It will be nice to meet her. From what Charlie says, she's very nice."

"Nice? What does that mean? You can have a nice meal but you wouldn't call a person 'nice.'"

"Why not? Alright, kind. Thoughtful. Just nice. Well, I know what I mean."

"As long as you do, that's alright. If I pass my test today I will ask Dad if I can use the car to drive us to go and see Charlie. And Gran and Summer too, of course. Okay? I can't do better than that."

"Promise?" said Daisy with her fingers crossed behind her back.

"Promise."

The driving instructor arrived an hour later and took Jake to the driving test centre. He was nervous at first but quietly confident.

"I'm pleased to tell you you have passed," the examiner said to Jake as he finalised the paperwork, still sitting in the car.

Jake couldn't wait for his father to get back from work and was hoping he was not going to make a detour to the pub first. Dean did go to the pub after work but only for a swift half. He came home to loud music and lots of animated talking. He could not believe his two children could make such a noise. It was just as if all three of them were in the house but he knew it was only just the two of them, Jake and Daisy. The noise was coming from the kitchen and as he put his head around the door the music became even louder.

"Turn it down!" shouted Dean over the noise. "Can't hear myself think!"

"I passed, Dad!" shouted Jake. Then he turned the music right down so they could talk. "I passed my A levels with good grades today and then I passed my driving test. This must be the best day ever."

"Well, I must congratulate you, son. I never thought you had it in you. No, that's a lie. I knew you had it in you. You worked hard at both your exams and your driving, I'm so pleased for you. You can take me down the pub now!"

"I knew you would say that! Mum's car? It's been in the drive all this time. Is it still insured?"

"How should I know? Your mother dealt with all that malarkey. You can have a look at the paperwork if you like, if you can find it, but I expect it's run out by now."

"What about the MOT and stuff like that?"

"Pass."

"Well, I can't take you down the pub then, can I?" said Jake. Dean folded his arms in semi-submission. "If I get all this sorted out for you, can I use the car when I want to? It's no use to you as you can't drive!"

"I could learn," said Dean. Jake was doubtful that his father would ever learn to drive. He was happier walking or taking the bus. He would never have the patience to drive a car.

"Yes, well anyway. I have more pressing things to do at the moment. I have to start looking to my future and universities. I don't think I want to go to Oxford or Cambridge anymore. I've had an offer to go to Bristol so I think I will take it up. It's not so far to go either. Just need to apply for my student loan."

"Good luck with that, son. You know I haven't got anything so make sure you apply for everything you need."

"I will, don't worry. And Uncle John has said he could put me up."

"Good luck with that too! He's got enough on his plate, I should think."

"I've spoken to him about it and apparently Auntie Vera is going to go into a care home pretty soon. He can't cope with her anymore as she is getting too disruptive. So by the time I need a place to stay she will be in the home and we could keep each other company. Well, some of the time anyway. Obviously I would be studying at uni in the daytime. And then in the evenings we could just hang out or go to the pub."

"What happened about going into halls for the first year?" asked Dean.

"I could do that but, since John has offered me a bed, I thought it would be rude to say no. And it could save me some money too. So it's a win–win situation, don't you think?"

"Sounds like you've got it all sorted then."

"Not quite. It still needs to be arranged. Are you going to able to look after Daisy on your own?"

"I should think we will cope. Give her a few more lessons in cookery and we'll be fine."

"I'm going to give both of you lessons in cooking. It's essential that you learn to cook, Dad, now more than ever."

"Okay, but Daisy will be the only female in the house so she should do most of the cooking and cleaning." Dean decided.

"Why? Just because she's female? That's just sexist. I don't agree with it, Dad. You must take responsibility as being the only adult in the house after I've gone."

"When did you get so wise, son?"

"Mum instilled it into me. You must do this, otherwise I shan't feel able to go away."

"We will muddle through. You mustn't let home life disasters influence what you're going to do. You go and don't look back."

"There's just one more thing I must run past you." Jake was a little apprehensive to bring up the subject of Charlotte knowing how his father had been with her. "Daisy and I would like to go and visit Charlie and the baby. By the way, did you know she has called the baby Summer? Charlie texted us a few days ago to tell us."

"Talk to the hand 'cos the face ain't listening!" Dean put up the flat of his hand.

"Dad! Be reasonable. I'm not really asking for permission. I'm telling you that that is what is going to happen and I'd like to take the car. You can come too, if you like." Jake threw in the last sentence to soften the blow of the one before.

"Not on your nelly! You go if you want to but leave me out of it," said Dean. Jake took that as acceptance that he could take the car. "What about your job? You can't leave that, can you?"

"A friend of mine is going to take it over. It's not rocket science; it's only putting deck chairs out and taking them in again! It's only for another week or so anyway 'cos it's the end of the season. And he needs the money. I've said he can take it over for the rest of the season if he wants."

Jake left it at that but the summer holidays were coming to an end for Daisy and arrangements had to be made for Jake and Daisy to go and visit their grandmother. He was a little apprehensive for two reasons. He had never driven as far as Surrey but he looked on that as a challenge and actually was looking forward to it. The second was the first meeting of his grandmother. How would she be towards them? Charlotte had said how kind she is but that was something for him and Daisy to find out for themselves. Then, of course, the cherry on the cake – to meet their niece, Summer.

Arrangements were made and agreed with Jan for the following week. A week before Daisy was due back to school. They would stay just two nights to get to know each other. Jake gave his father a short course of learning to cook simple things to start with and then later on he would teach him more complex recipes before he went off to Bristol University.

"You go off, the two of you, I'll be fine. I know where the chippie is!"

"I've put one or two things in the freezer for you; you just have to take them out and cook them but they're for emergencies only. There's a lasagne from Tesco's and also some other pasta-type food. They go in the microwave so you can't go wrong if you read the instructions," said Jake.

Jan made up the two spare bedrooms in readiness for the arrival of two more grandchildren. To say she was excited to meet them at long last was an understatement. She baked some scones and Lottie helped her. Lottie enjoyed Jan's company and was quite getting into helping out in the kitchen. It was better than doing housework in her view. She thought it was good to be able to eat the results of their hard work and Jan showed her lots of different things she never imagined could be cooked in a domestic situation. She thought fish and chips always came from a fish and chip shop. But actually everything tasted as good, if not better, when it was cooked at home. Jan introduced lots of fresh vegetables into their diet and Lottie was beginning to enjoy them.

Jake and Daisy arrived later in the morning. Jan opened the front door and felt overwhelmed and emotional. This day was a long time coming.

"Hello, you two! It's lovely to meet you at last." Jan greeted Jake and Daisy with a long hug. "I never thought this day would ever arrive. I'm so happy." She brushed away a tear and tried to hide her emotions.

Daisy felt like she should curtsy but then thought better of it and gave Jan a slightly embarrassed smile instead. Jake bent over to give Jan a peck on the cheek.

"We are pleased to meet you too." Jake spoke for himself and his sister.

"Come in, come in. Come and meet your niece. And see your sister too, of course." Lottie came to greet them outside with Summer in her arms before they could step indoors.

"Hiya," said Lottie to her two siblings, smiling all the while. She looked happier than she had ever been while at home, Jake noticed.

"Oh, she is gorgeous," cooed Daisy, looking at Summer and all but ignoring Lottie. She wanted to hold Summer and cuddle her but was too afraid as she had never held a baby before.

"Hi, Charlie," said Jake.

"I'm not called Charlie anymore," Lottie told him severely. "My new name is Lottie. Gran chose it for me because I said I didn't like Charlie. That's a boys' name and I always hated it. Did I never tell you?"

"No, never," said a surprised Jake.

"Come in," said Jan. She was aware that they were all still on the doorstep.

Lottie led the way and her siblings followed with Jan bringing up the rear, closing the front door behind her. Lottie put Summer in her carrycot and beckoned her brother and sister over to have a proper look at her.

"She's a little darling, isn't she?" said Jake, which surprised his sisters.

"Ooh, she's lovely," crooned Daisy and then asked. "Is she a good baby? Does she sleep through the night or do you have to get up and feed her every hour? That would do my head in!" She had read up on the internet all about babies and what to expect.

"She is nearly going through the night now. Her last feed is about midnight and Gran does that for me 'cos she goes to bed later than me," Jan nodded in agreement, smiling.

"That is Summer's and my time together without Mum. We have lots of cuddles," Jan confirmed, smiling.

They all stood around the carrycot and Jan let them finish their oohing and aahing over the baby before she suggested a light lunch before she showed Jake and Daisy to their rooms. She felt talking over the baby might break the ice. They all needed to get to know each other.

"Gran?" asked Daisy, once they had all started tucking into their lunch.

"Yes," Jan replied. She had got used to being called Gran by Lottie and now it was nice to hear someone else calling her that.

"What was our mum like when she was a child?" asked Daisy.

"Oh, that's a very easy question, I thought you were going to ask me something difficult! Your mum was the sweetest little girl, so kind and considerate. And when your Uncle Steven was born, your mum was three and bit, but she was so grown up. It was just like she was his mum. She would fetch me the nappies and rock him to sleep. He was a little devil when he was a baby. He cried and cried until he was about two. I loved them both so much." Jan was moved to tears when she remembered all that time ago when her babies were so young.

"Why did you leave them, then?" Daisy was determined to do some straight talking.

"Daisy!" Jake admonished her, but Jan continued.

"It's okay Jake, I don't mind," said Jan, kindly. "It's not as if I left them when they were babies. They were both grown up. You obviously don't know the background because your mum might have only told you what she thought from her side. My side of the story is that I left my husband, your granddad Geoff, because I was abused by him for many years. It's called mental abuse rather than physical abuse, where someone gets hurt. I can't go into details on that side, it would take too long, but it was over many years. Suffice to say, we had been married for nearly twenty-five years when I met Mike and left my husband, all within six or seven months. So that shows just how desperate I was. I took a huge gamble on Mike and we were very happy for just over twenty-two years. Luckily. It could have all gone pear-shaped but I was willing to take that risk. It's the happiest I've ever been in my life. He was my soul mate. But, of course, there was always something missing in my life."

There was silence around the table as Jan's words sunk in and they understood that she meant the absence of her children and then grandchildren. Them.

"The early years were the worst. After a while I got used to it. I tried to make contact with your mum and Uncle Steven many, many times, too countless to remember. When they did not respond, it dawned on me that they were never going to forgive me. I suppose they thought I had left them, but I tried to explain that it was my husband I left, not them. In a way Mike save my life because my life then, with Geoff, was so boring and awful. It was just so sad that I had to leave Louise and Steven too. They would not have wanted to come with me because they were settled in their jobs and they both had partners. I couldn't have disrupted them so I left on my own."

Daisy seemed to accept Jan's explanation and so Jan had a question of her own to Daisy. Jan thought that changing the subject might lighten the mood.

"Do you know what you want to do when you leave school, Daisy? What career you want to pursue?"

"Well, I'd like to be a vet or a vet's nurse. I love all animals but mostly dogs. If I don't get good grades to be a vet then I might have to fall back to just being a vet's nurse."

"Do you usually get good grades at school? If you keep up with your schoolwork, there is no reason why you can't achieve your goal."

"Yeah, not too bad."

"And what about you, Jake? I hear you are off to Bristol University soon? That's fantastic. John told me you are going to stay with him, is that right?"

"Yes," said Jake. "He offered so I said yes. I think he's a bit lonely right now, with Vera going into the care home."

"Yes, he is. That's very kind of you to think of him." Jan was impressed with Jake's empathy.

"Well, it helps me out too so it's a double whammy!"

"And do you know what you want to do, eventually, that is?" Jan asked Jake.

"Not sure, really. I'm taking mostly the sciences because that's what I'm most interested in, so I could think about being a doctor if my grades are good, although I would then have to go to med school."

"Yes, I know it all takes time. Five years to become a doctor and seven years to be a vet, I believe. Of course, there are other options which would not take so long. Have you thought of dentistry?"

"Don't think I like the idea of looking in people's mouths all day long. I haven't made up my mind yet; there's plenty of time."

"Gran?" Daisy was not finished with her questions.

"Yes, Daisy."

"Were you allowed to text your friends in class when you were at school?" Daisy had been told off for texting in class so she wanted to know how her grandmother used to contact her friends.

"Heavens no," Jan laughed. Jake and Lottie sniggered a little too because they knew what was coming next. They knew that Daisy had had her mobile phone confiscated more than once at school.

"Weren't you allowed to use your mobile phone at school in the old days? Could you only use it after school?" Daisy asked.

"There were no such things as mobile phones when I went to school. Don't forget that was over fifty years ago. Phones were only in people's homes."

"So did you have yours in your room? So you could speak to your friends."

"There was usually only one phone in the house and it was in the hall."

"So could you take it to your room if you wanted a private conversation with your friends?" Daisy persisted.

"It had a cord attached to it so it had to stay where it was connected to the wall." To this they all laughed, Daisy more than the others. They all looked quite perplexed and interested to hear more about life in the dim and distant past. There was lots of laughter around the table and this made it all the easier to get to know each other and the time disappeared very quickly. Before they knew it, it was the middle of the afternoon.

"Now, what would you like to do tomorrow?" Jan asked the three of them. We could go out in the car and I could show you around the area.

"We could go to the shops," said Daisy hopefully. She loved shopping, especially if she was buying clothes for herself.

There was only one clear day that Jake and Daisy were there and so they all decided to have a look around the area but to also concentrate on getting to know one another at home. Jan had learned a lot from Lottie already as she told her about her immediate family, of which Jan knew very little.

In the afternoon they all went for a walk to give Summer some fresh air. Jan was in two minds whether to go over the road to her favourite spot in a park beside a lake. This was the place that their mother lost her life when the tree came down, only ten months beforehand. Whenever Jan walked there on her own, it always reminded her of Louise. Should she say anything to them when they got there? She decided not to spoil their walk. They could go there in ignorance and only Jan would know the secret. She thought it would not do them any good knowing where their mother had died. It was all too sad.

One day and two nights went by in a flash and very soon they were saying their goodbyes.

"We must do this again; you are welcome to come anytime you like," Jan said to Jake and Daisy. They all kissed goodbye and Jan and Lottie waved them off. It was late afternoon so Jan hoped they would get back before it became dark.

"That was lovely," said Jan to Lottie. "I do hope they come again."

When Jake pulled up outside the house, he saw it was in darkness. He went in the house before Daisy and put on the lights. Dean was not at home. In the kitchen was a burnt smell and rubbish strewn all over the work surfaces. Dirty plates were stacked in the bowl. Dean had not bothered to put anything in the dishwasher.

Jake tutted but then started to clear up his father's mess. Daisy started to help him but then disappeared upstairs on the pretext that she needed to speak to her friends before they went back to school in a few days.

Jake guessed that Dean was at the pub and decided to go and fetch him. He could tell him off while he drove them home. He told Daisy where he was going and would not be long and checked she would be okay on her own.

"I'll be fine, I'm on the phone," Daisy called out. "Are you going to tell Dad off?"

"You bet!"

Jake arrived at his father's favourite local. He went in the door and found the pub was very busy and noisy. It was not Jake's preference to frequent the pub like his father did but he did like a beer occasionally. He asked Keith if Dean was there and Keith pointed over to where Dean was sitting on his own at "his" table, nursing a pint with a chaser.

"I'd like a beer, please, barman. Just a half," Jake asked Keith. He took his drink over to Dean's table and sat down.

"Oh, the wanderer returns!" hissed Dean nastily.

"Hi, Dad." Jake ignored his father's maudlin state. "I've come to pick you up and take you home. You left a right old mess in the kitchen, didn't you?"

"No, I didn't! I put things away. Okay, it might not be to your high standard but I did me best." Dean slurred most of his words so Jake could tell he had already had quite a bit of alcohol and just wanted to drink his beer and then go home.

"I see you cooked something because I could smell something had burnt," said Jake.

"Oh, that was me toast this morning. Mostly I had takeaways or I ate here. Keith's wife does a mean roast with all the trimmings, lovely it was." Dean started licking his lips.

"Good." Jake had heard enough. He felt that all he had showed his father before he left was a waste of time. He made a mental note to make sure he teaches him about clearing up after himself after cooking and making sure he does cook and not to rely on takeaways.

"Aren't you going to ask how your daughter is? And your granddaughter?" Jake asked.

"No! Why should I? They are better off without me, I expect."

"Come on, finish your beer and let's get out of here," said Jake, exasperated.

They arrived back in the house and Dean stumbled in the front door. Jake had to hold him up and help him into the house.

"One for the road? Or the stairs? I've got a delicious whisky in the cupboard with my name on it. And yours too, if you play your cards right! Would you like to try a wee dram?"

"I think you've had enough, don't you? I don't want any anyway. I think it's time for bed, don't you?"

Dean stumbled upstairs without his whisky. He went up two and down one but eventually made it to the top.

Daisy was in her bedroom with the door open. She was getting undressed ready for bed when Dean arrived at her bedroom door and stopped. He stood there for several seconds before he realised what he was thinking. They were unnatural thoughts that he tried very hard to suppress, what with Jake so close behind.

Jake came upstairs after locking up. He spotted his father watching Daisy momentarily and wondered what he should do, if anything. He helped his father to his bedroom and thought no more about it, thinking he must have imagined what he saw. At the back of his mind he started to worry about going off to university in September. He could not understand why he was worried.

28

Lottie settled into motherhood better than Jan was expecting. Summer thrived. Jan took them to the clinic for weekly check-ups, where they were pleased with Summer's weight and her health in general.

Lottie found her baby fat difficult to shift until Jan suggested on an exercise regime that they could do together with walking out, pushing the pram and all three of them getting plenty of fresh air. Jan always thought the summer was so short in England, from about June to September, when the weather was usually settled and warm. She loved the springtime herself, when the daffodils came out; they were her favourites. Then the bluebells arrived and that was usually the sign that summer was on its way. Mike's favourite flowers were bluebells so when they arrived this year they reminded her of him.

A lot had happened in the summer and September had arrived in no time at all, thought Jan. Autumn was not her favourite time of the year as it was the beginning of winter, which was definitely the season she hated the most. Christmas beckoned and she wondered if Lottie would want to be back with her family. She was not making any signs that she wanted to return home and Jan was glad of this. She was good company and had the makings of becoming a very good mother to Summer.

The days went by and there was always plenty to do when there was a baby in the house. Eventually Jan decided to broach the subject of Christmas. She was more than happy to spend it with Lottie and Summer but she wanted to give Lottie the option in case she wanted to go home and be with her father and siblings. It would not be fair of Jan to say to Lottie that she wished she would spend it with her. She need not have worried as Lottie was adamant. There was no way she wanted to go back to Devon. This was her home now.

Vicky arrived at Jan's house just before Gerry and herself went off on their cruise. But she had a little problem with which she was hoping Jan could help. She had the hiccups and could not get rid of them.

"I was getting worried about the cruise when *hic* this started. I was hoping *hic* that you could help *hic*. You told me once *hic* that someone told you a good remedy *hic*."

"You've come to just the right place." Jan was pleased to be able to help her friend. "Come into the kitchen and we will get you sorted out. Sit down."

"*Hic*. It's not one of these old wives tales, is it? *hic*."

"No, it's not. Someone told me the remedy years ago and it works every time."

Jan put a glass of water with a straw in front of Vicky and gave her some instructions.

"Now, you need to suck the water through the straw. At the same time put your fingers in your ears as far as they will go and hold them there so you will hear nothing but let me tell you everything before you start to do it! When you can hear nothing else you need to swallow the water quite slowly until it's all gone. So to reiterate, fingers in ears then suck and swallow."

"*Hic*. Are you sure this is going to work? *Hic*."

"We'll soon see, it doesn't take long. If it doesn't work at first then you can always try again," Jan averred.

"Thanks. *Hic*."

Vicky sipped the water through the straw and put her fingers in her ears and swallowed slowly as instructed. They both waited when finally she took her fingers out of her ears. There was a palpable silence. No more hiccups.

"That's amazing!" said Vicky "It's worked like magic."

"I know. It always works. Every time. And, if you find yourself without a straw, I find it still works if you just keep the water in your mouth and swallow slowly. The key is the fingers in your ears but don't ask me why it works, it just does. You sometimes get people saying hold your breath or drink water out of the glass from the other side or upside down but those are just old wives' tales which don't work. Now, don't worry about your cruise and, if you get hiccups again, you know what to do."

"I can't wait but I'm a little apprehensive after what you said about hurricanes," said Vicky to Jan.

"Oh, take no notice of me. You'll be fine, I'm sure of it. You go off and enjoy yourselves and let me know all about it when you come back. Actually I'm rather envious. I could do with a holiday myself."

"Thanks, Jan. I feel better now. Don't forget I want to babysit that young lady!"

Lottie was listening with interest and, when Vicky left, she jumped at the chance to offer Jan a chance to go on holiday.

"Why don't you go on holiday? You said you have friends in New Zealand and Thailand. It would make a great trip. I will be okay to hold the fort here." Lottie was not quite sure if she would be able to cope on her own but she was happy to make the offer.

"I wouldn't dream of leaving you here alone. Between you and me, I only went last Christmas because otherwise I would have been on my own. I have a lot of friends here who would have seen that I was okay. Don't let me stop you going back to Devon, though, but only if you want to."

"I don't want to. I want to stay here with you." Lottie was steadfast. Jan decided to leave the subject alone and go on to something different.

"I know! We could go on holiday together! Would you like that? Have you got a passport?" Jan asked.

"No, I've never been abroad so never needed one. Where do you think we could go?"

"Well, it would have to be somewhere that is suitable for babies. Not too far. Let me think about it. Summer is probably a bit too young to take away just yet but we could think of something for next year. What d'you think? We could go in the spring, somewhere with a bit of sunshine. It would make the winter a little shorter. We could do with it after the winter here, a bit of warmth on our skin, lovely."

"Lovely," said Lottie, not quite sure of what to expect and yet excited at the prospect.

"I know!" It was a light-bulb moment for Jan. "The best place I know which is not too far is Madeira. It is lovely there at any time of the year. Mike and I went there a few times when we felt like a bit of sunshine. It is very colourful and you would absolutely love all the flowers there."

Before Jan started thinking in earnest about a holiday in the new year she wanted to talk about Christmas again. Lottie was sure she was not going to go home so Jan started making plans in her head. She decided to invite her brother over as he would be on his own and she wanted to know if there was something special that she could buy Lottie. Something really special.

"I've always wanted a puppy. My sister has always been animal mad and she would take over whenever there was talk of having any sort of animals. I kept quiet because I never thought I'd get one because we were all too busy to be able to look after one. Daisy asked Granny Kath for a puppy last Christmas but it never materialised. She was mortified. I'd really, really like a puppy; they are so cute. And Daisy would be so jealous!" Lottie added the last sentence as an afterthought. Then she wondered if that sounded too mean.

"Don't forget puppies turn into adult dogs." Jan put on her sensible hat. And she chose to ignore Lottie's last sentence. "They do need a lot of looking after, you know? Don't you think you have enough to do with looking after Summer?"

"I s'pose so." Lottie pouted. "In fact, Granny Kath said the same to Daisy, that they need a lot of attention. Daisy was really upset. And she might be upset if I got one before her so maybe I'd better not; that was mean of me." Lottie was beginning to be more thoughtful and grown up and considerate of others and Jan appreciated that.

"It was, rather, but I think you were only joking," said Jan. "So, we won't rule it out if it is something you really want. I love dogs too. We used to have them. Actually, now you have suggested it, the more I like the idea. What sort were you thinking? Nothing too big, I hope!"

"I don't know about the different breeds. The Andrex puppies are always so adorable. Have you seen the ad where they steal the toilet paper and go miles and the man sitting on the toilet laughs at first and then he gets cross when the paper runs out? It's hilarious."

"Yes. And, yes, they are very cute when they are puppies but they turn out enormous! They're Labradors and I'm afraid I'm allergic to them because they moult. I was thinking of something a bit smaller that doesn't moult. Like a Westie or a miniature schnauzer. Now, they are cute and not too big. And Summer will grow up with a pet and that can only be good. I'll look into it."

Jan asked around. She found out that someone she knew had a Labrador bitch who had just become pregnant. Jan discounted a Labrador until she found out that the owners told her that the father was a poodle. If the puppy turned out to be a labradoodle with a coat like a poodle then Jan would be interested and she told the owner this. Unfortunately, the puppies would be born just before Christmas and so would not be sold until they were eight weeks old and weaned from their mother. She did not want to get Lottie's hopes up but Jan thought it would be a better idea anyway that Lottie could have a puppy for her birthday instead of Christmas.

"That would be fantastic." Jan had never seen Lottie's eyes light up with so much enthusiasm.

"Well, we will have to wait and see, won't we? We will know once they are born but we have been given first choice if that is what we decided."

"I do hope so."

Jan wanted to bring up the subject of Lottie's education as the autumn term had already begun. She told herself to just go for it and ask her.

"What about your education? Do you want to go back to school?" asked Jan tentatively.

"Not likely. How can I bring up a baby and go to school?"

"Well, I could have her in the daytime and then you can look after her when you come home. I do think you should finish your education, don't you? At the moment you have only missed one term. It's the only way you will be able to get a job."

"I'll think about it." The thought of going back to school was not Lottie's idea of fun and she was not pleased that Jan brought up the subject, although she saw that she had a point. She had no exam certificates to her name so how could she prove she had had any education at all? Lottie was no fool. "Yes, I've thought about it."

"Well, that was quick!" Jan was pleased that she had at least mulled over her suggestion.

"But I might leave it for a while before I go back. I need to bond with Summer; that's what I've read, anyway."

"Good. Okay, if that's what you want. As long as we are working towards a common goal. You bond with Summer for the time being and then maybe go back in the new year. You will have missed two terms by then so you could catch up if you work hard. Do you want me to look around at schools to see which is the most suitable?"

"No hurry for that. Anyway, I can do that."

Lottie could not think that far ahead. She was too excited thinking about having a puppy for her birthday. And a holiday. She definitely made the right decision to move and stay with her grandmother.

29

At the beginning of September, Daisy went back to school. She was in the last year before having to start work on her GCSEs, which would take another two and a half years. She enjoyed her schoolwork and was popular with the other girls. She held her own in most subjects and was a favourite with the teachers. She could not wait to become a teenager but that was going to be another couple of months. She already liked clothes and enjoyed shopping for them when she had enough money. Money was always tight and she had to go cap in hand every week to ask her father for her pocket money. Her mother always gave it to her without having to be asked. She wondered if he was going to give her a little more after her birthday.

Jake taught both Daisy and Dean all he knew about cooking. Daisy took to it easier than Dean but he did try.

"I can't get the hang of this! Why do you have to time everything?"

"Timing is really important. If you want a meal at say seven o'clock then you have to count back. So if you are doing say a roast chicken, which takes nearly two hours, you don't go putting the vegetables on at the same time or they will all be overcooked."

"Sounds daft to me," Dean complained. "Just put it all on and leave it to cook. Easy."

"It's not easy, Dad. Just listen, will you?" Jake felt like banging his head against a brick wall with his father's ignorance. *How did his mother put up with him?* he wondered.

"Don't worry, Dad," Daisy piped up. "I'll do the cooking as long as you look after the garden and do some of the other jobs around the house. Okay?"

"Deal." Dean went over to shake Daisy's hand.

"As long as you don't shirk your responsibilities." Daisy was concerned that she would be doing most of the donkey work around the house. She did not like to call him lazy but it was certainly what she was thinking. Dean walked away, happy to get out of the cooking but not really looking forward to the "other jobs" that Daisy mentioned.

"Time for me to go now, Dad. Are you going to wish me well?"

"Of course, I wish you all the best, son. Here, I've got something for you." Dean opened his wallet and took out two crisp £20 notes.

"Thanks, Dad. Where's Daisy?"

"Here I am." Daisy had been listening from upstairs. She flew down the stairs and into Jake's arms. "We will miss you."

"And I will miss you too."

"Good luck," said Dean and Daisy together as they waved Jake off in the car. He drove to Bristol and used the satnav to find John's house. He had never been to his house before. John was in a bit of state as Vera had gone into a care home only a few days beforehand.

"Welcome, Jake," said John. "I'm so pleased you have chosen to stay with me. We could be good company for each other."

"Thank you, Uncle John." Jake was not sure whether to call

him Great Uncle John, Uncle John or just plain John. John soon made it clear.

"Please, just call me John. It would be a lot easier. We're all adults, you know. So I hear you went to visit my sister in August? I bet that was a revelation after all this time. A first meeting and all that? Did it go well?"

"Oh, much better than expected actually. She is really lovely and made us so welcome."

"Grand job. I'm so pleased… for all of you. I think she loves having Charlie and Summer too now."

"Thing is, she's not called Charlie anymore. Gran suggested the name Lottie to her and she loved it. She never told us she hated Charlie, said it was a boys' name!"

"Well, I guess she's got a point. Charlie Chaplin. Charlie Drake and all that. Oh, yes, Charlie and the Chocolate Factory! He was a boy too, I believe. Charlie Bucket?"

"Yes, that's right," Jake confirmed.

They chatted together for quite some time before John showed Jake to his room. A big room overlooking a massive back garden. There was an old-fashioned wardrobe on one wall and a king size double bed with black and white striped covers. A man's room. There was also a large desk, which John thoughtfully added to help Jake with his studies. There was room for a computer and many books. Jake remembered to ask after Vera.

"Oh, she's doing okay. I visit her every day. The care home is only three miles away and it gets me out of the house. I do shopping or go to the library on the way there or the way back. I do miss her but I couldn't look after her anymore. I have not had time to feel lonely and now you are here it will help me as well as, hopefully, helping you out with a place to stay."

"It certainly does, yes. Thank you very much. We haven't talked of rent. Do you have a figure in mind?"

"Oh, dear boy, no. No rent. Just happy to help out. My kids finished uni a long time ago and have their own families and so I'm not short of a penny or two. I'm glad to help you out," John reiterated. "I'm sure you're not a rich student. Show me one that is!"

"Well, thank you again. I'd just like to say I'm very grateful. We don't have a lot of money, as you know. Dad only works in the factory and, of course, Mum's money stopped when she died so we have found it a bit of struggle. I managed to get enough together to get the car going with insurance, which is really expensive. And petrol too, of course. But at least the car was there ready to be used. At least I didn't have to find money to buy a car. And Dad had no use for it 'cos he can't drive."

"Can't drive? I didn't know that! No one ever told me that. I know Louise did the driving whenever we saw them but that was so rarely so I suppose I never noticed. By the way, well done for passing your test first time. That keeps it in the family!"

"What do you mean?" Jake was puzzled.

"Well, I passed first time, as did Jan and also Clare, our sister – you remember her? She's been gone five years now, bless her heart. Then Steven did and also Louise and that was all thanks to Jan. She took it upon herself to teach them both to drive. Her husband Geoff, your grandfather, wouldn't teach them. I think he thought it was beneath him, something like that. I don't know. Then my two passed first time too. Must be in the genes. My father and mother both drove but they never even took a driving test. It was before tests were compulsory. I think they just learned and then drove, just like that. Of course, there's more traffic on the roads these days, so the tests became compulsory. In about the mid-1930s, I believe. Then, when war broke out in 1939, no one was thinking of tests."

"I didn't know any of that."

"Stick with me, boy, and you will learn something new every day!"

"My mum always used to say that. That we should learn something new every day."

"Quite right! And did you know that your great-grandfather, my father, drove a racing car? He had his own car, which he built himself, with some help, I believe. For a businessman, he was a very good mechanic. Taught me everything I know about engines. I could teach you sometime too. Enough to service your own car; that could save you a fortune, my boy."

"That would be great, thanks a lot. I don't know much apart from where to put the petrol in and dip the oil. And you must tell me more about my great-grandparents. I never met my great-granddad because he died just before I was one year old and, with my great-grandmother, I think I only met her about three times before she died."

"She was a great character, my mum. She was diagnosed with manic depression when she was in her mid-forties. Nowadays it's a condition called bipolar. It affected the whole family but not in a good way. My father was head of the family business when my grandfather died and then, when my dad died, I became chairman. I can fill you in on all the family and more besides. We will have a great time, mark my words."

"Yes, I'm sure we will." Jake was not so sure now. Time will tell. Did he imagine it or did John like the sound of his own voice?

"I can't tell you how much I think it's nice to have another man about the house. My son left home to go to uni and never came back. He's now in his mid-forties and has only just started to have kids! At the age of forty he got married, to a lovely girl, I might add. They had to jolly well get on with it if they were going to produce any grandchildren for us. Anyway, they did get on with it mighty quickly and now they have two lovely boys. His wife is the same age as him and so lucky they found each other when they did; she's a beautiful girl. Well, woman I should say. My daughter produced boys too; there are three of them but they are somewhat older than my son's two. But none of them are as old as you. My sister started very young!"

"Yes. So I hear. Well, I'd better get myself together. I'm off to uni for my first day tomorrow and I've got stuff to sort out."

"Indeed. Freshers' week. You're going to love it at uni, I'm sure. I know I did. I usually cook supper for about 7pm but if you could just let me know when you are staying on to party; I won't mind a bit. You must make yourself right at home, dear boy, and please let me know your likes and dislikes. We're not a fussy family and don't expect others to be fussy either. You like most food?"

"Yes, I do. And thank you again for your hospitality. It's much appreciated."

Over a rather massive rump steak and chips they chatted again. John offered Jake large amounts of beer but Jake declined, wary of having to be compos mentis the next morning.

"Don't you drink, dear boy?" John asked, but when Jake looked askance he continued, "well, you don't take after your father, do you?"

"No, I don't. I do like a beer occasionally but I can't take it like he does. I like wine, though. But not in great quantities."

"Well, you should have said! I have wine! A whole cellar full, in fact. I'll get a decent claret for tomorrow night and we will quaff away. Well, I will and you can have as much or as little as you like. I meant to ask you, what subjects are you taking?" John changed the subject very smoothly.

"Biology, chemistry, science and medicine. The course is called applied anatomy."

"That's very specific. Do you want to be a doctor?"

"I do. Actually, I'd like to specialise and become a surgeon but I have to go through the whole course for becoming a doctor before I can do anything like that."

"Wonderful. Where do you get your brains from? Not from your father, methinks!"

"Maybe not but I've tried to work hard so I'd like to think it was on my own merit that I've got this far. How I hack it, we have yet to tell."

"You'll be fine, dear boy. You didn't have the best of starts when your mum was so upset and engrossed when her parents' marriage failed. I think your mum put all her energies into hating her mother and there wasn't much left for you kids."

"That all happened before I was born though!"

"I know but she kept it going all that time. It upset your gran no end that she was never able to meet you. She tried very hard but in the end she admitted defeat. She always said it was her husband she left, not her kids, albeit they were still living at home."

"But why did she leave in the first place?"

"Oh, that's an easy answer. Her husband, your grandfather, was a bastard, not to put too fine a point on it. They were far too young to get married; she was only nineteen. I think he liked the idea of being part of our family, son-in-law of a chairman of a successful family business. Small though it was. His father was a painter and decorator. Don't get me wrong, there's nothing wrong with that, but he was never going to set the world on fire. There was only a certain amount of money he was going to be able to earn. Geoff never had much ambition, a bit like your dad! He was a mechanic, a grease monkey to all intents and purposes. Nothing wrong with knowing about engines but he wasn't exactly going to rise through the ranks. So I think they struggled to bring up two children but Jan did a fine job, I have to say. She put up with a lot from him. I don't think she ever complained, not to me, anyway. She just got on with raising two fine children as best she could. There was never an escape route for her. Until Mike came along, that is. Some girls go back to their parents when there's trouble but Jan was never able to go to our parents. They more or less said "you made your bed, you lie in it!" That's because she got pregnant before she was married and in those days that was looked down on. I think he made her preggers just so she was then tied to him."

"Crikey. No one ever told me all that. Why did Gran never complain? Why didn't she go sooner?"

"Go where? She didn't have enough money to take the kids and go and live somewhere else. Like I say, our parents weren't prepared to help her out. So she was stuck. Stuck with a husband I'm not quite sure she loved. Or the love she did have soon waned. I'm convinced he loved her but it was a funny way of showing it. I think he was pretty nasty to her but there was no evidence because it would only happen behind closed doors but it's what she has confided in me since."

So the evening progressed in this vein until Jake made himself scarce and took himself off to bed fairly early to get a good start in the morning. He relished the stimulating, intellectual male conversation, something he had not really ever had. Also, he was pleased that John made the effort to ask about his studies, something his own father failed to do.

"Good luck on your first day at uni," said John to Jake the next day, just as Jake was starting off in his car.

"Thanks. I think it's mostly registration and getting to know the whereabouts of classes to start with and meeting with other students. A bit daunting really but I've been working towards this day."

"Quite. Well, good luck anyway. See you later. A word of

advice: take notes. Write down copious amounts of notes. That's what someone told me and it kept me in good stead."

Jake drove off, mindful he should arrive early on his first day. He would have to find out where to park the car and locate his meeting place.

30

Vicky and Gerry came back from their cruise full of the Caribbean and could not wait to tell their friends all about their exciting holiday.

"Shall we ask Jan around to dinner? And Lottie too? Actually, it would probably be better to be at lunchtime and then they can bring Summer. You've not met her yet; she's adorable!"

"You think all babies are adorable. I just think they all look like Winston Churchill! I bet you've offered to babysit too; you usually do," said Gerry.

"Oh, you! I have actually, but nothing has come of it as yet. I think they are enjoying getting to know one another, Lottie and Jan. I expect Jan could do with a holiday; it's the longest she has been without one." Vicky demurred.

"She went to Thailand and New Zealand last Christmas, didn't she?"

"She did, but maybe we can convince her a cruise would be good for someone on their own. Lots of eligible bachelors!" said Vicky.

"Lots of dirty old men, you mean! Rich old men with pots of money who just want a bit of arm candy!"

"Alright, alright, that's enough of that," said Vicky and changed the subject. "We could invite Giovanni and Rosa Lina along too and they could bring her father. Tino likes Jan, I'm sure of it."

"How was the cruise?" asked Jan when Vicky rang to ask her and Lottie over to lunch. "I hear the hurricane season ended almost as soon as it started and there was no damage. You were lucky. Did you enjoy it as much as you were hoping? What was the weather like? Warm?"

"If you stop talking I will tell you!" laughed Vicky. "No, actually I want to tell you face to face. Gerry and I want to ask you over for an informal lunch and bring Lottie and Summer too."

"Gosh, thanks. Are you sure? It's your turn to come to me although I haven't had any dinner parties since I've been on my own."

"Of course I'm sure. It was Gerry's idea," Vicky lied. It had been her own idea, as it usually was, but she thought it sounded better if Jan knew that Gerry had invited them. She did not mention anyone else and so Jan thought it would just be the four of them. "Come next Monday and we will tell you all about the cruise. Gerry said he thought it would be good if you went on a cruise. There were loads of women on their own there and they played bridge and danced together."

"That doesn't sound too thrilling to me." She was not convinced it was the sort of thing she would be keen on. "Think I might prefer something a bit more active."

"Are you going away at Christmas?" asked Vicky. "Last time you had such a great time. I just wondered if you were planning on going again to New Zealand or Thailand or both?"

"Not planning to, no. It's a bit late to start planning that now. I know I can always go at the last minute and I would be very welcome but with Lottie here now it's a bit up in the air.

I'm not sure if she is going to stay with me or if she is going home again. She seems adamant that she is staying here now. We get on so well, so much better than I was expecting and Summer is a real delight. She's growing so fast. Well, you will see her. Are you sure it's okay to bring her?"

"Of course. And Gerry wants to see her too, he said so." Now Jan knew Vicky was lying as she knew that Gerry did not like babies very much.

"He told me once that he thought they all looked like Winston Churchill! I had to laugh because I know exactly what he means. But actually, now she is a few months old, she has quite a lot of hair so you can tell Gerry she looks nothing like Winston 'cos he had very little hair. At least from what I remember of him. So is it a formal do? Do we have to dress up?"

"Oh, no, it's very informal, no dressing up." Vicky had in mind what she was going to wear: something she bought while in the Caribbean and a loud shirt for Gerry too. But she wanted it to be a surprise so said nothing about what clothes to wear. "We just want to tell you about our cruise and about the next one in the spring to the Far East. That's the one I'm really looking forward to."

"Any seasickness?" asked Jan.

"Oh, a little but we took your advice and took those seasickness pills and we were both fine. It did get a bit rough but every island was stunning. One island we couldn't land at because it was too rough but apart from that everything was wonderful. We met some lovely people too. One couple had the same deal we got and we are meeting them again on the next cruise! I'm telling you too much now, we will have nothing talk about. See you Monday." With that Vicky put the phone down and Jan went to tell Lottie.

"But I've got nothing to wear!" said Lottie as soon as Jan mentioned the lunch.

"Well, we had better go shopping then! Come on, we'll go now."

Jan usually hated shopping, but to buy something for her granddaughter would be far more exciting than buying clothes for herself. They took Summer along and she slept most of the time in her pram.

They bought an assortment of clothes so Lottie could choose what she would wear to lunch.

"I've never had a lunch at someone's house before," said Lottie. "Is that what you retired folk usually do?"

"Oh, yes, quite often," Jan replied. "Or otherwise it could be in the evening. I think they thought it would be easier for us to bring Summer along in the daytime. We will feed her and change her nappy before we go, keep her up until we get there and then put her down for her afternoon nap and then she should sleep through without too much trouble. We can probably put her in another room so it's quiet for her and we can take the baby monitor so we can hear her. Then we can relax."

They arrived at Vicky and Gerry's house in good time, with Summer in her carrycot.

"Just put her in the spare bedroom and leave the door open so we can hear if she cries," said Vicky to Lottie. Lottie took her up and placed the carrycot on the bed. She looked around the spare bedroom, which was beautifully decorated. It was only a small room with a single bed but the fittings and furniture had such style. She was beginning to appreciate the finer things in life, which Jan had taught her. She set up the monitor and closed the door so no noise would wake her.

"Is she okay?" Vicky asked Lottie as she came downstairs.

"I think she should sleep now. We kept her up and played with her to tire her out so she should be okay for a while. I've closed the door but put the baby monitor on so we will hear when she cries."

"Maybe I could have a cuddle when she wakes up. It's so lovely to have young people with us; we do miss our daughter and grandchildren."

"Where are they?" Lottie enquired.

"They emigrated. Some time ago now. The only time we see the grandchildren is on Skype or FaceTime. They are growing up so fast but we hope to see them early next year. Tell you all about it at lunch. Would you like a drink now?"

"Thanks. Can I have a Coke?"

"Of course you can. You go in with your gran and Gerry and I'll get it for you."

The doorbell rang and Vicky went to answer the door. It was Rosa Lina, Giovanni and Tino.

"Come in, come in," said Vicky, beckoning them in. She took their coats and led them into the sitting room. Lottie had taken a seat by the window and quietly sat there. When Jan saw the three Italians she went over to greet them.

"How lovely to see you. I didn't know you were coming! What a lovely surprise. Come and meet my granddaughter, Lottie."

Lottie stood up and shook them all by the hand and smiled demurely.

"Are you the one with the baby?' asked Rosa Lina and Lottie nodded. "Is she here? Can I see her?"

"Three questions in one, Rosa! Leave the poor girl alone," Giovanni remonstrated with Rosa Lina.

"Ah, Giovanni." Rosa Lina tapped her hand on her head as if to say, "leave me alone"! "You know I adore babies, I only want to see her. I won't touch her." Lottie beckoned to Rosa Lina to go upstairs with her.

"She sleeps very soundly so you won't disturb her." They crept into the spare bedroom and Rosa Lina looked over into the carrycot.

"Aah! Mamma mia, she is gorgeous!" whispered Rosa Lina. "Lovely fair hair. I want to kiss her but don't worry, I won't. But I might if she wakes up. Come on, I've taken up too much of your time. We will have a good afternoon with pleasant company, yes?"

"Yes." Lottie had nothing more to say. She was quite taken aback with Rosa Lina's typical Italianness. They arrived back in the sitting room and there was a Coke waiting for Lottie by the chair she occupied earlier. But, before she could get to it, the other two Italians, Tino and Giovanni, came to speak to her. Lottie had never had so much attention.

"Sorry for my wife," Giovanni began.

"Don't you go apologising for me," Rosa Lina interrupted Giovanni. "I am quite capable of doing that for myself, thank you very much!"

"As I said… my wife can be a little enthusiastic at times, especially where babies are concerned."

Jan heard all the commotion, even from the kitchen where she had been helping Vicky with the food. She decided to go and help Lottie in case she felt out of her depth. Gerry was getting drinks and came in with a tray at the same time as Jan arrived. They bumped into each other and the tray with all the drinks nearly slipped out of his hands. Tino came to the rescue as he had been looking out for when Jan would come back in the room.

"I've got it," said Tino, rescuing the tray from Gerry's hands.

"Thanks," said Gerry. "That was a near thing." He handed the drinks around and Tino went over to sit with Jan almost as soon as she sat down.

"How have you been?" Tino asked Jan tentatively.

"I've been just fine, thanks, Tino. And you? How are you? Been busy in the restaurant?"

"Oh, yes but we have missed you." Tino was careful to say "we" rather than "I" but he really meant he himself had missed her.

"Come and eat now," Vicky announced to all. No one took any notice and no one moved. Vicky nudged Gerry to start the ball in motion.

"Come on folks," Gerry cajoled each person in turn. "You can all talk later. Vicky has prepared a lovely lunch for us." His voice was in a crescendo.

They all trooped into the dining room and sat at the places where their names were placed. Vicky was not taking any chances. Jan was placed between Tino and Lottie on one side. Then Gerry, Rosa Lina and Giovanni on the opposite side of the table with Vicky at the head, nearest the kitchen.

Gerry poured the wine but, when he came to Lottie, he looked to Jan for approval.

"Lottie, would you like some wine?" Jan asked Lottie. She was well aware she might not have tried it before. "You can try it if you like, otherwise you can stick to Coke. What do you think? Would you like to try some wine?" Lottie nodded.

"I'd like to try just a little, thanks. No, I don't think I've ever had it before." She did not like to say she had tried other alcoholic drinks in the past but at least she could honestly say she had not tried wine.

Gerry poured her half a glass and whispered to her conspiratorially, "Let me know when you want a top-up!" Lottie smiled at him.

"We know you are dying to tell us all about your cruise." Rosa Lina broke the ice around the table and said what everyone else was thinking.

"Yes," said Jan. "We want to know everything and I am curious as to how you missed the hurricane season. You were very lucky."

"Well," started Gerry, before Vicky could get a word in. "That wasn't strictly true. We definitely saw the damage on some of the islands that Hurricane Isobel had caused. One or two were completely destroyed, or so it appeared to us but apparently they rebuild everything quite quickly. It's amazing how some islands are affected and not others. It was a period of consternation for us, knowing that we could have been caught up in a hurricane and, of course, some people don't know why they are called after a woman's name."

"Are they?" questioned Rosa Lina.

"Oh, yes, for obvious reasons." Gerry waited for effect before he told them the reason why hurricanes are named after women. Lottie for one had pricked up her ears because she did not know why and so Gerry put them at their ease and enjoyed telling them.

"It's because woman are so similar to hurricanes – stormy and unpredictable! Ha ha! Actually, they aren't only called after women these days but for about thirty years they used to be. Anyway, over to you, my dear, you can give them the details of our cruise."

Vicky was in her element and gave them all an account of their cruise from start to finish, with Gerry interjecting at appropriate moments. By the time they ended everyone had eaten their food. Apart from Vicky as she had become so engrossed with the tales of onboard shenanigans she almost forgot to put her fork in her mouth.

"We've never had such fun. Have we, Gez?" She had only just started to use this name but Gerry was not too pleased.

"Some Yanks aboard the cruise called me this and now she's calling me this stupid nickname all the time. It's driving me insane," said Gerry, fuming.

"So, next year," began Vicky again, once she finished her own food and ignoring everything Gerry was saying against her. "We are going to the Far East, a cruise around Singapore, which is where it begins. We have to fly there, of course. We sail all up the coast of Thailand and Malaysia then over to Indonesia and then Bali. We finish up in Papua New Guinea but we don't come home then!" Vicky waited for effect to make sure everyone knew what she meant.

"Oh?" said Jan, curious. "Where are you going after that?"

"Well, Gez wanted to come straight home then but I've persuaded him that we should go and visit our daughter and family in Melbourne after the cruise. After all, we are over halfway there and it would be a shame not to go and see them. We haven't seen them for ages, well, not in the flesh. We've FaceTimed them and seen them growing up but what an opportunity to see them properly, don't you think?"

"That's just the sort of thing Mike and I used to do! Whilst we were the other side of the world we might as well visit other places while we were there," said Jan, amused.

"Where do you think I got the idea from? You were always saying you were going here, there and everywhere and I was always so envious," said Vicky. Gerry looked on, glowering. Jan had the idea that he was not too pleased with Vicky. Or maybe he was not too pleased with her. She knew from years ago, when Mike and she went on holiday, Vicky would always remark to him that they should have better holidays. He put her off at the time, saying they would do so when he retired. Vicky never forgot his promise and now she was going to reap the rewards as he recently retired.

Tino took the opportunity to speak to Jan. They had hardly been able to speak more than a few words to each other with Vicky and Gerry hogging the conversation.

"Where in the world is your favourite place?" asked Tino.

"There are so many places, I don't think I have a definite favourite. When Mike first retired we went away for three months at a time. We pretty much did all of Australia and New Zealand over the course of about ten years, interspersed with other places, of course. We thought at the time that we would leave touring Europe until we got old so we concentrated on the Far East, Africa and the Americas. We've been to China, Japan, Malaysia, Thailand, India, South Africa, Peru, Chile, Canada. Loved Canada. The USA. Mike and I met in the USA." Tino stopped her there.

"You met him in America?" he enquired. "But I thought he was English?"

"He was! We were both on the same trip. I was with my husband and he was with his second wife. We exchanged addresses and phone numbers and he contacted me when we got home. He lived in Surrey and I lived in Devon. It's a long story; I don't want to bore you with it all now."

"I'd like to hear all about it," Lottie piped up. She had been quietly eating her meal and listening to the adult conversation but did not feel it her right to intervene.

"I'll tell you all about it one day, Lottie," Jan promised.

Vicky was starting to get annoyed that she might be being upstaged.

"Who's for pudding?" Vicky looked around to see who would be interested in one of her delicious home-made puddings. "I've got tiramisu, especially for the Italians, but I don't suppose it's as good as they make themselves! Ha ha." Vicky was the only one to get her own joke. "Or a family favourite, or at least one of Gez's faves, pineapple upside-down pudding."

Vicky looked around the table for affirmation that that was what was on offer and expected to get some sort of reply. Everyone looked a bit blank, going from exotic holidays and then being brought down to earth with a pudding.

"Lottie?" Vicky looked straight at Lottie. "I will start with the youngest. Oh no! I should have started with Summer. Oh well, she's not here in this room so I will start with you, Lottie. What would you like?" Lottie was a little taken aback. She wanted to hear more of her gran's exploits abroad.

"Oh, er, some pineapple upside-down, please." Vicky started attacking the pineapple pudding and at the same time asking the others what they would like.

"Rosa Lina, what about you?"

"I'd like some of the same if that's okay with you. I've had enough of Italian food. I'll have some typical English pudding. It's funny, isn't it? We Italians are not known for our desserts and yet people always assume we do because we do such brilliant ice cream I suppose. But we would normally have ice cream as a daytime snack rather than after a main meal. Do you know tiramisu was only invented in about the 1960s and sometimes it is a cake rather than a dessert, or pudding, as you English like to say. Some used to say it had aphrodisiac effects and it was served up to customers in brothels in Treviso."

"You're a fountain of knowledge, Rosa Lina. You're very clever," said an impressed Gerry. "Where is Treviso?"

"Oh, it's quite near Venice, in the north." Rosa Lina appreciated Gerry's remark.

"I'd like to go to Venice." Lottie finally found the courage to interject in the conversation. "It's the one place that sounds so romantic, all those gondolas and men in striped jerseys and flat hats singing as they push people along." Lottie had seen a programme on Venice quite recently and was glad to be able to add something to the conversation.

"They're called boaters," said Vicky, slightly sarcastically, wondering when the talk was going to get back to her Far East cruise and all that that entailed. She had not finished what she wanted to tell them.

"What, the hats or the men?" laughed Gerry. "I should say both, wouldn't you?" His pointed remark was to his wife.

"You're quite right, Lottie." This was Giovanni now, adding his twopenn'orth. "Although I have to say it is not that romantic there. The smell can be horrendous in the summer. Imagine all the tourists and all that they do! You can imagine where that goes! With all their rubbish too, that has to be dealt with. Phew, the pong!" He held his nose to show just what a smell it could be like.

Everyone laughed and Vicky became even more cross.

The Italians all chose the pineapple upside-down pudding and there was not enough left for Gerry. She decided that he would have to have the tiramisu and like it or lump it. She knew he did not really like it but she put it in front of him anyway, without asking him first. Then she helped herself to a small bowl of the same.

"As I said, we end up in Papua New Guinea where we are treated to a banquet in Port Moresby, the capital. I'm so looking forward to it. From there we fly straight down to Melbourne. We will be away a whole month," Vicky said, proudly.

"Papua New Guineans are cannibals, aren't they?" asked Tino.

"Of course, they're not!" said Vicky, indignantly.

"Well, they were the last time I heard about them. It's quite dangerous there too. Murders and sex assaults on tourists. Organised crime by gangs and robbery, so I've heard too."

"What utter nonsense! You're just trying to frighten me. I am your hostess and you're trying to get one up on me," cried Vicky. "Gerry, come to my aid, will you?"

"I'm sorry, Vicky," Tino placated Vicky. "I really am, but you need to look it up on the internet. I'm not kidding you. It is a very dangerous place."

"Have you been there, Gran?" Lottie interjected to try and keep the peace.

"I've not been there, no. I don't think it's on my bucket

list either. We came across cannibalism on Easter Island. But never mind about me," Jan said quickly, aware that her friend might get cross again. "Let's listen to what Vicky has to say. So you get down to Melbourne at about the end of March? It's a lovely city and that's a nice time to be there, weatherwise."

"I know you've been there," said Tino to Jan. "You told me all about going to the Australian Open tennis several times."

"I'd like to learn to play tennis," said Lottie to anyone caring to listen. "I love watching it, it was my mum's favourite sport and she tried to teach me once but I think I wasn't really interested at the time."

"Okay, I'll teach you," said Jan quickly to Lottie and then back to Vicky for fear of being lynched by her for people asking her questions. "Vicky, how are all the family over there? It's your daughter and son-in-law, isn't it? And two boys?"

Vicky started to get enthusiastic again when the conversation reverted back to her.

"Oh, yes, my daughter Catherine and her boys, Russell and Michael, oh and not forgetting my son-in-law, David. They absolutely love it there, love the outdoor life. I'd love to live there myself but Gezza won't budge."

"They wouldn't have us, dear," said Gerry. "Points and all that. You need points to emigrate to Oz and we don't have any."

"But they'd take us because we have family there, surely."

"Nope, don't think so. I'm an Englishman through and through and never want to go anywhere else to live. You'll have to kill me off first and then you can go. You can cast away on a ship and end up no-one-knows-where!"

To which they all laughed. Vicky decided to ignore Gerry's remarks and move on.

"Coffee anyone?" Vicky offered her assembled lunch party. They all nodded and Vicky trooped to the kitchen. Gerry took the opportunity, while she was out of the room, to put his side of the story.

"I wasn't keen on that cruise, between you and me," he said conspiratorially. He looked each person straight in the eye to make sure what he was saying was not going to go any further and then continued. "Lovely ship, mind you, but it was all so regimented. Breakfast between 7 and 10am, lunch between 12.30 and 2pm and then dinner between 7 and 9.30pm. Lots of snacks in-between. And tea, as if you needed that as well, was at 4pm sharp! The drinks were really expensive. No chance of getting drunk on board ship; it would cost a fortune! And the photos they take at every opportunity of everyone and anyone in all sorts of different places, poses and positions! At dinner, out on excursions, in the bar or at the most inappropriate moments! You name it and the photographer was there, almost as if he was in hiding ready to jump out when you least expected. And don't get me started on those extortionate excursions! We only did one or two. We could only afford one or two!"

"Could only afford one or two what, dear?" asked Vicky as she came in with coffee for everyone. She handed them out one by one, still awaiting a reply. Gerry could not think of a lie so came clean on the excursions part of his story.

"We only had one or two excursions because they were so dear. Not that they were that brilliant either. They mostly just took us around the island and told us about the history. We particularly wanted to do Barbados and St Lucia but with the others we just took ourselves off and wandered around on our own. We did meet another couple who actually are going to be on our next cruise."

"Yes, that'll be nice to see them again. They live in Scotland so we are not likely see them here. They could be our holiday buddies." With that remark there were one or two exchanged glances but nothing was said.

Summer started crying upstairs and Lottie jumped up. She left her coffee and went to the aid of her baby. She had had quite enough of holidays and cruises. She turned off the baby monitor, which was probably not needed with Summer crying so loudly.

"Crikey, she's keen," Gerry remarked.

"She's a very good mum." Jan jumped to Lottie's defence.

"I can see she is," Vicky added. "I, for one, can't wait to see Summer again properly. She's been so good to stay asleep for all this time while we've been making such a noise down here."

"You speak for yourself," said Gerry. "It's you who has hogged the conversation; no one else has been able to get a word in edgeways!"

"Oh, that's not fair." Vicky stormed out of the room and was met by Lottie, carrying Summer down the stairs, and then Vicky's heart melted. "Oh, she's just gorgeous. Can I hold her?"

"She's a bit wet. Can I just change her first and then you can feed her if you like?" said Lottie.

"Oh, I'd love to." Vicky was overwhelmed with delight at that suggestion. She showed Lottie to the kitchen, where she could change Summer's nappy, and showed her where everything was that she might need. "I'll come back in a minute."

Rosa Lina was in the middle of saying to her men that they ought to be going. It was their one day off and they needed to prepare for the next day. Tino was worried because he had hardly said anything to Jan and he had had thoughts earlier of all the things he wanted to say to her. He decided to ask for her phone number. She gladly gave it to him.

"I will ring you," said Tino, making his hand look like a telephone. Jan laughed and put her thumbs up. With that the Italians thanked their hosts and called goodbye to Lottie, who was still busy in the kitchen.

"She's ready now," Lottie said to Vicky. Vicky jumped up and took Summer with ease, took the bottle and sat down with her.

"She was hungry!" Vicky said after ten minutes of bottle feeding. She put her up against her shoulder and rubbed her back. "This is what I missed out on with my grandkids."

"Me too," said Jan sadly.

31

"What's for tea... er, I mean supper?" Dean asked Daisy. "God, if your mother caught me calling it tea, I would be for the high jump! It was always tea when I was at home and then your mother said tea was a cup of tea and a slice of cake at 4pm. The evening meal is supper. Or dinner. I always thought dinner was at midday, like school dinners." Dean continued to mumble. "I was so confused but I just went along with whatever she wanted to call it. It wasn't so important to me but my mum still calls it tea but we have to call it supper. What did I ask you? Oh, yes, what are we eating tonight?"

"Spag bol," Daisy responded, knowing the reply she would get so she switched off listening but she was ready with a quick retort.

"Oh, not again! That's what Jake kept making for us! I think I shall call it spag bog in future, 'cos that's the place it should be, in the bog!"

"If you don't like it, you know what the answer is. Cook something yourself. You could have a signature dish all of your own. What is it likely to be? Fish and chips? Anyway, we agreed that I would do most of the cooking but not all of it and we would share the housework. Why should I do everything?"

"Because, young lady, I've been hard at work all day and need a good solid meal to come home to."

"That was when you had a wife! I'm not your wife so that excludes that argument. And, anyway, I've been at school all day. It's not as if I've been lazing around doing nothing!" Daisy was indignant but she was learning to cope with her father and his lazy ways.

"No need to get on your high horse. I pull my weight, you know. And there's nothing wrong with good old fish and chips!"

"There's no good arguing with you. Let's just agree to disagree." Daisy harrumphed.

They muddled through week by week until it was time to talk about Daisy's birthday and, soon afterwards, Jake's homecoming and then Christmas. Daisy always loved Christmas but last year's was marred with her mother's demise, so not much fuss was made of her birthday or Christmas. This time Charlotte might be missing, although Daisy was ever hopeful that she would come home. She thought about asking Uncle Steven and Auntie Cheryl and her cousins if they would like to come over on Christmas Day for lunch. She would run it past Jake first, rather than her father.

On Daisy's thirteenth birthday, she woke up to find an envelope from her father with £20 inside, no card. It was no more than she expected but at least he had remembered. She did not think he could possibly forget as she had reminded him enough times, of the day it was and her age.

The doorbell rang and the florist handed her a large bouquet of flowers.

"They're from Gran and Charlie, oops... I mean Lottie," said Daisy to nobody in particular as her father had already left for work. She was reading the card on the flowers out loud. "I must ring them later to thank them."

The postman did not arrive until after she had left for school. The bus to the school left from the bus stop only a road away and it took her three minutes to walk. If she was a little late she could see it coming from the road beyond so by that time she knew she had to run.

"Happy birthday!" cooed all her friends on the bus. Then her best friend, Lucy, came over to give her a little present.

"It's not much, but it's something I know you will like."

"Oh, thank you," said Daisy, ripping the paper off her gift. It was an ornament of a unicorn with pink wings and a purple horn. "But I think I might have grown out of these now I'm thirteen!" She waited to see Lucy's face drop. "I'm kidding, I love it, but don't tell anyone!"

By the time Daisy arrived home from school she saw that the postman had delivered four cards for her. She recognised one by the writing which she opened first by ripping the envelope. It was from Granny Kath. There was a pretty card with flowers on the front and cash inside, in which she was more interested. It was a £20 note. She made a mental note to thank her. Louise had instilled into Daisy and her siblings that they must always acknowledge and thank everyone for anything that was given to them. It used to be "thank you" letters but as time went on it ended up as emails or texts or even a phone call but, as long as they thanked the person, Louise was happy. She could not bear it whenever she gave people presents and she never received any sort of acknowledgement. She thought that was the height of rudeness.

"Thank you, Granny Kath, for my birthday present," said Daisy as soon as she had opened her other envelopes. She thought she would get it over with and a phone call might be more personal. The other envelopes and cards were from

Uncle Steven and Auntie Cheryl with a gift voucher, one from Jake and one from Uncle John. He did not usually remember but as Jake was there to remind him he thought he had better send Daisy a card. He also slipped in a £20 note. The final one, from Jake himself, with no money but just promising a little something extra at Christmas. She knew he might not have any spare cash and quite understood. She set about sending texts to everyone else apart from Uncle John. She thought she had better send a little "thank you" note to him.

"There, that's all that done and out of the way. You would be pleased with me, Mum." Daisy said to herself but also as a message to her mother.

Dean came home early, missing out on a drink from the pub and suggested to Daisy that she might not want to cook tonight. He was going to treat her to fish and chips from the chippie for her birthday.

"Oh, thanks, Dad. And thanks for the money too," she said and went to put her arms around his neck. "Yes, fish and chips was just what I was thinking. Who's going to fetch them? I've got a lot of homework!"

"Oh, okay, I've got the message. I'll go and fetch them."

Dean went straight out and brought back fish and chips for them both. The local shops were easily walkable within five minutes and Dean enjoyed the walk.

"I'm going out later. Will you be okay?" Dean asked Daisy. "I expect you'll be busy with your homework, won't you? You can watch TV after your homework, as a special treat. It is your birthday, after all!"

"You go out, Dad, I know you're itching to have a drink." Daisy was aware that her father would pop out to the pub after she went to bed most nights. Even though it was her birthday, it was not really a very special day, at least she did not feel it to be. Just another day, she thought to herself, just like last year. She was starting to feel rather lonely. *What could she do to pep herself up a little?* she wondered. *Who could she ask?* She thought of her best friend, Lucy.

"Hi, Luce. What are you doing tonight?" Daisy asked her friend.

"Not much, just hanging out. Do you fancy doing something? What trouble can we get up to? Well, it is your birthday!" said Lucy.

"I know and I'm fed up. Dad's gone out."

"Come over here and we can dress up and try on my sister's make-up. She won't mind, she's got loads. I'll give you a makeover." Lucy loved make-up and wanted to experiment on her friend.

"That sounds like a plan, I'll be over in ten minutes. My homework can wait till the weekend."

Daisy changed into her semi-best skirt and top and arrived at Lucy's house in double-quick time.

"Happy birthday," said Lucy's mum as she opened the front door. Lucy rushed to the door but was just too late to open it to Daisy.

"Thanks, Mum, I'll get this." Lucy glared at her mother. "Is Tina in?"

"I don't think so, why?"

Lucy did not want her sister knowing she was going to borrow her make-up so she was not going to tell her mother.

"Just wondered," she said to her mother and then to Daisy. "Come on upstairs."

They rushed up to Lucy's bedroom and shut the door.

"I'll just go and get the make-up from Tina's room. Have a look through those clothes in that box, see if there's anything interesting you want to dress up in. I'm going to make you look beautiful, just you see if I don't!" Lucy crept to her sister's bedroom and picked up the make-up she thought they would need, came back to her bedroom and closed the door again. Lucy's mum stayed downstairs and heard lots of giggles coming from Lucy's room. Just teenage girls enjoying themselves, she thought.

"Hi, Dean, me ol' china, me ol' mate, how're you doin'? Pint, is it?" said Keith as he fetched a pint glass from the shelf above the optics like a robot; he was so used to the same actions. He was in a particularly good mood as he had had a win on the midweek races. "This one is on me, mate."

"Oh, I'll take that, thank you very much. To what do we owe the honour of this kind gesture?" Dean was surprised as he thought it was probably the first ever pint that anyone had ever bought for him. He was used to drinking alone and preferred it that way.

"I won a hundred and ten quid on the gee-gees! Mind you, it was on the cards that I had to win one day. This must be my lucky day. You're not usually in this early, not counting after work, of course."

"It's my daughter's birthday…"

"So you thought you'd treat her and have a drink with me? Get out of her hair? She must really thank you. I'm assuming it's the daughter that is at home with you? Not the daughter you…"

"No, not that one!" Dean cut Keith short. "I gave her fish and chips to save her cooking tonight."

"My, that was kind of you!" Keith laughed.

"I know, I'm all heart." Dean took Keith's remark seriously rather than the sarcasm that was meant.

"When will your other daughters come home to you?" Keith made an emphasis on the plural of daughters. "Or should I say daughter and granddaughter?" Keith liked to make trouble whenever he could, but only partly in jest. He laughed out loud.

"Ssh, will you? I don't want to broadcast about you-know-who. You said my secret was safe with you."

"It is. I promised, didn't I?" Keith went on to serve other customers and Dean went to sit at "his" table, on his own as usual. He stayed there all evening, just going up to the bar for more beers and the occasional chaser. Several beers later he went to stand up but stumbled over a chair. Keith took the decision not to serve him any more drink.

"Think you've had enough, mate!" said Keith to Dean.

"Just one for the road?"

"Nah, I don't think so, it looks like you've had enough, mate. Are you able to get home okay?"

"Of course. Are you sure I can't have another?"

"Sorry, mate, just closing up now. D'you want a lift home? Fred at the end of the bar came in for a swift half ten minutes ago and he's going your way."

"No, I'll be okay." Dean did not like to impose on anyone, especially if they were strangers. He promptly tripped up as he turned to go towards the door. Tripped by his own feet and ignominiously fell to the floor. He looked around to see if anyone noticed and got up on his knees and then his feet. He felt a little dizzy but decided to ignore this and walked rather unsteadily towards the door. Keith watched him and decided he would be okay.

Daisy had been back for about an hour before Dean rolled in the front door, making more noise than he expected. She had had a lovely evening with Lucy and was already in bed with the light off.

Dean took off his shoes, put them on the stairs and tiptoed in his socks to the kitchen to fetch a lager from the fridge. He put on the television and promptly fell asleep until the commercials started, more noisily than the programme, which woke him up. He switched everything off and decided it was time for bed.

He went upstairs, up two, back one, until he finally made it to the top. Slightly disorientated, he crept into Daisy's darkened room and fell onto her bed.

"Dad! What are you doing?"

"Ssh, it's fine." He started to drunkenly stroke her hair and let his hands fall to her tiny buds of newly forming breasts. Daisy jumped out of bed and put the light on. She did not like what she saw, her father sprawled on her bed with his trousers wet around the crotch area.

"You had better not have wet my bed!" Daisy shouted at him. "Go on, get out."

"Don't be like that, Dais. I only want a cuddle. Come on…"

"NO!" Daisy shouted again. "Get out of my room." She tried to help him up but he was like a dead weight. Eventually, with persistence, she managed to get him to her door and pushed him out of her room. She was shaking with rage. What a birthday this turned out to be, she thought.

Dean staggered to his own room but could not make it as far as the bed. He felt awful so made his way to the en suite just before puking all over the floor. He felt a little better and went to his bed and, still fully clothed, he dropped off to sleep. In the night he desperately needed to go to the toilet and, without putting any lights on, stepped into the en suite and slipped. He knocked himself out momentarily on the toilet. When he came around he wondered where he was. What was all this sticky stuff he had his hand in? *Was it blood?* he wondered. He got up and put the light on to see the mess all over the floor and realised it wasn't blood on his hands but vomit.

"Maybe the fish and chips were off," he said to himself. "Who's going to clear up this mess?" Knowing in his heart of hearts that it was going to have to be him. "God, I feel awful."

Next morning Daisy got up to ready herself for school. *Should she go and see if her dad was alright?* she wondered. She was still fuming with him for coming into her room so she decided not to wake him for work.

As she slammed the front door, Dean woke up. He had an almighty headache and wondered what on earth happened the night before. When he saw the mess in the bathroom he remembered some but not all. He cleared up the mess of vomit and took some paracetamols to alleviate the headache. He went downstairs and was surprised that Daisy had already left for school. Then he looked at the time and decided not to go in to work. He rang in to say he was not feeling very well and he would make up the time either later or next day. As it was flexitime, he could easily make up the time without loss of wages.

Daisy decided to ignore what had happened and was not sure even if her father remembered what had happened. She knew he had probably had too much to drink but she had never seen him so wasted as the night before. A birthday to remember? Probably, but not for the right reasons.

32

Jake was making good progress at university and was happy with how he was managing to keep up in the classes and lectures. It was just over a year ago that his mother had died when he had let go of his studies to cope with the backlash of the family's loss. John helped him tremendously too, with the uncertainty of being away from home for the first time. John remembered how he had coped with it himself and the mistakes he made. He was determined that Jake would be able to learn from his mistakes. Safe to say, they got on as well as any father and son might. The age difference did not matter; in fact, John relished the male company, although he had to keep up with modernity, to which he found he coped quite well under the circumstances. He had taught himself about the technology of the age and felt he could hold his own.

Christmas was mentioned in passing but neither man knew what the other was thinking. It was going to be odd for them both but more for John as he would be on his own now Vera was in the care home.

"What are you doing for Christmas, John?" asked Jake one day out of the blue. It had been on his mind that he might ask

John to spend Christmas with him and his family in Devon rather than be on his own. Christmas was over six weeks away but Jake was always a planner.

"Oh, I don't know, I haven't really thought about it. Vera will be well cared for so I hadn't thought much about myself. I don't know if I shall see my kids or the grandchildren. My son usually goes to his wife's mother and my daughter, I don't know, we haven't discussed it. They don't usually come home anymore for Christmas. I think they have other fish to fry."

"I haven't asked my dad yet but I was wondering if you would like to come and spend it with us," asked Jake, kindly.

"That's very kind of you, dear boy. Can I give it some thought? I'll get back to you on that. Do you need to ask your father in the meantime just in case I agree to it but then he says no. What do you think?" John always thought things through and reasoned things out.

"Good idea. I'll ask him. I don't know if Lottie will be there too. Maybe she will feel she wants to come home but she might be torn with staying with Gran too. Or maybe Dad might say no to her coming home."

"Too many ifs and buts, if you ask me!" John demurred.

Jake texted Daisy first to see what she thought about John coming for Christmas. She texted back to say, "The more the merrier." Jake texted again to say could she ask Dad? Then he waited for a reply but there was none for twenty-four hours. Then she texted back to say, "Dad says if he must! Whatever that means." Jake left it at that for the time being.

John came off the phone after speaking to Jan.

"My sister, your grandmother, has just asked me to come for Christmas! I can't believe I've got all these invitations. Never been so popular!" John laughed.

"Well, I guess we don't want you to have to spend Christmas all on your own. You never have and you might be a bit lonely on your own." Jake was empathetic to John's predicament.

"Oh, now I have a decision to make. I think I will sleep on it. No hurry for a reply is there?"

"None at all. You have to make the right decision so you must take your time."

Dean and Daisy were still muddling through with their household tasks. Jake rang occasionally to see how they were getting on and to offer advice.

"Did Uncle John decide to come for Christmas? If he is, then we need to get extra food in and we will need some help. Well, you can cook the turkey and I can do the veg and I expect Dad will help."

"All we need is a turkey about the same size as before, if Charlie's not coming." Jake was totting up in his head everything that would be involved with Christmas.

"Do you mean Lottie?" asked Daisy.

"Yes, I mean Lottie. I can't get used to calling her that, though. Have you heard from her lately?"

"We text each other quite regularly, why?"

"Well, we need to know if she's coming back home."

"Don't you think that's up to Dad? If he says 'no', then she doesn't have an option. I'll speak to her anyway to see the lie of the land. I do think she's as happy there as she has been for ages. If she sounds like she wants to come home, then I'll approach Dad if I can catch him in a sober moment!"

"Is he still boozing a lot?"

"Every night! He comes home from work stinking of beer. He has his meal, which, by the way, I always seem to be lumbered with cooking! Then he goes out to the pub. I hardly ever hear him come home." Daisy did not want to bother Jake by telling him about the time Dean came into her bedroom completely wasted. She had been worried he was going to do it again and wondered if she would be able to stop him. He was obviously a lot bigger and stronger than her. It had been playing on her mind recently but to tell Jake about it would only worry him when he had his studies on which to concentrate.

"What am I supposed to do? I can't do anything from here. I'll have a word with him at Christmas, man to man."

"Yes, you do that," said Daisy. As an afterthought she added, "Do you think we should invite Uncle Steven and Auntie Cheryl and the girls for Christmas? We went over to them last Christmas?"

"We went there to tea, if you remember. Yes, we can invite them to tea but not for Christmas lunch, I don't think I can cope with cooking for that many. I've seen a new recipe for a Christmas cake and I want to try it out. So, yes, invite them to tea."

"We mustn't forget Granny Kath but I expect Dad's already done that. He's been to see her more often lately, since she's not been too well."

"Oh, I didn't know that. Hope she's okay. Send her my love when you see her and make sure Dad has asked her for Christmas, like last year, although I don't suppose she will want to stay as long as she did last year."

John eventually made his decision regarding Christmas. He would see Vera on Christmas Eve but she had begun not to know him when he visited. His visits were not every day like they were when she first arrived at the care home. He would go every other day and then two or three times a week but every time was very strained and he began dreading visiting. He noticed a slight decline in her demeanour every time he saw her.

He planned to spend two nights, Christmas Eve and Christmas Day, with Dean, Daisy and Jake, then he would make the journey on Boxing Day to spend two nights with Jan, Lottie and Summer. He was very grateful for the offers. He made sure that everyone was going to enjoy their Christmas and went shopping in readiness, well before time. He bought presents for all and he thought that, even if he did not receive presents in return, that would be quite okay. What did a man of his age need? Nothing, he decided. This was going to be one of the best Christmases he would have spent in quite some time. He loved company but he would never put pressure on his own grown-up children and their respective families to spend it with their aging father anymore.

"I do miss you at the restaurant, Jan," said Tino on the telephone. He had summoned up the courage to ring her but he was a man of few words. He preferred to have eye-to-eye contact and found it difficult speaking on the telephone.

"Well, I miss it too." Jan was careful that she said she missed "it" rather than "him". She liked Tino but never thought anything serious was going to come of it. The conversation was very stilted and Tino, although he wanted to, decided he would wait to ask Jan out on a date. Small talk ensued and Tino told her of people who had come into the restaurant and Jan told him what Summer and Lottie had been up to.

Tino wondered when would be a good time to ask Jan out but his daughter's words to wait and see were still ringing in his ears. He was always afraid of his daughter and her high moral views.

"Why don't you want to see Tino?" asked Lottie innocently, after Jan had had the conversation with Tino on the telephone.

"I do, but I'm afraid that he probably wants more than I do. I like him as a friend."

"Go on, you could have fooled me! You fancy the pants off him!"

"Lottie!" Jan was aghast at the thought of what Lottie meant. "We are both a bit long in the tooth to start jumping in and out of bed at the merest opportunity."

"Well, I can tell he fancies the pants off you!" Lottie would not be stopped.

"Let him. I mean…" Jan stopped what she was about to say.

"Hah! That means you want to too!"

"Christmas," Jan announced out of the blue, desperate to change the subject. "Are you going to stop here for Christmas or do you want to go back to Devon?"

"This is my home now, our home." Lottie was careful to include Summer in everything on which she made a decision.

"Okay, and you know John is coming on Boxing Day for two nights?"

"Yes, that will be nice to see him and good for him too, to be with company rather than be stuck on his own. I know he is going to stay two nights with Dad and Jake and Daisy too before he comes here. Are we going to have Tino here too?" Lottie tried to get the conversation back to Tino.

"I expect he will want to spend it with his family, with his daughter and son-in-law. What I thought might be an idea was to have Gerry and Vicky over for Christmas Day lunch or Christmas Eve if they prefer. I know how much she's missing her family and they are on their own so that would be nice. I know she will make a fuss of Summer but you don't mind, do you?"

"I think that's a very good idea. I'm looking forward to it and I will help you as much as I can."

"I appreciate that, thank you."

John arrived at Dean's house at teatime on Christmas Eve.

"You're just in time for a drink," said Dean to John.

"I think he means a cup of tea," Jake interjected and welcomed John inside. "Daisy has put the kettle on." Dean looked a little disappointed but let it go.

"I've got bags in the car so I'll just bring them in." John went back to his car and brought in two huge carrier bags.

"We've got food," said Dean, as John dropped the bags into the hall and went back to fetch a small suitcase.

"I expect you have but I've got bags of goodies." John opened one of the carrier bags and brought out two bottles of claret and three of Sauvignon Blanc and gave them to Dean. Then John looked into the other carrier bag and took out crackers, dates, nuts and satsumas, plus chocolate boxes of differing sizes. He gave them all to Jake, who in turn put them in the kitchen. "The satsumas are a throwback from when we were at home with our parents. Our mother would always put a satsuma and a Brazil nut at the bottom of our Santa stockings but obviously I'm not pretending to be Father Christmas. Just put them in the fruit bowl and we can help ourselves. I've got something else in here." John pulled out three presents, all beautifully wrapped. Jake took them and put them under the tree.

"That's very kind of you, John," said Jake. "We asked you so we would be able to repay you for having me to stay. It really is incredibly kind of you and I've really enjoyed myself with you. So, from me to you, many thanks."

"And long may it continue! I've loved having you. It has smoothed the way since I had to put Vera into the care home."

"Shall we go to the late service at the church tonight?" asked Daisy, knowing her remark was going to fall on deaf ears and decided against it herself.

"I think not," said Dean, defiantly. "It will take up too much drinking time! In fact, it must be time for a beer. John, would you like a beer?"

"Ah, how could I possibly say no to a beer with you, Dean? That's very kind, thanks."

Dean took John into the sitting room after fetching two lagers from the fridge.

"I should have remembered you like beer, Dean. I should have brought some, never thought." John remonstrated with himself for forgetting to bring beer.

"When are you going to speak to Dad, Jake?" asked Daisy while they were preparing vegetables in the kitchen.

"Don't worry. I will, but not now. I shall monitor him over Christmas and see how it goes."

"Well, make sure you do it before you go back to uni."

"I will, I promise." Jake made a mental note of his promise.

A decision was made that they were going to push the boat out and would invite not only Granny Kath but also Uncle Steven and Auntie Cheryl, together with Milly and Poppy, to Christmas Day lunch as well as tea. The invitations were welcomed and so extra food was bought and prepared.

Dean's mother, Kath, arrived extra early on Christmas Day, to help out with the work in the kitchen. This year she was not prepared to stay away from her home after last year's debacle when she got home. The police reckoned it had been a rough sleeper who had broken into her house and slept in her bed. She had had to dispose of everything and buy a new bed. It had traumatised her for months.

"Merry Christmas, dear," said Kath to her son as he opened the door to her and gave her a peck on the cheek. "Merry Christmas, everyone," she called out to the whole household.

"Merry Christmas." Calls came out from the kitchen area, where Kath rolled up her sleeves and began to get to work.

Uncle Steven and his family arrived at the appointed time, soon after Granny Kath. Dean had taken on the responsibility of opening the front door and also looking after John and making sure that everyone had enough to drink. Including himself.

"Welcome. Merry Christmas. Come in," Dean said to the extended family, already with drink in hand.

"Merry Christmas, everyone," Steven and Cheryl called out.

Steven and Cheryl came bearing gifts for everyone. It was Poppy's job to put them under the tree. Dean took Steven aside, into the sitting room where John had taken an easy chair. He rose up to welcome Steven, while Dean put a can in his hand. The three of them made themselves comfortable, while Cheryl took the girls into the kitchen to see what needed to be done.

"It's all under control, thanks," said Jake. "Granny Kath came early and has been a tremendous help."

They had brought in the garden table to make an extension to the dining table and garden chairs to accommodate everyone. Daisy found tablecloths to cover. They were not very festive but she thought they would do.

Jake expertly carved the turkey, much to the surprise of his father.

"I see you remember everything I taught you," said John. John very often would cook a joint on a Sunday and he had showed Jake how to sharpen a carving knife to get the best result.

Jake smiled as he served up a beautifully cooked Christmas lunch. He had taken on the bulk of the work a few days beforehand, with Daisy as his helper and then Granny Kath on the day. They all tucked in to a delicious lunch and there was plenty for all.

Word soon turned to the absence of Charlotte.

"Have you heard from Charlie?" asked Milly.

"I got a text from her wishing us happy Christmas," said Daisy. "She is Lottie now. Apparently she hated us calling her Charlie so Gran suggested Lottie and she loved it."

"She told us she didn't like Charlie so we called her Charlotte. I wish she would make up her mind! So is she still staying with our grandma?" Milly was not going to let the matter drop. She was not happy when Charlotte stayed with them but she was still interested in how her cousin was coping. "And how is Summer?"

"They are all doing as well as can be expected, thanks." Dean tried to put an end to the conversation. "Who needs to have their glass filled?"

Cheryl had thought about her mother-in-law and wondered if now might be a good time to ask Steven if he was going to make it up with his mother, after all these years. She knew it would be like stirring up a hornet's nest but she had felt strongly lately that Steven was missing out on something. She felt that if she brought it up now, it would be difficult for Steven to dismiss it out of hand. *Here goes*, she thought, with fingers crossed.

"Now the subject of your mother has come up, do you think it would be a good idea to go and see her again, Steven? Last time was a disaster I know, but you haven't mentioned her since then."

Thoughts of the last time he saw his mother came to the fore of Steven's mind and the death of his sister in such awful circumstances. He carried on eating his turkey meal and did not answer at first. He was mulling over in his mind how he was going to reply. Meanwhile, John decided to join in the conversation. After all, it was his sister they were talking about and he wanted everyone to know what he thought about the situation.

"I know my sister would welcome seeing you again, Steven. You are her son, after all is said and done. Hasn't too much water gone under the bridge? It should be time to draw a line in the sand. Life's too short. I know, I know, too many clichés!" John laughed at himself.

"Come on, Dad." Poppy, the youngest around the table tried to cajole her father into an answer. "Milly and I want to meet our grandmother too, you know." Milly nodded but said nothing. Jake decided to intervene at this juncture.

"We went to see our gran for the first time last summer. I had just passed my driving test and Daisy persuaded me to drive us. I'm so glad we went. We stayed with her for two nights. We met Summer and she is a lovely baby. Also Lottie had grown up so much between the short time that she left home and the time we saw her again. Gran really is a lovely lady, nothing like the picture mum used to paint of what she was like. From what she used to say, I thought she was going to turn out to be like an ogre!" Daisy was nodding with everything that Jake was saying.

"What, like Shrek? I love Shrek!" Milly piped up, not to be outdone with putting in a point of view. "So you see, Dad, we are all agreed. Now it's up to you."

"Are you all trying to gang up against me?" This was all Steven was prepared to say on the matter.

"Will you at least think about it?" Cheryl asked.

"Okay, okay, I'll think about it." Steven took a huge gulp of his drink.

Two days of Christmas festivities went by all too quickly. John thanked Dean, Daisy and Jake for their company and left to spend two nights with Jan and Lottie. Something he was looking forward to more than he was with spending two nights in the company of Dean and his family. It would have been so different had Louise been there.

"Welcome," said Jan, opening the door to John on Boxing Day.

John had another two bags of goodies in the car, which he brought in with his small suitcase. He went to give Jan a hug and then Lottie appeared with Summer.

"Oh, hello?" he said to Lottie. "So this is the little mite? Isn't she beautiful?"

"You can hold her if you like," said Lottie. She read in a book all about how to bring up babies that the more people that were around them the more they thrive. John carefully took Summer in his arms and kissed her forehead. He walked around with her and then went to sit down.

"She's heavy! What have you been feeding her?" This broke the ice and Lottie sat down next to them.

"Just the usual. Formula plus real food now, just started last week because she seemed to be hungry after each feed. We cook up batches of food for her and freeze them and then we just have to blend them because she hasn't got any teeth yet."

"I should think not, although I don't suppose it will be long before she starts teething," he said, all the while looking in her mouth. He thought he spotted pale gums. "Looks like that might be sooner than you think!" Lottie jumped up to have a look in Summer's mouth.

"I must admit I had forgotten all I knew from when my kids were young," said Jan. "With not having the grandkids at all I have had to relearn everything from nearly fifty years ago!"

"Yes, I suppose so. This is nice," said John, sitting back in a comfortable armchair and making himself at home. "Thank you so much for having me. This is just like old times. Where has all the time gone? We haven't spent Christmas together almost since we were kids, have we?" John asked.

"We've a lot to catch up on. How are the Devon contingent? How is Dean coping without Louise? And Jake and Daisy? Are they all okay?"

"Oh, they are muddling along. I think Dean takes advantage of Jake's good nature. He's a hard-working young man. Not only at home: I mean when he's at uni. When he comes home he gets straight on with his studies in his room. I made sure he has a good solid desk for him to work at. He's always so appreciative, a real delight. I shall miss him when he goes. Daisy is a little sweetie too. She quietly gets on with things. Of course, I was only there the two nights over Christmas, so it was a sort of holiday atmosphere. They made me very welcome, especially Dean, always with a drink in hand!"

"Lottie had mentioned that he drinks a lot. Is he an alcoholic?"

"Oh, I don't know about that. He's had a lot to contend with, with losing Louise last year, so I don't blame him for turning to drink. I probably drink too much myself but I do have days off. I don't think Dean does. From what he says, it is the first thing he thinks about when he wakes up."

"Oh dear, that's not good." Jan agreed.

"Oh, guess what?"

"What?" Jan pricked up her ears to maybe hear some gossip.

"Steven and co came to Christmas lunch. Those girls are getting big now. I know I don't see them from one year to the next but they are fine specimens!"

"At least you do get to see them. Maybe I will one day," Jan said sadly.

"It's funny you should say that."

"Funny? Why?" Jan was intrigued.

"Well, I think the girls and also Cheryl were getting on to Steven to come and see you and possibly make up with you."

"Oh, I do hope so. When?"

"Hold your horses! I didn't say he agreed. It was Cheryl who brought up the subject and then the girls took over and started badgering him. I think they want to meet you. They say it's not fair that Lottie is here with you and yet they haven't even met you. So watch this space."

"Oh, I will," said Jan expectantly.

"What did you get for Christmas?" John asked Lottie.

"Gran gave me this lovely bracelet," said Lottie, showing John her arm adorned with a beautiful silver bracelet. "But that's not all! Gran has promised me a puppy but he isn't ready yet." Jan took over the conversation.

"We have not been to see it yet because the litter is only a few days old," Jan explained. "Actually, probably about a week old now: they were born just before Christmas. They're labradoodles and we can have the pick of the litter, so the owner says. We will go in the new year to choose one and then Lottie will have him or her for her birthday."

"I can't wait!" said Lottie excitedly.

"Labradoodles! Never heard of such a thing. Is that a breed of dog?" said John, puzzled.

"Yes. They're a cross between a Labrador and a poodle," Jan explained again.

"I guessed that much!" John was intrigued that there would be such a mixture.

"What is good is that they don't moult like Labradors and they're intelligent like poodles. D'you remember Nicky? I remember when Mum brought him home when I was fourteen. A ball of fluff he was and he grew almost to the size of a standard poodle but all his brothers and sisters were toy poodles, so Mum saved him. His owners were going to drown him."

"What! Drown him because he wasn't a toy?" Lottie was most perplexed. "You can't drown toys! They don't breathe!"

"No. You're quite right. I didn't explain properly. Toy and miniature poodles are breeds and then there is the standard poodle, which is a lot bigger. Nicky had big feet so they knew he wasn't going to be same as his brothers and sisters so he wasn't wanted. He was a lovely dog, so easy to train. I used to train him to keep a biscuit on his nose for ages and then, when you said it was okay, he would toss it up in the air and catch it and eat it."

"I wonder if we can train our new puppy to do that." asked Lottie.

"I don't see why not," Jan agreed.

"And Gran said we would be able to go on holiday in the new year too," Lottie continued to tell John.

"That'll be nice for you. Where are you going to go?" asked John.

"We haven't decided yet," Jan interjected. "It might be a bit more difficult with a dog so maybe later on, once the puppy has settled in. Maybe the owner might take it back for a week while we go away. For a little sunshine at the end of the winter."

"Gran's friends are going on a cruise over Easter," Lottie told John. "They came here on Christmas Day for lunch and were going on and on about it. I think she was more keen on going than he was, it was so funny."

"I don't think John wants to know about that. After all, he doesn't know them."

John's visit over Christmas was eventful and enjoyable and soon he was on his way home.

"Thank you so much for having me, I've really enjoyed myself."

33

New Year's Eve. Dean was going to the pub and Jake had a party to go to. Daisy was going to spend the evening at Lucy's house.

"What're you doing tonight, Daisy?" asked Jake.

"I'm going over to Lucy's house as there's nothing going on here," said Daisy. When her mother was alive she sometimes threw a party that involved the children and New Year's Eve. Nothing much happened last year because it was all too raw.

"Oh, yes, Lucy. Loo seat. Loose elastic. There are all sorts of combinations to her name." Jake and Dean laughed so hard it made Daisy cross with them.

"I suppose you think that's funny." She finally cracked a smile when she heard the guffaws of Jake and Dean. She thought they were being quite childish so she turned away from them and went to get ready.

Dean started getting himself dressed up, more than he usually would, to go to the pub. Entertainment was going to be provided and he was looking forward to that.

"What sort of entertainment, Dad?" Jake asked his father.

"Oh, I don't know, just entertainment. Probably be some karaoke or a comedian or both. I can't remember what Keith told me. I'll tell you tomorrow. They've never had entertainment before but someone offered so they took it up. There will be crowds there so I shall have to get there early to get my table."

"Do you never join up with friends there?" Jake was curious. He could not think of anything worse than just sitting at a table on one's own all evening.

"I've got friends!" Dean wondered to himself how many friends he could count. The only true friend he seemed to have was Keith, but he would be too busy behind the bar to be able to sit and drink with Dean. But Keith understood Dean. He told him so, but maybe because that was what Dean wanted to hear. Keith was a good listener.

"Hi, Dean, me ol' china, me ol' mate, how're you doin'? Pint is it?" said Keith as he fetched a pint glass from the usual shelf. "You're in early tonight. I bet you're here to get a good seat for the performance?"

"Yeah, thought I would. Many be in tonight?"

"I hope so, after the extortionate amount the comedian is asking. Well, I suppose they can ask what they like on New Year's Eve. I don't know what time he's coming though, probably about 9pm. After that we will have some karaoke, that always goes down well. I thought we might do a quiz but I don't sell so much booze then! They are all so intent on answering the questions they forget to drink! Probably be too much on New Year's Eve anyway to hold a quiz as well. There are one or two biggish groups coming in, I believe."

"Have one for yourself," said Dean, handing over a £20 note.

"Thank you very much, I'll just have a half, it's going to be a long night so I have to have my wits about me. I've an extra barmaid coming in soon. Between you and me, she's quite gorgeous. I shall have to mind my Ps and Qs and make sure the wife doesn't catch me ogling her!"

"I'll have to look out for her. Does she have big bazookas?" Dean was starting to get interested. Big boobs on a pretty and shapely woman was his fantasy.

"Dunno, mate. Why?"

"Well, you said she is gorgeous. I just thought that was what you meant."

"I meant she is pretty. At least that's what the agency said. I told them I didn't want an old hag. I need someone who is good with my customers, preferably young and pretty. They told me she was very good at her job and she is indeed pretty. And I believed them, although time will tell."

Dean took his pint to his table and watched as gradually more and more people started arriving through the door. He noticed the new barmaid arrive and saw Keith giving her instructions. Dean noticed that she wasn't as young as Keith had intimated but at least she was fairly pretty and she wore a typical barmaid blouse, with a plunging neckline showing plenty of cleavage. As more people arrived, he watched the barmaid tackle her job with aplomb. Very deftly she would serve more customers quicker than Keith himself. She coped with huge orders and added up as she went along, putting drinks on trays and delivering them. Keith was impressed, Dean could see, as an impression was also made upon himself.

Jake arrived at the party he had been invited to by an old schoolfriend. He noticed one or two people he knew. One girl in particular he recognised but could not put a name to the face. He decided to go straight over and ask her.

"Hello, I know you, don't I?" he began.

"Hi, Jake. Of course you know me! I'm Amelia, Charlie's friend. How is she?"

"Have you not heard from her? You know she's not called Charlie anymore!"

"News to me. She never told me that. Yes, I've been in touch with her and she's sent me photos of Summer. What name is she going under now?" asked Amelia.

"Lottie," Jake replied.

"Lottie! What sort of name is that?" Amelia laughed, pushing her hair off her face with a movement one would put down to flirting. "She seems happier now than she has ever been, what d'you think?"

"I think having a baby has calmed her down, taken the rebel out of her. She's a much nicer person now. So, what have you been doing?" Jake asked.

"Oh, this and that, you know. What about you?" This was a genuine question as Amelia liked Jake, she always had but thought of him as unattainable. She thought he was married to his studies and she knew him to be very ambitious.

"Well, I started at Bristol Uni in September, been working really hard, as usual. I am staying with my uncle at present and he has shown me around some of the interesting places I knew nothing about. Bristol is steeped in history, it's fascinating. Did you know Bristol was at the centre of the slave trade in the eighteenth century? And did you know Isambard Kingdom Brunel built the famous Clifton Suspension Bridge but he died before it was completed? He was only about fifty-three when he died. His ship, the SS *Great Britain*, is in dry dock there too." Amelia stifled a yawn but Jake continued regardless. "The first bungee jump in Britain was from the suspension bridge, although it is well known that people used to use the bridge to commit suicide from the time it was built. One woman in olden days, wearing a crinoline, jumped off the bridge but her skirt saved her life because it acted like a parachute." Jake was now noticing Amelia's eyes were glazing over so he changed the subject. "Would you like a drink, Amelia?"

"Now you're talking! Thank you. I'll have some of that rum punch everyone keeps talking about." Amelia took out her mobile phone and was still looking at it when Jake came back with her drink.

"Did you know that Bristol University developed the invention of the mobile phone?" said Jake.

"No, I didn't know that. Is there anything about Bristol that you didn't like?"

"Absolutely nothing! I loved all of it. I think I'd like to live there permanently. It's where our family originated from; our grandmother is from there."

"What, the one Charlie said you were not allowed to meet 'cos your mother wouldn't let you? The one that Charlie is staying with right now?"

"The very same one, yes. Daisy and I went to meet her in the summer after I passed my driving test."

"You passed your test?" Amelia was far more interested in the fact that Jake was able to drive. Jake nodded. "Maybe you'd like to drive me somewhere?"

"Where would you want to go?" Jake enquired curiously.

"Anywhere you like. You drive and I'll provide the picnic." In a roundabout way Amelia was angling for a date.

"It's a bit cold for a picnic, isn't it?"

"Not if we stay close together in the car, steam up the windows a bit, if you know what I mean." Amelia was trying to make it abundantly clear her intentions with innuendos rather than plainly asking Jake for a date.

"I've just spotted an old schoolfriend over by the bar. I'll see you later." Jake rushed over to where he thought there was someone he vaguely knew and Amelia was secretly relieved, thinking Jake had turned into a bit of a nerd.

Dean fought his way to the bar as the evening was progressing. The table next to him had been getting louder and louder, with people enjoying themselves in anticipation of the comedian, whose arrival was imminent. Dean did not want to sit with an empty glass so made sure he could get one in to enjoy with the expected entertainment.

"Hello, darling," said the barmaid. "What can I get for you?"

"Pint, please," said Dean, setting his glass down on the bar. The barmaid ignored his glass and proceeded to fill another. "I like this glass." Still the barmaid continued to ignore his glass so he lifted it up and shook it at her.

"I have to give you a fresh one," she shouted over the noise. "You can do what you like." So Dean proceeded to refill his own favourite glass with beer. He left the new glass on the bar and went back to his table. There he found the people on the table next to his had taken the three chairs from his table, leaving his one chair with his coat thrown over the back.

"Sorry, mate. Did you need those chairs? We were a bit short, thought you'd gone," said a man from the next table, which had expanded its circle. Dean tutted but said nothing and sat down. Alone as usual.

"Good evening," came a voice from the loudspeaker. "I'd like to introduce to you Jeffrey, our entertainment for this evening." Everyone clapped.

Dean could hardly hear the comedian with all the heckling and banter. He caught one or two bawdy jokes, which he reckoned he had heard before. Jeffrey liked the sound of his own voice but was not able to hold the attention of an audience. He was on for about an hour and at the end Dean decided he had had enough of sitting on his own, with no chance of anyone joining him with no chairs at his table. He fought his way to the bar again and found a vacant stool.

"Hello, darling," said the barmaid again. "What can I get for you?"

"Pint, please," said Dean. As an afterthought, he added. "And a whisky chaser."

The barmaid put his drinks in front of him.

"What's your name?" Dean bravely asked the barmaid.

"Doreen. What's yours?' she said. All the while she was clearing glasses and filling the dishwasher tray, as well as going along and busily wiping the bar down from spills, all in one deft movement.

"Dean."

"Hello, Dean, pleased to meet you. I won't shake hands 'cos mine are very sticky and the boss might not like me to take my eye off the ball."

Dean could not get out of his head that her name began with a D. They could be the DDs. Then for some reason his wife's bra size, 40DD, popped into his head. He looked down at Doreen's breasts and thought they were of a similar size. Louise would never have flaunted hers like Doreen was doing now and Dean enjoyed watching them bouncing around while she worked. Doreen noticed him looking at her cleavage and pushed them out further. She really enjoyed men looking at her and taking an interest. Dean put her at about forty, slightly younger than himself.

"Like what you see?" she asked Dean.

"Of course! Who wouldn't?" he said. This was the first time a woman had taken any interest in him in over a year. "Would you like to come home with me? We could have some fun with those." Doreen laughed at that and then Dean became self-conscious. He would not have been so daring without the large amounts of alcohol he had consumed.

"What would my husband say, I wonder."

"Sorry. Didn't know. Can I buy you a drink to make up for it?" Dean was disappointed but decided to stay at the bar for the rest of the evening. At least when it came to Auld Lang Syne he would be able to celebrate with his new friend Doreen and his old friend Keith.

"Don't worry about it. I'll have a small beer, thanks. Are you up for the karaoke? That's on next, I believe," asked Doreen as she took the money for her drink and poured it out.

"Yeah, I don't mind."

The rest of the evening went by in an alcoholic haze for Dean. When it was time to sing Auld Lang Syne he went to the toilet and when he returned someone had taken his stool. He was miffed at this action and looked around to see if he could find it but it had disappeared.

"Happy New Year, everyone," Keith called out to all his customers.

Daisy's evening with Lucy was mostly taken up with dressing up in vintage clothes, which they enjoyed. They also made up each other's faces with make-up from Lucy's sister's bedroom. Her parents and older sister had gone out with strict instructions to Lucy that they were to behave themselves and no alcohol.

"D'you want a drink?' asked Lucy.

"Okay. What have you got in mind? A Coke?"

"I think we can do better than that! Leave it with me."

Lucy dashed downstairs as Daisy was putting the finishing touches to her hair with some pretty purple ribbons she found in Lucy's dressing up box. Lucy looked in the cocktail cabinet. She reached to the back and found half of a bottle of gin, which she knew her parents never touched. It was kept for visitors, which was a rare occurrence. She poured a little in two glasses then found some ginger beer in the fridge and mixed the two together. She tried one and then added more gin to both and put the bottle back behind the other bottles.

"Here," she said, handing Daisy her glass.

"What's this?"

"It's ginger beer with a difference. Try it."

"I don't think I've had ginger beer before. Is it like beer?"

"No, silly! Ginger beer is non-alcoholic. I don't know why they call it beer. It's just a sweet gingery drink. My parents used to make it but there's loads of sugar in it. You can get low-sugar ones with that awful sweetener in it but we don't like that; it has an aftertaste, Mum says."

"It tastes nice, thanks."

Lucy waited for the effects of the alcohol to take effect but she thought it made no difference to her. She liked the taste with the gin in the ginger beer but Daisy did not know the difference because she had never tried ginger beer, either with or without alcohol. She wondered whether she should tell Lucy she had spiked the drinks but thought not.

"Shall we have some more ginger beer?" asked Lucy.

"Okay, thanks."

Lucy went again to the cocktail cabinet and poured more gin than last time into each glass, topped up with ginger beer. Daisy took a swig but then puckered her lips.

"Oh, what have you put in it? It doesn't taste the same!"

"I've just put a little extra in there to pep it up. Don't you like it?" Lucy asked.

"It's okay. Mmm, I quite like it actually." Daisy finished the glass and stood up from sitting on the floor. She swayed a little but put that down to getting up too quickly.

"Gin," Lucy announced. "That's what I put in our glasses. Mum and Dad won't miss it. Hope not, anyway. Their preferred spirit is whisky but they usually just go for wine."

"When you come over to mine, I'll find something different for you! There's loads of drink at the back of a cupboard in the kitchen. Mum used to stash it there and I found it one day when I was cooking and looking for something to add to the cooking. I put some brandy in and it tasted great. Don't know if Dad ever noticed, though. I didn't tell him but he ate it and said nothing. I think they use alcohol to make meat less tough, so I believe, anyway. I'd better be going home soon: Dad and Jake will be home and I want to get home before them."

"Why?"

"Well, I just do that's all. I will wait until midnight and wish you happy new year and then I'll go."

Daisy arrived home and went straight to her bedroom to get undressed. She cleaned her teeth in the bathroom and then heard the front door click. She knew it was her father by the stomping around he usually did when he had had a few beers. She heard the television being turned on and the news blaring out. She crept to her bedroom, got into bed and turned off the light.

She was asleep when she was awakened by footsteps in her room. She felt a heavy body lie on top of her bed beside her but she kept quiet for the time being. Then she felt something tickle her feet under the duvet.

"Ugh, you disgust me," she screamed as loudly as she could and shoved the whole duvet plus the body onto the floor. Thud! The whole room shook. "Get out! Go on, get out!"

"What on earth is going on in here?" Jake turned on the main light switch and the room flooded with light. There he saw his father's body twisted around Daisy's duvet. Jake wrestled the duvet away from his father's legs and gave it back to Daisy, then helped Dean up on to his feet. Jake had had a few himself but he was not so drunk as Dean. Jake almost pushed his father out of Daisy's room and into his own bedroom. He left him there and went back to Daisy's room.

"Are you okay?"

"I'll live!" Daisy did not want to worry Jake by telling him this was not the first time it had happened. She had her own method in mind. She would put a chair up against her door when she went to bed in future but she was telling no one of her plan. "Maybe now is the time to have a word with him about his drinking?"

"I will, I promise. But just not now. I will speak to him tomorrow."

In the morning Daisy was up bright and early. There had been a scattering of snow and she was hoping to go out and make a snowman but sadly there was not enough snow for that. Jake emerged around mid-morning and eventually Dean surfaced at lunchtime. He had no recollection of what had happened in Daisy's room. All he could remember was chatting up Doreen. He really liked her and planned to go to the pub and hoped that he would see her again. Jake had other ideas when his father mentioned going to the pub.

"You're not going there again, are you? Don't you think you've had enough alcohol for the time being?"

"Don't be silly. It's still Christmas and New Year. Holiday time. We drink in holiday time. It's called eat, drink and be merry. And I intend to be merry," said Dean.

"Seriously, Dad. I've seen enough over the holidays. You're drinking far more than you used to. You are bordering on being an alcoholic."

"Rubbish! I can stop any time I want to. I just don't want to." Dean was adamant.

"But why?" Jake was perplexed at his father's attitude. "I want you to just try one day without a drink before I go back to uni. Would you do that for me? Then I won't worry about you."

"Okay, if that makes you happy. Just not today. I'm going to meet Doreen down the pub. At least I hope I am. Come with me if you like. On second thoughts, maybe not, you might cramp my style."

"Will you try out a dry day tomorrow, then?" Jake pleaded.

"Okay. Tomorrow I will stay at home and be a good boy, if that makes you happy." Dean then disappeared to the pub.

34

Jan met up with Tino one evening between Christmas and New Year's Eve. He had been ringing her every other day and she finally relented to seeing him for a drink at her local pub. She was keeping him at arm's length, not wanting to encourage him too much.

"But I like you and want to be with you, Jan," said Tino, at the end of their evening out.

"I like you too, but the timing is not right. I have to concentrate on looking after Lottie and Summer. And we will soon have a new arrival."

"Not another baby?"

"Sort of! A new puppy. It is Lottie's birthday present but I expect I shall have to help her with looking after it."

Lottie would have liked to go out and meet friends but she did not have any. She had concentrated so much with looking after her baby, other pursuits were kept on the back burner. She started wondering if she should go to school and then she would at least start to make new friends. She texted her friend Amelia but Amelia had moved on with other friends and was not so interested in Lottie anymore. She was beginning to go out with boys from the sixth form. When she told Lottie this,

Lottie was wondering where she went wrong. Should she go back to Devon? Carry on where she left off? She felt a little dejected. Then she remembered she was about to become the owner of a new puppy. Another life to look after.

"We must go and choose which puppy you want. There are two girls and a boy available," Jan told Lottie. "The breeder said we can go and choose one now they are two weeks old. They are very vulnerable when they are born so the breeder is being cautious. Quite right too."

They went to the kennels to meet the litter of puppies. The breeder, Mrs Brown, only had the one dog, which she bred.

"I think I might have said you could have the pick of the litter," said Mrs Brown, a big woman in her fifties. "I'm afraid my family have rather taken a shine to these so they have to come first and have taken one boy and one girl pup. I still have two girls and a boy. Come and have a look."

They followed Mrs Brown into an outhouse, from where they could hear noises. There in the corner in a metal cage they could see five puppies suckling on their mother. Lottie was carrying Summer in a papoose on her front but she could not wait to rush over to see the puppies.

"Ooh, aren't they gorgeous?" Lottie was mesmerised at the sight of the puppies. "Can I pick them up?"

"I think if we wait until they finish their feed first, that would be a good idea." Mrs Brown pointed out the two that were already taken. She then suggested to Lottie that Jan held the baby while Lottie only held one at a time after Mrs Brown had picked it up. If he or she didn't take to her, then she can choose another one. Lottie took off the papoose and gave Summer to Jan in readiness to choose a puppy.

"Mmmumm." Jan and Lottie looked at Summer in astonishment. Lottie believed that that was Summer's first word but Summer was just playing. It was too early for words.

"That's her first word," said Lottie, smiling. "Come on, Summer, say Mum again." But Summer stayed silent.

"How old is she?" asked Mrs Brown.

"She's six months old," Lottie told Mrs Brown. "Wow, I can't believe it, she's called me Mum for the first time." Jan was not so sure if it was her first word but let Lottie believe this for she did not want to burst her bubble.

"Lovely." Mrs Brown wanted to get back to the job in hand.

The puppies fell off the Labrador mother one by one and Mrs Brown pointed to the only available boy pup, which was the closest to her and the colour of gold apricot. All the others were a caramel colour.

"Come on, mister," Mrs Brown said kindly to the boy pup, reaching into the cage for him and placing him gently in the arms of Lottie. He snuffled into her and appeared very comfortable.

"Oh, I love him," said Lottie, stroking the puppy and immediately ignoring the rest of the litter. "I adore his colouring. It's so different from the others." If she decided against this first one, then she knew she could choose another.

"Just to check with you, they won't moult, will they?" Jan asked. She explained to Mrs Brown that she suffered with asthma and was allergic to dogs that moulted.

"No. This is the second litter we've had," explained Mrs Brown to Jan while Lottie was cooing over the puppy. "It was a mistake the first time round but because it went so well we decided to try it again. The labradoodles are so popular these days mostly for the same reason as you, because some people are allergic to the Labrador coats. The father is our neighbours' dog, a standard poodle, not a crossbreed. In fact, at one time he won medals for a competition like Crufts. Not Crufts itself but something similar. I'm not sure. But he's got a lovely temperament, just like Mum here. She's called Betty and the father is called Reggie, after our neighbour's father. It gets very confusing when he calls round!" Jan laughed.

"I don't want to let him go," Lottie said meaningfully.

"Is he the one?" asked Jan. "I bet he weighs a bit less than Summer. She's getting quite heavy now. Is there anything we should watch for, with puppy being around a small child?" Jan asked Mrs Brown.

"I've always thought that the two go hand in hand very nicely as they grow up together. It's a lovely combination, a girl child with a boy dog. I'm not biased or anything and I'm not trying to persuade you to have the boy. Would you like to hold one of the girls now?"

"I think you ought to, just to make sure," Jan said to Lottie.

Lottie reluctantly gave back the puppy in her arms and then took one of the others from Mrs Brown, a girl puppy.

"She is sweet but I think I've bonded with the boy now. We felt very comfortable with each other." Lottie had decided she wanted the boy and gave the girl back to Mrs Brown.

"Looks like that is the decision, then: the boy it is," said Jan.

"I will have all the paperwork for you when you come to collect him and he will have had his vaccinations and microchip all done. I shall also give you some special puppy feed that he will be used to. He will actually be ready in six weeks, although if you could leave him for a wee bit longer with Mum that would be better for him. Say seven or eight weeks would be ideal."

"That's perfect. He will be with us just in time for your birthday, Lottie," said Jan.

"I can't wait that long!" Lottie was very excited.

"I'm afraid you'll have to," said Mrs Brown. "Which birthday will you be celebrating?"

"Seventeen," said Lottie.

"Oh, lovely. Are you going to get your driving licence and have some lessons too?" asked Mrs Brown.

"I don't know. I hadn't thought about that." Lottie looked at Jan.

"That was going to be a surprise!" said Jan, smiling. "I was going to get your driving licence for you and then give you lessons for your birthday."

Lottie looked pleasantly surprised and pleased.

"Your mum is awfully good to you, isn't she?" said Mrs Brown to Lottie.

Lottie was just about to say, "She's not my mum," but thought better of it. She just smiled and nodded.

"Did you really mean that about driving lessons?" Lottie asked Jan when they got back in the car.

"Of course! I don't make promises and then not carry them through. That's one thing that my father did for us when we were seventeen. He made sure we could all drive. I had my own car, which my father bought for me out of money left to me by my godfather. I passed first time when I was seventeen and more recently I passed the advanced driving test."

"I didn't know that. You see, because my mum refused to let us meet you, we have all missed out on knowing about our own family. Because you're older, you know more and can tell us. But we would have known about things a lot sooner if Mum hadn't been so pig-headed," said Lottie.

"Quite. I could tell you all sorts of things if you're interested, things about the family that your mum wouldn't have known about. Things my parents told me about elderly relatives that I can just about remember. Things like a great-uncle of mine who had the first car in Bristol, who had been a friend of Isambard Kingdom Brunel. Things like that and stuff that obviously your father wouldn't have known about either. Hopefully he has told you about his side of the family. Your grandmother on your father's side is a widow, isn't she?"

"Yes, Granny Kath. She's an okay sort, a hard worker because she has had to be. Would do anything for you, very kind, she would give you her last penny. Salt of the earth, you could say. D'you know what I mean?"

"Yes, I do. Talking of salt of the earth, that is how Tino talked about himself! I had to laugh. It's not really something you say about yourself. It is something that you say about someone else, just like you did about your Granny Kath."

"You do like Tino, don't you?" asked Lottie. "You should go out with him again. I think he's a real catch."

"Yes, I do, but I don't want to leave you on your own."

"I shall be okay. I think you're just using me as an excuse!" Lottie laughed. "I shall be quite alright to be left on my own. I'm not a child anymore, you know. I'm an adult with a baby of my own. I've had to grow up fairly quickly."

"Yes, and a good job you've made of it. I am very proud of you. Summer is so lucky to have such a lovely mum."

"You're being too kind to me and you're also getting off the subject of going out with Tino!"

"No, I'm not!" They both laughed. "What do you suggest I do? Ask him out? I think he's given up on asking me."

"Just go for it. When we get back you could give him a ring," said Lottie.

"Better than that. We could go to the restaurant and have lunch there as a special treat. Summer is big enough now to sit in the high chair. I'm sure they have high chairs there. The Italians are very family-orientated and would like to see us, I'm sure."

Jan drove straight to the restaurant.

"Ah, welcome, how lovely to see you again," said Rosa Lina. "Come, come, I have a lovely table for you over here in the corner and I will fetch a high chair for Summer. She is growing so fast." She kissed all three of them.

"Yes, it's nice to see you too," said Jan, all the while nonchalantly looking around the restaurant but hoping not to be too obvious. "This is the first time we have brought Summer to a restaurant."

"I'm sure it will not be the last," said Rosa Lina, noticing Jan looking around. "Tino isn't here at the moment!"

"Oh!" said Jan, blushing slightly. She started looking at the menu and showing Lottie that there was a special lunch menu. "What shall we have?" she asked Lottie. And then to Rosa Lina, "Could we have something soft for Summer and not too highly spiced?"

"I have just the thing for Summer. We always keep special baby food in store. We are always having families in. Tino will be back later. He's gone to the wholesalers. He will be pleased to see you, I'm sure." Jan blushed again and tried to ignore the remark. Rosa Lina went off to the kitchen to give Giovanni their order and then went to the bar for their drinks. As she brought them their drinks, Lottie was bubbling over with excitement.

"We're getting a puppy soon," she told Rosa Lina. "We've just been to choose him and he will be ready just in time for my birthday!"

"That's lovely. No wonder you are so excited. What sort are you going to get?" Rosa Lina asked.

"He's a labradoodle and he's a lovely golden apricot colour."

"I love dogs but I don't know this breed."

"It's a mix between a Labrador and a poodle. Hence labradoodle," said Jan. Rosa Lina laughed. She thought it was a joke.

"Oh, you English are so funny. Why not just get a Labrador? They are adorable."

"Well, the labradoodles are even more adorable, you wait and see. I am allergic to Labradors but this one has the coat of a poodle."

Giovanni was in the kitchen but he made the time to come out and see Jan and Lottie and Summer, bringing their food and serving them himself.

"Not so busy now; you've caught us on a day that is not too hectic," said Giovanni. "Tino is at the wholesalers. He likes to go when we are not too busy." Giovanni drew up a chair and sat with them.

"Yes, Rosa Lina said that," said Jan. "How are you keeping?" She was hoping to change the subject away from Tino but it just kept winging right back.

"We are fine. Tino is having trouble with his teeth but the dentist is sorting him out. He hadn't been to a dentist, was not even registered with one, since he left Italy. So that serves him right, as you English say. In fact, you English have lots of funny sayings." Lottie laughed.

"Yes, we do," Jan agreed.

Rosa Lina saw the last of their customers out of the door and brought a chair over to sit with them.

"Dad should be back soon," she said. She sometimes referred to her father as Tino, as she had earlier, and sometimes as just plain Dad. She suddenly disappeared to the kitchen and phoned Tino to ask him how long he was going to be. She was hoping Jan would still be here when Tino came back.

"I shall not be long," said Tino into his mobile phone. "I am just at the checkout now. I will be about half an hour, I expect. Why do you ask?"

"No reason," said Rosa Lina, nonchalantly. She was not going to say that Jan was at the restaurant. "But come straight back, won't you? There is stuff that I need urgently," she lied.

"Okay, I'm on my way," Tino confirmed.

Summer finished her food and started grizzling and banging her spoon on her tray.

"I think she's tired. She needs her nap," said Lottie. "I think we had better go."

As Rosa Lina wanted to keep them there until her father returned she brought coffees over for Jan and Lottie as soon as it looked like they were about to leave.

"Coffee on the house," said Rosa Lina, putting cups down in front of Jan and Lottie.

"Oh, thank you, that's very kind," said Jan. "But we ought to go soon; Summer is playing up."

Rosa Lina picked up Summer and waltzed her all around the restaurant, dancing to steps she enjoyed. Everyone laughed and Summer gurgled.

Tino arrived just as Jan and Lottie were putting on their coats.

"Oh, hello," said Tino. "I nearly missed you! I'm so glad to see you." He directed this to Jan. "Please don't go."

"Sorry, Tino," said Jan. "We have to get Summer back for her nap."

"I'll call you," Tino called to Jan's disappearing back.

35

"Dad's got a black eye!" Lottie announced to Jan and showed her a photo on her phone. Lottie and Daisy texted each other almost daily.

"Oh dear," said Jan. "How did he get that?"

"Apparently he was after the barmaid at the pub just as her husband arrived. Daisy thinks it is hilarious. She says he's drinking too much. What's new, I ask myself?"

"Did he always drink a lot when you were at home with him?"

"Not really. Well, not every day like Daisy says he is. It got worse after Mum died. Of course, they used to go out but Mum was the steadying influence on him and now he's out of control, I reckon. He met the barmaid on New Year's Eve and went back the next day. She wasn't there but she helped out occasionally, usually weekends when it was busy. I think Dad really took a fancy to her. Sad, really. He doesn't have many friends, let alone women friends. It was just unfortunate that the time he upped his game and tried it on with her was when her husband just happened to walk in!"

"That was bad luck but men will be men. They get it into

their heads that they are God's gift, when in reality they aren't. Shame, really, but you have to laugh."

"I meant to ask you, how was your evening out with Tino last night?" asked Lottie.

Jan had had a second date with Tino, this time for a meal out. He fetched her in his old car and they went to the old established Indian restaurant in the village. Tino would have liked to have supported his daughter and son-in-law's business but he felt uncomfortable if he thought they would have been spying on him. In time, his intention was to use the family business but for now he was happier going somewhere else.

"Oh, you know. It was good, lovely food. I enjoyed the evening. He is very intense but I'm not ready for a steady relationship."

"He's obviously got over his wife quicker than you got over Mike."

"Yes, I guess so. We are just going to take it easy. See each other platonically for a while and see how it goes from there. I'm not going to rush things. I've got enough on my plate with preparing for the new puppy. Have you thought of any names yet?" He was due on Lottie's birthday, just as Jan had arranged, in just three weeks' time.

"Well, I can't call him Jet like I was going to call my baby if it was going to be a boy. Jet just doesn't suit him, not with that colour. What about Apricot? Or Peaches? Maybe not; that sounds like a girl's name. Apple? No. Plum? Pear?"

"Why a fruit?"

"Dunno, really. Have you got any suggestions?"

"I think it should be your choice. If you have several ideas, then you could write them all down on separate bits of paper and then just pick one."

"Great idea. I'll do that." Lottie took herself off and was gone for ages. Jan went to answer the telephone when it rang.

"Hello?"

"Hi, Jan. I need your help, I'm desperate!" Vicky was in the throes of preparing for their cruise, which was imminent.

"What do you need help with?" Jan enquired.

"You've travelled a lot. You can help me with choosing what to take. I've bought a load of clothes, much to the annoyance of Gerry. He says I've got far too much stuff and I'm beginning to think he might be right. Please help me. Pretty please."

Jan went to Vicky's as commanded. She suggested Vicky take layers. Jan always swore by layers and separates. One or two dressy dresses for evening on the cruise but mostly smart casual clothes and nothing too bulky. It was going to be warm in the Far East, sometimes bordering on hot. Then they were going on to Melbourne, where the temperatures would be in the mid-twenties.

Jan came home to chaos. There were bits of paper strewn all around the sitting room and Summer sitting in the middle of the mess, crying.

"What on earth is going on?" Jan started picking up the bits of paper but Lottie stopped her.

"No, no. There's method in my madness! I've done what you suggested and written down lots of names on separate bits of paper. Then I've put them all down on the floor and I wanted Summer to choose one for me. She doesn't understand and just keeps muddling them all up."

"Well, aren't they meant to be muddled up? So she can pick one out?"

"Not really. I've put them in some sort of order and I was hoping she was going to pick one of the ones I like."

"Do you mean you have put in names that you don't like?"

"Yes, just to pad it out. I tried to get her over to the ones I wanted her to pick from but she insisted on going to the ones I didn't like very much."

"Oh dear, this isn't going to work, is it? Take out the ones you're not keen on and just leave the rest."

Lottie picked up the bulk of the papers and left two.

"That should make it easier for her now," said Jan, amused that Lottie should make life difficult for herself, and for Summer. Summer suddenly lunged forward and fell on her nose and started crying again. She made a grab for one piece of paper and Lottie took it from her.

"That's it! It's my favourite as well! Yippee!" Lottie shouted out after reading the piece of paper.

"Well, what is it?" After all the excitement Jan couldn't wait to hear what the puppy was going to be called. Lottie handed her the paper and Jan read it aloud.

"Sandal. Oh, yes, I like it."

"I love it! Sandal, Sandal," Lottie kept calling the name out loud as if the dog were already there.

Jan sent away for Lottie's driving licence so it would arrive in time for her seventeenth birthday. It was going to be a birthday to remember and Jan was getting as excited about it all, as Lottie was going to be too.

"Happy birthday!" said Jan to Lottie as she pulled back her bedroom curtains and set down a cup of tea on her bedside table. "As a special treat I've sorted Summer out and she is bathed and dressed and ready for the day. Your day. Your special birthday." Lottie was overwhelmed. She had never had such treatment.

"Thanks, Gran," said Lottie, most grateful and also excited that they were going to pick up her special birthday present. She jumped out of bed and into the shower, singing as she went. Jan had never seen her so animated. Summer was happy playing with her toys.

"Here are all your cards. Luckily the postman delivered most of them yesterday so I put them away for you." Jan put her special card on the top and Lottie opened it first. She knew she was going to get her driving licence but she didn't know she would get it on her birthday. "Surprise!" said Jan with glee as Lottie opened her card, and the licence dropped out. Jan loved to see Lottie's eyes light up. She knew then what she had missed over all these years.

"Ah, my driving licence! Thank you so much." Lottie went to give Jan a big hug. "I can't believe it. This is the best day of my life. Well, it will be later when we pick up Sandal. I love you, Gran." Jan could hardly believe her ears; she never thought she would ever hear those words from a grandchild of hers. It was the best sound. She never thought that would ever happen and it was more than she could ever have hoped for, even just a year ago.

"Well, we had better go and fetch him then," Jan suggested. "Mrs Brown has asked that we get there this morning around 10am so we need to leave now."

"Yes, please, I can't wait! Let's go."

Lottie fidgeted all the way to the kennels. She kept looking around at Summer, who was napping in her baby seat.

"You know who is going to want to see the new puppy?" asked Jan.

"I can't think. Who?"

"Vicky. She adores all animals but in particular she loves dogs. All dogs. In fact, I wouldn't be surprised if she went out and bought one for herself. I think she doesn't like it when someone has something that she wants. I think Gerry has kept her in check but I reckon she will try and persuade him after she sees Sandal. You mark my words."

"Can I have my first driving lesson? Today? You can take me, can't you?"

"Oh, I'm sorry but I'm going to have to say no. I'm going to get you some proper lessons to start you off with. I've a friend who is a driving instructor and he has agreed to take you on. After you've had a few lessons I will gladly take you out. I need to sort out insurance for you and you need to get on with reading the Highway Code." Jan had given her the Highway Code as part of her birthday present with her driving licence. "Let's just concentrate today on getting Sandal today. That's enough for you to think about, don't you agree?"

"Yes, you're quite right."

Mrs Brown was ready and waiting for them to arrive and came out with Sandal in her arms, plus a bag of goodies.

"Everything you need is in the bag, including his pedigree certificate showing his parents, plus some puppy food that he is used to. He's had his jabs and he is microchipped with all your details. Have you thought of a name for him yet?"

"Sandal," said Lottie immediately.

"Oh, how lovely. I will just add that to his certificate." Mrs Brown gave Sandal to Lottie and pulled a pen from her pocket. "There, that's done now. Goodbye, Sandal, lovely boy. You've a good home to go to. Please keep me informed of his development," she said to Jan and Lottie.

"We will. Thank you and goodbye." They all shook hands and Mrs Brown turned her back and was gone.

Lottie sat in the back and had Sandal between her and Summer. Sandal started licking Summer's hand and she giggled. Jan drove very carefully and they were home in what seemed no time.

"Take him into the garden and see if he wants a wee. We might have some accidents but we need to praise him when he does pee in the garden." Jan said to Lottie. Jan had given Lottie a book on looking after puppies and she had read it from cover to cover.

The phone rang and Jan went inside to answer it.

"Have you got him?" Vicky asked. "Can I come over?"

"Yes, of course you can. We don't want to overwhelm him but I'm sure one more person would be fine."

Vicky arrived ten minutes later.

"Oh, isn't he gorgeous?" Vicky gushed as she came through into the back garden. "You were right about the colour: it is most unusual, so pretty." Sandal was running about the garden and then he started biting at Lottie's heels.

"Aargh, get off me, will you?" Lottie shouted in alarm, running away. The more she ran away, the more Sandal thought she was playing.

"Happy birthday, Lottie," Vicky called out. Lottie started screaming and probably did not hear what Vicky was saying.

"Gerroff!" shouted Lottie. "Go away and stop biting me, will you?" She kept running away and Sandal kept up, still biting at her heels.

"Are you stopping? Would you like a coffee?" Jan asked Vicky. "Hey, guess what? We think Summer said her first word today or we might have imagined it as she's kept mum ever since! She said what sounded like mum. Or mmmummm. Anyway, it's a milestone in her development. I had forgotten when they started to talk and I do think girls develop a little quicker than boys. I remember my daughter did things a lot earlier than my son did, but then he soon caught up."

"He's a lovely chap," said Vicky to Lottie. "Can I pick him up?"

"You can if you can catch him! Be my guest." Lottie continued running away from his sharp teeth around her ankles and then when she turned around to catch him he would run away. He thought it was a wonderful game and the more Lottie screamed the more Summer enjoyed the fun too, from her pushchair. She had been most curious since they arrived home with Sandal and rocked herself back and forth, giggling.

"Maybe I will pick up Summer first. She hasn't got such sharp teeth and probably won't bite me anyway." Vicky was loving the interaction between Summer, Lottie and Sandal. She took Summer out of her pushchair and cuddled her. "It's lucky it's such a nice day to be outside, although it's getting slightly chilly now."

Sandal thought it was great fun, biting Lottie's ankles, until Jan decided enough was enough as she could see that Lottie was getting distressed. Jan went straight over, took Sandal gently by the scruff of his neck with one hand and showed him the flat of her other hand.

"No," she said, sharply. Sandal backed off but then tried again to bite at Lottie's ankles.

"No," Jan said again to Sandal, and then to Lottie. "We must show him who is boss and what is unacceptable. It will be part of his training, I can assure you. When he does it again, you must turn around to him and do the same. The more you run around and let him bite, the more he thinks that it's a game." Jan remembered training dogs she had had in the past and that was the only way.

Jan came back to Vicky and watched as Lottie copied Jan's sharp words to Sandal.

"No!" Lottie raised her voice to Sandal. "No, you're not to keep biting me. It hurts!"

Vicky and Jan laughed.

"It's not funny. It does hurt, it really hurts and, look, there's blood." Lottie showed Jan and Vicky a tiny speck of red on her sock.

"Maybe while he's in this mischievous mood you should try wearing boots," Jan suggested. "Then he can't bite your ankles, can he? We must persevere and he will stop, I can assure you." Sure enough, after her third attempt, he backed away and never bit her ankles again.

"I think we will bring Summer in now and we'll have coffee in the conservatory. We can still watch them outside and Lottie can bring Sandal in when she's ready." Jan pushed the pushchair inside and Vicky carried Summer. Jan made coffee and took it on a tray into the conservatory.

"Are you going to say 'mum' for me, Summer?" asked Vicky. Summer looked blank and just gurgled. "I don't believe she said mum!" Vicky said to Jan.

"Me either but don't tell Lottie. She is convinced she said mum."

"I'm so glad to see the puppy before we go off on our cruise next week. By the time we get back he will have grown quite a bit."

"That time has gone by so quickly. It doesn't seem any time at all since you were on the last cruise, to the Caribbean. I sort of envy you and yet I have everything I have ever wanted now. My granddaughter and great-granddaughter and now a little puppy. I'm so happy. And it looks like Daisy and Jake will visit again over Easter as soon as they break up from school. Lottie is in constant touch with them so that is nice. Her father doesn't seem to take any notice at all but Lottie is happy here and hasn't missed him. I was trying to get her to finish off her education and I think she is coming around to that idea. Maybe in the summer. She will have missed a year but it's important to get her exams if she's going to get a job later on."

"Does she know what she wants to do?" asked Vicky. Summer was now asleep in her arms and she was trying to sip her coffee around the prostrate baby, so as not to spill it on her.

"I think she is quite keen on teaching. When she was younger she was telling me she and a friend wanted to be famous! They wanted to be a girl group and sing, a bit like the Spice Girls or Little Mix. Actually, she does have a nice voice. I've heard her sing when she didn't know I was listening. She sings along to her favourite songs when she's got headphones on."

"That's what all young things want to be these days – famous. Famous for doing nothing, I always think. They don't really want to put the work in but they want loads of dosh and want the fame and fortune that entails. How little they know!"

"Quite. Still, one can dream, I suppose."

Lottie came into the conservatory with Sandal hot on her heels, but not biting them anymore.

"There, it looks like you have trained him. That didn't take too long, did it?" Jan was so pleased to see that Lottie was happier now.

"Yes, I didn't need the boots after all. Who's a lovely boy?" Lottie smiled to Sandal and then noticed Summer asleep in Vicky's arms.

"You could give him a treat, if you like," said Jan. "When dogs do things you want them to you should reward them. Lottie fetched the doggie treats and gave him one.

"Good boy," they all said to him in unison when he finally sat down to enjoy his treat. Lottie sat down too, exhausted.

"So, are you all ready for the holiday of a lifetime?" Jan asked Vicky.

"Oh, just about, yes. Gerry keeps faffing about non-important stuff. He did ask me to ask you if you would keep an eye on the house. If you're happy about that, I will give you a key. If you could just take the post away from the front door and make it look a bit lived in, then Gerry will be happy. We've got lights that come on at dusk and go off again about midnight."

"Of course, no probs, as they say in Australia."

"Do they? Oh, I see; that means no problem, I assume."

"Yes." Jan was amused by her friend's naivety. "So you get back at the end of March, just in time for Easter?" asked Jan.

"Unless I can persuade Gerry to stay on longer in Melbourne, for Easter."

"Okay, well, you have a great time and we want to hear all about it when you get back."

36

Jan and Lottie continued to enjoy each other's company tremendously. The relationship was very similar to a mother and daughter without the huge age gap, which was hardly noticed by either of them. They enjoyed the same television programmes and because Jan had kept up with technology she was able to hold her own when Lottie talked about some new gadget or other that she liked.

They talked long into the evenings about all sort of things in which they were both interested. They took it in turns to feed Summer and look after her, both helping each other in great harmony. Also, with Sandal, they enjoyed good long walks with him as he became older and stronger, taking it in turns with one holding the lead and the other pushing the pushchair with Summer.

The phone rang and Jan answered it. She came back and told Lottie who had rung.

"It was Tino," said Jan excitedly. "He's got us tickets to see a play I've wanted to see for ages. It's on at our local arts centre. He has suggested we have a meal out first."

"Italian, by any chance?" Lottie laughed out loud. "Got to keep it in the family."

"No, actually. I think he was talking about going to that new Thai restaurant that opened last year. Mike and I used to love trying out new restaurants, although he was fairly conservative about foreign food. He loved Italian food but he was a bit wary of Indian and Thai food. He thought it would be too hot for him but I always tried to explain that spicy did not always mean hot. Anyway, I love all of it and I'm looking forward to it. We are going in a couple of weeks."

"That will be fun for you. You haven't been out much in all the time I've been here," said Lottie.

"I've just had a strange text from Vicky," Jan told Lottie. "They've only been away two weeks but she doesn't seem to be enjoying it very much. She talks of being confined to barracks, whatever that means. They have to stay in their cabin and food is brought to them. I've no idea what on earth is going on."

"Maybe they're not well." Lottie was good at finding simple solutions.

"That must be it. We must get prepared for Easter as it's not long now. Jake and Daisy are coming to stay. Is there anything you would particularly like to do with them?" asked Jan.

"I think the main thing they want to do is to meet Sandal and also see Summer again. She's grown up a lot since they saw her last summer. Now she's starting to find her feet."

"Yes, her legs are strong. Must be something to do with that bouncy exerciser she loves so much. Your mum used to love that." Jan transported herself back to the days of looking after her own children when they were babies. "And Steven. Louise walked by the time she was a year old and Steven was a bit later, I seem to remember. Boys generally are behind girls in the development stages, but they soon catch up. You might find Summer walking by the time she has her first birthday."

"That will be good. What was Mum like as a baby?" Lottie enquired.

"Oh, she was lovely. Apart from the day I brought her home from hospital, when she cried and cried, almost to the point of screaming. I was at my wit's end not knowing what to do with her. Being a new mum, I had no idea how to look after a baby. My husband was useless too, although he did ring the doctor for advice. Our doc was a real old-fashioned family doctor with old-fashioned ideas and values. He arrived within minutes and was more worried about me than Louise. He had to give me a sedative to keep me calm. Actually, that did the trick. Because I was calmer, that made baby calm too. I was breastfeeding her so Geoff wasn't able to take that over from me. Anyway, I remember feeding her and changing her nappy. As I was sedated I just fell into a deep sleep. I think Geoff put her in her cot and she slept too. All was well after that."

"She didn't cry again?"

"Well, I'm sure she must have done but not as much as when we first brought her home. She was a very contented baby after that initial hiccup. And when I had Steven, Louise was three years and three months old. She behaved like she was the mother. She fetched me the nappies and talcum powder and I made sure I included her in everything I did with him." Jan had a tear in her eye as she remembered those times.

"Sometimes siblings get jealous, don't they? I remember being jealous of Daisy when she came along. It had been just Jake and I for so long and suddenly another little body appeared, demanding attention that belonged to me and Jake!"

"Yes, you're right; that can happen but certainly not in my experience with my two."

"I think Daisy might have been a bit of a mistake but Mum and Dad never said as much. Actually, she wasn't too bad and I'm really glad to have her now."

"That's good."

"Mmmummm," Summer started to gurgle. "Mmumm, mmum, mum."

"Yes, I'm your mum!" Lottie picked up Summer and gave her a kiss. She started wriggling in Lottie's arms and as soon as she put her down she started to crawl. A few tentative moves at first before she fell over and started giggling. Up she got again and again until she had perfected crawling. It took a few goes but by the end of the afternoon she could move from one end of the room to the other.

"Crawling and talking all at once! My, she is going through an important developmental phase," said Jan, so pleased when she saw the beaming face of Lottie marvelling at her daughter.

Over the next few days Summer improved her crawling technique and even tried the stairs. Jan eventually put a gate to stop her trying the stairs on her own but then would let her there under supervision. She soon got the hang of the stairs.

"I've had another peculiar text from Vicky. She says they are moored off of a place in Bali but I can't pronounce the name of it! T-A-N-J-U-N-G B-E-N-O-A," she spelt out off the text. "Tanjung Benoa. I don't know what is special about that place. She says she can see a lovely beach area but they are not allowed off the ship. There is some virus or other, which she says someone picked up in Malaysia. It sounds horrendous. They aren't even allowed out on their balcony. They paid extra to have that balcony. What on earth is going on, I wonder?"

Within days Jan and Lottie were going to know all about the virus, on the news, which was winging its way all around the world. Apparently it had started in China, in a meat market several months earlier. Jan knew all about the Chinese meat markets from a visit many years ago. She had been quite appalled, at the time, at what she saw. She saw chickens running around with their heads cut off and snakes crawling all around the filthy floors. Plus all sorts of bugs in containers. Some sort of cross-contamination had occurred and a very infectious virus had escaped.

Jan watched the news avidly every day and each day it became more and more serious especially when the word "pandemic" was mooted. Soon enough there were cases in UK as well as other parts of Asia, Europe and the Americas. It was unbelievable that it could spread so fast.

One day she saw on the world news that a cruise ship had been isolated and it was not allowed to move anywhere. Someone had brought the virus aboard the ship and it was utter chaos. Everyone had to stay in their cabins. The ones in inner cabins were allowed out on deck, one at a time, to exercise. The ones with balconies were not allowed to use them. All food for the day was brought to cabins and left outside the cabin door. There was to be no face-to-face contact with anyone else. So the cabins could neither be cleaned nor beds made nor any laundry collected. Jan's realisation dawned on her that this cruise ship was the one that Vicky and Gerry were on.

Vicky's texts were becoming more and more desperate. They did not want to catch the dreaded virus so they were doing exactly as they were told. But they were so bored. They could see a lovely beach but they could not go ashore. One day they were given antiseptic wipes with their food and told to clean their cabins with the wipes and keep on washing their hands.

The pandemic was soon to take hold of the whole world. It was a crazy time.

Every day there was a Downing Street press conference

where the law was being laid down by the politicians. Everyone was to stay home and self-isolate for however long it took. It could take weeks or even months. Even years, if it went wrong. Unbelievable.

Working people were told to stay home and work from home if they were able. Everyone else was furloughed and the government paid eighty per cent of their wages. It was going to cost the country billions. All through a silly mistake in a Chinese market. The virus was affecting mostly older people and people with underlying conditions like asthma as it appeared to attack the lungs. If anyone found they had developed a new cough and had a temperature they had to stay home and dial a number for help. Other symptoms were loss of smell and taste.

"Right, well, we will have to stay home," Jan told Lottie. "Nothing more to be done about it. I definitely can't go out with my asthma. We will get food delivered and stay in for as long as is needed."

"But you've got your date with Tino at the Thai restaurant," said Lottie.

"Just have to forget about that. The theatres and cinemas and pubs are all closing too. There are lots of things I shall have to cancel. Daisy and Jake won't be able to come at Easter either."

"Daisy says that Jake is coming home from uni and her school is closing. Also Dad has been furloughed. He isn't allowed to work. That'll please him!"

"Oh dear, what a mess. I see on the news that the cruise ship that Gerry and Vicky are on can still not go anywhere. They are due to go to Melbourne soon to see the family but that's looking unlikely now. Vicky will be disappointed."

"The Krakenvirus is what they're calling this dreadful thing," Jake told Dean and Daisy. "I heard it on the news."

Jake had just arrived home, as soon as the university closed its doors and Daisy was home from school. He turned on the radio so they could all hear the dreadful news.

"What utter nonsense," Dean harrumphed. "Self-isolate? What's that all about?" Never heard of such a thing. I don't believe it."

"Well, it is here and you'll just have to believe it. We have to self-isolate ourselves. That means no going out. We have to stay home for as long as it takes."

"They are saying three weeks," said Daisy. "We can manage that, surely. We can only go out for food and essentials."

"Yes, of course we can; we will just have to pull together," said Jake. "Of course, it could take a lot longer; we will just have to wait and see."

They made preparations for being stuck at home for at least three weeks. Jake made a shopping list and left it out to be added to as things ran out.

"Well, at least I'm getting paid, but there's nothing to spend it on as the pubs are closed!" said Dean.

"Maybe that's a good thing, Dad," said Jake.

"My teacher says I have to be homeschooled, Dad. Are you up for that?" said Daisy.

"On yer bike, I've never homeschooled in my life, whatever that means!" Both Daisy and Jake laughed out loud. It was the exact reaction they were expecting.

"Don't worry, Dad, I've got homework that's been set so there's no need! I think I knew what the answer was going to be," said Daisy. "What about you, Jake, have they given you work to do?"

"It's all on the computer. Yes, I can get on with it but let's just see what happens after Easter. I've been told there's a new way of being taught by your teacher via a new app called Zoom. I expect your teachers will start using that too, Daisy."

Jake was being pragmatic as usual. "You never know, it might all be over by then." Neither Jake nor Daisy believed that, but it was worth wishing.

"Oh, yes, Easter!" cried Daisy. "We are supposed to be going to see Gran and Lottie. And not forgetting Summer and Sandal. I don't suppose we can go now, can we, Jake?"

"Sorry but no, I'm afraid not. Only essential travel. Apparently you can get fined if they find out you have gone against their instructions.

"From what I hear it could go on for months. I can't afford to be out of work all that time," said Dean. "I could use it as a sort of holiday, a paid holiday at that! If the weather is nice we could go down the beach and mooch about. Don't know what else we are supposed to do."

"It's called lockdown for a reason, Dad!" said an exasperated Jake. "We are supposed to stay indoors. If we go out and spread the virus, then we will never get rid of it. All the shops are shut except for essentials like food and medicines."

"Oh, damn, yes, I need a new pair of shoes," said Daisy. "What am I going to do about that?"

"You will just have to wait, like everyone else. You don't need new shoes to walk about the house, do you? No." Jake answered his own question.

"It's a shame we won't be able to visit Gran and see Lottie and Summer over Easter. I was dying to see the new puppy as well. Lottie's so lucky to have a puppy of her own. She knows I always wanted one! We will have to FaceTime them and then we can see how Summer has grown and see Sandal as well. Will you want to see Lottie and Summer, Dad? On FaceTime? Did you know that Charlie changed her name to Lottie?" asked Daisy.

"Leave me out of it," said Dean. He went upstairs to his bedroom and lay down on his bed. *I hate it when they talk about Charlie and our baby. They obviously still don't know. I'm surprised Charlie hasn't told them our secret. It's been well over a year now; I'm really surprised it hasn't got out. Well, they won't hear it from me but I'm afraid if Charlie sees me on that screen, she might just blurt it out. She could say to me "here's your baby" and then it would be out. Our secret. I can't let that happen. God, I need a drink and the pub's shut. What did Daisy say about Charlie changing her name? Lottie? What sort of name is that? And she's called our baby Summer! Is that some sort of hint that she was conceived in the winter? Poor little mite was premature. Probably 'cos Charlie was so young. She was fifteen and that would mean I could go to prison. It was lucky she had her sixteenth birthday when she had the baby. Oh God, what have I done? I need a drink. There are lagers in the fridge; I'll have one of them.*

Dean went downstairs when it was quiet and helped himself to a lager from the fridge. Jake and Daisy were quietly getting on with their studies.

"Who's going shopping?" Dean called out, then saw the shopping list. "We are short of lagers. I'll add it to your list, Jake."

"Okay, then, now you could go to the shops and get the other things on that list I left out," said Jake. "Or we could all go. I'm not sure if we have to wear masks. We could go and find out. At least we have the car so that should save us carrying the shopping too far. We need quite a bit to last a week or two."

They made the trip to the supermarket and were shocked to see a queue outside the shop that snaked around the square opposite. There must have been over 200 people waiting their turn to go into the supermarket. There was someone on the door to make sure not too many people went inside at once. The queue was not like any other queue anyone had ever seen because people were spaced about six feet apart.

"There will be nothing left by the time we get in there!" Dean complained.

"We will just have to try. Come on." Jake parked the car and the three of them stood in the long queue. They noticed people coming out with trolley loads of food and toilet rolls.

"They must be bulk buying, stocking up," Daisy noticed.

"Panic buying, more like." Dean sulked, thinking his lagers might all be gone.

"Only one of you allowed in at a time," said the officious supermarket man on the door. "I see you haven't got a mask. Do you want one? I think they might still be in stock. And soap, antiseptic hand wash, sanitiser and antibacterial wipes are all in short supply. You'd better be quick: they are going faster than a rat up a drainpipe! And there's no toilet rolls left, I know that." The man took great delight telling people over and over what might not be available.

"Here's some money, Jakie boy. You go in, you know what we need," said Dean, handing Jake a wodge of cash and then retreating away with Daisy. "We'll wait out here for you. Don't forget the lagers. Get plenty."

Dean had been to the ATM but was slightly worried that the money in the bank was going down significantly quicker than usual. He was drawing out the same as he usually did but since being furloughed he was only being paid approximately eighty per cent of his usual pay.

Jake took the trolley, which a girl had recently wiped with antiseptic. He found it difficult maintaining a two-metre distance from other people but managed as best he could.

He went methodically through his list and arrived at the queue for the checkout. He could still hear the man on the door telling people to go in one at a time and that toilet rolls had run out. He finally got to the front of the queue and put everything on the conveyor belt.

"Only contactless credit cards," said the checkout girl, after she had scanned everything and Jake was stuffing his shopping into carrier bags.

"But I've only got cash," said Jake, despondently, with crisp new £20 notes in his hand. "I don't have a credit card!"

The girl tutted and rang a bell. The supervisor came over and they had a whispered conversation of which Jake was not privy to the details.

"Okay, just this once," she said. As she took the money, she put it in a separate container and then proceeded to put antibacterial gel on her hands. "Should've brought gloves," she said to herself. "Must remember them tomorrow."

"It's a bit manic, isn't it?" Jake enquired. The girl looked at him as if he was an alien.

"Next!" she called.

37

Jan was preparing for lockdown herself, together with Lottie, Summer and Sandal. She made a shopping list and proceeded to the computer to get a food delivery.

"This is mad," said Jan, clicking away on the computer. "There are hardly any slots left. I reckon everyone is doing the same thing. I'll get on with it and order as much as I can."

"Are you able to get baby food, nappies and dog food? As well as food for us, of course?" Lottie asked.

"Yes. There's a delivery next week, I'll take it. I'm not allowed to the shops with my condition. My doctor has told me I should shield myself and not go out at all."

"I could always go, couldn't I?" asked Lottie. "I mean, if you can't get another delivery."

"Well, yes, but if you get the virus and bring it home, that rather defeats the object. Let's see how this goes."

"I don't know how it goes, I've never lived through a pandemic before," said Lottie. She had looked up what the word meant.

"Neither have I!" said Jan. "The last one was a hundred years ago! They seem to go in hundred-year cycles. Anyway, all I do know is that we need to have a plan of action. I'll draw up some guidelines and run them past you, see what you think. We must use this time wisely. Okay?"

"Okay." Lottie was rather sceptical and wondered what was in store for her. "What about my driving lessons?"

"Oh, yes. Well, they will have to wait, I'm afraid. The driving instructor can't work while this is on and anyway we can't go out in the car. There are more important things to do at the moment. When my driving instructor friend is back at work, we will arrange for him to take you for lessons. Is that okay?" Lottie grudgingly nodded her assent, even though she was disappointed. There was no choice and she knew it in her heart of hearts.

Jan went off to make a list and came back within minutes, hardly time for Lottie to draw breath.

"I've been thinking about Sandal. I can look up on the internet as to how we can make a start in training him. It'll be fun. I've had dogs in the past so I know the basics. We can't take him to a training school so we can do it here. We could start right away. Okay with you?"

"Yes," said Lottie. She did not realise that puppies needed training but Jan made a list of the things that needed to be done. They included sitting to order, being put on a lead and walking to heel for starters. By the time Lottie had read the list for what needed to be done to train Sandal, Jan had started on another tangent.

"Now, you've missed a year of school, how about I homeschool you? Bring you up to speed and then you could take your exams. Later on, I mean. I could find out where you had got up to and then see what there is on the internet. A friend of mine used to homeschool her daughter and, although it's not easy, I'm up for the challenge. Mike and I used to do loads of quizzes and I have missed them. You would be surprised how much you learn. I could teach you everything I know; it would be fun." Lottie was not so sure, it sounded like hard work to her.

"What were your fave subjects at school, Gran?" Lottie asked.

"English and geography. I loved them! Geography was Mike's favourite subject too. Which is why we liked to travel so much. I would really love to try and teach you. I'm not too bad on history and the sciences but my only downfall would be maths. I could never get on with maths but most of the other subjects I reckon I can cover. We can do it when Summer is asleep or when she is playing in her playpen. Please say you will give it a go."

"Okay. We'll try it." Lottie wondered where her grandmother got her enthusiasm. At a difficult time like this. "Actually, maths was the one subject I was quite good at."

"That's grand. It would be an ideal opportunity while we are stuck at home and can't go out. We won't be bored, I can assure you." Jan then tried another tack to keep Lottie interested. "Apart from that, you could help me with my travelogue: that's been on the back burner for ages. I started it about a year ago but never got very far. It just means doing some research and then putting words around photos of all the places Mike and I went to. I wrote journals at the time so that should be quite easy and you will learn something about the places. It's all done on the computer and we can do it together so it should be easy-peasy," said Jan, with complete faith in Lottie.

"I reckon I will enjoy that."

"Plus, there are some really old photos I've been meaning to put into albums. Old photos of your mum and Uncle Steven, probably ones you've never seen before. When I left Devon all that time ago I brought with me loads of negatives that I had. Most of the photos were already in albums and I left them behind for Geoff to have. I had all the negatives developed so that I could have a full range of my children growing up. Unfortunately, I never had time to put them into albums. That would be a great help if we can do it together and then you can see photos of your mum when she was little. I can't wait to see them again."

"That'll be nice. Okay. Well, we've put a few things in place now. Is that all?"

"Well, you could help me clean out some cupboards and there's lots of stuff in the attic that needs chucking out. Old files that Mike had that are donkey's years old and not needed anymore. Failing that, the only other thing I can think of, for now anyway, is to teach you to cook. It is so important. I know you used to help Jake out but you haven't really shown any inclination to cook here. How would you like that? We could start with simple baking and then get on to the more difficult things like a roast or a pie. Have you followed a recipe before?"

"Not really. I was really only Jake's helper. He seemed to know everything. Mum taught him but never got around to teaching me or Daisy."

"Okay. We could start today if you like. We'll make a sponge cake, a Victoria sandwich."

"Why is it called that?" asked Lottie.

"I've no idea why it was called a sandwich but it was named after Queen Victoria because she made afternoon tea popular and she liked sponge cake. They seem to name a lot of things after her. There, you see, you've learned something new already! I always reckon you should learn something new every day."

"Yes." Charlotte was a little dubious but agreed all the same.

Dean was bored. It had only been three weeks into lockdown. Jake and Daisy were either busy with homework or they were in the kitchen, trying out new recipes. Every time Dean turned on the television he found it was either the news, which was never pleasant, always about more new rules and how many more deaths there had been, or repeats of programmes and films he had already seen.

Easter came and went but every day was the same. There were no weekends to speak of and nothing planned. They noticed, however, that it was probably the best weather they had ever known at Easter time. It was unseasonably warm and they were grateful for that. It showed that it was definitely the end of winter. Although that could change but they felt they ought to be optimistic as there was little else to which they could be cheerful.

"How monotonous is this? I'm fed up. I'm going out," said Dean.

"You can only go in the garden," Jake told his father. "The weather is nice; you could do some gardening, couldn't you?"

"Well, I could sunbathe. It's almost warm enough. At least I could get a bit of a tan. Your mum always liked it when we had some sun on our bodies. She liked me with a tan."

"That wasn't quite what I meant. I meant you could do some work in the garden. Mow the lawn. Pull some weeds. Do some DIY in the garage. You've got a perfectly good workbench in the garage. Make something useful." Jake kept suggesting ideas to keep Dean occupied to stop him going out.

"Couldn't I just go out for a walk? I won't meet anybody so I can't spread the virus," Dean asked, childlike.

"I guess that won't hurt." Jake thought it would be okay as the pub was not open. News guidelines stipulated that one could go out locally for exercise, near to home but to keep away from other people for fear of spreading the virus.

Dean went out for a walk. He walked down to the deserted beach. It was a sunny day and one that would normally attract a lot of people to the beach. There were one or two people walking their dogs and they kept out of Dean's way. Other than that, Dean did not encounter many people. It was weird. Everything was weird. Surreal. When he got home he looked at the lawnmower, then he looked at the grass.

"That isn't going to mow itself. Jake doesn't look like he's going to help in the garden anytime soon so I shall have to do it, I s'pose." Dean was disposed to talking to himself lately.

"First cut of the season," said Dean when Jake went outside to make sure he was not seeing things. "Your mother would be proud of me. She always liked to do the first cut of the year herself."

"Well done, Dad. I'm proud of you, as Mum isn't here. We've got scones for tea. Daisy has just made her first batch, under my expert tuition and guidance!"

Dean finished the grass and thought to himself he deserved a beer but there was only a cup of tea on offer. He drank the tea and ate a scone.

"Hey, Daisy, that ain't half bad! You can cook them again."

"Thanks, Dad. It's nice to get a bit of praise now and again."

Jan took on the training of Sandal, teaching Lottie to cook, the homeschooling and the gardening, as well as helping Lottie to care for Summer. There was never a dull moment for any of them. They had sorted out the cupboards in just a couple of days and put all the photos in albums in half the time it would have taken Jan on her own. Lottie was ecstatic to see photos of her own mother when she was a child. The travelogue was something to be proud of and Jan thanked Lottie for her input and expertise on the computer. She was ever curious as to some of the photos she had seen.

"Where is this? It looks very exotic, with elephants and all," Lottie enquired. Jan leaned over to see and was delighted to be transported back over the years.

"Those are our wedding photos! In Sri Lanka. Oh, that was a wonderful time, so romantic. They made me the most beautiful bouquet of colourful orchids and made a super wedding cake for us. The ceremony took place on a little island between two swimming pools. We couldn't have it on the beach because it was high tide and the rollers were breaking on the shore. The little island was ideal; it was decorated with orchids and banana leaves, so beautiful. I've got a video too. I'll show it to you. We became friendly with an Italian man there and he said he would take a video of our wedding with our own video camera. It was hilarious because, with his broken English, he gave a running commentary. We would see him at odd spots around the area. He would pop out from behind bushes or trees and he even went into the swimming pool to get a good shot of us taking our vows!"

"What is it with you and Italian men?" Lottie giggled and Jan smiled.

"Then, when we had taken our vows, they opened champagne and we had to cut the cake. The Italians joined us in our celebrations; we had champagne and the cake. We were given a plate of cake each with a little fork. Then we were told we had to cut off and give a little to our new spouse. It was very tempting to smear the cream over Mike's face, just for a giggle, of course." Jan laughed as she remembered those days that seemed so long ago now.

"And did you?" asked Lottie.

"No, of course not. One had to have a little decorum. We couldn't have the Sri Lankans thinking we were heathens who didn't know how to behave properly! And then the elephant arrived! He had a most garish orange covering, like a big sheet, with a blue and white diamond pattern. He had a plaque around his neck saying "Just Married". Then we had to climb onto him. Luckily there were steps up but my dress was quite tight and I had to ride astride his neck with Mike sitting behind me. We must have looked very comical. We only went along the beach path and back. We didn't eat all the wedding cake so I gave the rest of it to some locals who turned out to watch. We went back ten years later and they remembered us! That was amazing."

Lottie was mesmerised. She loved hearing stories about all the photos she was looking at, but especially her gran's wedding. Jan was delighted to be able to show Lottie the photos and also to tell her all about them.

"For our honeymoon, we went 'on safari' to the local national park for a few days and then up into the hills to the tea plantations. It is fabulous to see the rolling hills, which are covered with the tea bushes that look like velvet from afar."

"I want to get married somewhere exotic," said Lottie, imagining herself with a long, flowing white dress in a far-off country, with beautiful flowers in her hair and the warmth of the sun on her back. Jan was afraid to burst her bubble but had to bring her back to earth with a bump.

"I think you need to think about things as they are now, don't you? I had to wait a long time before I did anything like that, with a second husband."

"Did you get married in church the first time around?" asked Lottie.

"Yes, I did. But only because Geoff, your granddad, and his mother wanted it. I would have been happy with a register office wedding because I was already pregnant, you see? I had a white dress too, which actually was strictly taboo. Only virgins were supposed to wear white. I know that's a load of nonsense these days because there are not many virgin brides nowadays."

"No! And rightly so." Lottie was indignant. "No one in their right mind should marry someone without living with them first, I always think. How do you know if he doesn't have really bad habits that you can't bear?"

"Well, I have to say you have a point there. I didn't live with Geoff before we were married but actually he didn't have any bad personal habits. He just had other bad habits. He was very jealous and possessive and didn't let me breathe and be myself. With Mike, we lived together for six years and got married on the same date that we met, only six years later. He was very easy-going and I was able to blossom and be myself without having to worry about what I said or did. He joked some years later, saying I was like a mouse when he met me and then I turned into Frankenstein's monster! He was joking, of course."

Lottie was browsing some more of the photos on the computer.

"I love this place! Where is it?" said Lottie and Jan looked over at the screen.

"Oh, that's Venice. Yes, I can see why you would like it there. It really is a most unusual place with all the buildings built around the canals. It's beautiful; I love it there. I'll take you there one day; it's not too far to go. We'll go when Summer is older. It would not be easy with a pram or even a pushchair, with all the steps. Maybe next year when she is walking properly and this virus is not so prevalent. And, of course, I haven't forgotten that you need a passport. I hear that they are really behind at the passport office, some several tens of thousands, so, as it is not vitally important, we can wait before we apply for one, once everything gets back to normal."

"You say you have been to Australia loads of times?" asked Lottie and Jan nodded. "Why did you need to go so many times? Didn't you get bored just going back to the same old place?"

"Bored? Never! It's a very big country and so diverse."

"What are the best things about it?" Lottie could only imagine what this place is like at the other end of this wonderful planet.

"Oh, what a question! How could I begin? The first time we went, we took a trip on the Indian Pacific train, which, correct me if I'm wrong, has the longest stretch of straight track, some 3,000 miles long, I believe. All across the Nullabor Plain, with miles and miles of nothing! That might sound boring but it was very exciting. Then there is the Great Barrier Reef, where I went snorkelling for the first time; that was fantastic. We walked over the Sydney Harbour Bridge, which was an experience, and we also got to watch the fireworks on New Year's Eve from a boat in Sydney harbour. Then there's Tasmania, which is the little island off the south-eastern tip of Australia, which is mostly forest. We also went to the Australian Open tennis a few times. A bit like Wimbledon but much more laid back. I could go on because we pretty much did the whole of Australia, around the coast and up the middle to Ayers Rock and Alice Springs. And Coober Pedy, where they mine opals and we stayed in an underground hotel room. The temperature there goes to over fifty degrees!"

"Crikey! I don't think I want to go there if it gets that hot!" said Lottie.

"No, not all the time. They are very lucky with their weather; it is much better than we get here. Although, having said that, the weather here has been fantastic lately."

The weather had been beautiful and everything was growing faster than Jan could cope with. She was so pleased to have Lottie to help her in the garden because the part-time gardener was not able to come because of the virus lockdown. The supplies of food were spasmodic. Sometimes Jan could get a delivery but she had to be wily and ahead of the game and it was not always easy.

"What, no eggs again?" Lottie would hear Jan shout at the computer occasionally. Sometimes there was no flour either.

There were toilet rolls and then there weren't any. It was all quite surreal.

"I can't make a Victoria sponge cake without eggs or self-raising flour! We will have to make some flapjacks instead." Jan resigned herself with having to make do. "This must be just like it was in the war. Do you know they had dried eggs then, to make cakes with?" Jan asked Lottie.

"No! Dried eggs? How on earth would you have a boiled egg? What else do you know about the war? I don't know very much because Mum and Dad never told me."

"I don't know that much either. I was born four years after it ended. I did have a ration book though, apparently. They were in being for quite a few years after the end of the war. And I've no idea how they had a boiled egg. I guess they still had proper eggs for that and I just know that they had dried eggs for baking."

One thing that was still bothering Jan was the fact that Gerry and Vicky were being kept in a hospital in Bali and she was very worried about them. News was very sketchy but she gathered that they had caught the dreaded virus and had to stay in hospital for weeks. Gerry was affected worse than Vicky and he had to be put on a ventilator in the intensive care unit. They never made it to see their daughter and family because no one was allowed into Australia at that time. Vicky emailed Jan when she could but the Wi-Fi was intermittent and it all seemed very muddled. It appeared they would be home very soon, much to Jan's relief.

Vicky and Gerry arrived home and Vicky phoned Jan to tell her what had happened to them and why they were home so late.

"Gerry nearly died!" Vicky was ever the drama queen.

"No, I didn't." Jan could hear Gerry's voice in the background.

"Well, I'm really glad you're home now. That was a bit

traumatic, wasn't it?" Jan asked. She was worried about asking that question for fear of Vicky rambling on and making mountains out of molehills.

"I should say so! You don't know the half of it. I'll come round soon and I'll fill you in, without Gerry interfering."

"No! You can't come round!" Jan almost shouted.

"Whyever not?" Vicky was intrigued.

"We are in quarantine, self-isolating. No one can come here. Although I think they are going to relax the rules slightly soon and you might be able to come into the garden via the back gate. You must watch the press conference; it's on every day. We've been on lockdown ever since it started. Almost like your lockdown on the ship."

Vicky then proceeded to tell Jan what it was like on the ship and in the hospital. Jan was no wiser at the end of the call because she switched off. She did not really want to hear all Vicky's tales of woe; it was just too much for her to take in. She was just happy that they were home now, safe and well.

No sooner had Jan put the phone down from Vicky than it rang again. She picked it up and almost said, "What have you forgotten to tell me?" She did not say that and she was glad she did not because it was her brother's voice, which sounded quiet and crackly.

"Hello, Jan. I tried you a couple of times just now but it was engaged," said John.

"Oh, that was my friend and her husband. They've been caught up with that cruise ship in Bali. Did you see it on the news? They caught the virus and have been in hospital ever since. They've only just got home. They were telling me all about it."

"And I have to tell you that Vera caught the virus too, in her care home. I'm afraid she… wasn't so… lucky…" John left the words dangling. He could not bring himself to say the word he was dreading, hoping if he did not say it, it might not be true.

"What d'you mean?" There was silence at the other end. "Are you telling me Vera died?" asked Jan.

"Yes," said John, his voice breaking up. "Sorry, can't speak. I'll ring you later."

"Vera's died!" Jan told Lottie.

"Oh no! Of the virus?"

"Yes, I think so. Oh, poor John. This is awful and I can't go and comfort him. Damn this bloody virus; it's so cruel."

"Social distancing! What's that all about?" Dean was baffled. "I can't get my head around all these rules!"

"We must obey the rules, Dad. Mum always told us that. That means you have to too," said Jake. "If we don't stay indoors and we want to exercise outside we can, but we have to keep two metres away from everyone else. Apart from us, that is, because we are from the same household. And you can only go out once a day."

"Two metres? What's that in old money?" asked Dean.

"Two metres is a bit more than six feet. So just think six feet and you will be okay. Okay?"

"If you say so. I'm getting bored with this now, week after week. Bloody government. Bloody lockdown. Times like this I would be glad to get back to work. Just have to watch another repeat on tele. It's alright for you lot that's got work set out for them. It's driving me crazy."

Week by week the monotony was getting Dean down. He would go for a walk nearly every day but he would try and find a different route for a change of scenery to alleviate the boredom. Sometimes Jake and Daisy would walk with him, otherwise they had no other exercise. Jake had joined a gym at university and he was missing that.

"I'm getting fat," Dean exclaimed, feeling all around his waistline and slapping his tummy.

"It's hardly surprising," said Jake. "The food we are cooking is not very healthy. You won't eat a salad and you want chips with everything! That and all the beers I see disappearing from the fridge, it's not at all unexpected!"

"My hair is driving me crazy," Daisy piped up one day. "I need a haircut."

"I'll cut it for you. It doesn't look like the hairdressers are going to be able to open any time soon. Nor anything else, for that matter," Jake told Daisy. "It's just lucky we have the nice weather. Just imagine if this was winter coming on instead of the summer. We've got a garden too. Think about all those poor people in high-rise flats in the middle of a city. With heaps of kids, to boot! I can't imagine what they must be going through, can you?"

"You're ever the optimist, Jake," said Daisy.

"Well, someone's got to be. I don't think the schools will be back before the end of the summer term and then we've got the summer holidays. We ought to have some sort of a plan of what we are going to do. We can't sit indoors watching old repeats all the time. We could play some board games or get those old jigsaws out that Mum used to like."

"Boring," Dean interjected. "Boring, boring, boring! I'd rather see the repeats than do a jigsaw. And I don't like board games so don't ask me to play. Cluedo, Monopoly and Scrabble. They were your mum's favourite games. I think she only had you lot so she had someone to play games with!"

"Dad!" Jake was horrified to hear this.

"I'm only kidding." Dean went to fetch himself another lager from the fridge. "Hey, these are running a bit low. Shall we go to the shops?"

"They don't take cash and only one person in the shop at a time. I told you that the last time we went shopping. Have you got a contactless credit card?"

"I do, but I've forgotten the pin number. We used it so rarely. But if it's contactless that means you don't need the pin number. I think you just wave it at the till. I've seen young lads in the pub doing it," said Dean, getting enthusiastic to know they might be able to get fresh supplies of his beer. "Cash is going out of date with you young people, it seems. It's always credit card this or debit card that, Oyster cards for going on the trains, topping up cards for this, that and the other. It's no wonder people don't think so much about cash these days."

"And I think they have upped the limit for contactless since this virus business. But that still isn't enough for what we need. You will have to find out the pin number, Dad. Or you will have to go to the ATM and get some more cash. I'm sure they won't really turn down good old-fashioned money, will they?"

"I'll go and look in your mother's files. She was meticulous in keeping records of everything. All her passwords are on a sheet of A4. Every time she ordered something online she had to make up a new password. It's ridiculous the number of different passwords she had. Leave it with me, I'll go and look."

Dean took himself off to his bedroom to root around in all the paperwork. It gave him something to do and his interest kept a focus when he thought about his beers. The whisky bottle had taken a hammering too and he had his sights set on a new bottle of scotch.

"That should keep him quiet for an hour or two," Jake whispered to Daisy. "What shall we play? Scrabble?"

"Why not?" said Daisy.

Summer had begun to pull herself up, holding on to the furniture. Eventually she took her first tentative steps, holding on to chairs and the sofa and eventually without any visible means of support.

"Look, Gran! Summer can walk on her own now," Lottie shouted to Jan. Jan came rushing out of the kitchen to see Summer greeting her in the hall, albeit a little wobbly.

"Oh, wonderful! Well done, Summer. Just in time for your first birthday. Just like your grandmother did."

"Mumm," said Summer. "Mum, mum, mum." And then she fell down and giggled.

"Oopsie-daisy. Yes, here's your mum," said Jan, as Lottie came to rescue Summer by picking her up and giving her a kiss on her tummy.

"Who's a clever girl?" She put her down on the floor again but Summer crumpled her legs and landed on her knees. "Come on, Summer, are you going to try again for mummy?"

"Mum, mum, mum," said Summer.

"Next we'll have to teach her to say Gran," said Lottie smiling. "I'm so happy. Thank you for helping to make me happy, Gran." That came out of the blue and surprised Jan.

"No. Thank you," said Jan. "You have lightened my life no end so it's me thanking you. If it wasn't for you I would not have met any of my grandchildren or my great-granddaughter and I might not have had a puppy either. He's a lovely boy, isn't he? His training is going well and he's growing so fast. It's lovely to see him and Summer reacting to each other. It'll be nice now she can walk and she can play with Sandal out in the garden, under supervision, of course. We can't let them out of our sight for one second. With Sandal getting bigger, he could easily push her over and we don't want to frighten her now she has found her feet. And we are so lucky with this beautiful summer weather."

38

By the time the Krakenvirus pandemic was just over three months old, over 40,000 people had died in the UK. In America the numbers were quadruple and still advancing: there were tragic losses day by day. In the world, the death toll was reaching the half a million mark and there were new spikes happening all the time. New lockdowns were having to be reapplied wherever the new spikes were.

"This is getting very serious," said Jan to Lottie. "Where will it all end, I wonder."

"They say they are trying to get a vaccine, aren't they?" Lottie asked.

"Yes, but that could take months or even years. We will have to keep our fingers crossed that something will turn up. Meanwhile, we are okay here, aren't we? We can still get deliveries of food and all our essentials. Between us we can look after Summer and Sandal. I'm so glad you came to me when you did. I'm so happy." Jan could not believe her luck. She had waited years to be able to meet her grandchildren and now at least one was actually living with her and she was loving and appreciating every minute.

"Otherwise you would be on your own now and that's

not so good in these times when you can't go out or see your friends or anyone." Lottie was starting to become a sensible young adult.

"You are so right. I've got my mind occupied and that is a good thing. It's Summer's first birthday coming up. I'd really like to buy her a book. I know that sounds strange but when your mum was very young someone bought her the book *The Tiger Who Came to Tea*. I must have read it to her a hundred times; she absolutely loved it and always went to fetch it for me to read to her. When she was about three, some friends came to stay and our party piece was that I would start reading the book and, as I turned the pages, Louise would say the words on the page, just as if she was reading them. Our friends were gobsmacked that Louise could read but, of course, she had only memorised them and could say them parrot fashion. It was hilarious," said Jan, instantly transported back to the days when her own daughter was so very young.

Lottie smiled and could only imagine her mum at that age.

"Did your mum ever read it to you when you were young?" Jan asked Lottie.

"No, I don't think so. She did read some things to us but I don't remember that one."

"Is there anything you'd like to do for Summer's birthday? We obviously can't see anyone so we could put it on hold for the time being. I don't suppose she will notice!" said Jan. "We could have a party for her when all this is over. In fact, we could have a party for ourselves too. A double celebration. I can't wait!"

Lottie agreed. There was too much going on to worry about anything like that just yet.

Dean had sunbathed in the garden every day that the sun was out. He was rather enjoying not having to go to work but he soon became bored. After much searching he had found the pin number for the credit card so Jake was able to go shopping again and Dean made sure his lagers were at the top of the list. Jake was very careful and wore gloves and a mask when he went to the supermarket. Then he washed his hands religiously as soon as he arrived home.

"I'm afraid your favourite lagers weren't available, Dad." Jake said to Dean when he came home with the shopping. "So I'm afraid you will have to do without this time."

Dean was almost apoplectic. He was furious and went red in the face.

"Well, you'll just have to go somewhere else..." Dean began as Jake continued.

"So I got these instead." He showed Dean the supermarket own-label beers and laughed so hard when he saw his father's red face.

"Oh, they're rubbish. Not very strong at all. Gnat's pee is what they are!" Dean said disappointingly. "You could try at another supermarket, couldn't you?"

"No! You'll just have to make do." Jake shrugged.

"I'm going out. I'm fed up," said Dean.

Dean went out for a walk. He decided on a different track and ended up, after a circuitous route, at his favourite pub. It was the first time he had been this way and was disappointed to see how dowdy it looked, with paint coming off the door and dirty windows. Trestle tables and picnic tables with seats were stacked up against the wall at the front and he just stood there staring. He noticed someone waving at him from one of the dirty windows. He waved back but he did not know to whom he was waving. The door suddenly popped open after a bit of force as it was sticking.

"Hi, Deano, me ol' china, mate," said Keith, looking a little dishevelled. He rushed over to where Dean was standing.

Keith put out his hand as a natural reaction to meeting someone but he soon put it away when he remembered he could not shake hands with anyone. "No hugs and no kisses", he kept having to remind himself, so put out his elbow to bump with Dean's. Dean looked askance and wondered what on earth he was doing. He realised after a little time that he was supposed to reciprocate, which he eventually did, shoving his elbow at Keith's and missing in the process. They both laughed at this.

"I've never done that before!" said Dean, still laughing and feeling cheered to see a friendly face.

"How have you been? Been keeping yourself occupied?" Keith asked.

"Oh, you know, a bit fed up after all this time. How's it going with you? You must be losing a lot with not being able to open?" Dean enquired.

"Yeah, you could say that! Bit of an understatement really, I don't know how much longer I can keep going with no income." Keith started to take down a picnic table and offered Dean a seat. "This is a fine howdidoo, isn't it? Is this the new normal, I ask myself?"

"Dunno, really. It's mighty annoying, I know that."

"It's really great to see you, mate. Sit tight and I'll be right back."

Keith rushed indoors and came back carrying two bottles. He gave one to Dean and that put a smile on his face. He took one large swig and the bottle was nearly empty.

"Thanks, mate," said Dean. "Cor, that hits the spot. Now I know what I've been missing. How much do I owe you?" he asked, rooting around in his pocket but knowing that there was nothing in there. With no shops open, he did not take any money with him.

"That's alright, mate. Have it on the house. One beer isn't

going to make any difference. You can buy me one when we finally open again."

"How much longer, d'you think?" Dean enquired.

"Well, they are talking about lifting restrictions but not anytime soon for our type of business. It looks like we are over the peak now, fingers crossed. Did you know my old lady had the virus? Quite poorly, she was. She had to go to hospital but she's home now. I think I might have had it but only mildly; I had very few of the symptoms that they talk of."

"No, I didn't know she had been to hospital. Glad she's okay now. With not seeing anyone, you don't get any gossip or news or anything that you would normally get while out and about. So, did you have a take a test?"

"Nah, didn't bother. Must have picked it up on the last day we were open. Either I gave it to her or she gave it to me, we will never know."

"I suppose you're rather in the firing line, with people you don't know coming in and out of the pub." Dean was being practical in working out how Keith might have got the virus.

"Yeah, I reckon you're right. See those tables over there?" Keith pointed to the tables stacked up. "Nearly every morning some of the tables are taken down and strewn around here. At least no one's stolen them yet! I don't know why they take them down. Kids messing around, I suppose."

"Do you hear anything of Doreen?" Dean asked.

"What, since your black eye incident from her hubby?" Keith laughed, but not unkindly. "I did feel for you, mate. It's not as if you were kissing her or fondling her! Maybe he knew that that was what you were thinking and he was reading your mind! Maybe it was the drool down your chin that gave you away and gave him the clue that that was what you wanted to do!" Keith laughed even more.

"It's not *that* funny, is it? Yes, I fancied her but I knew she was married and nothing was going to come of it. Actually, I don't remember that much – apart from fancying her, that is."

"Well, I guess she is now safely ensconced at home, with her hubby."

"Well, I'd better get back. The kids will be worried. Thanks for the drink and I hope to see you very soon."

"It'll be a while yet, I think. Might be a couple of weeks or maybe more. It's all so uncertain. They have to be careful that there isn't a spike, in which case everything will take longer to open up. Meanwhile I'm not making any money and the landlord is still insisting on his rent!"

"Bad luck, Keith." Dean commiserated. "I shall be first through that door when you do open, you can take that as the honest truth."

"Thanks, mate. I might even give it a lick of paint, especially for you!"

Dean wended his way home and thought no more about his unexpected encounter with Keith.

"What's for supper?" asked Dean.

"Whatever you would like to cook. I think it's your turn, isn't it? There's plenty in the cupboards now I've done the shopping for you," said Jake.

"I would have done the shopping but only one can go in at a time and you've got the car. It makes more sense that you do the shopping. Eh?"

"If you say so. So what are you going to cook for us?" asked Jake.

"Yes, Dad, what's for supper?" asked Daisy.

"Are you trying to gang up against me? I don't know. Fish and chips?" Dean knew that was the easiest thing he could cook, with fish and chips straight out of the freezer. All he had to do was lay it out on a tray and cook it all in the oven at a high temperature. "I can do mushy peas too, if you like, as long as there's a tin in the cupboard."

"This is starting to get a bit monotonous, not going out," said Lottie to Jan. "At least we can take Sandal for walks and that is allowed as long as we keep our distance from other people."

"Yes, I know it's a bit boring. But hopefully things will be starting to ease up pretty soon now the peak is flattening out. We just have to be patient. We've been managing to stay safe, staying at home with food deliveries. What I can't understand is why all my clothes are so tight. I think there must be something wrong with the washing machine; it's shrinking my clothes!"

"I've put weight on and I expect you have too. They say it's because we are not doing the things we are used to doing."

"I expect so, yes. And we've probably done more baking than we would normally do, with fattening things like cakes and puddings. But at least you have learned more with all the lessons I've been giving you. You should be able to get back to school and get your exams now. What is the capital of New Zealand?" Jan asked Lottie.

"Wellington." Lottie was pleased with herself that she actually enjoyed learning and was very keen on geography since Jan's enthusiasm had rubbed off on her. Jan would ask her the odd question and, if she did not know it, she liked to be able to go and look it up, rather than have Jan tell her. She reckoned that was a better way of remembering facts. She needed to see it written down. Sometimes she would ask Jan a quiz-type question and loved it when she could baffle her gran with science. "How many chromosomes does a human have?"

"Ah, I know this one." Jan thought for a bit. "Twenty-three pairs of chromosomes in a human."

"Correct. And how many bones does a human have?" asked Lottie, enjoying the game.

"206 bones. And did you know that a baby has about 270 bones when it is born?"

"No, I didn't know that. How come?" Now Lottie was puzzled, so Jan took great pleasure in making the explanation.

"Well, a baby has many more bones when it is born, which is why they are a bit floppy. As the baby grows, their bones fuse together, so by the time they are about three years old they end up with 206. And do you know what the top of a baby's skull is called? The soft part. You remember when Summer was born, you thought it was odd that there was a soft part on top of her head?"

"Yes, but I'm not sure it is called anything."

"It is. It's called the fontanelle. It soon grows over and the skull becomes stronger."

These question and answer sessions would sometimes go on throughout the day between Lottie learning to cook, training Sandal in how to behave and teaching Summer to walk and talk.

Jan heard that her yoga class was starting again soon and she was looking forward to that. She had shelved it for the last year but was keen to return as it kept her supple. They were only taking on a few people because they needed to keep their distance and it was going to be outdoors to begin with, then indoors when the weather was inclement.

Jan rang John to find out how he was coping. It had been on her mind for several days but had been dreading the call for fear of not knowing what to say to her brother.

"How are you?" asked Jan, kindly. "I've been worried about you."

"I can't even have a funeral for Vera!" said John, despondently.

"Oh no! How come?" asked Jan.

"Well, there is such a backlog and, even when it comes to it, only five people can attend. That's awful."

"Yes, it is. I'm so sorry, John. But how are you in yourself?"

"I feel wretched. I can't sleep. Basically, I miss her. I know we weren't together in the end, what with her at the care home. I wasn't able to visit her because the virus was there. It's just awful that she had to go this way. At least, I don't suppose she knew anything about it. That's one good thing."

"Yes. You have to look at the positives. And I can't even come and see you although they are now talking about a family bubble. If you've been self-isolating and not seen anyone else, you could come here. I'll look after you."

"I don't need looking after!" said John indignantly. "Sorry, Jan, that came out all wrong. I'm very grateful, I really am. All I'm thinking about at the moment is getting this funeral arranged. I must do my best for my Vera. I feel I've let her down."

"I quite understand but you mustn't feel you have let her down. You looked after her at home for as long as you were able. She was grateful to you for that, I'm sure. Just let me know if you would like to come here. Anytime. We are family so we must stick together."

"Thanks."

39

"What's this muck you've cooked up?" Dean pushed his plate away, disgusted. He started coughing and choking. He wondered if the cigarette he had had earlier was making him cough. He had given up cigarettes over ten years ago but all this uncertainty and boredom made him start again, but only in secret. He did not want his children to start nagging at him again like they used to. They used to say, "Oh Dad, not another fag! It makes you smell. It's a horrible habit. Mum doesn't like it either." He gave up for Louise because she was borderline asthmatic and was starting to have to take inhalers.

"It's just the usual spag bol! I've not done anything different, Dad. Promise." Jake wondered what was the matter with his father.

"Well, I can't taste it. It tastes just like papier mâché!"

"I bet you don't even know what that tastes like!" said Jake, amused with himself for having a ready answer to his father. "That cough of yours is getting worse too. Have you got a cold?"

"Nah, don't think so. Come to think of it, I'm not feeling so good."

"Have you got the virus?" asked Daisy, not in the least

expecting that he did have. "All points to the virus. Your sense of smell: you didn't smell the burnt toast this morning. Your sense of taste: you didn't like the taste of Jake's spag bol. Hardly surprising, really! If I had made it, it would taste much better!" Daisy smiled at Jake. There was always friendly banter between the two siblings.

"Come to think of it… *no*, I don't have the blessed virus! But I'm going to bed to watch something on tele and maybe have a sleep. I haven't been sleeping all that well lately. There you are, you can add that to all my other symptoms! Put that in your pipe and smoke it!"

Dean coughed his way up the stairs and shut his bedroom door.

"He'll be alright, won't he?" asked Daisy, now seriously a little concerned for her father.

"Yeah, of course he will," Jake confirmed, but slightly sceptical. "I'll check on him later." Jake went in later and found the television on and Dean fast asleep. He turned off the television and left his father sleeping.

Dean had not surfaced by the morning and so Jake went in with a cup of tea.

"Christ, Dad, you're sweating! Look, your bedclothes are soaked through."

"Leave me alone. I'm okay. Just resting."

Jake went downstairs and found a telephone number so that he could order a home testing kit for the virus. The testing kit was delivered and Jake read all of the instructions. He did not want to alarm his father but he was going to have to take a swab from his mouth and then send it back to the special testing centre.

"I think we are all going to have to be tested, aren't we, Jake?" Daisy asked. "We are all together here so I'm sure that's what's going to have to happen, even if we don't have symptoms. If Dad's picked up the virus then there is every likelihood that we have it too!"

Dean's test came back positive and his condition worsened. Against his will he was taken to hospital. Jake and Daisy were also tested positive and Daisy was taken to hospital as a precaution as she had breathing problems. Jake stayed home and self-isolated. He could not go and visit for fear of spreading the virus that was still in him.

"This is a right pain," Jake was telling Lottie on the phone. "You are in the best place. We racked our brains to try and think where it could have come from. We've not been out, apart from me doing the shopping, but I've always been very careful, wearing gloves and a mask in the supermarket. Then when I get home I wash my hands meticulously, like they show you on the tele. Apart from that, Dad has been out walking but he doesn't meet anyone."

"So what's it like? The virus, I mean. Is it as bad as they say?" Lottie asked Jake. Something suddenly sparked Jake's memory and he was quiet for a while.

"I've just remembered something. Dad came back one day and he mentioned seeing the pub looking dowdy and he met with Keith. I wonder if he touched anything. He never washes his hands when he comes back like they tell you to." Jake pondered this for a while, almost talking to himself as he remembered back. He continued, his head still in another place. "Well, Dad's quite poorly. They were talking about putting him in intensive care if he gets any worse and that means a ventilator, I think. I've not heard him cough so bad, just like when he was smoking. His breathing was labouring. Daisy is not so bad but her breathing was starting to suffer. It's so frustrating, not being able to visit. I'm so lucky, I've had no symptoms at all."

"Give them my love if you do see them. Have you heard

from anyone else? How are Granddad and Lynda? And Uncle Steven and Auntie Cheryl and Milly and Poppy? Are they all okay? Oh, and Granny Kath?"

"Yes, as far as I know. With not being out and about, you don't get to hear about anyone else. It's like being in a little bubble. I will ring around and make sure and let you know," Jake confirmed.

"Oh, that reminds me. Uncle John rang the other day and he said that Auntie Vera died. The care home was riddled with the virus and she was especially vulnerable. He is cross 'cos he can't arrange a proper funeral for her. He's obviously upset as well," Lottie added.

"Oh no! That's awful. I will ring him to make sure he's okay. Thanks for telling me."

Slight easing of restrictions was starting to take place fourteen weeks after the start of lockdown, with some businesses able to reopen.

"Gran?" asked Lottie tentatively.

"Yes, dear." Jan wondered what was coming.

"You remember you promised me driving lessons for my birthday?"

"Of course! I haven't forgotten. I will organise it as soon as driving instructors are able to take on beginners. I don't think they can at the moment because it is in too close proximity, in the car."

"And then there was the holiday you talked about. We were going to try Venice or Madeira?"

"All in good time. We can't do that yet; it is not safe to travel. We can't risk getting the virus for just a holiday after I've been shielding all this time. But we will, I promise, just as soon as it is safe to do so. The virus isn't going to just go away so we have to take our own precautions."

Jan and Lottie were both pleased when the hairdresser was able to open again and that was when they first ventured out.

"You look lovely, Gran," said Lottie, looking at Jan's hair. "The shorter style does suit you. I only wanted mine tidied up to take off the split ends. I like to have it long so I can put it up. You can do so much more with long hair."

"I know! I was young once, you know! I had really long hair, all down my back. Then, when I had your mum – I was only twenty – I had to have it cut because her sticky fingers got entangled in it. It was quite yuk. I've had it short ever since."

"I see. I didn't know that. When should we have Summer's hair cut? Do you think we should let it grow long?" Lottie asked.

"She's got beautiful fair hair; it would be a shame to cut it just yet," said Jan "It will suit her long, don't you think? At the moment it hasn't grown that much, it's a bit in-between. She's a real girly girl so will probably like to have long hair. But you're her mum so you must decide for her."

It was the middle of summer and all the seeds that Jan and Lottie planted were coming to fruition. The weather had been perfect, probably the best weather Lottie had ever experienced in her lifetime. Watering took the two of them nearly an hour to complete, with having had no rain for weeks.

"We will have beans coming out of our ears at this rate!" said Jan. "The tomatoes are ready and some cucumbers too. I love a nice salad."

Lottie was not so sure about the salad but she did like runner beans. She really enjoyed helping Jan in the garden. Summer watched them from her playpen and she could also see Sandal running about the garden, in and out of the shrubs. He was very happy to play on his own, although he preferred to be chasing and fetching a ball. Lottie would sometimes leave Jan to the plants and play with Sandal. Summer had also started to know the difference between her mum and her gran. Except, of course, Jan was her great-grandmother, but she copied Lottie in calling her Gran.

"Gan!" she would shout to Jan. She started enjoying the sound of her own voice. "Gan, gan!"

Lockdown was much less of a burden now and everything was more or less back to normal, with restaurants and other non-urgent shops starting to open up. Some were never to open again, having succumbed to the virus, mostly for financial reasons.

Lottie's mobile phone rang. She picked up when she saw it was Jake. Jan saw her sit down and look very serious. Then she started to cry. Jan went over to see what the matter was after she finished the call. She could not speak for several minutes, which worried Jan.

"It's Dad... he's... dead! He died of the virus, Jake just told me." Lottie took out a hankie and cried into it. Summer looked concerned for her mum. She put her arms around her, even though she did not understand what was the matter. Jan put her arms around them both.

Daisy came home on the same day that Dean died. She had recovered sufficiently but was in shock, as was Jake. Jake picked her up and they just sat in the car park for a long time, not saying anything. Both were deep in their thoughts.

"Are you feeling better?" Jake managed. Daisy cried. Jake hugged her, understanding her completely. It reminded him of the time their mother died and he was the one to comfort her. "We had better get home." Silence ensued as Jake drove them home.

Daisy went into the house first. It was strange. It was her home and yet it was different. Empty, somehow. She felt empty. She cried.

"Come on," Jake comforted her again. "A cup of decent tea? I don't suppose hospital tea is up to much."

"No. I mean yes. Please." Daisy nodded to a cup of tea. "And can we have fish and chips tonight? I shall always remember Dad and his fish and chips. He loved them so much."

"Yes, he did." Jake made the tea and they sat outside in the garden. "This is where Dad used to sit and sunbathe."

"Yes. Nice tea, thanks. The food wasn't as bad as you might think and the nurses were really lovely. So kind. It is a definite calling to be a nurse; it takes a certain something."

"Is that what you want to be, then?" Jake asked.

"Oh no. I don't have that certain something. I told you I want to work with animals. To be a vet or something like that. Anyway, I don't want to talk about that now. We have some things to sort out and loads of decisions to make."

"They can wait until tomorrow."

"No, I want to talk to you now. I can't live here on my own when you go back to uni. Where am I going to go? And what about the mortgage? We just can't afford to live here, can we? Without Dad's wages, I mean."

"No, you're right, we can't. What do you suggest?"

"I don't know but I shall think of something."

40

Jan noticed that Lottie was on the phone almost constantly, talking to Daisy or to Jake. She realised they must be trying to sort things out between them. She was hoping that did not mean that Lottie was going to have to go back but she knew she must not be selfish. If Lottie had to go back to look after Daisy, then so be it. She could not be on her own, especially after Jake went back to university. That was some time away, at the end of September. It was towards the end of August now and Jan had been about to suggest that Lottie go back to school. She had made tentative enquiries and there were places available at the local comprehensive. She had missed a year but she hoped that with the homeschooling she had had she was in a better position. She could just take the last year again to be able to take her exams. Meanwhile, Jan would look after Summer. All was up in the air until everything was sorted out between them.

"Everything sorted now? Is there anything I can do?" Jan took the opportunity of asking Lottie after a particularly long conversation. Lottie looked a little sheepish.

"Can I ask you a question?" asked Lottie, straightforwardly.

"Of course, you can ask me anything. I think you know me by now. I would give you an honest and trustworthy answer.

What is it?" Jan had her fingers crossed and hoped it did not mean what she thought it was going to mean. That Lottie would have to move back to Devon.

Lottie prevaricated. "What would you say if Daisy came to live here with us? And Jake too, when it's his holidays from uni?" In the end Lottie just had to come right out with it and she had her fingers crossed for good measure.

"Well, of course! I'd be absolutely delighted to have them. There is absolutely no way I would object and, of course, as they have already had the virus, they will have some immunity and some of those antibodies which everyone is talking about."

"Yes, that's what I was thinking. Even though the virus is still about, I think it is easing a little but we will still have to be careful."

"We can arrange for Daisy to go to the same school as you," said Jan. "She has missed so much with the pandemic but I do think it's important she doesn't miss any more school. All the kids have to go back to school now. I'll look into it, if you like." Daisy had not been to school since lockdown in March but she had kept up with her studies at home.

"Yes, please. Thank you so much. I was so worried about asking you."

Jan was thankful she never moved to a smaller house, for a single person. Now her four bedrooms were really coming into their own and being used for the purpose they were meant for, a family.

"Well, you need worry no more," Jan assured her.

All was arranged and within a week Daisy and Jake had packed their belongings and moved to Surrey. Jake was awaiting going back to university and Daisy and Lottie happily attended the local comprehensive school. The siblings all back together was one thing they missed.

Dean's funeral was put on hold but they were told it would be at least six to eight weeks. Jake worked out that he would be back at university by then but he planned that he would have to take a day off to attend. He would take Daisy and Lottie out of school to attend their father's funeral. Meanwhile, he left it with the funeral directors to make the arrangements but he said he would keep in touch meanwhile.

Jan enjoyed Jake's company in the month before he was due back at university. He helped around the house and the garden as well as keeping up with his studies. Jan appreciated having a man about the house once again.

"What's going to happen to the house in Devon?" Jan asked.

"We can't keep up the mortgage repayments so it'll be on the market pretty soon. That was one thing I had to do before we came here. I went to an agent and put it all in their hands. They have a key so they can start the proceedings. I shall have to go down there and will go and see them. I shall also arrange to clear it out but I might have to go there again before I go back to uni. There might be something of Mum's that you would like? I could bring back some of her personal things and you must choose something. I shall go one day next week."

"That's very kind of you, yes, that would be nice, thank you, Jake. And, of course, the girls must both have a keepsake of your mum's, and you too. I have a friend coming to lunch on Thursday next week. She's called Rachel and she is new to my yoga class and I would really like you to meet her."

"Okay. I had planned on going down early on Tuesday as the traffic shouldn't be too bad then and I shall stay over for two nights. Two days to sort things out should be enough." Jake had a lot of arrangements to make before he went back to university. "I'll be back on Thursday afternoon. Hopefully I shall be back in time to meet Rachel."

Jake made the journey back to Devon. He was glad to be on his own as he could then get on with sorting out everything. As he went into the house, it was eerily quiet. It was exactly as he and Daisy had left it, in a bit of a hurry. It was not left in a mess but if a person went in there they could tell someone had left hurriedly. They had had a week to get their belongings together, enough to tide them over until such a time as this, when Jake had more time. Daisy had given Jake a list of the extra things she needed. He made sure he packed them first before he got on with stuff that he needed himself. His university course started in a couple of weeks and so he was glad to have this time, whereas Daisy did not have that extra time.

The schools were open again, where they had been closed for several months, since the beginning of lockdown, and Daisy had been anxious to get in to her new school on the first day. This meant she needed a new school uniform, as did Lottie too. Jan was happy to take them shopping to get them both kitted out with everything they needed, just in time for their first day.

The bedrooms that Jan gave to Jake and Daisy were sufficiently large for their things and they both had fitted wardrobes to keep their clothes tidy. Jake was anxious not to take too much but he did promise his gran a keepsake of his mother's. He rooted around and found just the thing for her. His mother's beloved framed photo collage with a collection of photos from when the children were young. *Gran will love that*, he thought. There must have been about a hundred photos ranging in sizes. He also took his mother's jewellery, which was still in Dean's bedroom, exactly in the place where his mother had left them before she passed away. *The girls can choose whatever pieces of jewellery they would like and maybe give Gran a piece too.* He did not think that there was anything of his mother's that he would keep for himself but he looked for something that belonged to his father. He looked all over the house, seeing only things that reminded him of his mother. Then he suddenly thought about his father's pride and joy, something that he had won in a raffle many years ago. Something that may or may not be worth something one day, but he did not care how much it was worth. To Jake it was priceless because it belonged to his father.

He went to his parents' bedroom, as that was the last time he remembered seeing it, on the wall above the bed. It was not there. He seemed to remember his parents arguing about it one day and his mother winning the argument. She did not want such a thing over her bed but Dean could never understand why she made such a fuss. To his eyes it was a thing of beauty. Needless to say, she had had her way and the thing in question was put away. But where?

Jake looked in their wardrobes but it was not there. He looked in the cupboard under the stairs but to no avail. He went to the shed in the back garden. Not there. The only place he had not looked was the garage. The garage had been a dumping ground for years and he grimaced when he knew it would be gone into a skip in the blink of an eye once the house clearance people came. He must find it.

Boxes and boxes from the last house move were still stacked in a corner of the garage. No one had looked in those boxes for ages. He wondered what was actually in there. He did not have the time or the inclination to look. He knew the thing he was looking for was too big to be in a box. But where was it? Old garden furniture he moved aside, plus broken toys and the lawnmower. The lawnmower was about the only thing in the garage that was of any use as far as he could see. He moved stuff from one side of the garage to the other.

There. There it is. On the floor, leaning up against the wall, covered over with old curtains. Jake picked it up and looked at it. Not really a thing of beauty, as his father had called it, but of sentimental value, now more than ever it was. It was in a large, ungainly even ugly, frame. Inside was the back of a football shirt with a number seven on it purporting to have belonged to David Beckham in the 90s, with his signature at the bottom of the frame. He had in mind that he would get it valued but then thought better of it in case it was worthless. He had heard of fakes and there were a lot around. No, he wanted it because his father liked it.

He tidied the garage as best he could, stacking most of it all together in one corner, in case potential buyers wanted to look in there, but he hoped not. The rubbish might put them off. But he had promised it would all be cleared by the time completion would take place and he might be able to come again to sort through some boxes to see if there was anything else they might want to keep.

Jake went to see the estate agents to see if there had been any interest.

"Not yet, but it is starting to pick up now," said the estate agent. "It has been pretty dead all through the summer and the pandemic. Everything was put on hold, I think. I will contact you just as soon as we have a buyer."

"Thank you. You will see that I have come back and tidied a bit better than before! Sorry that I had to leave it in a bit of a hurry. Obviously, I will come back again and arrange for a house clearance company to come and take away everything else, before completion."

"I always think it is better that furniture etc is still in place. Some people take everything away and then it always looks so empty and sad. Also, carpets show where furniture had been, with indentations, which is not a pretty sight. You are lucky not to need the furniture where you are. Well, we have the keys and we've taken some good photos. We have written up the particulars and we're ready to put it on the internet for all to see. We have already emailed around to people who are on our books that we know who want that type of house, but there has been little interest as yet."

Next job was the funeral directors. Jake called in to see if they had a date for his father's funeral.

"There is such a backlog, you have no idea what it has been like. It's been absolute mayhem!"

"I can imagine you have been a bit busy." Jake knew that was an understatement but did not know any other words to put it politely.

He took one last look around the house to see if there was anything he had missed. He methodically went into every room. He had a gut feeling there was something else but promised himself he would make at least one more journey before going to university. Maybe he would go on a weekend and take his sisters so they could take one last look.

He packed everything he needed into the boot of the car, including his precious framed football shirt. He felt sad but somehow elated that this was the start of a new life rather than the end of an era.

Rachel and Jan enjoyed a lovely lunch in the late September sunshine. Rachel finished the last dregs of wine in her glass.

"I must really make a move. Thank you so much for our socially distanced lunch and I look forward to the time when we can have a normal meal together without having to keep several feet apart. No hugs and no kisses, it really is tough."

"I agree. It's been so weird these last few months. I look forward to when we get the vaccines that have been promised and the sooner the better. I've heard it shouldn't be long now. I promised to show you what is inside the door of the owl. Come on, I'll show you."

Jan took Summer by the hand and they walked over to the sculptured owl. Jan let go of Summer's hand and bent down to open the creaky door. Summer was intrigued; she stood behind Jan and peered into the darkness. Jan took out an urn, which contained Mike's ashes.

"Mike loved the owl sculpture so I thought it was fitting that he should be buried here."

Jan was showing the urn to Rachel and Summer when there was a commotion by the side of the house. Jake had come back from Devon early and had gone to fetch Daisy and Lottie from school. They all came rushing over, their face masks in hand.

"I didn't get around to telling you about Jake and Daisy but I didn't realise they were going to come home together!" said Jan to her friend. She introduced Lottie first.

"Your grandmother has told me all about you, Lottie. Your daughter is a lovely little girl, you must be very proud," said Rachel and Lottie blushed as she picked up Summer.

"And this is Jake and Daisy, my other two grandchildren, who are living with me now. They came to stay with me after their father died of the virus. It's been an awful time for them, losing first their mother nearly two years ago and then their father just a few weeks ago."

Rachel felt a little overwhelmed as they all gathered around but still keeping their distance to keep everyone safe.

Jan continued. "It's just such a pity it has taken all this time for me to meet my family. I loved my daughter but I hated what she did to this family." Jan was in tears as she was remembering her daughter, who had been such a kind, loving child.

"I'm so pleased to meet you all," said Rachel, smiling and liking the picture of this happy family, which seemed so close and loving. "Can't shake hands, I'm afraid!"

"They are such a delight to have and now my family is complete," said Jan.

Jake took centre stage after the formalities of being introduced to Rachel.

"Not quite, Gran. We've got a surprise for you. Come round the front of the house; there is someone who wants to see you."

"I'm not sure what you mean, Jake." Jan was perplexed but she was ready to go along with Jake's plans.

Jake made sure that Jan went first through the side gate and there, standing in the drive was her son, Steven, with his wife and two teenage children. Jan could not believe her own eyes and blinked twice to make sure what she was seeing was real.

"Hello, Mum," said Steven, wiping away a tear in his eye. "I'd like to introduce you to Cheryl, Milly and Poppy."

Jan was overcome with emotion and lost for words. She was so happy. Her whole family reunited at last, after a quarter of a century.